最重要的100個英文字首字根

最重要的
100個 英文字首字根

100 ENGLISH PREFIXES
& WORD ROOTS

許章眞 編著
(Chang-chen Hsu)

修訂再版序

　　《最重要的100個英文字首字根》初版印行後，頗受歡迎，不旋踵即已售罄。茲藉再版之便，修訂若干小錯誤，並且增加一些星記號（*）。本書初版前言中曾作說明，書中所錄單字屬於高程度者，均以星記號標於該字右上角。初版之後，發現許多未標星記號的單字，仍可歸屬於高程度字彙範圍，因此補上一些星記號。

　　標有星記號的單字增多，有兩大好處。首先，程度偏高的單字盡數標出之後，讀者學習時，可先掌握未標星記號的基本字彙，俟基本字彙讀熟後，再進一步學習較高程度的單字。這點對一般讀者幫助最大。其次，有志留學的讀者也可藉此增進學習效率。GRE 部分字彙程度較低，也屬於托福字彙範圍。這一部分單字在初版中均未標上星記號，目前修訂再版，已全部標上。準備考托福的讀者，可先看未標星記號的托福基本字彙，等到這些單字記熟之後，再學習標有星記號的部分。若是考 GRE，則須掌握全書的字彙，因為 GRE 不但常考書中標有星記號的單字，比較基本的字彙也不時出現。另外，準備參加SAT、GMAT 等留學考試的讀者，和準備 GRE 測驗一樣，也應熟讀全書，方可應付裕如。

　　本書雖經修訂勘正，恐怕仍有未盡完善之處，尚祈讀者諸君不吝指正。

許　章　眞

1988 年 10 月・台北

最新增訂本
增訂說明

　　本書這次修訂，是要把書中字根與字幹（root 與 stem，或稱詞根與詞幹）的問題說明白。本書原來所說的字根，若依照現代語言學的觀念言之，十居其九都是字幹。比方在〈前言〉中，作者許先生解釋構詞的道理時，以英文字 predictable 爲例，他說在字首 pre 和字尾 able 中的 dict 是字根；其實這個 dict-是拉丁動詞 *dicere* "說話" 的過去分詞詞幹。除了這幹，*dicere* 另有現在式詞幹 dic(e)-，它也能構造新詞。

　　本書原版中各章裡頭常見的一個錯誤，是把同一個拉丁動詞的不同性質的詞幹，以及在拉丁和法語中的變體，稱爲幾條詞根，這與語言學的學理有所牴觸。按語詞的詞根是基本語意的所在，一條詞根可以生出多個語詞——既生出動詞，又生出名詞和形容詞，乃至其他詞類，每類都可能不止一個；但是一個語詞不會有多過一條詞根。（例外的少數是那些 "異根互補" 的拼合詞，如英文動詞 go 的現在式 go、過去分詞 gone 與動詞 wend 的過去式 went，拼合而成 go，went，gone。）

　　關於詞根和詞幹的分辨及其他問題，可參閱本版附錄中〈詞根與詞幹〉一文。附錄的另一文〈英語簡說〉是代替許先生原著〈英語發展簡史〉。除了這兩篇，本版對七十章講字根的說明部份酌加了一些補正（見 601 頁，附錄前）。但其餘的內容，包括所有的選字和例句，書首的構詞型態與用法說明，前三十章字首的說明及書末的

字尾表等等，都沒有更動。

　　原編著者許章眞先生的語文天份很高，他的托福成績是個紀錄，多年來無人能破。他英年早逝，遇難於出國進修語言學的前夕；這個修訂版爲他作一些補足，諒是他泉下樂見的。我們儘量保存本書的原貌，以表對他的懷念。在講字根的七十章中，我們保留他原來的說明，因爲語詞溯源是一種推測，在我們認爲須給他補正的地方，也不好完全肯定他是錯的。而即使他錯了，也不必太著意爲他隱諱，因爲推想錯誤實在是史不絕書，無論是語言學史或別的學術史。學術上的錯誤，對後之來者是很有啓發性的。

　　這本書倘若不加修訂，雖有謬誤，卻也不是一無用處的。讀者大可藉它之助來學習英文單字，得到優良成績，如同許先生當年，以及他在南北各地補習學校所敎過的千百學生一般。書林也可以繼續出版發行而營利。但蘇正隆先生知道這書稍有違反學術之處，就寧可負擔重新排版的費用也要加以修正，這種負責的態度是很值得稱道的。

孫述宇　識

最重要的 100個 英文字首字根

目　　錄

最重要的 70 個字根 243

前　言

　　字首字根是學習英文字彙最重要的方法。英文中上程度的字彙，大部分以源自希臘語、拉丁語、古英語等古語的字首、字根，加上字尾所構成。可見這種構詞法 (word-formation) 舉足輕重，若能掌握，必可使英文程度突飛猛進①。

　　什麼是字首、字根、字尾呢？茲舉托福字彙經常考出的predictable a.「可預知的」為例說明：

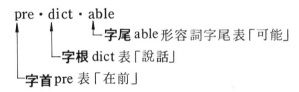

由以上分析可知，字首顧名思義，列於單字開頭位置，可決定單字的部分意義。字根一般置於字首之後，其後或接字尾或不接字尾，如上述 predictable一字的動詞原型 predict「預知」，便僅有字首pre-與字根 dict 而已。字尾則附著於單字尾部，主要功能在決定單字的詞類，此外並沒有太大的作用。一般談構詞成分，多以字首和字根為主，字尾數量較少，功能也不大，泰半只是附帶一提而已②。字

---

①英語字彙與希臘語、拉丁語等古代語言的字彙，關係非常密切，讀者欲進一步瞭解，請參閱本書附錄一「英語簡說」。

②本書共整理有 103 個最常用的字尾，以簡明扼要的方式，列於附錄二「英文常用字尾一覽表」中，供讀者參考。此外，欲詳知字首、字根、字尾常見的構詞型態，請參閱 xi 頁至 xvi 頁的「英文字首、字根、字尾常見的構詞型態」。

首字根的構詞功能極爲重要，茲以上述 predictable 一字爲起點，舉一連串單字說明如下：

predictable a.可預知的（字首 pre = before, 字根 dict = say, 字尾 able）

edict n. 詔令、敕令（字首 e = out, 字根 dict = say)

expedite v. 使加速（字首 ex = out, 字根 ped = foot, 字尾 ite)

impede v. 妨礙、阻礙（字首 im = in, 字根 ped = foot)

impel v. 推進、逼迫（字首 im = in, 字根 pel = drive）

compel v. 強迫（字首 com = together, 字根 pel = drive）

commit v. 委託、犯（字首 com = together, 字根 mit = send)

submit v. 使屈服、提出（字首 sub = under, 字根 mit = send)

suppose v. 推測、假定（字首 sup = under, 字根 pos = place)

dispose v. 處置、使傾向（字首 dis = away, 字根 pos = place)

distract v. 分心、擾亂（字首 dis = away, 字根 tract = draw)

contract v. 收縮、感染（字首 con = together, 字根 tract = draw)

這一連串「字鍊」裏，都是托福常考的單字，以及英文最常用的字首、字根。這些字首、字根可組成的單字極多，眼前列出的不過九牛一毛罷了。可見要將英文字彙學好，決不可忽視字首字根。

事實上，英文較常用的重要字彙，特別是大專以上程度常用的字彙，多以字首、字根組成。本書收列了英文最重要的30個字首，和70個字根，列出例字達 3,500 個以上，每字均附有音標、例句、

中譯、同義字、字源解釋。英文的字首多達兩百以上，字根則可達數百，其中有的比較常見，組成的單字極夥，有的却十分罕見，不但組成的單字偏難，而且也多半是一般不易用到的科學用語。有鑒於此，本書收列的 100 個字首字根，均是最常見、最基本的構詞要素，俾使讀者藉此學到最佳方法，得探英文字彙的堂奧。此外，每個例字後所附的例句與同義字，請萬勿忽視。一般人學習英文字彙最感困擾的問題，就是記了單字，懂了意思，知道唸法和詞類，可是到了寫作、會話，必須派上用場的時候，却躊躇起來，生怕不甚了解該字的涵義，而鬧出笑話。因此，學習單字時，不可沒有例句，否則只知中文翻譯，不了解實際用法，仍是一知半解而已。至於同義字，也是了解單字不可或缺的一環。漂亮的英文文章中，常有許多同義字，以免同一個字使用過多，使文章變得枯燥無味。學習同義字除了可以增進寫作能力，並能幫助學習者深入掌握這一批字的涵義，提昇字彙能力。總之，書中列出的例句和同義字極為重要，盼望讀者能切實把握。

　　本書不但可供一般人士進修英文使用，更適合準備托福、GRE、GMAT、SAT 等留學考試參考。本書 100 個字首字根組成的單字，多半是大專以上程度常用的重要字彙，而上述各種留學考試所考的字彙，正以這種字首字根組成的居多。書中所收的 100 個字首字根，乃英文最基本的構詞成分，因此列出的例字絕多屬托福範圍，而且幾盡是托福常考字彙③。GRE 的字彙程度較托福為高，但是要取得高分，仍須先將比較基礎的字彙記熟。本書例字除了大部分是托福重要字彙外，另有部分程度偏難，以星記號 ＊ 標出於該字右上角。準備 GRE 考試的讀者，不但須將未標星記號的基本字彙讀熟，以鞏固基礎，更得留意標星記號的GRE 字彙。

　　本書編撰期間，承蒙好友賀一平鼎力相助，書中各例字條下所

---

③請參閱拙著「托福字彙研究」（台北書林出版公司，1988 年）中「電腦統計 1980–87 年托福常考字彙排名」與「托福字彙命題最新趨勢」二節。

列音標及中譯，均出自賀兄之手，謹在此致上萬分謝意。此外，版面設計打字蒙全疊打字公司李秋月、張佩芬兩位小姐費心安排，謹此一併致謝。作者識力有限，本書謬誤之處，冀盼同道先進，不吝批評指正。

許　章　眞
1988 年 5 月●台北

本書英文摘要

100 English Prefixes
& Word Roots

Chang-chen Hsu

ENGLISH ABSTRACT

Word roots and affixes are essential to the study of English vocabulary. Anyone familiar with just a score of these basic combining forms can learn a large number of words with extraordinary celerity. It was this expedience in learning that inspired the author to write the present volume on English prefixes and word roots with a view to helping Chinese students increase their English vocabulary.

English vocabulary is composed largely of words formed by prefixes and word roots which are indispensable for the learning of these words. With concision in mind, the author has chosen 30 prefixes and 70 roots that are among the most fundamental combining forms of English. Once familiarized with these 100 prefixes and roots, the student is fully equipped to memorize more than 3,500 important words, an encouraging breakthrough for anyone wishing to acquire a proficiency in English vocabulary.

In this book each of these 3,500 words is accompanied by one or more sentences, which are considered instrumental in vocabulary study. Equally helpful are the two synonyms attached to each word since synonyms play a key role in the understanding of words. This book also contains three appendixes on the subjects of suffixes, word-formation, and the development of the English language respectively. These articles are meant to aid the reader in his study by outlining the origins and common features of English affixes and word roots.

Though originally designed for the general reader who wishes to efficiently acquire an English vocabulary for all purposes, this book can also help those preparing to take the TOEFL, the GRE and other English tests. The vocabulary essential to English is equally essential to such tests. Therefore, the 100 prefixes and word roots in this book can likewise be of immense help to those whose desire is to achieve high scores in tests.

英文常見的構詞型態

　　字首、字根（或字幹）、字尾構詞法是學習英文字彙最重要的方法。這些源自希臘語、拉丁語、古英語、古法語等古代語文的構詞要素，一個個神通廣大，可組成的單字佔英文字彙一大部分，如能靈活貫通，必可將英文程度提高甚多。

　　字首、字根（或字幹）、字尾是構詞的三個要素，本文僅將最常見的十四種型態分述如後，各型態所舉的例字，均是一般常用的單字。

● 第1型態　字首＋字根

conclude v. 結束、下結論 (字首 **con** = together, 字根 **clud** = close)

expound v. 解釋 (字首 **ex** = out, 字根 **pound** = place)

incite v. 刺激、鼓勵 (字首 **in** = in, 字根 **cit** = rouse)

predict v. 預知 (字首 **pre** = before, 字根 **dict** = say)

reduce v. 減少、降低 (字首 **re** = back, 字根 **duc** = lead)

註：承王家聲教授提出寶貴意見，指出字也可以如字根一般做為另一字的結構基礎，所以本文中許多類型的結構可進一步簡化如下：

$$(字首) + \begin{Bmatrix} 字根 \\ 字根+字根 \\ 字 \end{Bmatrix} + (字尾)$$

〔說明〕小括弧內的字首與字尾不一定要具備，但大括弧內的三者必須有其中之一。

● 第2型態　字首＋字首＋字根

coincide v. 巧合、協調（字首 co = together, 字首 in = in, 字根 cid = fall)

discompose v. 使不安、使慌亂（字首 dis = away, 字首 com = together, 字根 pos = place)

malcontent a./n. 不滿的、不滿的人（字首 **mal** = bad, 字首 con = together, 字根 **tent** = hold)

predispose v. 使傾向、使偏愛（字首 **pre** = before, 字首 **dis** = away, 字根 **pos** = place)

recollect v. 想起（字首 re = back, 字首 col = together, 字根 lect = select)

● 第3型態　字首＋字根＋字尾

diffident a. 羞怯的（字首 **di** = away, 字根 **fid** = trust, 字尾 -ent)

excessive a. 過度的（字首 **ex** = out, 字根 cess = go, 字尾 -ive)

incessant a. 不斷的（字首 **in** = not, 字根 cess = cease, 字尾 **-ant**)

pertinent a. 恰當、有關的（字首 **per** = through, 字根 **tin** = hold, 字尾 **-ent**)

requirement n. 需要的事物、必要條件（字首 **re** = back, 字根 **quir** = ask, 字尾 **-ment**)

● 第4型態　字首＋字首＋字根＋字尾

inadvertent a. 不注意的（字首 in = not, 字首 ad = to, 字根 vert = turn, 字尾 **-ent**)

insufficient a. 不足夠的（字首 in = not, 字首 suf = under, 字根 fic = make, 字尾 **-ent**)

irrevocable a. 不能取消、更改的（字首 ir = not, 字首 re = back, 字根 voc = call, 字尾 -able)

overabundance n. 過多、多餘（字首 **over** = over, 字首 **ab** = away, 字根 **und** = wave, 字尾 **-ance**)

unexpected a. 意外、未預料的（字首 **un** = not, 字首 **ex** = out, 字根 **spect** = watch, 字尾 **-ed**)

● 第 5 型態　字首＋字根＋字根＋字尾

dispossession n. 強奪、剝奪（字首 **dis** = away, 字根 **pos** = be able, 字根 **sess** = sit, 字尾 **-ion**)

emancipate v. 解放、釋放（字首 **e** = out, 字根 **man** = hand, 字根 **cip** = take, 字尾 **-ate**)

insignificant a. 無意義、無關重要的(字首 **in** = not, 字根 **sign** = sign, 字根 **fic** = make, 字尾 **-ant**)

remanufacture v./n. 再製造（字首 **re** = again, 字根 **manu** = hand, 字根 **fact** = make, 字尾 **-ure**)

unequivocal a. 明白、易分辨的（字首 **un** = not, 字根 **equ** = equal, 字根 **voc** = voice, 字尾 **-al**)

● 第 6 型態　字首＋字根＋字尾＋字尾

compassionate a. 表示同情的（字首 **com** = together, 字根 **pass** = feel, 字尾 **-ion**, 字尾 **-ate**)

differentiate v. 區分、辨別（字首 **dif** = away, 字根 **fer** = carry, 字尾 **-ent**, 字尾 **-ate**)

incidental a. 偶發、附帶的（字首 **in** = in, 字根 **cid** = fall, 字尾 **-ent**, 字尾 **-al**)

inequality n. 不平等（字首 **in** = not, 字根 **equ** = equal, 字尾 **-al**, 字尾 **-ity**）

posthumously adv. 死後地(字首 **post** = after, 字根 **hum** = earth, 字尾 **-ous**, 字尾 **-ly**)

● 第7型態　字首＋字首＋字根＋字尾＋字尾

incompatibly adv. 不能相容地 (字首 **in** = not, 字首 **com**=together, 字根 **pat** = feel, 字尾 **-ible**, 字尾 **-ly**)

indefinitely adv. 不明確、模糊地 (字首 **in** = not, 字首 **de** = down, 字根 **fin** = end, 字尾 **-ite**, 字尾 **-ly**)

indifferently adv. 冷淡、不在乎地 (字首 **in** = not, 字首 **dif** = away, 字根 **fer** = carry, 字尾 **-ent**, 字尾 **-ly**)

unprecedented a. 無先例的 (字首 **un** = not, 字首 **pre** = before, 字根 **cede** = go, 字尾 **-ent**, 字尾 **-ed**)

unsuspiciously adv. 不覺得懷疑的 (字首 **un** = not, 字首 **sus**=under, 字根 **spic** = watch, 字尾 **-ous**, 字尾 **-ly**)

● 第8型態　字根

claim v./n. 要求、主張 (字根 **claim** = cry out)

core n. 核心、中心 (字根 **cor** = heart)

fuse v. 鎔化、鎔合 (字根 **fus** = melt)

luster n. 光澤、光亮 (字根 **lustr** = light)

pend v. 未決、未定 (字根 **pend** = hang)

● 第9型態　字根＋字根

artifact n. 人工製品 (字根 **art** = skill, 字根 **fact** = make)

facsimile n. 複製、摹本 (字根 **fac** = make, 字根 **simil** = like)

homicide n. 殺人、兇殺 (字根 **hom** = human, 字根 **cid** = kill)

solicit v. 懇求、懇請 (字根 **sol** = entire, 字根 **cit** = rouse)

suicide v./n. 自殺 (字根 **sui** = self, 字根 **cid** = kill)

● 第10型態　字根＋字尾

dictate v. 口授、命令 (字根 **dict** = say, 字尾 **-ate**)

fortify v. 加強（字根 **fort** = be strong, 字尾 **-ify**）

fraction n. 碎片、小部分（字根 **fract** = break, 字尾 **-ion**）

tractable a. 溫順、易處理的（字根 **tract** = draw, 字尾 **-able**）

vertical a. 垂直的（字根 **vert** = turn, 字尾 **-ical**）

● 第11型態　字根＋字根＋字尾

equanimity n. 平靜、鎮定（字根 **equ** = equal, 字根 **anim** = mind, 字尾 **-ity**）

equivocal a. 模稜兩可的（字根 **equ** = equal, 字根 **voc** = voice, 字尾 **-al**）

magnificence n. 壯麗、堂皇（字根 **magn** = great, 字根 **fic** = make, 字尾 **-ence**）

manufacture v./n. 製造（字根 **manu** = hand, 字根 **fact** = make, 字尾 **-ure**）

solicitous a. 擔心、渴望的（字根 **sol** = entire, 字根 **cit** = rouse, 字尾 **-ous**）

● 第12型態　字根＋字尾＋字尾

clamorous a. 吵鬧、喧嘩的（字根 **clam** = cry out, 字尾 **-or**, 字尾 **-ous**）

currently adv. 一般、現今（字根 **cur** = run, 字尾 **-ent**, 字尾 **-ly**）

dictator n. 口授者、獨裁者（字根 **dict** = say, 字尾 **-ate**, 字尾 **-or**）

equality n. 平等（字根 **equ** = equal, 字尾 **-al**, 字尾 **-ity**）

sequential a. 連續、結果的（字根 **sequ** = follow, 字尾 **-ent**, 字尾 **-al**）

● 第13 型態　字根＋字根＋字尾＋字尾

equanimously adv. 平靜、鎮定地（字根 **equ** = equal, 字根 **anim** = mind, 字尾 **-ous**, 字尾 **-ly**）

equivalently adv. 同等、等量地（字根 **equ** = equal, 字根 **val** = be strong, 字尾 **-ent**, 字尾 **-ly**)

equivocally adv. 模稜兩可地（字根 **equ** = equal, 字根 **voc** = voice, 字尾 **-al**, 字尾 **-ly**)

magnificently adv. 壯麗、堂皇地（字根 **magn** = great, 字根 **fic** = make, 字尾 **-ent**, 字尾 **-ly**)

manipulation n. 操縱（字根 **man** = hand, 字根 **pul** = fill, 字尾 **-ate**, 字尾 **-ion**)

● 第 14 型態　字根＋字尾＋字尾＋字尾

clamorously adv. 吵鬧、喧嚷地（字根 **clam** = cry out, 字尾 **-or**, 字尾 **-ous**, 字尾 **-ly**)

momentarily adv. 短暫地（字根 **mom** = move, 字尾 **-ent**, 字尾 **-ary**, 字尾 **-ly**)

rectifiably adv. 可修正、矯正的（字根 **rect** = straight, 字尾 **-ify**, 字尾 **-able**, 字尾 **-ly**)

sedentarily adv. 久坐、定居地（字根 **sed** = sit, 字尾 **-ent**, 字尾 **-ary**, 字尾 **-ly**)

sequentially adv. 連續、結果地（字根 **sequ** = follow, 字尾 **-ent**, 字尾 **-al**, 字尾 **-ly**)

本書用法說明

一、本書收錄的每個字首、字根，均附有一篇數百字的說明，分析該字首、字根的起源，並介紹各種不同的拼法。例字中如有意義衍變比較特別的單字，也一併在說明中詳加解釋。讀者開始讀例字前，請先參閱說明。

二、書中所用略語 (abbreviations)，請參考下表說明：

n. = noun　名詞	**prep.** = preposition　介系詞
v. = verb　動詞	**n.m.** = noun masculine　陽性名詞
a. = adjective　形容詞	**n.n.** = noun neutral　中性名詞
adv. = adverb　副詞	**n.f.** = noun feminine　陰性名詞

（希臘、拉丁文名詞有陽、中、陰性之分，因此後三項僅用在希臘、拉丁文上。）

三、每個字首字根的例字部分，共分「單字‧音標‧詞類」、「例句」、「中譯‧同義字」、「字源分析」四段，由左至右分四欄排列，以方便閱讀。讀者初讀一遍或數遍後，再次複習時，可以直尺或手掌遮住右欄「中譯‧同義字」部分，目視例字，設法想出其意義與同義字。如此反覆練習，效果極佳，請切實把握。此外，各欄間尚有若干細節必須介紹，茲以「最重要的30個字首」 **1. ab‧abs** 第一頁例字為例，說明如下頁表。

四、本版於正文後新增孫述宇教授對 70 個字根的補正，用以釐清原先普遍對字根的一些誤解。如需進一步認識字根與字幹分辨的原則，可以參考附錄二「詞根與詞幹」。此外，孫教授所撰「英語簡說」是一篇簡要的英語發展史，敍述英語與其它印歐語言的互動及英語本身結構、聲韻、語彙等變動，極具參考價值。附錄三「英文常用字尾一覽表」則列出 103 個最常用的英文字尾，對字尾研讀有興趣的讀者可加利用。

五、本書最後附有「本書英文字彙索引」，書中所錄一切單字，均
以字母排列順序收錄於此，對閱讀幫助極大，請善加利用。

單字・音標・詞類	例　　句	中譯・同義字	字源分析
abdicate v. ˈæbdəˌket	When the king *abdicated*, his brother succeeded him on the throne.	讓位、放棄 relinquish renounce	dic(say)
abduct v. æbˈdʌkt	The millionaire's children were *abducted* yesterday.	綁架、綁走 carry off kidnap	duct(lead)
aberration n. ˌæbəˈreʃən	The *aberrations* of his youth had long been forgotten.	離正、越軌 deviation eccentricity	err(wander)
abhor v. əbˈhɔr	They *abhorred* cruelty to animals.	憎惡、痛恨 detest loathe	hor(horror)
abject* a. æbˈdʒɛkt	He is poor but not *abject* in his manner.	卑鄙、卑屈 mean base	ject(throw)
abjure v. əbˈdʒʊr	Some of the Roman Emperors tried to make Christians *abjure* their religion.	（發誓）放棄 renounce retract	jur(swear)
abnegate v. ˈæbnɪˌget	The surfs would never *abnegate* the idea of freedom.	放棄 renounce abjure	neg(deny)
abnormal a. æbˈnɔrml	It is *abnormal* for a man to be seven feet tall.	畸形、異常的 singular anomalous	norm(rule)
abominate v. əˈbɑməˌnet	The faithful townsfolk *abominated* sin.	痛恨、痛惡 abhor loathe	omin(omen)

例字欄右上角標有
＊記號者，表示該
字程度偏難，雖屬
於常用字彙範圍，
却比較不易見到。

字源分析欄內所列
字首字根，以粗體
字表示者，屬於本
書最重要的 100 個
英文字首字根範圍
，讀者可一併參閱
書中介紹該字首字
根部分。

字尾除可決定單字
的詞類之外，一般
比較不重要，因此
字源分析欄內一律
不列字尾，讀者如
欲進一步了解，請
參閱書後附錄二「
英文常用字尾一覽
表」。

最重要的30個字首

1

AB·ABS

away, from

分離

　　字首 ab, abs 源自拉丁文介系詞 ā, ab ，原在拉丁文便有 away, from 的意思，如「離開義大利」這句話，拉丁文便作 "ab Italiā"。這個介系詞在拉丁文較常見的形態，有 ā, ab, abs 三種，後接名詞為子音開頭者用 ā，母音開頭者用 ab，子音 t 與 q 開頭者用 abs，拼法之所以不同，和語音配合有極大的關聯。原在拉丁文便已當字首使用，如下文的 aberration n.「越軌」、abduct v.「綁架」、absence n.「缺席」等，即出自拉丁文的 aberrāre, abdūcere, absēns 等字。英文中較常見的拼法為 ab 與 abs, a 的形態則極為罕見，一般字彙書也絕少列出，比較重要的例字就只有 averse 「厭惡的」和 avert 「避開」（請參閱本書「最重要的 70 個字根」**65. vers·vert** 部分）。下文 abominate v.「痛恨」，字根有 ill omen 「凶兆」的意思，因此「視為凶兆而遠離」，便成了「痛恨」。absolve v. 和 absolute a. 源自同一字根 solv, solu「放鬆」，因此 absolve 有「解除」的意思，absolute 為「鬆開而自由分離」，便成了「完全的」。

單字‧音標‧詞類	例　　句	中譯‧同義字	字源分析
abdicate v. ˈæbdəˌket	When the king *abdicated*, his brother succeeded him on the throne.	讓位、放棄 relinquish renounce	**dic**(say)
abduct v. æbˈdʌkt	The millionaire's children were *abducted* yesterday.	綁架、綁走 carry off kidnap	**duct**(lead)
aberration n. ˌæbəˈreʃən	The *aberrations* of his youth had long been forgotten.	離正、越軌 deviation eccentricity	err(wander)
abhor v. əbˈhɔr	They *abhorred* cruelty to animals.	憎惡、痛恨 detest loathe	hor(horror)
abject* a. æbˈdʒɛkt	He is poor but not *abject* in his manner.	卑鄙、卑屈 mean base	**ject**(throw)
abjure* v. əbˈdʒʊr	Some of the Roman Emperors tried to make Christians *abjure* their religion.	（發誓）放棄 renounce retract	jur(swear)
abnegate* v. ˈæbnɪˌget	The serfs would never *abnegate* the idea of freedom.	放棄 renounce abjure	neg(deny)
abnormal a. æbˈnɔrml	It is *abnormal* for a man to be seven feet tall.	畸形、異常的 singular anomalous	norm(rule)
abominate v. əˈbɑməˌnet	The faithful townsfolk *abominated* sin.	痛恨、痛惡 abhor loathe	omin(omen)

單字·音標·詞類	例　　句	中譯·同義字	字源分析
aboriginal a. ˌæbəˈrɪdʒənḷ	The anthropologists have studied the *aboriginal* inhabitants of the area.	土著的 native indigenous	original
abrade v. əˈbred	Drifting sand *abrades* rocks.	磨損、摩擦 scrape erode	rad(scrape)
abrogate v. ˈæbrəˌget	This law has now been *abrogated*.	取消、廢止 abolish annul	rog(ask)
abrupt a. əˈbrʌpt	The van took an *abrupt* turn in the road.	突然、陡峭的 sudden precipitous	rupt(break)
abscond * v. æbˈskɑnd	The dishonest cashier *absconded* with the bank's money.	潛逃、逃亡 escape flee	cond(conceal)
absence n. ˈæbsṇs	His long *absence* from work delayed his promotion.	缺席、缺乏 non-attendance deficiency	ence(be)
absolute a. ˈæbsəˌlut	*Absolute* alcohol has no water in it.	純粹、完全、絕對的 complete peremptory	solu(loose)
absolve v. æbˈsɑlv	I was *absolved* of blame in the matter.	免除、赦免、解除 discharge acquit	solv(loose)
absorb v. əbˈsɔrb	A blotter *absorbs* ink.	吸收 consume imbibe	sorb(suck)

單字・音標・詞類	例　　句	中譯・同義字	字源分析
abstain v. əbˈsten	Athletes usually *abstain* from smoking.	戒絕 withhold refrain	**tain**(hold)
abstract v. æbˈstrækt	Metal can be *abstracted* from ore.	抽出、提煉、摘要 draw epitomize	**tract**(draw)
abstruse a. æbˈstrus	*Abstruse* questions are usually hard to answer.	難解、深奧的 enigmatic recondite	**trus**(thrust)
absurd a. əbˈsɝd	The young men's request is absolutely *absurd*.	荒謬的 irrational preposterous	surd(deaf)
abundant a. əˈbʌndənt	This island country is *abundant* in natural resources.	豐富、充足的 ample copious	und(wave)
abuse v. əˈbjuz	A good rider never *abuses* his horse.	虐待、辱罵 maltreat upbraid	use

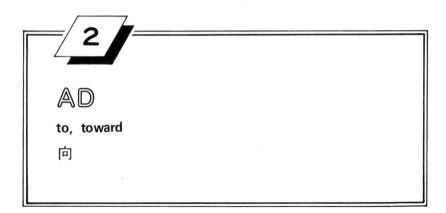

2

AD

to, toward

向

　　字首 ad 源自拉丁文介系詞 ad，拉丁文原義即爲 to，表方向。美國堪薩斯州 (Kansas) 建州箴言 "Ad Astra per Aspera" (To the Stars Through Difficulties) 中，ad 便有 to 的意思（其餘各拉丁字 astra 爲 stars, per 爲 through, aspera 爲 difficulties）。ad 的拼法變化相當複雜，爲了與字根配合，第二個字母 d 或消失或同化，而衍生出 a, ac, af, ag, al, an, ap, ar, as, at 各種形態，如下文的 accustom v.「使習慣於」、affix v.「黏上」、allocate v.「撥出」、append v.「附加」等等，均是這種情形。ad 原意在表示方向，但與字根配合之後，卻已沒有多大作用，因此以字首 ad 組成的單字，其字義一般視該字的字根而定。例如，accelerate v.「加速進行」一字，由字首 ac 加上字根 celer（快速）而成，字根的意思正也是該字的意思。再如 adapt v.「使適合」，由 ad 與 apt「適合的」組成，apt 的意思便成了該字的字義。

單字・音標・詞類	例　　　句	中譯・同義字	字源分析
accede v. æk'sid	I will never *accede* to her request.	同意、答應 consent comply	cede(yield)
accelerate v. æk'sɛlə,ret	The riots on the streets *accelerated* the fall of the government.	催促、加速進行 speed expedite	celer(speed)
accost* v. ə'kɔst	I was *accosted* by a beggar.	招呼、搭話 greet address	cost(rib)
account n. ə'kaʊnt	Please give me an *account* of your trip to Africa.	敘述、說明 narration explanation	count
accredit v. ə'krɛdɪt	They *accredit* these views to him.	將（言語等）歸於 ascribe attribute	cred(believe)
accumulate v. ə'kjumjə,let	By buying ten books every month, he soon *accumulated* a good library.	積、積聚 gather amass	cumul(heap)
accustom v. ə'kʌstəm	A good traveler can *accustom* himself to almost any kind of food.	（使）習慣於 habituate inure	custom
adapt v. ə'dæpt	The young man quickly *adapted* himself to the new customs of the country.	使適應、使適合 adjust conform	apt

單字・音標・詞類	例　　　句	中譯・同義字	字源分析
adhere v. ədˈhɪr	Although he was warned of the danger, he *adhered* to his plans to go alone.	堅持、黏著 glue stick	her(stick)
adjourn v. əˈdʒɝn	The meeting was *adjourned* for a week.	延期、休會 defer prorogue	journ(day)
adjure v. əˈdʒʊr	I *adjure* you to speak the truth.	懇請、祈求 beseech invoke	jur(swear)
adjust v. əˈdʒʌst	These desks and seats can be *adjusted* to the height of any child.	調節、使適於 regulate accommodate	just
administer v. ədˈmɪnəstɚ	We need the best men to *administer* the affairs of the state.	管理 conduct superintend	minister
admire v. ədˈmaɪr	His cleverness is much *admired*.	欽佩、歎賞 respect regard	mir(wonder)
admonish v. ədˈmɑnɪʃ	The policeman *admonished* him not to drive too fast.	警告、訓戒 chide reprove	moni(warn)
adopt v. əˈdɑpt	They *adopted* a strong attitude towards this matter.	採取、收爲養子 assume foster	opt(option)
adore v. əˈdor	We *adored* him for his integrity and brilliant diplomatic achievements.	敬重、敬愛 esteem venerate	or(speak)

單字・音標・詞類	例　　　句	中譯・同義字	字源分析
adorn v. əˈdɔrn	Their house was lavishly *adorned*.	裝飾 decorate embellish	orn(decorate)
adulterate v. əˈdʌltəret	The milk we bought had been *adulterated* with water.	摻混、使品質變壞 deteriorate vitiate	alter(other)
affable a. ˈæfəbḷ	He is *affable* to the poor.	和藹可親、殷勤的 amiable courteous	fari(speak)
affiliate n. əˈfɪlɪˌet	The hospital is *affiliated* with that university.	聯合、加入、合併 associate incorporate	fili(son)
affirm v. əˈfɝm	The Bible *affirms* that God is love.	斷言 declare asseverate	firm
affix v. əˈfɪks	The little boy has learned how to *affix* stamps to letters.	黏上、貼上、附加 append attach	fix
afflict v. əˈflɪkt	He is *afflicted* with the gout.	使痛苦 torment pang	flict(strike)
affront v. əˈfrʌnt	The boy *affronted* the professor by making a face at her.	侮辱、冒犯 offend outrage	front

單字・音標・詞類	例　　　句	中譯・同義字	字源分析
aggrandize v. ˈægrənˌdaɪz	The king sought to *aggrandize* himself at the expense of his people.	提高、增大（權力等） exalt augment	grand
aggravate v. ˈægrəˌvet	His bad temper was *aggravated* by his headache.	加重、激怒 intensify exasperate	grave
aggregate v. ˈægrɪˌget	The money collected will *aggregate* US$1,000.	合計、聚集 heap accumulate	**greg**(group)
aggrieve* v. əˈgriv	He was *aggrieved* at the insult from his friend.	使苦惱、使受屈 grieve wrong	grieve
align v. əˈlaɪn	He *aligned* himself with the liberals.	使合作、排列成行 form in line array	line
allay v. əˈle	His fears were *allayed* by the news of the safety of his family.	使和緩、使鎮靜 assuage soothe	lay
alleviate v. əˈliviˌet	The doctor gave the patient something to *alleviate* the pain.	減輕、使緩和 assuage mollify	lev(light)
allocate v. ˈæləˌket	They will *allocate* funds for housing.	撥出 deal allot	loc(place)

單字・音標・詞類	例　　　句	中譯・同義字	字源分析
allot v. əˈlɑt	When the profits of business were *alloted*, I received a lot of money.	分配 dispense allocate	lot
alloy n. ˈælɔɪ	Brass is an *alloy* of copper and zinc.	合金 mixture of metals	lig(bind)
allure v. əˈlʊr	Rewards *allure* men to brave danger.	引誘 decoy entice	lure
ally v. əˈlaɪ	Great Britain was *allied* with France during the World War.	聯合、結合 unite associate	lig(bind)
ameliorate v. əˈmiljəˌret	The politicians were trying to *ameliorate* the workers' conditions.	改善 better improve	melior(better)
amenable a. əˈminəbḷ	We are all *amenable* to the law.	有責任、應服從的 responsible liable	men(lead)
amend v. əˈmɛnd	The regulations must be *amended*.	修正、改良 reform rectify	mend
annex v. əˈnɛks	Japan *annexed* Korea in 1910.	併吞、附加 affix subjoin	nec(tie)
annihilate v. əˈnaɪəˌlet	Our soldiers *annihilated* a force of three hundred enemy troops.	消滅 destroy exterminate	nihil(nothing)

單字・音標・詞類	例　　　句	中譯・同義字	字源分析
annotate v. 'æno͵tet	Shakespeare's plays are often *annotated* to make them easier to understand.	評註、註解 comment elucidate	note
announce v. ə'naʊns	The engagement will be *announced* soon.	正式宣佈 declare proclaim	**nounc**(announce)
annul v. ə'nʌl	The judge *annulled* the contract because one of the signers was too young.	取消、廢止 abolish nullify	null(none)
apparatus n. ͵æpə'retəs	We need some chemical *apparatus* for the laboratory.	儀器 equipment instruments	para(prepare)
appeal n. ə'pil	The game has lost its *appeal*.	吸引力、懇求 attraction invocation	peal(call)
appease v. ə'piz	The angry king was soon *appeased* after seeing the beautiful princess.	使平靜、緩和 pacify soothe	peace
append v. ə'pɛnd	Amendments are *appended* to the Constitution of the United States.	附加 attach affix	**pend**(hang)
appertain* v. ͵æpɚ'ten	Forestry *appertains* to geography, to botany, and to agriculture.	屬於、與⋯有關 concern pertain	pertain

單字・音標・詞類	例　　句	中譯・同義字	字源分析
apportion v. ə'porʃən	The father's property was *apportioned* among his sons after his death.	分攤、分配 allot dispense	portion
appraise v. ə'prez	An employer must be able to *appraise* ability and character.	鑑別、評價 rate estimate	price
apprehend v. ˌæprɪ'hɛnd	The outlaw was *apprehended* early this morning.	逮捕、憂懼 arrest dread	prehend(seize)
approbate* v. 'æprəˌbet	The act was *approbated* by the committee.	認可、贊成 approve endorse	prob(prove)
appropriate v. ə'proprɪˌet	Congress *appropriated* money for the new naval bases.	撥（款）、撥作 （某目的）之用 assign allocate	proper
arouse v. ə'rauz	Their terrible experience *aroused* our pity.	引起、激起 excite rouse	rouse
arrange v. ə'rendʒ	I came here to *arrange* business.	處理、調解 settle adjust	range
assail v. ə'sel	He was *assailed* by his political opponents.	攻擊 attack assault	sal(leap)
assault v. ə'sɔlt	The enemy *assaulted* us at darkness.	攻擊 attack assail	sal(leap)

單字·音標·詞類	例　　　句	中譯·同義字	字源分析
assemble v. əˈsɛmbl̩	The students were *assembled* in the school hall.	集合、聚集 gather congregate	sembl(together)
assent v. əˈsɛnt	I do not quite *assent* to your point of view.	同意、贊同 consent accede	**sent**(sense)
assert v. əˈsɝt	His friends *asserted* that he was innocent.	斷言 affirm asseverate	sert(bind)
assimilate v. əˈsɪml̩ˌet	The U.S. has *assimiliated* people from most of the countries of Europe.	同化、使類似 、吸收 make similar absorb	simil(similar)
associate v. əˈsoʃɪˌet	He *associated* himself with good company.	結交、聯合 combine affiliate	soci(join)
assort v. əˈsɔrt	Stay here and *assort* the papers on your desk.	分類 arrange classify	sort
assortment n. əˈsɔrtmənt	We have quite an *assortment* of goods today.	各色俱備之物 、物品總集 varied collection miscellany	sort
assuage v. əˈswedʒ	One must learn to *assuage* his passions.	緩和 smooth appease	suave
assume v. əˈsjum	He *assumed* that the supervisor would be on time.	假定、假裝 suppose affect	sum(take)

單字・音標・詞類	例　　句	中譯・同義字	字源分析
assure v. əˈʃʊr	I *assure* you there is no danger whatsoever.	確告、保證 certify embolden	sure
attach v. əˈtætʃ	He *attached* labels to all his bags.	繫、附加 fasten affix	tach(nail)
attain v. əˈten	The boy tried so hard to *attain* honor.	得到 obtain procure	**tain**(hold)
attaint* v. əˈtent	The gentleman's honor was *attainted* when he was accused of stealing.	污辱、羞辱 disgrace defame	taint
attemper* v. əˈtɛmpɚ	The bartender *attempered* the wine by adding some water.	沖淡、使緩和 moderate mitigate	temper
attend v. əˈtɛnd	The meeting was well *attended*.	出席、到、注意 frequent heed	**tend**(stretch)
attest v. əˈtɛst	The man's ability was *attested* by his rapid promotion.	證實 exhibit manifest	test
attune v. əˈtjun	She is *attuning* her violin to the piano.	使合調、使一致 harmonize accord	tune
aver v. əˈvɝ	She *averred* that the event actually happened.	斷言 assert asseverate	ver(true)

單字・音標・詞類	例　　　　句	中譯・同義字	字源分析
avow* v. əˈvaʊ	The man finally *avowed* his guilt.	公開承認、坦白承認 admit confess	**vow**
awake v. əˈwek	The noise of the car *awoke* him.	吵醒、喚起 awaken arouse	wake

3

BENE·BON

good

良好

　　拉丁文名言 "Dē mortuĭs nil nisi bonum" (Of the dead nothing but good should be said.) 中，bonum 一字便有這個字首。原拉丁文已有兩種拼法，bonus（經過性別變化可有 bona、bonum 形態）為形容詞，意思和英文的 good 一樣，而 bene 則為副詞，有 well 的意思。bene、bon 其實也應該視為字根，只不過一般字彙書多已習慣稱之為字首，原因是 bene、bon 均出現在單字的字首位置，無一例外。下文例字拼法比較特別的，有 boon n.「恩賜」、bounty n.「獎金」、bounteous a.「慷慨的」、bountiful a.「豐富的」，皆由 bon 變音而成。其中 bounty, bounteous, bountiful 同一字源，均由拉丁文 bonitās (goodness, n.) 變來，目前的拼法在十四世紀末葉已經形成。

benediction n.　At the end of the church　祝禱、恩賜　**dict**(say)
ˌbɛnəˈdɪkʃən　service the minister gave　blessing
　　the *benediction*.　　beatitude

benefaction* n.　The college owed much　捐助　**fact**(do)
ˌbɛnəˈfækʃən　to the *benefaction* of its　contribution
　　financial supporters.　　charity

beneficial a.　The medicine had a　有益的　**fic**(do)
ˌbɛnəˈfɪʃəl　*beneficial* effect.　favorable
　　　　advantageous

beneficiary n.　Joyce was the only　受惠者　**fic**(do)
ˌbɛnəˈfɪʃɛrɪ　*beneficiary* of her　one who
　　husband's insurance　　receives benefits
　　policy.

beneficence n.　The scholarships were　善行、仁慈、　**fic**(do)
bəˈnɛfəsn̩s　funded by the　慈善
　　beneficence of the　kindness
　　alumni.　generosity

benefit n.　I am doing this for your　利益　**fit**(do)
ˈbɛnəfɪt　*benefit*.　good
　　　　advantage

benevolent a.　She had a *benevolent*　慈善、仁慈的　vol(wish)
bəˈnɛvələnt　attitude toward her　kindhearted
　　staff, always giving them　philanthropic
　　bonuses.

benign a.　The growth proved to be　良性、良好、
bɪˈnaɪn　*benign* rather than　親切的
　　malignant.　favorable
　　　　complaisant

單字·音標·詞類	例　　句	中譯·同義字	字源分析
benignant a. bɪˈnɪgnənt	A *benignant* ruler is always loved by his subjects.	仁慈、親切的 gracious amiable	
bonus n. ˈbonəs	The employer does not like to give too many *bonuses* to his staff.	紅利、獎金 dividend premium	
boon* n. bun	Parks are a great *boon* to people in big cities.	恩物、恩賜 blessing gratuity	
bounty n. ˈbaʊntɪ	The municipal govern-ment gave a *bounty* of $10 for each fox killed.	獎金、慷慨好施 reward beneficence	
bounteous a. ˈbaʊntɪəs	The millionaire has a *bounteous* nature.	慷慨的 generous beneficent	
bountiful a. ˈbaʊntəfəl	The hungry soldiers were happy to receive the *bountiful* supply of food.	豐富、大方的 liberal plentiful	

4

CATA

down, complete

下降 • 完全

---

cata 源自希臘文 *κατα* (kata)，原有副詞、介系詞兩種用法，意思原即 downward, completely。由 cata 組成的英文單字，最初完全由希臘文引進，十五、十六世紀時的英文著作中，已可見到這些單字。例如，cataclysm n. 原希臘文作 *κατακλυσμος* (kataklysmos)，本即有「洪水」的意思；catalog(ue) n. 源自 *καταλογος* (katalogos)，原已有「統計、目錄」的意思；catastrophe n. 源自 *καταστροφη* (katastrophē)，原有「變動、滅亡」的意思。歐洲希臘文等古語文對英文影響之深，可見一斑。由 cata 組成的字彙中有不少專門用語及科學用語，較為偏難，不適合本書收錄，僅在此一語帶過，供讀者參考：catabolism n.「分解作用」、catachresis n.「字語誤用」、catacomb n.「地下墓穴」、catagmatic a.「斷骨的」、catalase n.「接觸酵素」、catalepsis n.「癲癇」、catalysis n.「催化作用」、catapult n.「投石機」、catatonia n.「緊張症」等等。

單字・音標・詞類	例　　句	中譯・同義字	字源分析
cataclysm* n. **ˈkætəˌklɪzəm**	World War II was a *cataclysm* for all of Europe.	洪水、劇變 deluge upheaval	clysm(wash)
catalog(ue) n. **ˈkætlˌɔg**	The card *catalog* in the library lists titles of books.	目錄 list register	**logue**(say)
cataract* n. **ˈkætəˌrækt**	The writer has made a beautiful description of the *cataracts* of the Nile.	大瀑布 waterfall cascade	ract(break)
catastrophe n. **kəˈtæstrəfɪ**	A big earthquake is a natural *catastrophe*.	災禍 disaster calamity	strophe(turn)
category n. **ˈkætəˌgorɪ**	What *category* of books are you looking for?	種類 class sort	egory(assembly)

5

CIRCUM

around

環繞

　　字首 circum 源自拉丁文介系詞 circum，原已有 around 的意思。拉丁文 circā (around, adv., prep.), circus (circle, n.m.), circuitus (circuit, n.m.)，和英文的 circle n.「圓圈」、circular a.「圓的」、circulate v.「循環」等字，均與 circum 同源。字首 circum 與字根 scrib「寫」組合，而成 circumscribe v.（拉丁文原作 circumscrībere, v.），原義為「畫圓圈」，後引申為「限制」。與字根 spect「看」組合，而成 circumspect a.（拉丁文 circumspectus, a.），由「環視」的意思，而引申為「小心、慎重的」。與字根 sta「站立」組合，而成 circumstance n.（拉丁文 circumstatia, n.f.），表示「周圍所立之物」，而有「情況」的意思。

單字・音標・詞類	例　　　句	中譯・同義字	字源分析
circuit n. ˈsɝ·kɪt	The newspaper boy made his usual *circuit*.	巡行、巡迴路線 path route	
circuitous a. sɚˈkjuɪtəs	Her speech was full of *circuitous* arguments which are hard to grasp.	間接、迂曲、繞行的 winding roundabout	
circumference n. sɚˈkʌmfərəns	The *circumference* of the earth at the equator is about 25,000 miles.	圓周、周圍 boundary perimeter	**fer**(carry)
circumlocution*n. ˌsɝ·kəmloˈkjuʃən	The speaker used a lot of *circumlocutions* in his speech.	婉轉曲折的說法 indirect way 　of expressing	**loc**(speak)
circumscribe v. ˌsɝ·kəmˈskraɪb	The rules of the private school *circumscribed* the students' daily activities.	限制、立界限 limit confine	**scrib**(write)
circumspect a. ˈsɝ·kəmˌspɛkt	He must learn to be *circumspect* about making suggestions to his boss.	慎重、小心的 cautious heedful	**spect**(look)
circumstance n. ˈsɝ·kəmˌstæns	Under no *circumstances* will I consent to sell the building.	情況 condition situation	**sta**(stand)
circumstantial a. ˌsɝ·kəmˈstænʃəl	Minor details are *circumstantial* compared with the main fact.	不重要、間接、推論的 indirect inferential	**sta**(stand)

單字・音標・詞類	例　　句	中譯・同義字	字源分析
circumvent* v. ˌsɝkəmˈvɛnt	The melodrama's heroine is *circumvented* with various perils.	包圍、勝過 surround outwit	**vent**(come)

CO·COM·CON

with, together

一起 • 共同

　　字首 co, com, con 源自拉丁文介系詞 cum，原義即爲 with。古羅馬作家西塞羅 (Cicero, 106–43 B.C.) 的名言 "Parēs cum paribus facillime congregantur" （「物以類聚」，英文可作 "Birds of a feather flock together"）中，便有這個介系詞 cum。co, com, con 是極爲重要的英文字首，共有五種拼法，除了 co, com, con 之外，並有 col 和 cor 兩種。跟隨在字首之後的字根，第一個音若是母音、半母音或 h，一般拼作 co，如下文的 coalesce v.「合併」、cohere v.「凝結、結合」等均是。若是 p、b、m 三個雙唇音(bilabial)之一，便拼作 com，如 compress v.「壓縮」、combat n.「戰鬥」、commend v.「稱讚」等。後面若接 l 或 r，則分別拼作 col 或 cor，如 colleague n.「同事」、correspond v.「調合」等。其他情形則拼作 con，如 condone v.「寬恕」、confer v.「賜與」、conquer v.「征服」、consecrate v.「奉爲神聖」等等。

單字・音標・詞類	例　　句	中譯・同義字	字源分析
coalesce v. ˌkoəˈlɛs	The thirteen colonies in North America *coalesced* to form a new nation.	合併、聯合 combine amalgamate	alesce(grow up)
coalition n. ˌkoəˈlɪʃən	The two parties formed a *coalition* government.	聯合、聯盟 league alliance	alesce(grow up)
coerce v. koˈɝs	Her parents *coerced* her into marrying the man that she did not love.	強迫 force compel	erce(restrain)
coeval* a. koˈivl̩	This university is *coeval* with the nation.	同時期、同時代的 coexistent comtemporary	ev(age)
coexist v. ˌko·ɪgˈzɪst	Orange trees have *coexisting* fruit and flowers.	共生、共存 exist together	exist
cogitate v. ˈkɑdʒəˌtet	He did not *cogitate* long before he made the decision.	思考、沈思 contemplate brood	agit(consider)
cohere v. koˈhɪr	The particles making up a brick *cohere*.	凝結、結合 connect unite	her(stick)
coherent a. koˈhɪrənt	A sentence that is not *coherent* is hard to understand.	連貫、一致的 corresponding intelligible	her(stick)
coincide v. ˌko·ɪnˈsaɪd	My views do not *coincide* with those of my employer.	符合、一致 agree concur	in(on) cid(fall)

單字・音標・詞類	例　　　句	中譯・同義字	字源分析
collaborate v. kəˈlæbəˌret	The two students have *collaborated* in preparing the term paper.	合作 work together cooperate	labor
collapse v. kəˈlæps	The house *collapsed* on account of the earth-quake.	倒塌、崩潰 fall break down	lapse(fall)
collateral* a. kəˈlætərəl	Cousins are *collateral* relatives.	旁系、附屬的 related subordinate	lateral
colleague n. ˈkɑlig	My *colleagues* would not believe what happened to me on this trip.	同事 co-worker associate	league
collect v. kəˈlɛkt	I have *collected* enough material for my report.	收集 gather compile	lect(choose)
collide v. kəˈlaɪd	The two trucks *collided* on the highway.	互撞、衝突 clash conflict	lid(strike)
colloquial a. kəˈlokwɪəl	One has to learn *colloquial* English to live in the United States.	口語的 conversational informal	loqu(speak)
collusion* n. kəˈluʒən	The police and the criminals appeared to be working in *collusion*.	共謀、串通 conspiracy deceit	lus(play)
combat n. ˈkɑmbæt	The troopers are in *combat* now.	戰鬥 battle skirmish	bat(fight)

單字・音標・詞類	例　　　句	中譯・同義字	字源分析
combine v. kəmˈbaɪn	Quicklime *combines* with water to form slaked lime.	化合、結合 connect blend	bin(two)
commend v. kəˈmɛnd	His work was highly *commended* by everyone.	稱讚 laud eulogize	mand (command)
commensurate＊a. kəˈmɛnʃərɪt	Nothing in this life is *commensurate* to our desires.	相當、同量的 equivalent tantamount	mensur (measure)
commingle v. kəˈmɪŋg̣ḷ	Fact is inextricably *commingled* with fiction.	混合、混雜 mingle amalgamate	mingle
commiserate＊v. kəˈmɪzəˌret	The colleagues have *commiserated* his misfortune.	憐憫、同情 sympathize compassionate	miser(misery)
commission n. kəˈmɪʃən	I have several *commissions* for you if you are going to India.	委託代辦的事、委託 trust errand	miss(send)
n.	A *commission* of three experts was sent to the site.	委員會、代表團 committee delegation	
commit v. kəˈmɪt	You have to *commit* yourself to the doctor's care.	委託、付與 entrust deliver	mit(send)
v.	The madman *committed* suicide when they tried to break into his room.	作、犯 do perpetrate	

單字・音標・詞類	例　　　句	中譯・同義字	字源分析
compact a. kəm'pækt	Her speech was rather *compact*.	簡潔的 terse succinct	pact(fasten)
companion n. kəm'pænjən	Who were your *companions* on your journey?	同伴、朋友、伴侶 friend partner	pan(bread)
company n. 'kʌmpənɪ	She has come here to keep me *company*.	陪伴、同伴 companionship partnership	pan(bread)
compare v. kəm'pɛr	She *compared* several samples of silk for her dress.	比較、匹敵、競爭 compete parallel	par(equal)
compartment n. kəm'pɑrtmənt	The pencil box has several *compartments* for holding different things.	格、隔間 section subdivision	part
compass n. 'kʌmpəs	A prison is within the *compass* of its walls.	周圍、範圍 boundary range	pass(pace)
compassion n. kəm'pæʃən	She did not show much *compassion* toward the poor man.	同情、憐憫 pity sympathy	passion
compatible a. kəm'pætəbḷ	Accuracy is not always *compatible* with haste.	能共存、一致、符合的 consistent congruous	**pat(feel)**

單字・音標・詞類	例　句	中譯・同義字	字源分析
compel v. kəm'pɛl	I was *compelled* to believe every word they had said.	強迫 force coerce	**pel**(push)
compensate v. 'kɑmpən‚set	The hunter *compensated* the farmer for killing his cows.	賠償、補償、報酬 atone remunerate	**pens**(weigh)
compete v. kəm'pit	The prize was open to all, but few *competed*.	競爭、比賽 contest vie	**pet**(seek)
compile v. kəm'paɪl	These tables were *compiled* from actual observations over the years.	編纂、編輯 gather amass	**pile**
complacent a. kəm'plesṇt	The winner's *complacent* smile annoyed some people.	洋洋自得、自滿的 satisfied arrogant	**plac**(please)
complaisant a. kəm'plezṇt	His *complaisant* manners pleased the elders.	謙恭、有禮、順從的 polite compliant	**plais**(please)
complement v. 'kɑmplə‚mɛnt	Two discussions from different points of view may *complement* each other.	補足、補充 make complete	**ple**(fill)
complex a. 'kɑmplɛks	Life is getting more and more *complex*.	複雜、錯綜的 complicated intricate	**plex**(fold)

單字・音標・詞類	例　　句	中譯・同義字	字源分析
complicate v. ˈkɑmpləˌket	That will only *complicate* the matter.	使複雜 confuse entangle	**plic**(fold)
comport* v. kəmˈport	His conduct did not *comport* with his high position.	適合、相稱 accord correspond	**port**(carry)
comprehend v. ˌkɑmprɪˈhɛnd	One can use a word correctly only when he *comprehends* the word.	了解 understand grasp	prehend(seize)
v.	Canada and New Zealand were *comprehended* in the British Empire.	包括、包含 include comprise	
comprehensive a. ˌkɑmprɪˈhɛnsɪv	The term's work ended with a *comprehensive* review.	廣博、廣泛的 wide extensive	prehens(seize)
compress v. kəmˈprɛs	The men are asked to *compress* two months' work into one.	壓縮、減縮 condense abbreviate	**press**
comprise v. kəmˈpraɪz	The United States *comprises* 50 states.	包括 include comprehend	pris(press)
compromise v. ˈkɑmprəˌmaɪz	Sooner or later she will have to *compromise* with her husband.	和解 settle arbitrate	**promise**
compulsory a. kəmˈpʌlsərɪ	*Compulsory* measures have been taken to conserve energy.	強迫、強制的 obligatory mandatory	**puls**(push)

單字・音標・詞類	例　　　句	中譯・同義字	字源分析
compunction* n. kəm'pʌŋkʃən	I have little *compunction* in doing that.	良心不安、 懊悔 penitence contrition	punc(prick)
compute v. kəm'pjut	Mother has *computed* the cost of my study abroad.	計算 count reckon	put(think)
concave* a. kɑn'kev	The palm of one's hand is slightly *concave*.	凹的 hollow depressed	cave
concede v. kən'sid	We meant to conciliate and *concede*.	讓步、承認 yield acknowledge	**cede**(go, yield)
conceit n. kən'sit	No one admires a man who is full of *conceit*.	自負 vanity complacency	**ceit**(receive)
concentrate v. 'kɑnsn̩,tret	The commanders had to *concentrate* their troops in this area.	集中、濃縮 converge condense	center
concoct v. kɑn'kɑkt	They have *concocted* a plot to overthrow the military government.	計畫、調製 prepare contrive	coct(cook)
concord n. 'kɑnkɔrd	The stars move in harmony and *concord*.	和諧、一致 agreement harmony	**cord**(heart)
concourse* n. 'kɑnkors	The fortress was built at the *concourse* of the two rivers.	會流、合流 confluence convergence	**course**

單字・音標・詞類	例　　句	中譯・同義字	字源分析
condense v. kən'dɛns	He *condensed* the paragraph into only one line.	使簡潔、縮短 contract abridge	dense
condescend* v. ˌkɑndɪ'sɛnd	Some people never *condescend* to help their wives with the house-work.	屈尊 submit stoop	**descend**
condole v. kən'dol	I *condole* with you upon the loss of your mother.	同情、慰問 sympathize console	dole(grieve)
condone v. kən'don	The offense was soon *condoned*.	寬恕、原諒 forgive overlook	don(give)
conduce v. kən'djus	Insecurity often *conduces* to fear.	引起、有助於 lead promote	**duc**(lead)
confederate n. kən'fɛdərɪt	The thief was arrested, but his *confederates* got away.	共犯、同謀者 companion accomplice	fed(league)
confer v. kən'fɜ˞	The university *conferred* an honorary degree upon the illustrious educator.	頒給、賜與 grant bestow	**fer**(carry)
confide v. kən'faɪd	The girl always *confided* in her mother.	告以秘密以示 信賴、交託 reveal in trust entrust	fid(believe)

單字·音標·詞類	例　　句	中譯·同義字	字源分析
confident a. ˈkɑnfədənt	I am *confident* that we will win.	確信的 sure positive	fid(believe)
configuration n. kənˌfɪgjəˈreʃən	Geographers study the *configuration* of the surface of the earth.	形狀、輪廓、外貌 outline contour	figure
confine v. kənˈfaɪn	He *confines* his activities in educational circles.	限制 limit circumscribe	**fin**(end)
confirm v. kənˈfɜm	What I have seen *confirms* my suspicions.	證實 assure corroborate	firm
confiscate v. ˈkɑnfɪsˌket	The government *confiscated* the property of the traitors.	充公、沒收 seize sequester	fisc(treasury)
conflict n. ˈkɑnflɪkt	The underlying *conflicts* between the two nations cannot be easily solved.	衝突 clash collision	flict(strike)
confluence* n. ˈkɑnfluəns	We built a cabin at the *confluence* of the two rivers.	滙流處、合流 concourse	**flu**(flow)
conform v. kənˈfɔrm	The stranger has learned to *conform* his ways to ours.	使順應、使一致 adjust accord	form

單字・音標・詞類	例　　句	中譯・同義字	字源分析
confound v. kən'faʊnd	Her husband's cruelty amazed and *confounded* her.	使惶恐、使混淆 astound baffle	**found**(pour)
confuse v. kən'fjuz	She was *confused* by her father's remarks.	使混亂 disorder bewilder	**fus**(pour)
congeal v. kən'dʒil	Water *congeals* into ice.	凝結、凍僵 freeze curdle	**geal**(freeze)
congenial* a. kən'dʒinjəl	It is sometimes difficult to find *congenial* companions.	意氣相投、友善的 agreeable complaisant	**genial**
congenital* a. kən'dʒɛnətḷ	The baby was born with *congenital* deformity.	天生的 existing at birth	**genital**
congest v. kən'dʒɛst	The streets are often *congested* at Christmas.	擁塞 overcrowd	**gest**(carry)
conglomerate* v. kən'glɑmə‚ret	People always *conglomerate* around her.	聚集 gather amass	**glomer**(globe)
congregate v. 'kɑŋgrɪ‚get	Cattle *congregate* during a storm.	聚集 assemble amass	**greg**(group)
congress n. 'kɑŋgrəs	He is attending the International *Congress* of Medicine at Montreal.	會議、大會 convention convocation	**gress**(go)

單字・音標・詞類	例 句	中譯・同義字	字源分析
conjunction n. kənˈdʒʌŋkʃən	He opened a store in *conjunction* with his relatives.	結合、連結 connection combination	**junc**(join)
conjure* v. ˈkʌndʒɚ	The old woman declared that she could *conjure* up the spirits of the dead.	以咒召魂、變魔術、懇求 juggle implore	jur(swear)
connect v. kəˈnɛkt	The two towns are *connected* by a railway.	連接 join link	nect(fasten)
connote* v. kəˈnot	The word "tropics" *connotes* heat.	含意、暗示 suggest implicate	note
conquer v. ˈkaŋkɚ	The maritime people was finally *conquered* by the invading nomads.	征服、克服 overcome subjugate	**quer**(seek)
conquest n. ˈkaŋkwɛst	The Romans succeeded in the *conquest* of the Phoenicians.	征服 subjection subjugation	**quest**(seek)
conscience n. ˈkanʃəns	Decide the matter according to your own *conscience*.	良心 awareness of right and wrong	sci(know)
conscientious a. ˌkanʃɪˈɛnʃəs	He is a *conscientious* judge.	正直、有良心的 honorable straightforward	sci(know)
conscious a. ˈkanʃəs	She is *conscious* of her own mistakes.	自覺、知道的 aware knowing	sci(know)

單字・音標・詞類	例　句	中譯・同義字	字源分析
consecrate v. ˈkɑnsɪˌkret	This battlefield is *consecrated* to the memory of the soldiers who died.	奉爲神聖 hallow sanctify	secr(sacred)
consecutive a. kənˈsɛkjətɪv	Four, five, and six are *consecutive* numbers.	連續的 successive following in order	secu(follow)
consensus n. kənˈsɛnsəs	The *consensus* is against revision.	一致的意見 agreement unanimity	sens(feel)
consent v. kənˈsɛnt	My father could not *consent* to my leaving school.	允許、同意 permit accede	sent(feel)
consequence n. ˈkɑnsəˌkwɛns	Do you realize the possible *consequences*?	結果 result outcome	sequ(follow)
conserve v. kənˈsɝv	One must learn to *conserve* one's energy.	保全、保存 preserve retain	serv(keep)
consist v. kənˈsɪst	Cake *consists* of flour, sugar and some other ingredients.	爲…所製成、組成 be formed be composed	sist(stand)
console v. kənˈsol	His grief was *consoled* by time.	安慰 relieve assuage	sol(solace)
consolidate v. kənˈsɑləˌdet	The politician has tried to *consolidate* his power for years.	鞏固 stabilize solidify	solid

單字・音標・詞類	例　　　句	中譯・同義字	字源分析
consonant a. ˈkɑnsənənt	The quality of this suit is quite *consonant* with its price.	一致、相稱的 compatible congruous	son(sound)
consort v. kənˈsɔrt	The soldiers of this unit liked to *consort* with local women.	結交 associate fraternize	sort(share)
constant a. ˈkɑnstənt	They received *constant* complaints from their customers.	不斷、持久的 incessant perpetual	sta(stand)
constellation* n. ˌkɑnstəˈlɛʃən	Ursa Major is the most conspicuous *constellation* in the northern sky.	星座、星群 group of stars	stella(star)
constitute v. ˈkɑnstəˌtjut	Seven days *constitute* a week.	構成、任命 compose appoint	stitute(stand)
constrain v. kənˈstren	Hunger *constrained* the protesters to eat.	強迫 impel coerce	strain(strain)
construct v. kənˈstrʌkt	The engineers have *constructed* a bridge.	建築 build erect	struct(build)
construe v. kənˈstru	His remarks were wrongly *construed*.	解釋、翻譯 render interpret	stru(build)
consume v. kənˈsum	He had *consumed* the best years of his life in prison.	消耗、浪費 waste absorb	sum(take)

單字・音標・詞類	例　　句	中譯・同義字	字源分析
consummate v. ˈkɑnsəˌmet	His ambition was *consummated* when he won the first prize.	完成 accomplish effectuate	sum(sum)
contact n. ˈkɑntækt	A club is a place to make frequent *contacts* with friends.	接觸 touch union	**tact**(touch)
contagious a. kənˈtedʒəs	Scarlet fever is a *contagious* disease.	傳染性的 infectious pestilential	**tag**(touch)
contain v. kənˈten	Books *contain* knowledge.	包含、容納 hold comprise	**tain**(hold)
contaminate v. kənˈtæməˌnet	The waste from that factory *contaminated* the river nearby.	污染 pollute vitiate	**tamin**(touch)
contemporary a. kənˈtempəˌrɛrɪ	We can check the *contemporary* records to decide when he was born.	同時代的 coexisting coeval	tempor(time)
contend v. kənˈtɛnd	Thirty students are *contending* for the prize.	競爭 contest vie	**tend**(stretch)
content v. kənˈtɛnt	Nothing *contents* her; she is always complaining.	使滿足、使滿 意 satisfy delight	**ten**(hold)

單字・音標・詞類	例 句	中譯・同義字	字源分析
contest n. ˈkɑntɛst	Shall we begin the *contest* now?	比賽、爭鬥 competition struggle	test
contiguous a. kənˈtɪgjʊəs	A fence showed where the two farms were *contiguous.*	接觸、鄰近的 adjoining adjacent	**tig**(touch)
contort v. kənˈtɔrt	The *contorted* face of the clown pleased the children.	扭歪、歪曲 twist distort	**tort**(twist)
contour n. ˈkɑntʊr	The *contour* of the Atlantic coast of America is quite irregular.	輪廓、外形 outline configuration	tour(turn)
contract v. kənˈtrækt	In talking we usually *contract* "do not" to "don't."	縮短、省略 shorten abbreviate	**tract**(draw)
contribute v. kənˈtrɪbjʊt	Everyone was asked to *contribute* suggestions for the trip abroad.	貢獻、捐助 supply furnish	trib(allot)
convene v. kənˈvin	They will *convene* a meeting on coming Monday.	召開、召集、集合 convoke congregate	**ven**(come)
converge* v. kənˈvɜdʒ	These lines *converge* at a certain point.	集中於一點、使聚合 concentrate gather	**verg**(turn)
converse v. kənˈvɜs	They *conversed* like gentlemen about the racing season and the hunting.	談話 talk discourse	**vers**(turn)

單字·音標·詞類	例　　句	中譯·同義字	字源分析
convert v. kənˈvɝt	The Smiths have *converted* their old mansion into a new one.	改變 change alter	**vert**(turn)
convey v. kənˈve	I owe him more than I can *convey* in words.	傳達、運送 transport communicate	**vey**(way)
convict v. kənˈvɪkt	The man was *convicted* by the jury.	宣告有罪 sentence condemn	**vict**(conquer)
convince v. kənˈvɪns	I am *convinced* that what she has said is true.	使相信、說明 persuade assure	**vinc**(conquer)
convivial* a. kənˈvɪvɪəl	They were gentlemen of the *convivial* sort and lovers of horses and scenery.	歡樂、快活的 jovial mirthful	**viv**(life)
convoy v. kənˈvɔɪ	The ships were *convoyed* into the harbor.	護送 accompany escort	**voy**(way)
convulse v. kənˈvʌls	His face was convulsed with rage.	痙攣、抽搐 shake agitate	**vuls**(prick)
v.	The island was *convulsed* by an earthquake.	震撼、使不安 disorder derange	
cooperate v. koˈɑpəˌret	The two companies have *cooperated* with each other for years.	合作、協同 combine conspire	operate

單字・音標・詞類	例　　句	中譯・同義字	字源分析
coordinate a. koˈɔrdn̩ɪt	This officer is *coordinate* in rank with that one.	同等的 equal equivalent	ordin(order)
correct v. kəˈrɛkt	These wrong spellings must be *corrected*.	改正、修正 adjust rectify	**rect**(direct)
correlate v. ˈkɔrəˌlet	She has tried to *correlate* this year's figures with last year's.	使相關連 relate together show relationship	relate
correspond v. ˌkɔrəˈspɑnd	Her white hat and shoes *correspond* with her white dress.	調合、符合 agree harmonize	respond
corroborate v. kəˈrɑbəˌret	Witnesses *corroborated* the policeman's statement.	證實 verify authenticate	robor(robust)
corrode v. kəˈrod	Rust has *corroded* the steel rails.	腐蝕、侵蝕 erode canker	rod(gnaw)
corrugate* v. ˈkɔrəˌget	The old lady *corrugates* her forehead whenever she feels annoyed.	使起皺紋 wrinkle rumple	rug(wrinkle)
corrupt v. kəˈrʌpt	One corrupt apple *corrupts* many sound ones.	使腐壞、敗壞 spoil defile	**rupt**(break)

7

CONTRA·CONTRO· COUNTER

against

相對 • 反對

　　字首 contra, contro, counter　源自拉丁文 contrā，原爲介系詞與副詞，意思即爲「相對、反對」。拉丁文本即將 contrā 和 contrō 視作字首，下文 contradict v.「矛盾」、contrary a.「相反的」、controversy n.「爭論」等字，原來便是 contrādīcere, contrārius, contrōversia　等拉丁字所轉成。英文拼法的 counter　，在十三世紀已大致形成，到了十六世紀之後，便固定下來。下文各例字中，比較特別的是 counter v.「反對、對抗」，以字首形態單獨演變成一個動詞。

單字・音標・詞類	例　　句	中譯・同義字	字源分析
contradict v. ˌkɑntrəˈdɪkt	The candidate has *contradicted* a statement which he made previously.	否認、矛盾 oppose gainsay	**dict**(say)
contrary a. ˈkɑntrɛrɪ	What she told us is *contrary* to the facts.	相反的 opposite perverse	
contrast n. ˈkɑntræst	The *contrast* between the two brothers is remarkable.	差異 difference distinction	
contravene v. ˌkɑntrəˈvin	A dictatorship *contravenes* the liberty of individuals.	抵觸、否定、反駁 oppose contradict	**ven**(come)
controversy n. ˈkɑntrəˌvɝsɪ	This question has aroused much *controversy*.	爭論、辯論 dispute contention	**vers**(turn)
controvert* v. ˈkɑntrəˌvɝt	The statement of the last witness *controverts* the evidence of the first two.	否定、反駁、爭論 dispute argue against	**vert**(turn)
counter v. ˈkaʊntɚ	He *countered* my proposal with one of his own.	反對、對抗 oppose confront	
counteract v. ˌkaʊntɚˈækt	The doctor gave him some medicine to *counteract* the effects of the poison.	消解、抵消 offset annul	**act**

單字・音標・詞類	例　　　句	中譯・同義字	字源分析
counterattack v. ˌkaʊntərəˈtæk	The enemy is preparing to *counterattack*.	反攻、反擊 attack in 　　opposition	**attack**
counterbalance v. ˌkaʊntəˈbæləns	The boy's earnest effort *counterbalanced* his slowness at learning.	彌補、使抵消 offset neutralize	balance
counterfeit v. ˈkaʊntəfɪt	He was put in jail for *counterfeiting* ten-dollar bills.	偽造 duplicate forge	**feit**(do)
a.	Be careful; that might be *counterfeit* money.	贋造、假冒的 bogus spurious	
countermand v. ˌkaʊntəˈmænd	He *countermanded* his instructions to his staff.	撤回、取消 revoke repeal	**mand** (command)
counterpart n. ˈkaʊntəˌpart	This twin is her sister's *counterpart*.	極相似的人或 物、互相配對 的東西 match duplicate	part
countervail* v. ˌkaʊntəˈvel	This force has been *countervailed* by another.	抵消、對抗 oppose thwart	**vail**(be strong)

8

DE

down, complete

降下 ● 完全

字首 de 源自拉丁文，原在拉丁文也是字首，有 down, complete 的意思。以 de 組成的英文單字，有部分直接借自拉丁文，部分間接由法文傳入，甚至有部分在英國「土生土長」而成。de 除了上述的意義，也可引申為否定或加強語氣的意思。下文例字 decrepit a.「破舊、衰老的」，字根 crep 拉丁文原作 crepāre v.，有「爆裂」的意思，全字源出拉丁文 dēcrepitus，本即有破裂殆盡而至於「破舊、衰老」的意思。deliberate v.「考慮」源自 dēlīberāre v.，字根來自拉丁文名詞 lībra n.f.「天平、磅」（英文 pound 可寫成 lb.，便是源自 lībra），因此「將事物定下來掂算重量」，自然有了「考慮」的意思。凡事若是經過深思熟慮才做，必然有一定目標，因此作形容詞時，意思便又轉成了「有意、存心的」。英文另有一單字 liberate v.「使自由」，字形與 deliberate 相似，但字義、字源均不同，須特別留意。liberate 出自拉丁文 līberāre v.「使自由」，原拉丁文拼法與上述的 lībra「天平、磅」頗有不同，進入英文之後演變成相同的拼法，不過純屬巧合。

單字·音標·詞類	例　　　句	中譯·同義字	字源分析
debar v. dɪˈbɑr	He was *debarred* from entering the contest for presidential nomination.	禁止 prohibit interdict	bar
debase v. dɪˈbes	If you do that to her, you will only *debase* yourself.	貶低 disgrace degrade	base
debate v. dɪˈbet	This question has often been *debated*.	討論、爭論 dispute contend	bate(batter)
deceased a. dɪˈsist	The *deceased* general was a great soldier.	已故、死亡的 dead departed	cess(go)
declaim* v. dɪˈklem	He was often chosen to *declaim* on private and public occasions.	演說、高聲朗誦 speak loudly recite loudly	claim(cry)
declare v. dɪˈklɛr	When will the results of the polls be *declared*?	宣布 pronounce promulgate	clar(clear)
decline v. dɪˈklaɪn	The wall *declined* slightly on account of the earthquake.	傾斜 lean languish	clin(bend)
v.	I invited her to dinner but she *declined* my invitation.	拒絕 refuse reject	
decrepit a. dɪˈkrɛpɪt	The old couple had only a *decrepit* bed and some other furniture.	破舊，衰老的 aged crippled	crep(creak)

單字・音標・詞類	例　　　句	中譯・同義字	字源分析
decry v. dɪˈkraɪ	The minister *decried* gambling in all its forms.	譴責 denounce rail against	cry
dedicate v. ˈdɛdəˌket	Only a foolish man can *dedicate* his life to the pursuit of pleasures.	獻身、致力、奉獻 devote consecrate	dic(say)
deduce v. dɪˈdjus	John's mother *deduced* from his loss of appetite what had happened to the cookies.	推想、推論 conclude infer	duc(lead)
deduct v. dɪˈdʌkt	He *deducted* the price of the cup I broke from the amount that he owed me.	扣除 remove subtract	duct(lead)
deface v. dɪˈfes	Who has *defaced* the desk by marking on it?	傷毀(外表) tarnish mar	face
defer v. dɪˈfɝ	Do you always *defer* to your parents' wishes?	順從 yield succumb	fer(bear)
deflate v. dɪˈflet	The boy has *deflated* one of the tires of his bicycle.	放出空氣、使坍陷、減消 collapse lessen	flat(blow)
deject v. dɪˈdʒɛkt	Bill has looked *dejected* ever since he came back from his date tonight.	使沮喪 sadden depress	ject(throw)

單字・音標・詞類	例　　句	中譯・同義字	字源分析
delay v. dɪˈle	Our journey was *delayed* because of bad weather.	延期 postpone defer	lay(leave)
deliberate v. dɪˈlɪbəˌret	He spent some time *deliberating* the question before he made an answer.	熟思、考慮 contemplate cogitate	liber(weigh)
dɪˈlɪbərɪt　a.	She told her parents a *deliberate* lie.	有意、存心的 intentional premeditated	
demean v. dɪˈmin	The baron's son would not *demean* himself by working to earn a living.	貶抑、降低 debase disgrace	mean
demerit n. dɪˈmɛrɪt	Everyone has his merits and *demerits*.	短處、過失、缺點 fault defect	merit
demise n. dɪˈmaɪz	The *demise* of the king caused great sorrow among his subjects.	死亡 death decease	**miss**(send)
demoralize v. dɪˈmɔrəlˌaɪz	The army was *demoralized* by these defeats.	使沮喪、敗壞 dishearten corrupt	morale & moral
demote v. dɪˈmot	He was *demoted* because of the scandal.	降級 lower in rank	**mot**(move)
demure* a. dɪˈmjʊr	She gave him a *demure* smile.	佯作端莊、端莊的 modest coy	mure(mature)

單字·音標·詞類	例　　　句	中譯·同義字	字源分析
denominate v. dɪˈnɑməˌnet	The Spaniards *denominated* their navy the Invincible Armada.	命名 name call	nomin(name)
denote* v. dɪˈnot	A quick pulse often *denotes* fever.	表示、指示、意指 indicate signify	note
denounce v. dɪˈnaʊns	He was *denounced* as a rascal.	當眾指責 condemn decry	**nounc** (announce)
deny v. dɪˈnaɪ	She has *denied* all charges against her.	否認、不承認 oppose disavow	neg(deny)
depict v. dɪˈpɪkt	The writer has *depicted* in his travelogue the scenery of the Himalayas.	描寫、敘述 describe delineate	pict(paint)
deplore v. dɪˈplor	The woman is *deploring* the loss of a dear friend.	悲痛 mourn lament	plor(weep)
deposit v. dɪˈpɑzɪt	He always *deposited* half of his salary in the bank.	存儲、放下、置下 put place	pos(place)
deprave* v. dɪˈprev	The major defeat had *depraved* the morale of the troops.	使敗壞 debase degenerate	prav(crooked)
depredation* n. ˌdɛprɪˈdeʃən	Depredations went on unchecked during the civil war.	劫掠、搶奪 plunder pillage	pred(plunder)

單字・音標・詞類	例　　句	中譯・同義字	字源分析
depress v. dɪˈprɛs	The government was forced to *depress* the price of wheat.	降低、壓下 lower reduce	**press**(press)
v.	The rainy days always *depress* me.	使沮喪 dispirit deject	
deprive v. dɪˈpraɪv	They were *deprived* of their right to vote.	剝奪 strip divest	priv(remove)
derelict a. ˈdɛrəˌlɪkt	They found a *derelict* ship in the ocean.	被棄的 abandoned deserted	relict (relinquish)
deride v. dɪˈraɪd	Some people *deride* patriotic rallies and parades.	嘲笑、嘲弄 ridicule flout	rid(laugh)
descend v. dɪˈsɛnd	The sun slowly *descended* over the western hills.	降 fall sink	scend(climb)
design n. dɪˈzaɪn	This theatre seats over 1,000 people but the *design* is poor	設計 plan outline	sign(mark)
designate v. ˈdɛzɪgˌnet	The company has *designated* Mr. Jones to be in charge of the department.	指派、任命 appoint assign	sign(mark)
desolate a. ˈdɛsl̩ɪt	The sailors found a *desolate* island north of the peninsula.	荒涼、荒蕪的 bleak barren	sol(sole)

單字・音標・詞類	例　　句	中譯・同義字	字源分析
despicable a. ˈdɛspɪkɪbḷ	To spit in public places is *despicable*.	可鄙、卑劣的 contemptible abject	**spic**(watch)
despise v. dɪˈspaɪz	The man was *despised* for the things that he had done.	輕視、蔑視 disdain spurn	**spic**(watch)
despoil* v. dɪˈspɔɪl	He was *despoiled* of his right to appeal.	奪取、掠奪 strip deprive	**spoil**(strip)
destitute a. ˈdɛstəˌtjut	When Mr. Michaelson died, his wife and children were left *destitute*.	窮困的 impoverished indigent	**stitute**(stand)
destroy v. dɪˈstrɔɪ	The house was *destroyed* during the bombardment.	毀壞、毀滅 ruin demolish	**strue**(build)
determine v. dɪˈtɝmɪn	They have *determined* to do it at any cost.	決心、決定 decide resolve	**termin**(limit)
dethrone v. dɪˈθron	The king was *dethroned* during the revolution.	廢(君) depose oust	**throne**
detonate* v. ˈdɛtəˌnet	The terrorist was killed when he tried to *detonate* the bomb at the airport.	使爆炸 explode fulminate	**ton**(thunder)
detour* n. ˈditʊr	The main road was blocked so we had to make a *detour*.	繞行之路 roundabout way	**tour**(turn)

單字・音標・詞類	例　　　句	中譯・同義字	字源分析
devaluate v. dɪˈvæljʊˌet	The U.S. dollar has *devaluated* several times during the year.	（使）貶值 devalue depreciate	value
devastate v. ˈdɛvəsˌtet	The towns were *devastated* by war.	破壞、蹂躪 desolate ravage	vast(empty)
devoid a. dɪˈvɔɪd	A well *devoid* of water is useless.	缺乏、無的 vacant void	**void**
devolve* v. dɪˈvɑlv	The director has *devolved* certain work on a subordinate.	移交、委任 deliver consign	**volv(roll)**

9

DE·DI·DIS

away, off, not

分離 • 否定

---

de, di, dis 是英文最重要的字首之一，組成的單字數量極大。de 與前述 8. de 字首有關，原義爲 down, complete，引申而有 away, off 的意思，因此爲方便計，歸列於 di, dis 之中（字首de的其他用法，請參閱本書「最重要的 30 個字首」 8. de ）。di, dis 源出拉丁文字首 dī, dis：後接字根的第一個字母若是 d、g、l、m、n、r、v 之一，則拼作 di；若是 c、p、q、s、t 之一，便拼作 dis。除了上述 de, di, dis 三種最常見的拼法之外，並有 dif 一種，字根的第一個字母若是 f，便用這拼法，如下文的 differ v.「不同」、difficult a.「費力的」、diffident a.「羞怯的」等均是。

單字・音標・詞類	例　　　　句	中譯・同義字	字源分析
decadence n. dɪˈkedns	The *decadence* of morals is bad for a nation.	墮落、衰落 decline deterioration	**cad**(fall)
decapitate v. dɪˈkæpəˌtet	The prisoners were *decapitated* at dawn.	斬首 behead execute	**capit**(head)
decay v. dɪˈke	What caused the Roman Empire to *decay*?	衰亡、逐漸衰弱 decline degenerate	**cad**(fall)
deceive v. dɪˈsiv	She would not let anyone else *deceive* her.	欺騙 dupe beguile	**ceiv**(receive)
decide v. dɪˈsaɪd	Have you *decided* yet?	決定、決心 determine resolve	**cid**(cut)
decipher v. dɪˈsaɪfɚ	The historical linguists were asked to *decipher* the ancient scripts.	解釋、譯解 interpret decode	cipher
decode v. diˈkod	The assistant has already *decoded* the message.	譯解 translate decipher	code
decompose v. ˌdikəmˈpoz	Organic compounds *decompose* on heating.	分解、腐爛 disintegrate rot	**compose**
decrease v. dɪˈkris	His interest in women gradually *decreased*.	減少 lessen dwindle	**creas**(grow)

單字・音標・詞類	例　　　　句	中譯・同義字	字源分析
decree n. dɪˈkri	He needs to act by executive *decrees* in the next two months.	命令 mandate ordinance	cree(see)
defame v. dɪˈfem	The presidential candidate was *defamed* on account of the scandal.	損毀名譽、誹謗 disgrace detract	fame
default n. dɪˈfɔlt	In *default* of tools, she used the heel of a shoe as a hammer.	缺乏、怠忽 lack lapse	fall(fail)
defeat v. dɪˈfit	We *defeated* the enemy in the battle.	擊敗 overcome vanquish	**feat**
n.	Our team has never yet suffered any *defeat*.	失敗 failure frustration	
defect n. dɪˈfɛkt	I could find no *defect* in what he has done.	缺點、過失 shortcoming flaw	**fect**(do)
v.	The pilot has *defected* to the West.	投奔敵方、變節 rebel revolt	
defend v. dɪˈfɛnd	The people are willing to *defend* their own country.	保衛、保護 protect safeguard	fend(strike)
defer v. dɪˈfɝ	Examinations were *deferred* because of the typhoon.	延期 delay postpone	**fer** (carry)

單字·音標·詞類	例　　句	中譯·同義字	字源分析
deficient a. dɪˈfɪʃənt	A mentally *deficient* person is one who is weak-minded.	有缺點、不足的 insufficient inadequate	**fic**(do)
deficit n. ˈdɛfəsɪt	Huge trade *deficits* have forced the president to leave office.	赤字、不足(額) deficiency in 　amount	**fic**(do)
define v. dɪˈfaɪn	A dictionary *defines* words.	定義、詳細說明 expound specify	**fin**(end)
definite a. ˈdɛfənɪt	I want a *definite* answer: yes or no?	明確、確定的 assured positive	**fin**(end)
definitive a. dɪˈfɪnətɪv	The legislators will have to give the protesters a *definitive* answer.	確定、最後的 final conclusive	**fin**(end)
deflect v. dɪˈflɛkt	The bullet struck a wall and was *deflected* from its course.	使偏斜、使轉向 deviate diverge	**flect**(bend)
deform v. dɪˈfɔrm	The girl has a *deformed* foot.	使不成形、使醜 disfigure distort	**form**
defraud v. dɪˈfrɔd	That man was *defrauded* of his estate.	欺騙、詐欺 deceive dupe	**fraud**

單字·音標·詞類	例　句	中譯·同義字	字源分析
defy v. dɪˈfaɪ	The protesters have *defied* the law by attacking a number of passers-by.	違抗、不顧、挑激 disregard challenge	fid(faith)
degenerate v. dɪˈdʒɛnəˌret	His health *degenerated* rapidly after that winter.	惡化、變壞 worsen deteriorate	**gen**(beget)
dehydrate v. diˈhaɪdret	Serena wanted me to buy some *dehydrated* castor oil.	脫水、使乾 dry desiccate	hydr(water)
delegate v. ˈdɛləˌget	Each club *delegated* one member to attend the state meeting.	指令…爲代表、委派 appoint depute	leg(send)
delinquency n. dɪˈlɪŋkwənsɪ	The sociologist has studied the juvenile *delinquency* in this area.	犯罪、違法 wrongdoing misdemeanor	linqu(leave)
delirious a. dɪˈlɪrɪəs	The winners were *delirious* with joy.	狂喜 frantic frenzied	lir(line)
deliver v. dɪˈlɪvɚ	May God *deliver* us from all evil spirits.	拯救 liberate extricate	liver(free)
v.	A postman *delivers* letters and parcels.	遞送 distribute	
delude* v. dɪˈlud	The young knight was *deluded* to folly by her enchanting beauty.	迷惑、欺騙 mislead cozen	lud(play)

單字・音標・詞類	例　　　句	中譯・同義字	字源分析
deluge n. ˈdɛljudʒ	Livestock drowned in the *deluge*.	洪水 flood inundation	lug(wash)
demarcation* n. ˌdimɑrˈkeʃən	The two countries have drawn a *demarcation* line along the river.	界限、界線 boundary confine	marc(mark)
demonstrate v. ˈdɛmənˌstret	How can you *demonstrate* that the earth is round?	證明、演示 indicate manifest	monstr(show)
	v.	The workers marched through the streets *demonstrating* against the union leaders.	作示威運動 protest	
demur* v. dɪˈmɝ	They *demurred* at working on Sundays.	反對、猶豫 object waver	mur(delay)
denude v. dɪˈnjud	Most trees are *denuded* of their leaves in winter.	剝下、脫去、剝奪 strip divest	nude
depart v. dɪˈpɑrt	The soldiers are ready to *depart*.	離開、放棄 leave quit	part(divide)
deplete v. dɪˈplit	Illness may *deplete* a person's strength.	耗盡、使空竭 exhaust drain	plet(fill)
deploy v. dɪˈplɔɪ	The nuclear missiles were *deployed* along the western border.	部署、展開 spread out	plic(fold)

單字・音標・詞類	例　　句	中譯・同義字	字源分析
deport v. dɪˈport	The spy was first imprisoned and then *deported* from the country.	放逐、驅逐出境 banish expel	**port**(carry)
depose v. dɪˈpoz	The king was *deposed* by the revolution.	廢除 dethrone oust	**pos**(place)
deprecate* v. ˈdɛprəˌket	Lovers of peace *deprecate* war.	反對、不贊成、鄙視 disapprove of belittle	prec(pray)
depreciate v. dɪˈpriʃɪˌet	The price of wheat has greatly *depreciated*.	跌價、貶值 devalue devaluate	prec(price)
v.	He objected to scholars who *depreciated* craftsmen.	輕視、毀謗 undervalue disparage	
depute v. dɪˈpjut	The teacher *deputed* a student to take charge while she was gone.	委託（某人）為代理 appoint entrust	put(cleanse)
deputy n. ˈdɛpjəˌtɪ	He is my *deputy* during my absence.	代表 agent commissioner	put(cleanse)
derange* v. dɪˈrendʒ	Sudden illness in the family *deranged* our plans for a trip.	擾亂、使錯亂 confuse confound	range

單字·音標·詞類	例　　　句	中譯·同義字	字源分析
derive v. dəˈraɪv	Many French words are *derived* from Latin and Greek.	起源、獲得 obtain draw	riv(stream)
descant* v. dɛsˈkænt	She *descanted* on the things she had seen on her trip to Sri Lanka.	詳述 discuss expatiate	cant(sing)
describe v. dɪˈskraɪb	Please *describe* the looks of the bank robber.	形容、描寫、敘述 depict relate	**scrib**(write)
desert v. dɪˈzɝt	He *deserted* his wife and children.	遺棄、放棄 abandon relinquish	sert(join)
despair n. dɪˈspɛr	He was filled with *despair* as she refused his proposal.	失望、絕望 desperation despondency	sper(hope)
desperate a. ˈdɛsprɪt	The situation of that country is becoming *desperate*.	絕望、不顧死活的 irretrievable headstrong	sper(hope)
despondency n. dɪˈspɑndənsɪ	They found him in a state of *despondency*.	意氣消沈、失望 dejection depression	spond(promise)
detach v. dɪˈtætʃ	The watch was *detached* from the chain.	分開 separate disconnect	tach(nail)

單字・音標・詞類	例　　　句	中譯・同義字	字源分析
v.	A regiment was *detached* to cut off the enemy's retreat.	派遣 send dispatch	
detail n. 'ditel	Please let me know all the *details*.	細節、細部、詳述 part account	tail(cut)
detain v. dɪ'ten	The men were *detained* by the military police.	拘留、扣押 keep arrest	**tain**(hold)
detect v. dɪ'tɛkt	They *detected* him in the act of breaking into their neighbor's house.	發現 discover reveal	tect(cover)
deter v. dɪ'tɝ	This paint can *deter* rust.	防止 check hinder	ter(terror)
detract* v. dɪ'trækt	It *detracts* nothing from the credit due to him.	減損、責難 take away disparage	**tract**(draw)
detrimental a. ˌdɛtrə'mɛntl̩	Lack of sleep is *detrimental* to one's health.	有害、傷害的 harmful deleterious	trim(rub)
develop v. dɪ'vɛləp	The government has made up plans to *develop* natural resources.	開發、進展、發展 progress cultivate	velop(wrap)
deviate v. 'divɪˌet	The students have *deviated* from the subject under discussion.	離題、逸出正軌 stray digress	via(way)

單字・音標・詞類	例　　句	中譯・同義字	字源分析
devious * a. ˈdivɪəs	His *devious* nature was shown in half-lies and small dishonesties.	不正直、有偏差的 deviating erratic	via(way)
devote v. dɪˈvot	She *devoted* large sums to the care of the poor.	奉獻 dedicate consecrate	vote(vow)
devout a. dɪˈvaʊt	He has always been a *devout* supporter of Capitalism.	忠誠、虔誠的 devoted pious	vout(vow)
differ v. ˈdɪfɚ	The twin sisters are alike in appearance but *differ* in disposition.	不同、意見不合 vary dispute	fer(carry)
differentiate v. ˌdɪfəˈrɛnʃɪˌet	A botanist is able to *differentiate* varieties of plants.	辨別、區分 distinguish discern	fer(carry)
difficult a. ˈdɪfəˌkʌlt	They are now undertaking a *difficult* task.	艱難、費力的 laborious arduous	fic(do)
diffident a. ˈdɪfədənt	Amanda is a *diffident* girl.	羞怯的 timid bashful	fid(trust)
diffuse v. dɪˈfjuz	The printing of books *diffuses* knowledge.	傳播 spread disseminate	fus(pour)
dɪˈfjus a.	Readers are never fond of *diffuse* writers.	冗長的 verbose prolix	

單字·音標·詞類	例　　　句	中譯·同義字	字源分析
digest v. dəˈdʒɛst	Some foods are *digested* more easily than others.	消化、吸收、分類 assimilate systematize	gest(bear)
digress v. dəˈgrɛs	The members of the board have *digressed* from the subject under discussion.	離開本題 deviate diverge	**gress**(go)
dilapidate* v. dəˈlæpəˌdet	We saw a *dilapidated* castle on our journey.	使部分毀壞、使破損 ruin demolish	lapid(throw stones)
dilate v. daɪˈlet	The pupils of your eyes *dilate* when the room suddenly becomes dark.	擴大 expand distend	lat(wide)
diligent a. ˈdɪlədʒənt	He is the most *diligent* student of the class.	勤勉的 industrious assiduous	**lig**(choose)
dilute v. dɪˈlut	Strong acids are often *diluted* before they are used.	稀釋、變淡、使變弱 thin down weaken	lut(wash)
dimension n. dəˈmɛnʃən	What are the *dimensions* of this room?	尺寸、大小 measure bulk	mens(measure)
diminish v. dəˈmɪnɪʃ	The management had tried to *diminish* the cost of production.	減少 reduce abate	**mini**(small)

單字·音標·詞類	例　　句	中譯·同義字	字源分析
diminutive a. dəˈmɪnjətɪv	The man we saw was sort of *diminutive* in stature.	小的 minute minuscule	**minu**(small)
direct v. dəˈrɛkt	The officer *directed* his men to advance slowly.	命令、指導 guide conduct	**rect**(rule)
a.	This is the *direct* route to the railway station.	直接、坦白、絕對的 straight absolute	
disable v. dɪsˈebḷ	*Disabled* soldiers should be cared for by the state.	使殘廢、使無資格 disqualify cripple	**able**
disadvantage n. ˌdɪsədˈvæntɪdʒ	The hungry soldiers were fighting at a *disadvantage*.	不利情況、缺點、傷害 drawback detriment	**advantage**
disaffect v. ˌdɪsəˈfɛkt	The workers were *disaffected* by paid agitators.	使生惡感、使生二心、使疏遠 alienate estrange	**affect**
disagree v. ˌdɪsəˈgri	The conclusions *disagree* with the facts.	不一致、爭論 differ dispute	**agree**
disapprove v. ˌdɪsəˈpruv	I must *disapprove* of your action.	非難、不准許、不贊成 disallow condemn	**approve**

單字・音標・詞類	例　　句	中譯・同義字	字源分析
disarray v. ˌdɪsəˈre	Communication was *disarrayed* by the severe snow storm.	使亂 confuse derange	**array**
disaster n. dɪzˈæstɚ	They have recorded major earthquake *disasters* of the country.	災禍 calamity catastrophe	aster(star)
disavow* v. ˌdɪsəˈvaʊ	The prisoner *disavowed* any share in the plot against the king.	否認、不承認 deny refute	**avow**
disband v. dɪsˈbænd	The army was *disbanded* when the war came to an end.	解散 dismiss dissolve	band
discard v. dɪsˈkɑrd	The people were told to *discard* their old believes.	摒除、棄絕 remove reject	card
discern v. dɪˈsɝn	One must be able to *discern* good and bad.	辨別、看見 perceive discriminate	cern(separate)
discharge v. dɪsˈtʃɑrdʒ	The man was *discharged* because they were not sure what he had done.	開釋 release dismiss	charge
v.	The servant was *dis-charged* for being dishonest.	開除 remove expel	
v.	Where do the sewers *discharge* their contents?	放出、流出 eject emit	

單字・音標・詞類	例　句	中譯・同義字	字源分析
disclaim v. dɪsˈklem	He *disclaimed* the ownership of the bulldog.	否認、拒絕承認 disown renounce	**claim**
disclose v. dɪsˈkloz	This letter *discloses* a secret.	揭露 reveal unveil	close
discomfit* v. dɪsˈkʌmfɪt	He had thought his plan could *discomfit* his opponents.	挫敗、使困惑 frustrate baffle	comfit (prepare)
discomfort n. dɪsˈkʌmfət	One has to bear a little *discomfort* while traveling.	不舒適、不快 uneasiness unpleasantness	**comfort**
disconnect v. ˌdɪskəˈnɛkt	He *disconnected* the electric fan by pulling out the plug.	使分離 disjoin detach	**connect**
disconsolate a. dɪsˈkɑnslɪt	The little girl was *disconsolate* because her kitten had died.	哀傷、孤獨的 forlorn melancholy	**console**
discontent n. ˌdɪskənˈtɛnt	The *discontent* of the people gave rise to much trouble.	不滿 displeasure dissatisfaction	**content**
discontinue v. ˌdɪskənˈtɪnjʊ	The train has been *discontinued*.	停止 cease interrupt	**continue**
discord n. ˈdɪskɔrd	These two answers are in *discord*.	不一致 disagreement dissonance	**cord**(heart)

單字・音標・詞類	例　　句	中譯・同義字	字源分析
discount n. **ˈdɪskaʊnt**	We give 10% *discount* for cash payment.	折扣 deduction rebate	count
discourage v. **dɪsˈkɝɪdʒ**	The wet weather *discouraged* people from going to the theater.	阻止、使沮喪、妨礙 dishearten deter	**courage**
discourse* n. **ˈdɪskors**	They have printed the philosopher's *discourses* with the students.	演講、談話、論文 talk dissertation	cours(run)
discourteous a. **dɪsˈkɝtɪəs**	Her *discourteous* remarks caused much displeasure among the guests.	無禮貌、粗魯的 impolite rude	courteous
discover v. **dɪˈskʌvɚ**	Columbus *discovered* America.	發現、洩露 find disclose	cover
discredit v. **dɪsˈkrɛdɪt**	His theories were *discredited* by fellow scientists.	懷疑、不信任 doubt disbelieve	**cred**(believe)
discreet a. **dɪˈskrit**	She has always tried to be *discreet* when he is around.	言行謹慎、小心的 heedful prudent	creet(separate)
discrepancy n. **dɪˈskrɛpənsɪ**	There was considerable *discrepancy* between the two accounts of the battle.	矛盾、不同 difference distinction	crep(creak)

單字·音標·詞類	例　　　句	中譯·同義字	字源分析
discrete* a. **dɪˈskrit**	Human traits and abilities are not *discrete*, but interact with each other.	分立、各別、不相關連的 unrelated distinct	cret(separate)
discriminate v. **dɪˈskrɪməˌnet**	The child could not *discriminate* between good and bad.	辨別 judge discern	crimin(separate)
discursive* a. **dɪˈskɝsɪv**	This is a sprawling book, with *discursive* and prolix paragraphs.	散亂無章的 rambling erratic	**curs**(run)
disdain v. **dɪsˈden**	A great man should *disdain* flatterers.	鄙視 contemn spurn	dain(deign)
disease n. **dɪˈziz**	Everyone is afraid of this *infectious* disease.	病、疾痛 sickness malady	ease
disembark v. **ˌdɪsɪmˈbark**	The troops have *disembarked*.	登岸、離船、卸貨 leave unload	**embark**
disengage v. **ˌdɪsɪnˈgedʒ**	The sailor has *disengaged* the rope from the gear.	解開、放開 release disentangle	**engage**
disentangle v. **ˌdɪsɪnˈtæŋgḷ**	She is trying to *disentangle* the threads of the plot.	解開 disengage extricate	**entangle**
disfavor n. **dɪsˈfevɚ**	He looked upon the project with *disfavor*.	不贊成、不喜歡 dislike disapproval	favor

單字·音標·詞類	例　　句	中譯·同義字	字源分析
disfigure v. dɪsˈfɪgjɚ	Beautiful scenery is often *disfigured* by ugly advertising signs.	破壞（姿容、形狀等） deform stain	figure
disfranchise * v. dɪsˈfræntʃaɪz	A *disfranchised* person cannot vote or hold office.	褫奪…之公權 deprive of a　right	franchise
disgorge v. dɪsˈgɔrdʒ	Day after day the tourist buses *disgorged* their multitudes at the site.	吐出、流出、噴出 spew belch	gorge
disgrace n. dɪsˈgres	Honest poverty is no *disgrace.*	恥辱 dishonor infamy	grace
disguise v. dɪsˈgaɪz	He *disguised* himself as a woman in an attempt to escape.	假扮、偽裝、掩飾 mask dissemble	guise
disgust n. dɪsˈgʌst	From that day to this he never smelled cooking beans with *disgust.*	厭惡 antipathy abhorrence	gust(taste)
dishearten v. dɪsˈhɑrtn̩	The long drought has *disheartened* the farmer.	使沮喪、使氣餒 discourage depress	heart
dishevel * v. dɪˈʃɛvl̩	The wind tugged at and *disheveled* her.	使凌亂 disarrange rumple	chevel(hair)

單字・音標・詞類	例　　句	中譯・同義字	字源分析
dishonest a. dɪsˈɑnɪst	The employer has fired the *dishonest* clerk.	不誠實、欺詐的 treacherous fraudulent	honest
dishonor n. dɪsˈɑnɚ	He would rather die than live in *dishonor*.	恥辱、不名譽 disgrace degradation	honor
disillusion n. ˌdɪsɪˈluʒən	The critic laments the facile *disillusion* of the romantic intellectuals.	幻滅 disenchantment	illusion
disincline v. ˌdɪsɪnˈklaɪn	The old man was *disinclined* to accept his story.	(使)不願、厭惡 make reluctant make averse	**incline**
disinfect v. ˌdɪsɪnˈfɛkt	The house was thoroughly *disinfected* after he had had scarlet fever.	消毒 purify cleanse	**infect**
disintegrate v. dɪsˈɪntəˌgret	Time has caused the old books to *disintegrate* into a pile of fragments.	崩潰、分裂 crumble disunite	**integrate**
disinter* v. ˌdɪsɪnˈtɝ	The plays had remained unknown until they were *disintered* by a critic.	發現、從墳墓中挖出 unearth exhume	**inter**
disinterested a. dɪsˈɪntərəstɪd	A judge should be *disinterested*.	公正、無私、漠不關心的 unbiased indifferent	**interest**

單字・音標・詞類	例　　　句	中譯・同義字	字源分析
dislike n. dɪsˈlaɪk	Many women have a *dislike* for snakes.	嫌惡 distaste aversion	like
dismantle v. dɪsˈmæntḷ	The old warship was sent to the docks to be *dismantled.*	拆卸、剝脫 strip raze	mantle
dismiss v. dɪsˈmɪs	The soldiers were *dismissed* after a little while.	解散、開除 discharge disperse	**miss**(send)
disorient v. dɪsˈɔrɪˌɛnt	By the time he had made three turns, he was totally *disoriented.*	使失去方向感 、使迷惑 confuse baffle	orient
disown v. dɪsˈon	The man *disowned* the gun when he found it had been used to kill a woman.	不承認爲己所 有、否認 disclaim renounce	own
disparage* v. dɪˈspærɪdʒ	The coward *disparaged* the hero's brave rescue of the girl.	貶抑、毀謗、 輕視 belittle detract	parage(rand)
disparate* a. ˈdɪspərɪt	The young lady is said to have three *disparate* personalities.	不同的 unequal dissimilar	par(equal)
dispatch v. dɪˈspætʃ	The commander quickly *dispatched* a messenger.	派遣、速辦 send hasten	**ped**(foot)

單字·音標·詞類	例　　　句	中譯·同義字	字源分析
dispel v. dɪˈspɛl	The wind soon *dispelled* the fog.	吹散、驅散 disperse dissipate	**pel**(push)
dispense v. dɪˈspɛns	The kindhearted lady has been *dispensing* alms among the poor.	分與、分配 distribute apportion	**pens**(weigh)
v.	The young man was *dispensed* from his obligations.	免除 excuse exempt	
disperse v. dɪˈspɝs	The police *dispersed* the crowd.	驅散、消散 dispel dissipate	**pers**(strew)
displace v. dɪsˈpleˑ	The war has *displaced* thousands of people.	使離鄉背井、免職 remove oust	place
v.	Nowadays barns are being *displaced* by garages.	取代、代替 replace supplant	
display v. dɪˈsple	They are *displaying* goods for sale.	陳列、展示 show exhibit	**ply**(fold)
displeasure n. dɪsˈplɛʒɚ	The little girl never showed her *displeasure* in front of her mother.	不滿、不悅 disgust aversion	pleasure
disport* v. dɪˈsport	The sea lions bark and *disport* themselves before a gallery of enthusiasts.	嬉戲、娛樂 amuse divert	**port**(carry)

單字·音標·詞類	例　句	中譯·同義字	字源分析
dispossess v. ˌdɪspə'zɛs	The poor man was *dispossessed* of his goods and chattels.	強奪、剝奪 divest deprave	**possess**
disprove v. dɪs'pruv	The defendant's claims were *disproved* by the evidence.	證明為誤、反駁 refute confute	prove
dispute n. dɪ'spjut	They always have a lot of *disputes*.	爭吵、爭論 quarrel contention	put(think)
disquiet n. dɪs'kwaɪət	The agitators know how to spread suspicion and *disquiet*.	不安、動搖 disturbance restlessness	quiet
disregard n. ˌdɪsrɪ'gɑrd	They acted with complete *disregard* of danger.	忽視、輕視、不理 disrespect indifference	regard
disrobe v. dɪs'rob	The medical officer requested that the patient *disrobe* himself.	脫衣 undress divest	robe
disrupt v. dɪs'rʌpt	She would hate to have the job because it will *disrupt* her domestic coziness.	瓦解、中斷、使分裂 interrupt rupture	rupt(break)
dissect v. dɪ'sɛkt	The subject or object of a Miltonic sentence is often hard to *dissect*.	分辨、切開、分析 cut apart analyze	sect(cut)

單字・音標・詞類	例　　　句	中譯・同義字	字源分析
disseminate v. dɪˈsɛməˌnet	Various journals usually *disseminate* information of scientific discoveries.	傳播、散布 spread promulgate	semin(sow)
dissent v. dɪˈsɛnt	I *dissent* strongly from what the speaker has said.	不同意 disagree differ	sent(feel)
dissertation n. ˌdɪsɚˈteʃən	John is writing his Ph.D. *dissertation*.	論文、演講 treatise discourse	ser(join)
dissidence n. ˈdɪsədəns	The government has arrested people for political *dissidence*.	異議、不一致 dissent contention	sid(sit)
dissimulate* v. dɪˈsɪmjəˌlet	He is a man trained to conceal or *dissimulate* all strong feeling.	掩飾、假裝 dissemble affect	simulate
dissipate v. ˈdɪsəˌpet	The morning sun had *dissipated* the night mists.	使消散、驅散 dispel disperse	sip(throw)
dissolute* a. ˈdɪsəˌlut	The writer is critical of the *dissolute* aspects of human nature.	放蕩、淫樂的 wanton licentious	solu(loosen)
dissolve v. dɪˈzɑlv	Her smiles have helped to *disslove* some of their rancor.	消除、消滅 destroy dispel	solv(loosen)
v.	Both salt and sugar *dissolve* easily in water.	溶解 melt liquefy	

單字・音標・詞類	例　　句	中譯・同義字	字源分析
dissonance n. ˈdɪsənəns	The mingling of bitter comedy and stark tragedy produces sharp *dissonances* in the play.	不協調、不調和 discord jarring	son(sound)
dissuade v. dɪˈswed	They are trying to *dissuade* a friend from making a mistake.	勸阻、阻止 discourage deter	suade(persuade)
distant a. ˈdɪstənt	The *distant* mountain looks like a huge monster.	遙遠、遠離的 faraway secluded	sta(stand)
distaste n. dɪsˈtest	She has developed a *distaste* for work.	嫌惡 dislike abhorrence	taste
distend v. dɪˈstɛnd	The bat's body was so *distended* that it appeared spherical.	擴張、膨脹 expand dilate	**tend**(stretch)
distinct a. dɪˈstɪŋkt	These are things similar in effect but wholly *distinct* in motive.	相異、各別、清楚的 individual obvious	stingu(prick)
distinguish v. dɪˈstɪŋgwɪʃ	He has nothing in his dress to *distinguish* him from his workmen.	區別、辨別、認明 differentiate discern	stingu(prick)
distinguished a. dɪˈstɪŋgwɪʃt	His name was placed on the roster of *distinguished* statesmen.	傑出、著名的 illustrious celebrated	**distinguish**

單字・音標・詞類	例　　句	中譯・同義字	字源分析
distort v. dɪsˈtɔrt	They do not want to *distort* their writings to conform to the values of any group.	扭曲、曲解 twist contort	**tort**(twist)
distract v. dɪˈstrækt	The musicians were irritated and *distracted* by the late entrance of a few people.	分心、困惱 harass divert	**tract**(draw)
distraught a. dɪˈstrɔt	In his *distraught* state, he allowed himself to be struck by a passing truck.	心神分散、發狂的 distracted frantic	**distract**
distress n. dɪˈstrɛs	The company has been in great *distress* for money.	窮困、困難、痛苦 hardship anguish	**stress**(stretch)
distribute v. dɪˈstrɪbjʊt	The prizes were *distributed* among five winners.	分送、分配 apportion dispense	**trib**(allot)
disturb v. dɪˈstɝb	He does not want to be *disturbed* now.	打擾、擾亂 derange agitate	**turb**(stir)
diverge* v. dəˈvɝdʒ	These two roads *diverged* like the branches of a Y.	分歧、逸出正軌 fork deviate	**verg**(turn)
diverse a. dəˈvɝs	This is the most *diverse* group of politicians.	各色各樣、種類不同的 differing varying	**vers**(turn)

單字・音標・詞類	例　　句	中譯・同義字	字源分析
diversify v. dəˈvɝsəˌfaɪ	They plan to *diversify* the educational program by introducing new subjects.	使多樣化、使變化 alter vary	**vers**(turn)
divert v. dəˈvɝt	He was trained as a surgeon, but later *diverted* to diplomacy.	轉入、轉向 deviate deflect	**vert** (turn)
v.	The people *diverted* themselves with games.	自娛、消遣 entertain amuse	
divest v. dəˈvɛst	The trees are *divested* of their summer finery.	脫去、剝除 strip deprave	vest(dress)
divorce v. dəˈvors	They have been *divorced* for several years.	離婚、分開 dissolve sunder	**vers**(turn)
divulge* v. dəˈvʌldʒ	They knew of the conspiracy, but did not *divulge* it.	洩漏、揭穿 disclose expose	vulg(make public)

10

DIA

through, between, across

穿越 ● 居中

　　字首 dia 源起希臘文介系詞與副詞 $\delta\iota\alpha$ (dia)，原義即爲through 或是 between。這個字首在希臘文本已形成不少單字，後來又有小部分被羅馬人借入到拉丁文。如下文例字裡的 dialect「方言」，原希臘文爲 $\delta\iota\alpha\lambda\epsilon\kappa\tau o\varsigma$ (dialektos)，後來引進拉丁文而成 dialectus，即是一例。由此也可看出，羅馬文化與希臘文化本即一脈相傳，現代的西洋文明之所以昌盛，溯本究源，仍得歸功於希臘人和羅馬人。下文的 dialect n.「方言」和 dialectical a.「辯證的」同字源，意義却截然不同。原因是 dialect 源自希臘文 $\delta\iota\alpha\lambda\epsilon\kappa\tau o\varsigma$「方言」，而 dialectical 的名詞 dialectic「辯證」源起 $\delta\iota\alpha\lambda\epsilon\kappa\tau\iota\kappa\eta$ (dialektikē)「辯證」，兩字在希臘文均由同一字根 $\lambda\epsilon\kappa\tau$ (lect「說話」) 組成，而解釋不同，以致到了英文也出現如此差異。

單字・音標・詞類	例　　　句	中譯・同義字	字源分析
diacritic* a. ˌdaɪəˈkrɪtɪk	The professors like students of superior *diacritic* powers.	能分辨、區別的 distinguishing discerning	crit(separate)
diagnosis n. ˌdaɪəgˈnosɪs	A doctor cannot treat a patient until he has made a *diagnosis*.	診斷 identifying a disease	gnos(know)
diagonal* a. daɪˈægənḷ	There are a number of *diagonal* lines on this map.	對角線的 slanting between two opposite corners	gon(angle)
diagram n. ˈdaɪəˌgræm	The engineer has drawn a *diagram* to show how the machine works.	圖樣、圖表 sketch graph	gram(write)
dialect n. ˈdaɪəˌlɛkt	He speaks several *dialects*.	方言、同語系的語言 tongue provincialism	lect(speak)
dialectical* a. ˌdaɪəˈlɛktɪkḷ	All educational situations are *dialectical* at the core.	辯證的 rhetorical argumentative	lect(speak)
dialog(ue) n. ˈdaɪəˌlɔg	The novel contains some good writing but the *dialogue* is poor.	對白、對話 conversation discourse	log(speak)
diameter n. daɪˈæmətɚ	The *diameter* of the earth is about 7,926 miles.	直徑 measurement through the center of a circle	meter(measure)

單字・音標・詞類	例　句	中譯・同義字	字源分析
diaphanous* a. daɪˈæfənəs	Fish can be clearly seen through this *diaphanous* water.	透明、清澄的 transparent pellucid	phan(show)
diatribe* n. ˈdaɪəˌtraɪb	No one would be irritated or offended by such *diatribe*.	苛評、漫罵、爭論 abuse disputation	trib(rub)

11

E·EC·EX·EXTRA

out

向外

---

　　e, ec, ex, extra　是英文最重要的字首之一。其中 e, ex　源自拉丁文介系詞ē, ex，ec 源自希臘文介系詞ἐκ (ek), ἐξ (ex)，均有 out, outside 的意思；而 extra　則來自拉丁文副詞與介系詞extrā，原有 outside, except, without　的意思。這個字首的拼法除上述四種之外，並有兩種比較少見的變音。後面所接的字根第一個音是 f 子音時，往往會同化成 ef，如下文的 efface　v.「消除」、effect　n.「效力、影響」等均是如此。字根的第一個字母若是 c，則有部分會同化為 es，如 escape　v.「逃脫」、escort　n.「護送」等均是。字首拼作 ex　時，字根的第一個字母若是 s，則一律同化在字首的 x 字母中，因此這些字均不見有 s 字母，如 execute v.「執行、處決」（字根 secu「跟隨」）、exist v.「存在」（字根 sist 「站立」）、expire v.「死亡、滿期」（字根 spir「呼吸」）等等，均是如此。但有趣的是，這些字的拉丁文字源，如exsequor, exsistere, exspīrāre 等，却仍保有字根中的 s 。

單字・音標・詞類	例　　句	中譯・同義字	字源分析
ebullient* a. ɪˈbʌljənt	The opera offered three acts of *ebullient* breezy music.	興高采烈、沸騰的 boiling agitated	bull(boil)
eccentric a. ɪkˈsɛntrɪk	His goods were so *eccentric* that only he could sell them.	古怪的 aberrant anomalous	centric
eclipse v. ɪˈklɪps	The writer's sudden death *eclipsed* the gaiety of so many of his faithful readers.	使晦暗、遮掩 obscure extinguish	lips(leave)
ecstasy n. ˈɛkstəsɪ	Speechless with *ecstasy*, the little girl gazed at the beautiful dolls.	心醉神迷、狂喜 rapture frenzy	histana(place)
educate v. ˈɛdʒəˌket	He wanted all his sons and daughters to be well *educated*.	教育、培育 instruct cultivate	duc(lead)
educe* v. ɪˈdjus	People usually want to *educe* and cultivate what is best and noblest in themselves.	引出 elicit extract	duc(lead)
efface v. ɪˈfes	He had left a mark of the affairs of the state which would not be easily *effaced*.	消除、沖淡 erase obliterate	face
effect n. ɪˈfɛkt	The *effect* of morphine is to produce sleep.	效力 power efficiency	fect(do)

單字・音標・詞類	例　　　句	中譯・同義字	字源分析
n.	Penalty did not seem to have much *effect* on him.	影響 influence sway	
v.	The reform was *effected* peacefully.	實現 execute perform	
effectual a. əˈfɛktʃuəl	Quinine is an *effectual* preventive for malaria.	有效的 effective valid	**fect**(do)
effectuate v. əˈfɛktʃuˌet	They strove successfully to *effectuate* a settlement not by force but by reason.	使實現、實踐 accomplish perform	**fect**(do)
effete a. ɪˈfit	He is rather critical of the *effete* literary critics and dogmatic professors.	失去活力、枯竭、衰弱的 exhausted decayed	**fet**(productive)
efficacious a. ˌɛfəˈkeʃəs	There is not yet an *efficacious* cure for the deadly disease.	有效的 effective adequate	**fic**(do)
efficient a. əˈfɪʃənt	We have to adopt more *efficient* methods for this task.	有效、有能力的 competent effective	**fic**(do)
effort n. ˈɛfət	She had made great *efforts* to appease her mother.	努力 endeavor exertion	**fort**(strong)

單字·音標·詞類	例　　　　句	中譯·同義字	字源分析
effuse v. ɪˈfjuz	The room *effused* an atmosphere of un-happiness and discontent.	發散、流出 shed emanate	**fus**(pour)
ejaculate* v. ɪˈdʒækjəˌlet	The crowds were angry, *ejaculating* unfinished sentences.	突然說出、叫出 utter suddenly exclaim	**jac**(throw)
eject v. ɪˈdʒɛkt	He was *ejected* for taunting the performers.	逐出 expel oust	**ject**(throw)
elaborate v. ɪˈlæbəˌret	Newton's idea of mechanical energy was *elaborated* by those who followed him.	使擴大、完美 improve refine	labor
a. ɪˈlæbərɪt	He began an *elaborate* calculation on his fingers.	複雜 intricate complicated	
elapse v. ɪˈlæps	Ten years had *elapsed* before she met him again.	(光陰)逝去、溜走 pass slip by	**laps**(glide)
elate v. ɪˈlet	It was a fine sunny day, the sort of day that *elates* the heart of young and old.	使興奮、欣喜 elevate exhilarate	**fer**(carry)
elect v. ɪˈlɛkt	The man was *elected* twice in ten years.	選舉、推選、選擇 select choose	**lect**(choose)

單字‧音標‧詞類	例　　句	中譯‧同義字	字源分析
elegant a. ˈɛləgənt	Every young man in the party kept staring at the *elegant* attractive lady.	文雅、高雅的 graceful tasteful	leg(choose)
elevate v. ˈɛləˌvet	He *elevated* his eyebrows, and looked at the girl in amazement.	提高、舉起 lift heave	lev(lift)
elicit v. ɪˈlɪsɪt	Without a word the young girl started to *elicit* harmonious sounds from her instrument.	引出 draw out educe	lic(entice)
elide v. ɪˈlaɪd	These figures should be *elided* wherever possible.	略去 annul suppress	lid(strike)
eligible a. ˈɛlɪdʒəbļ	The book is not *eligible* for copyright in this country.	合格、適當的 qualified desirable	lig(choose)
elite n. ɪˈlit	This is a store catering only to the *elite*.	社會名流、精華 choice part	elect
elongate v. ɪˈlɔŋget	He *elongated* his face as he heard their story.	拉長、延伸 lengthen extend	long
elope v. ɪˈlop	She *eloped* with her second cousin and they got married immediately afterwards.	私奔、逃亡 escape flee	lop(run)

單字・音標・詞類	例　　　句	中譯・同義字	字源分析
eloquent a. ˈɛləkwənt	The *eloquent* candidate moved many hearts.	雄辯的 expressive vocal	**loqu**(speak)
elucidate v. ɪˈlusəˌdet	This pamphlet is printed to *elucidate* the policy of the government.	闡明、說明 clarify expound	**lucid**
elude v. ɪˈlud	They have tried to *elude* their responsibilities.	逃避、規避 evade sidestep	**lud**(play)
emaciate* v. ɪˈmeʃɪˌet	The poor little girl reached out her *emaciated* bony hands at the strangers.	使瘦弱 cause to become lean	**maci**(lean)
emanate* v. ˈɛməˌnet	Much of the criticism against him *emanated* from defeated candidates.	發出、流出 flow emerge	**man**(flow)
emancipate v. ɪˈmænsəˌpet	His greatest wish was to *emancipate* the slaves in the country.	解放 liberate extricate	**man**(hand) **cip**(receive)
emerge v. ɪˈmɝdʒ	The sailors burst into crying when land first *emerged* from the sea.	出現 appear rise	merge
emigrate v. ˈɛməˌgret	The Russian Jews have *emigrated* to other countries.	移居 move migrate	migrate
eminent a. ˈɛmənənt	His *eminent* services to the party will forever be remembered.	傑出的 prominent outstanding	**min**(project)

單字・音標・詞類	例 句	中譯・同義字	字源分析
emissary n. ˈɛməˌsɛrɪ	The warring states have sent *emissaries* to discuss possible peace terms.	使者 agent representative	**miss**(send)
emit v. ɪˈmɪt	Gamma rays may continue to be *emitted* for years.	放射、噴出 eject discharge	**mit**(send)
emotion n. ɪˈmoʃən	Love, hate, and fear are *emotions*.	情感、情緒、感情 feeling passion	**mot**(move)
enormous a. ɪˈnɔrməs	The war cost an *enormous* sum of money.	巨大的 huge gigantic	norm
eradicate v. ɪˈrædɪˌket	These perennial creeping rootstocks are not easy to *eradicate*.	連根拔除、撲滅 uproot exterminate	radic(root)
erase v. ɪˈres	He has *erased* the pencil marks in his notebook.	擦掉、抹去 efface obliterate	ras(scrape)
erect v. ɪˈrɛkt a.	A monument has been *erected* in memory of the deceased hero. The natives on this island usually bury their dead *erect*.	建立、豎立 establish elevate 直立的 upright standing	rect(make straight)
erode v. ɪˈrod	The mountain range has been *eroded* into low hills.	侵蝕、腐蝕 corrode canker	rod(gnaw)

單字・音標・詞類	例　　　句	中譯・同義字	字源分析
erudite a. ˈɛrʊˌdaɪt	The captain knew about sea fighting in a fashion too informed to be *erudite*.	迂腐、拘泥、博學的 learned pedantic	rudit(rude)
erupt v. ɪˈrʌpt	The volcano has *erupted* three times during the last decade.	爆發 break out explode	rupt(break)
escape v. ɪˈskep	Three of the prisoners *escaped* in the revolt.	逃脫 flee abscond	cap(cloak)
escort n. ˈɛskɔrt	Under heavy *escort* the ship made the dangerous trip through the Panama Canal.	護送、護衛 protection convoy	**correct**(make straight)
v. ɛˈskɔrt	The prisoner was *escorted* back to his cell.	護送、護航 accompany convoy	
evacuate v. ɪˈvækjʊˌet	The people threatened by the forest fire were soon *evacuated*.	撤離、撤空 withdraw vacate	vac(empty)
evade v. ɪˈved	Wisdom consists in learning when to *evade* and when to oppose head on.	規避、逃避 elude dodge	vad(go)
evaluate v. ɪˈvæljʊˌet	They used trained observers to visit and *evaluate* teachers in the classrooms.	評估 rate appraise	**value**

單字・音標・詞類	例　　句	中譯・同義字	字源分析
evanescent* a. ˌɛvəˈnɛsn̩t	He could feel her breath on his neck, slight and *evanescent* like an April breeze.	短暫、易逝的 fleeting transient	vanesc(vanish)
event n. ɪˈvɛnt	We made careful plans and awaited the *event*.	結果 outcome consequence	**vent**(come)
n.	The discovery of America was a great *event*.	發生的事、事件 happening incident	
eventual a. ɪˈvɛntʃʊəl	After several failures, his *eventual* success surprised everyone.	最後的 final conclusive	**event**
evict v. ɪˈvɪkt	A heavy counterattack *evicted* the enemy from the town.	逐出 remove eject	vict(conquer)
evident a. ˈɛvədənt	It is quite *evident* that someone has been in the house.	明顯的 obvious manifest	**vid**(see)
evoke v. ɪˈvok	His remark *evoked* nothing, not even curiosity.	喚起、引起 elicit educe	**vok**(voice)
evolve v. ɪˈvɑlv	Hitler and his disciples *evolved* a racial myth out of their writings.	引出、發展 develop unfold	**volv**(roll)
exacerbate* v. ɪgˈzæsɚˌbet	Foolish words could *exacerbate* a quarrel.	使加劇、激怒 provoke aggravate	acerb(sour)

單字・音標・詞類	例　　句	中譯・同義字	字源分析
exact v. ɪɡˈzækt	An extremely delicate task may *exact* any scholar.	需要、堅持要求 demand extort	**act**
a.	I don't know the *exact* number yet.	精確的 precise correct	
exaggerate v. ɪɡˈzædʒəˌret	She was only *exaggerating* when she said that to you.	誇大、使擴大 overstate enlarge	agger(heap)
exasperate v. ɪɡˈzæspəˌret	She's a good child but her slowness often *exasperates* me.	激怒 enrage inflame	asper(rough)
excavate v. ˈɛkskəˌvet	They have *excavated* a tunnel under the river.	挖掘 dig trench	cave
exceed v. ɪkˈsid	Their failures *exceeded* all expectations.	超過、勝過 surpass surmount	**ceed**(go)
excel v. ɪkˈsɛl	The charming child instinctively *excelled* other children in all aspects.	優於、超過 exceed surpass	cel(rise)
except v. ɪkˈsɛpt	Those who passed the first test were *excepted* from the second.	免除、除外 exclude omit	**cept**(receive)
prep.	We all went to the party *except* Teresa.	除…之外 but excluding	

單字・音標・詞類	例　　　句	中譯・同義字	字源分析
excerpt n. ˈɛksɝpt	The doctor read *excerpts* from several medical books.	摘錄 quotation extraction	cerpt(pick)
excess n. ɪkˈsɛs	During March there was an *excess* of imports over exports.	超額、超過數 surplus residue	cess(go)
a.	The body tends to rid itself of its *excess* nitrogen.	額外、超過的 excessive exorbitant	
exchange v. ɪksˈtʃendʒ	They *exchanged* gifts at Christmas.	交換 swap barter	change
excise v. ɪkˈsaɪz	The surgeons have *excised* the tumor.	切去、除去 cut out extirpate	cis(cut)
excite v. ɪkˈsaɪt	The news of success *excited* everybody.	鼓舞、引起 rouse animate	cit(call)
exclaim v. ɪkˈsklem	The tourists *exclaimed* with wonder when the view unfolded.	驚呼、呼喊 cry shout	claim(shout)
exclude v. ɪkˈsklud	Immigrants must be screened to *exclude* the small fraction of undesirables.	拒絕、排除 debar eliminate	clud(close)
excrete* v. ɪkˈskrit	The skin *excretes* sweat.	排泄 give off discharge	cret(separate)

單字・音標・詞類	例　句	中譯・同義字	字源分析
exculpate* v. ˈɛkskʌlˌpet	They *exculpated* the man after a thorough investigation.	使無罪、證明無罪 release exonerate	culp(fault)
excursion n. ɪkˈskɜ·ʃən	He is rather excited about his summer *excursions* to the Colorado Rockies.	旅行 journey tour	**curs**(run)
excursive a. ɪkˈskɜ·sɪv	His *excursive* remarks annoyed his host.	散漫、無連貫的 rambling digressive	**curs**(run)
excuse v. ɪkˈskjuz	We *excused* him for being late.	原諒 pardon forgive	cus(charge)
execrate* v. ˈɛksɪˌkret	He was *execrated* as a murderer and adulterer.	咒罵 damn curse	secr(sacred)
execute v. ˈɛksɪˌkjut	The king's will has been well *executed.*	執行 perform transact	**secu**(follow)
v.	The prisoner was *executed* at dawn.	處死、處決 kill behead	
exempt v. ɪgˈzɛmpt	The man was *exempted* from military service.	使免除（責任等） remove exclude	empt(take)

單字・音標・詞類	例　　　句	中譯・同義字	字源分析
exert v. ɪgˈzɜˈt	He had to *exert* all his strength to move the stone.	運用 labor endeavor	ser(join)
exhale v. ɛksˈhel	The woman *exhaled* a sigh when she saw the poor couple strolling down the street.	發出、呼出 breathe emit	hal(breathe)
exhaust v. ɪgˈzɔst	You will be *exhausted* if you don't stop jumping.	使力竭、耗盡 drain fatigue	haust(draw)
exhibit n. ɪgˈzɪbɪt	There is an *exhibit* of American colonial pottery at the students' center.	展覽 show display	hib(hold)
v.	In all cultures we know, man *exhibits* an aesthetic sense.	顯示、展覽 show display	
exhilarate v. ɪgˈzɪləˌret	The sun and the wind on the traveler's back somehow *exhilarated* him.	使高興 gladden cheer	hilar(glad)
exhort v. ɪgˈzɔrt	We have been *exhorted* to drive all negative fears out of our minds.	勸告、力勸 urge stimulate	hort(urge)
exhume* v. ɪgˈzjum	The body of the murdered man was *exhumed* and sent to the police.	從墓中挖出 dig out disinter	hum(earth)

單字·音標·詞類	例　　　句	中譯·同義字	字源分析
exigency* n. ˈɛksədʒənsɪ	The president is the sole judge of the *exigency* demanding the use of troops.	緊急、迫切 urgency pressure	**ig**(act)
exile n. ˈɛgzaɪl	The man was sent into *exile* after the revolution.	放逐 banishment expatriation	
v.	The *exiled* generals were all called back to the country.	放逐 banish ostracize	
exodus* n. ˈɛksədəs	The book is on the *exodus* of the cotton mills from New England to the South.	大批離去、 (移民)出國 departure emigration	hod(way)
exonerate* v. ɪgˈzɑnəˌret	There is no reason for *exonerating* anyone from the duties of a citizen.	免除 disburden exempt	oner(burden)
exorcise v. ˈɛksɔrˌsaɪz	The elderly woman tried to *exorcise* the girl's feeling of alarm.	去除 cast out expel	horc(oath)
exotic a. ɪgˈzɑtɪk	The man has many *exotic* plants in his garden.	外來、外國產的 outlandish alien	
expand v. ɪkˈspænd	The children *expanded* their lips and stared with distended eyes.	張開、擴大、 使膨脹 enlarge dilate	pand(spread)

單字・音標・詞類	例　　　句	中譯・同義字	字源分析
expatiate* v. ɪkˈspeʃɪˌet	His knowledge of the country enabled him to *expatiate* on its strategic situation.	詳述、漫遊 range enlarge	spati(walk)
expatriate v. ɛksˈpetrɪˌet	The writer *expatriated* himself for years at the Cape of Good Hope.	移居國外、放逐 banish exile	patr(fatherland)
expect v. ɪkˈspɛkt	I did not *expect* to see you here.	預期、預料 anticipate foresee	**spect**(watch)
expedient a. ɪkˈspidɪənt	In time of war, governments often take *expedient* measures.	權宜、方便的 convenient advisable	**ped**(foot)
expedite v. ˈɛkspɪˌdaɪt	The admininstration measure was intended to *expedite* the shipbuilding program.	使加速 hasten accelerate	**ped**(foot)
expeditious a. ˌɛkspɪˈdɪʃəs	Our workmen are spirited, diligent, and *expeditious*.	敏捷、迅速的 speedy brisk	**expedite**
expel v. ɪkˈspɛl	The secret agents were *expelled* after their identity was discovered.	驅逐、逐出 oust eject	**pel**(push)
expend v. ɪkˈspɛnd	Part of the public revenue is *expended* on social services.	花費、消耗 spend consume	**pend**(weigh)

單字・音標・詞類	例　　句	中譯・同義字	字源分析
expense n. ɪkˈspɛns	The *expense* of a good education is great.	費用 expenditure cost	**pens**(weigh)
expire v. ɪkˈspaɪr	The old man was carried home by two servants and soon *expired*.	死亡 die perish	spir(breathe)
v.	His term of office as President will *expire* next year.	滿期、終止 cease terminate	
explain v. ɪkˈsplen	Will you be able to *explain* why you were late?	解釋、說明 expound explicate	plain
explicable a. ˈɛksplɪkəbl̩	The reason for my being late is absolutely *explicable*.	可說明、可解釋的 explainable	**explicate**
explicate v. ˈɛksplɪˌket	They were asked to *explicate* the mystery of her disappearance.	解說、說明 explain elucidate	**plic**(fold)
explicit a. ɪkˈsplɪsɪt	It is sometimes hard to have an *explicit* notion of that which is infinite.	明確的 express definite	**plic**(fold)
explode v. ɪkˈsplod	The bomb *exploded* when the policeman wanted to examine it.	爆炸、發作 burst fulminate	plod(applaud)
exploit n. ˈɛksplɔɪt	The hero's *exploits* have been lauded ever since.	功蹟 accomplishment feat	**ploit**(fold)

單字・音標・詞類	例　　　句	中譯・同義字	字源分析
v. ɪkˈsplɔɪt	The government has planned to *exploit* the natural resources of the country.	開發、利用 use utilize	
explore v. ɪkˈsplor	Geologists and archeologists were summoned to *explore* the cavern.	探險、探測、研究 investigate scrutinize	plor(cry)
exponent n. ɪkˈsponənt	He is the best-known *exponent* of the science of anthropology.	解釋者 explainer expounder	**pon**(place)
export v. ɪksˈport	China *exports* tea and silk.	外銷、輸出 ship out	**port**(carry)
n. ˈɛksport	Last year our *exports* exceeded our imports in value.	輸出品 something shipped out	
expose v. ɪkˈspoz	The commander's decision would dangerously *expose* the troops.	暴露、揭穿 bare reveal	**pos**(place)
expound v. ɪkˈspaʊnd	The physicist was asked to *expound* on his new theory.	解釋、說明 explain explicate	**pound**(place)
express v. ɪkˈsprɛs	It is not difficult to *express* what you already have in mind.	表達 utter couch	**press**(press)
a.	He was the *express* image of his father.	正確、明確的 definite precise	

單字·音標·詞類	例　　句	中譯·同義字	字源分析
a.	The train was traveling at *express* speed.	快速的 fast rapid	
expulsion n. ɪkˈspʌlʃən	Their *expulsion* from Germany had cost them their homes.	逐出 ejection banishment	**puls**(push)
ex quisite a. ˈɛkskwɪzɪt	The night-blooming cereus is an *exquisite* white blossom with a spicy fragrance.	纖美、精緻的 delicate perfected	quis(ask)
ex tant a. ɪkˈstænt	This is one of the oldest works *extant* on that subject.	現存的 currently 　existing	sta(stand)
ex temporaneous* ɪkˌstɛmpəˈrenɪəs a.	His is one of the funniest *extemporaneous* wits of our time.	即席、臨時作成的 impromptu improvised	tempor(time)
ex temporize v. ɪkˈstɛmpəˌraɪz	Her rarely *extemporizes* on serious occasions.	即席演說、即席作曲 improvise	tempor(time)
ex tend v. ɪkˈstɛnd	They are thinking of *extending* their stay to one month.	延長 expand prolong	**tend**(stretch)
ex tenuate* v. ɪkˈstɛnjʊˌet	Nothing can *extenuate* his guilt.	減輕 reduce diminish	ten(thin)
ex terior a. ɪkˈstɪrɪɚ	The *exterior* design of the building is poor.	外在的 outer external	

單字·音標·詞類	例　　　句	中譯·同義字	字源分析
n.	The house has an old *exterior*.	外面、外表 outside	
exterminate v. ɪkˈstɝməˌnet	The rats in this field were *exterminated*.	消滅 annihilate expel	termin(limit)
external a. ɪkˈstɝn̩	He does not think the *external* aspect of a religion is important.	外表、形式上 、外部的 outer extrinsic	
extinct a. ɪkˈstɪŋkt	The book deals with *extinct* prehistoric animals.	滅種、熄滅了 的 vanished extinguished	stingu (extinguish)
extinguish v. ɪkˈstɪŋgwɪʃ	One failure after another *extinguished* her hope.	滅絕、熄滅 annihilate stifle	stingu(ex- tinguish)
extirpate v. ˈɛkstɚˌpet	Many precious species have been *extirpated* from the volcanic region.	滅絕、連根拔 起 uproot eradicate	stirp(root)
extol v. ɪkˈstɑl	The deeds of the hero were *extolled* by poets.	頌揚 laud eulogize	tol(raise)
extort v. ɪkˈstɔrt	The official was accused of *extorting* bribes.	勒索 squeeze extract	**tort**(twist)
extra a. ˈɛkstrə	We don't need any *extra* money for the trip.	額外、特別的 additional special	

單字‧音標‧詞類	例　句	中譯‧同義字	字源分析
extract v. ɪkˈstrækt	He *extracted* a letter from his pocket and started to read it.	抽出、取出 draw produce	**tract**(draw)
v.	They could *extract* happiness from what many would consider a humdrum existence.	引出、得到 draw derive	
extradite v. ˈɛkstrəˌdaɪt	The prisoner was *extradited* from Panama back to the United States.	引渡 banish exile	tradit(sur- render)
extraneous a. ɪkˈstrenɪəs	There should not be any *extraneous* light in a camera.	外來的 additional extrinsic	
extraordinary a. ɪkˈstrɔrdṇˌɛrɪ	Her performance in school was *extra-ordinary*.	傑出、驚人的 singular marvelous	ordinary
extravagant a. ɪkˈstrævəgənt	These dialogues best describe the *extra-vagant* language of a lover.	過度的 immoderate excessive	vaga(wander)
extreme n. ɪkˈstrim	The temperature in the desert ranges astonishingly between the *extremes* of heat and cold.	極端、極端之 事物 end termination	
a.	The police had resorted to *extreme* measures to combat crime.	極端、最遠、 極度的 farthest excessive	

單字・音標・詞類	例　　句	中譯・同義字	字源分析
extricate v. ˈɛkstrɪˌket	The horse could not *extricate* its foot from the mudhole.	解脫、救出 free disentangle	tric(vexation)
extrinsic a. ɛkˈstrɪnsɪk	The government has looked for *extrinsic* aid to search for the missing plane.	外來、外在的 outside external	
extrude* v. ɪkˈstrud	The offender was *extruded* as unworthy of an honorable calling.	逐出 eject expel	**trud**(thrust)
exuberant a. ɪgˈzjubərənt	She had an *exuberant* capacity for pleasure.	豐富、充溢的 profuse extravagant	uber(fruitful)
exude v. ɪgˈzjud	Beads of moisture *exuded* from the clamming walls.	滲出、流出 ooze discharge	sud(sweat)
v.	He has a voice that *exudes* confidence.	流露 emit emanate	
exult v. ɪgˈzʌlt	They have *exulted* over their good luck since they found the bag full of cash.	大喜、耀武揚威 rejoice taunt	sult(leap)

12

EM·EN·IM·IN

in, upon

進入 • 在上

字首 em, en, im, in 也是英文非常重要的構詞成分，組成的單字極多，必須留意。四種拼法之中，em 與 en 源自希臘文的副詞與介系詞 *ἐν*，im 與 in 來自拉丁文的介系詞 in，有 in, within, upon 的意思。後面所接的字根第一個音，若是 p, b, m 三個雙唇音之一，則拼作 em 或 im，以雙唇音接雙唇音，方便發音，如下文的 embargo n.「禁止入港」、empirical a.「實驗上的」、imbibe v.「吸收」、immerse v.「浸入」、impart v.「傳遞、給與」等字均是。字根的第一個音若不在雙唇音之列，則拼成 en 或 in，如 enamor v.「迷住」、incise v.「刻、雕」等等，均是這種情形。這個字首組成的單字，意義大半和 in「進入」有關，只有少數須將字首視為 upon 來解釋。例如 impale v.「以尖物刺住」，字根 pale 意思是 pole「竿子」，便必須想成是「刺在竿上」。再如 imprecate v.「詛咒」，字根 prec 有 pray「祈求」的意思，因此可想做是「祈求讓事情落在某人身上」。此外，字首 im, in 尚有否定的用法，但本書並未列出討論，因此讀者諸君如想進一步了解，請自行參閱一般的辭典。

單字・音標・詞類	例　　　句	中譯・同義字	字源分析
embargo n. ɪmˈbɑrgo	The Port of London laid an *embargo* on all ships coming from the Baltic.	禁止入港、禁止、阻礙 restriction bar	bar(bar)
embark v. ɪmˈbɑrk	The soldiers have *embarked* for the island.	乘船 go aboard	bark(small boat)
v.	She had no hesitation about *embarking* on a new career.	從事、著手 begin engage	
embarrass v. ɪmˈbærəs	Don't feel *embarrassed* when you say that to her.	使困窘、使侷促不安 abash confound	bar(bar)
embed v. ɪmˈbɛd	The tales of the hero's prowess have become *embedded* in folklore.	嵌入、深植 set enclose	bed
embellish v. ɪmˈbɛlɪʃ	There are faults with which nature has generously *embellished* us all.	美化、裝飾 decorate adorn	bel(beautiful)
emblem n. ˈɛmbləm	A balance is an *emblem* of justice.	象徵、徽章 symbol badge	blem(throw)
embody v. ɪmˈbɑdɪ	The statesmen have attempted to *embody* basic democratic principles in their treaty.	具體表現、編入 incarnate comprehend	body

單字・音標・詞類	例　　　　句	中譯・同義字	字源分析
embrace v. ɪmˈbres	The reuniting relatives *embraced* one another.	擁抱 hug huddle	brace(arm)
v.	This book *embraces* many subjects.	包含 include comprehend	
v.	He *embraced* his father's belief and settled down to be a country gentleman.	接受 receive undertake	
embroil* v. ɛmˈbrɔɪl	Her emotions were forever *embroiling* her intellect.	使混亂 disorder confound	broil(dirty)
empathy* n. ˈɛmpəθɪ	Without *empathy* an artistic emotion is purely intellectual and associative.	共感、神入 sympathy	**path**(feeling)
emphasize v. ˈɛmfəˌsaɪz	You have to *emphasize* your sincerity when you talk to him.	強調 stress accentuate	phas(show)
empirical a. ɛmˈpɪrɪkļ	This is merely an *empirical* treatment of a disease little known.	實驗上的 hypothetical tentative	pir(trial)
employ v. ɪmˈplɔɪ	They have *employed* a lawyer to straighten the legal tangle.	僱用 hire commission	**ply**(fold)
v.	He *employed* most of his leisure in reading.	利用、使用 use engage	

單字・音標・詞類	例 句	中譯・同義字	字源分析
empower v. ɪmˈpaʊɚ	The department was *empowered* by the legislature to begin courses in medicine.	授權與 authorize warrant	power
enact v. ɪnˈækt	A lot of history has been *enacted* within the historian's view.	演出 play perform	**act**
enamor v. ɪnˈæmɚ	We met the beautiful Indian girl with whom he was *enamored*.	迷住 captivate enchant	amor(love)
encase v. ɪnˈkes	Each of the products was *encased* in leatherette.	納入套內、納入箱內 enclose in a case	case
enchant v. ɪnˈtʃænt	The scene *enchanted* her to the point of tears.	使迷住、迷惑 charm bewitch	chant(sing)
enclave* n. ˈɛnklev	An *enclave* is a tract enclosed within foreign territory.	被包領土 territory 　surrounded 　by another	clav(key)
enclose v. ɪnˈkloz	The town is *enclosed* by mountains.	圍繞 surround encircle	close
encompass v. ɪnˈkʌmpəs	A thick fog *encompassed* the building.	包圍 besiege beset	**compass**
encounter v. ɪnˈkaʊntɚ	I *encountered* an old acquaintance on the street.	邂逅、遭遇 meet confront	**counter**

單字・音標・詞類	例　　　句	中譯・同義字	字源分析
encourage v. ɪnˈkɝɪdʒ	I do not *encourage* you to do that.	鼓勵、激勵 hearten embolden	**courage**
encroach v. ɪnˈkrotʃ	They *encroached* on the territory of the neighboring country.	侵佔、侵入 intrude trespass	croach(hook)
endeavor v. ɪnˈdɛvɚ	However much he *endeavored*, the goal stayed unattained.	努力 try struggle	deavor(duty)
endemic* a. ɛnˈdɛmɪk	The islands have a number of interesting *endemic* species.	某地特有的 native indigenous	dem(people)
endorse v. ɪnˈdɔrs	He *endorsed* his name on the check.	背書 sign inscribe	dors(back)
v.	Parents heartily *endorsed* the plan for a school playground.	贊同 support sanction	
endow v. ɪnˈdau	Nature *endowed* him with good eyesight.	賦與 provide furnish	dow(give)
endure v. ɪnˈdjur	If help does not come, we must *endure* to the end.	忍受、忍耐 tolerate abide	dur(hard)
v.	His fame will *endure* for ever.	持久 last abide	

單字・音標・詞類	例　　句	中譯・同義字	字源分析
energy n. ˈɛnɚdʒɪ	It is hard to believe that she has so much *energy*.	精力、活力 vigor stamina	erg(work)
enfold v. ɪnˈfold	She seemed to be *enfolded* in an unbearable atmosphere.	圍繞、籠罩、包封 envelop contain	fold
enforce v. ɪnˈfors	His comment is enough to *enforce* the significance attributed to a free ballot.	加強、力勸、迫使 urge constrain	force
engage v. ɪnˈgedʒ	His family had been *engaged* in trade for generations.	從事、忙於 occupy engross	gage
engender v. ɪnˈdʒɛndɚ	Angry words *engender* strife.	釀成、產生 generate beget	**gen**(bear)
engrave v. ɪnˈgrev	The mason has *engraved* an inscription on the stone.	刻、銘記（於心） carve imprint	grave(cut)
enhance v. ɪnˈhæns	Our pleasure was *enhanced* by our hostess's care.	增加、提高 elevate augment	alt(high)
enjoin* v. ɪnˈdʒɔɪn	His leader had sternly *enjoined* him to avoid any weakness.	命令、禁止 command forbid	join

單字・音標・詞類	例　　　句	中譯・同義字	字源分析
enjoy v. ɪnˈdʒɔɪ	To tell the truth, I do not *enjoy* her company.	歡喜、享受 like relish	joy
enlist v. ɪnˈlɪst	He *enlisted* for three more years of service in the navy.	服役、從軍 enroll engage	
enrage v. ɪnˈredʒ	The audience became *enraged* when the songstress did not show up on time.	激怒、使暴怒 anger infuriate	range
enrapture v. ɪnˈræptʃɚ	The boy was *enraptured* when Susan promised to have a date with him.	使狂喜 delight entrance	rapture
enrich v. ɪnˈrɪtʃ	His expeditions *enriched* the museum's collections of tropical fauna.	使豐富、充實 、裝飾 aggrandize embellish	rich
enroll v. ɪnˈrol	Nearly 10 percent of our population is *enrolled* in the elementary school.	入學、登記、 入伍 register enlist	roll
enshrine* v. ɪnˈʃraɪn	A fragment of the Cross is *enshrined* in the cathedral.	奉祀於廟堂中 、奉為神聖 worship sanctify	shrine
enshroud v. ɛnˈʃraud	Darkness began to *enshroud* the earth.	覆蓋、遮蔽 cover conceal	shroud

單字·音標·詞類	例　　句	中譯·同義字	字源分析
enslave v. ɪnˈslev	Millions of people were held in subjugation, *enslaved* by poverty and illiterarcy.	奴役 subdue subjugate	slave
ensnare* v. ɛnˈsnɛr	She was *ensnared* by some sharpers.	誘入陷阱 trap dupe	snare
ensure v. ɪnˈʃʊr	Careful planning and hard work *ensured* our success.	保證 assure secure	sure
entangle v. ɪnˈtæŋgḷ	The speaker has *entangled* his listeners in a maze of sophistries.	使困惑、使陷入 entrap perplex	tangle
enthrall* v. ɪnˈθrɔl	His ringing laugh and humorous anecdotes *enthralled* his companions.	迷住 fascinate captivate	thrall
entice v. ɪnˈtaɪs	The man had a vivid dark face that *enticed* attention.	吸引、引誘 attract allure	tice(burning brand)
entitle v. ɪnˈtaɪtḷ	The new book is *entitled The Russians in Afghanistan.*	給與名稱 name designate	title
v.	You are not *entitled* to sit here.	使有資格、使有權利 qualify empower	

單字・音標・詞類	例　　　句	中譯・同義字	字源分析
entrance* v. ɪnˈtræns	The beauty of the land *entranced* the settlers.	使出神、使神魂顛倒 enrapture ravish	trance
entreat v. ɪnˈtrit	I must *entreat* both your patience and your attention.	懇求 beseech implore	**treat**(draw)
entrench v. ɪnˈtrɛntʃ	The enemy *entrenched* himself strongly along the river.	挖壕溝以保護 surround with 　trenches	trench
v.	This thought is firmly *entrenched* in the minds of many people.	確立 establish confirm	
entrust v. ɪnˈtrʌst	I do not feel like *entrusting* him with my money.	交託 commit	trust
envelop v. ɪnˈvɛləp	Large black clouds were *enveloping* the moon.	包圍、圍繞 enclose encircle	velop(wrap)
environment n. ɪnˈvaɪrənmənt	I know little about his home *environment*.	環境 surroundings	viron(circuit)
environs* n.pl. ɪnˈvaɪrənz	Subsequent administrative developments further enlarged the *environs* of these towns.	周圍、郊外 compass suburbs	viron(circuit)

單字・音標・詞類	例　　　句	中譯・同義字	字源分析
envisage v. ɛn'vɪzɪdʒ	The philosopher *envisaged* man as simply the locus of a polytheism.	想像、設想 visualize contemplate	**vis**(see)
envision v. ɛn'vɪʒən	She *envisioned* a career in teaching and research.	擬想（未來） foresee envisage	**vis**(see)
envoy n. 'ɛnvɔɪ	The mutineers sent an *envoy* to deal with the ship's captain.	使者 agent representative	**voy**(way)
imbibe v. ɪm'baɪb	Plants can *imbibe* as much nourishment through their leaves as via their roots.	吸收、飲 absorb drink	**bib**(drink)
immanent* a. 'ɪmənənt	In social evolution one must consider both *immanent* and external factors.	內在的 indwelling inherent	**man**(remain)
immerse v. ɪ'mɝs	Test the temperature before *immersing* yourself in the pool.	浸入、埋首熱衷於 dip engross	merge
immigrate v. 'ɪmə͵gret	The Stanislavskies have *immigrated* to this country for many years.	移居入境 move migrate	migrate
impair v. ɪm'pɛr	You might *impair* your health by wild living.	損害、減少 damage lessen	**pair**(worse)

單字・音標・詞類	例　　　句	中譯・同義字	字源分析
impale* v. ɪmˈpel	The butterfly has been *impaled* by a pin.	以尖物刺住、圍起 fix confine	pale(pole)
impart v. ɪmˈpɑrt	His very position *imparted* a political significance to whatever he did.	傳遞、給與、告訴 confer relate	part
impeach* v. ɪmˈpitʃ	The testimony of the witness was *impeached*.	非難、指責、檢舉 challenge denounce	pedic(fetter)
impede v. ɪmˈpid	Storms *impeded* the vessels.	阻礙 hinder hamper	**ped**(foot)
impel v. ɪmˈpɛl	He felt *impelled* to tolerate what he intensely disliked.	驅使、逼迫 force compel	pel(push)
imperil v. ɪmˈpɛrəl	The investments of the people were *imperiled* in the recession.	危及、使陷於危機 hazard jeopardize	peril
impetuous a. ɪmˈpɛtʃʊəs	He is a man of a very warm and *impetuous* nature.	衝動、猛烈的 furious impulsive	impetus
impetus n. ˈɪmpətəs	The man is trying to discover the *impetus* behind all this activity.	原動力、衝力、刺激 impulse incentive	pet(rush)

單字・音標・詞類	例　　　　句	中譯・同義字	字源分析
impinge* v. ɪmˈpɪndʒ	A strong light *impinged* on his eyes and caused sudden pain.	衝擊、打擊 strike dash	ping(strike)
implant v. ɪmˈplænt	The preacher has *implanted* in the people the idea that the end of the world is near.	灌輸、注入 ingraft infuse	plant
implement n. ˈɪmpləmənt	They need an *implement* to help roll the heavy logs.	工具、器具 tool instrument	ple(fill)
v. ˈɪpləˌmɛnt	I wondered how he could best *implement* his purpose.	實現、完成 fulfill accomplish	
implicate v. ˈɪmplɪˌket	There is evidence *implicating* many high officials in the conspiracy.	牽連、暗示 involve imply	**plic**(fold)
implicit a. ɪmˈplɪsɪt	The artistic standards of our time are *implicit* rather than codified.	暗示、隱含的 implied inferred	**plic**(fold)
implore v. ɪmˈplor	The accused had *implored* another chance to prove his innocence.	懇求 entreat beseech	plor(cry out)
import v. ɪmˈport	The government *imported* wheat during the grain shortage.	輸入 bring introduce	**port**(carry)
n. ˈɪmpɔrt	The chief *imports* of this country are machinery and vehicles.	輸入品 merchandise brought in	

單字・音標・詞類	例　　　句	中譯・同義字	字源分析
impose v. ɪmˈpoz	A tax was *imposed* on all unmarried men.	課（稅）、強使 enjoin set	**pos**(place)
imposing a. ɪmˈpozɪŋ	The man's *imposing* appearance impressed every guest.	儀表堂堂、宏偉的 grand commanding	**impose**
impound v. ɪmˈpaʊnd	They have caught and *impounded* a number of stray dogs.	關於欄內、扣留 confine imprison	**pound**(place)
imprecate* v. ˈɪmprɪˌket	The writer *imprecated* the weather when the ink froze in his fountain pen.	詛咒 curse execrate	**prec**(pray)
impress v. ɪmˈprɛs	The carpenter has *impressed* an odd design on the wood.	銘刻、壓印、蓋印 stamp imprint	**press**(press)
v.	The altered manner of his son *impressed* him strangely.	印入記憶、使感動 move affect	
imprint v. ɪmˈprɪnt	They have a machine to *imprint* code numbers on metal merchandise.	印刻、蓋印於 impress mark	**print**
n. ˈɪmprɪnt	The teacher left her *imprint* on several generations of students.	不可磨滅的影響 effect influence	

單字・音標・詞類	例　　　句	中譯・同義字	字源分析
impromptu adv. ɪmˈprɑmptu	The man was able to speak *impromptu* and at length on any given subject.	即席、毫無準備地 without previous preparation	prompt(ready)
a.	He made a short *impromptu* speech, thanking the performers for their work.	即席、立刻的 offhand improvised	
improve v. ɪmˈpruv	He is trying to *improve* his health by exercising.	增進、改善 better ameliorate	prov(profit)
impulse n. ˈɪmpʌls	The writer's successful novels are derived from the same *impulse* as his poetry.	靈感、動機、刺激 impetus motive	**puls**(push)
inborn a. ɪnˈbɔrn	Man has an *inborn* desire to fly.	天生的 innate inherent	born
incarcerate* v. ɪnˈkɑrsəˌret	The man had been *incarcerated* for seven years.	監禁、下獄 jail confine	carcer(cell)
incarnate v. ɪnˈkɑrnet	We need an international organization that *incarnates* our hopes for lasting peace.	使具體化、使化身 embody personify	carn(flesh)
incense v. ɪnˈsɛns	Such careless waste *incensed* the old lady.	使發怒 inflame enrage	cens(burn)

單字·音標·詞類	例　　　句	中譯·同義字	字源分析
incentive n. ɪnˈsɛntɪv	Money is still a major *incentive* in most occupations.	誘因、刺激、動機 motive stimulus	cant(sing)
inception n. ɪnˈsɛpʃən	The *inception* of the plan was due to him.	開始 beginning start	cep(receive)
incident n. ˈɪnsədənt	Conflict is an inevitable *incident* in any active system of cooperation.	附帶的事物、事件 event happening	cid(fall)
incipient a. ɪnˈsɪpɪənt	We have begun to see the *incipient* light of day.	剛開始、初期的 beginning commencing	cip(receive)
incise v. ɪnˈsaɪz	They have *incised* an inscription on the monument.	刻、雕 carve engrave	cis(cut)
incisive a. ɪnˈsaɪsɪv	The critic has an *incisive* mind.	敏銳、尖刻的 sharp acute	incise
incite v. ɪnˈsaɪt	The agitator has *incited* the people to rebel.	鼓動、引起 rouse instigate	cit(rouse)
incline v. ɪnˈklaɪn	She *inclined* toward the speaker to hear more clearly.	傾、傾斜 lean bow	clin(lean)

單字・音標・詞類	例　　　句	中譯・同義字	字源分析
v.	Dogs *incline* toward meat as a food.	傾向、性近、愛好 tend predispose	
include v. ɪn'klud	Many subjects are *included* in the curriculum.	包含、包括 contain comprehend	**clud**(close)
incorporate v. ɪn'kɔrpəˌret	The committee recommended that we *incorporate* several new rules into the bylaws.	編入、合併、具體表現 include embody	**corpor**(body)
increase v. ɪn'kris	Her interest *increased* as she was shown better ways to study the subject.	增加、增大 augment enhance	**creas**(grow)
incriminate* v. ɪn'krɪməˌnet	He *incriminated* the other boys to the teacher.	控告 accuse charge	**crime**
incubate* v. 'ɪnkjəˌbet	He *incubated* the new idea for a while before giving it to his supervisor.	熟慮、深思、籌策 brood contemplate	**cub**(lie)
inculpate* v. ɪn'kʌlpet	The man *inculpated* his brother to escape punishment himself.	歸罪、控告 blame incriminate	**culp**(blame)
incur v. ɪn'kɝ	The woman had *incurred* large debts to educate her children.	招致 bring entail	**cur**(run)

單字・音標・詞類	例　　　　句	中譯・同義字	字源分析
indebted a. ɪnˈdɛtɪd	He was heavily *indebted* to the bank for the loans extended to him.	負債的 owing money owing gratitude	debt
indent v. ɪnˈdɛnt	She has *indented* the pillow with her head.	留凹痕於 form a 　depression	dent(tooth)
indicate v. ˈɪndəˌket	What do these strange signs *indicate*?	指示、顯示 manifest demonstrate	**dic**(say)
induce v. ɪnˈdjus	The antivitamin was shown to *induce* gross malformation in the young.	引起 cause effect	**duc**(lead)
infatuate* v. ɪnˈfætʃʊˌet	You have *infautated* this boy in such a way that he will agree with you on anything.	使(人)迷戀 inspire with a 　foolish love	fatu(foolish)
infer v. ɪnˈfɝ	A child can *infer* the existence of an environment which is not part of itself.	推斷出、推知 、暗示 imply conclude	**fer**(carry)
infiltrate v. ɪnˈfɪltret	Many Hebrew idioms have *infiltrated* into various Jewish dialects.	滲入、浸透 seep permeate	filtrate
inflame v. ɪnˈflem	The unpleasant events had combined to irritate and *inflame* him.	使動怒、激怒 incense exasperate	flame

單字·音標·詞類	例　　句	中譯·同義字	字源分析
inflate v. ɪnˈflet	The balloon has been *inflated*.	使脹大、使得意 distend with air elate	flat(blow)
inflect v. ɪnˈflɛkt	Profound feeling for music has *inflected* all his major works.	轉向、改變 bend modulate	**flect**(bend)
inflict v. ɪnˈflɪkt	The workers are still out, and the industry is *inflicted* with a kind of paralysis.	使痛苦、施加（傷害等） impose afflict	flict(strike)
influence n. ˈɪnfluəns	He has much *influence* on each of his children.	影響（力）、權勢 sway ascendancy	**flu**(flow)
influx* n. ˈɪnˌflʌks	The city is expecting an *influx* of holiday visitors.	湧到、流入 inflow	**flu**(flow)
infringe v. ɪnˈfrɪndʒ	The marching troops have already *infringed* the peace treaty between the nations.	侵犯、違背 violate transgress	**fring**(break)
infuriate v. ɪnˈfjʊrɪˌet	His book will *infuriate*, enlighten, and rejoice different types of readers.	激怒 enrage aggravate	fury
infuse v. ɪnˈfjuz	They have *infused* an aviation curriculum into some forty universities.	灌輸、鼓舞 impart inspire	**fus**(pour)

單字・音標・詞類	例　　　　句	中譯・同義字	字源分析
ingenious a. ɪnˈdʒinjəs	An *ingenious* English clergyman invented the knitting frame.	有發明天才、靈敏的 clever resourceful	**gen**(bear)
ingenuous a. ɪnˈdʒɛnjʊəs	At times he was astoundingly *ingenuous,* which perplexed everyone.	坦白、老實、誠樸的 natural unwary	**gen**(bear)
ingrained* a. ɪnˈgrend	She could never overcome her *ingrained* prejudice.	根深蒂固、深染的 deep-seated inveterate	grain
ingredient n. ɪnˈgridɪənt	There are various *ingredients* in a man's character.	要素、組成分子 component constituent	**gred**(go)
ingress* n. ˈɪngrɛs	The *ingress* of im-migrants was checked for a few months.	進入 entrance entry	**gress**(go)
inhabit v. ɪnˈhæbɪt	The isolated island is *inhabited* by a rich fauna and flora.	居住、棲息於 reside dwell	hab(live)
inhale v. ɪnˈhel	They *inhaled* the fragrance from their cupped fingers till their cheeks bulged.	吸入 breathe in	hal(breathe)
inherent a. ɪnˈhɪrənt	There are shortcomings *inherent* in our approach.	固有的 essential intrinsic	her(stick)

單字・音標・詞類	例　　句	中譯・同義字	字源分析
inherit v. ɪnˈhɛrət	The eldest son will *inherit* the title.	繼承 receive succeed	her(heir)
inhibit v. ɪnˈhɪbɪt	Wrong desires or impulses are usually *inhibited.*	抑制 check repress	hib(hold)
initial a. ɪˈnɪʃəl	These are the *initial* symptoms of the disease.	初期、最初的 first incipient	it(go)
initiate v. ɪˈnɪʃɪˌet	They have *initiated* a new road-building program.	發起、開始 begin commence	it(go)
inject v. ɪnˈdʒɛkt	The author is able to *inject* both color and humor into this rather dull subject.	加入 drive into introduce	ject(throw)
injunction* n. ɪnˈdʒʌŋkʃən	The Hindu religion has no *injunctions* against birth control.	訓令、命令、禁令 order prohibition	junc(join)
inlet n. ˈɪnˌlɛt	An *inlet* may be a narrow passage of water running into the land.	灣、海口 creek orifice	let
innate a. ɪˈnet	There are several *innate* defects in the plan.	固有、生來的 natural inborn	nat(be born)
inner a. ˈɪnɚ	The news soon got around the *inner* circles of the administration.	內部、內在的 interior intrinsic	

單字・音標・詞類	例　　句	中譯・同義字	字源分析
innovation n. ˌɪnəˈveʃən	This book deals with the technical *innovations* of the agrarian revolution.	革新之處、革新 change novelty	nov(new)
inquire v. ɪnˈkwaɪr	They do not have the right to *inquire* into the activities of the teachers.	探究、調查 ask investigate	**quir**(ask)
inquisitive a. ɪnˈkwɪzətɪv	Her *inquisitive* nature has brought her much trouble.	好管閒事、好問、好奇的 questioning curious	**quis**(ask)
inroad n. ˈɪnˌrod	The farmers are protecting their crops of barley from the *inroads* of sparrows.	襲擊 raid foray	road
inscribe v. ɪnˈskraɪb	The mason *inscribed* the name on the tombstone.	刻銘 carve engrave	**scrib**(write)
inseminate* v. ɪnˈsɛməˌnet	The teachers have *inseminated* the minds of the young with practical ideals.	播種、使受精 impregnate imbue	semin(seed)
insert v. ɪnˈsɝt	The mother told the child to *insert* the key noiselessly into the lock.	挿入 put place	ser(join)
insight n. ˈɪnˌsaɪt	The novelist has an amazing *insight* into the complexity of women's emotions.	洞察力、洞察 understanding penetration	sight

單字·音標·詞類	例　　句	中譯·同義字	字源分析
insist v. ɪnˈsɪst	She still *insisted* on coming despite the objection of her mother.	堅持 demand persist	sist(stand)
inspect v. ɪnˈspɛkt	Let us *inspect* your motives.	檢查、審查 examine supervise	spect(watch)
inspire v. ɪnˈspaɪr	These books have *inspired* countless generations.	啓發、鼓舞 stimulate arouse	spir(breathe)
install v. ɪnˈstɔl	The old man has *installed* himself in the big chair before the fire.	安置 place establish	stall(place)
instance n. ˈɪnstəns	The young man's act was an *instance* of true heroism.	實例、例證 example case	sta(stand)
instant a. ˈɪnstənt	Mrs. Roper does not like to drink *instant* coffee.	即溶、立刻的 immediate prompt	sta(stand)
instigate v. ˈɪnstəˌget	They were *instigating* a plot to overthrow the government.	鼓動、煽動 incite actuate	stig(prick)
instill v. ɪnˈstɪl	Courtesy must be *instilled* in childhood.	灌輸 implant introduce gradually	still(drop)
institute v. ˈɪnstəˌtjut	The man has *instituted* some reforms on lexicography.	創立、制定、著手 organize initiate	stitut(stand)

單字・音標・詞類	例　　句	中譯・同義字	字源分析
instruct v. ɪnˈstrʌkt	Have you been *instructed* when to start?	下命令於、教 、通知 teach inform	struct(build)
instrument n. ˈɪnstrəmənt	The university is the *instrument* for preserving and disseminating knowledge.	工具、器械 tool implement	stru(build)
instrumental a. ˌɪnstrəˈmɛntḷ	Mr. Rockhill is *instrumental* in finding a job for George.	有幫助的 helpful auxiliary	instrument
insult v. ˈɪnsʌlt	His impertinences *insulted* his sister's guests.	侮辱、對…無 禮 offend affront	sult(leap)
insurgent* n. ɪnˈsɝdʒənt	The *insurgents* were soon defeated and executed by government troops.	叛徒、起事者 rebel traitor	surge
intense a. ɪnˈtɛns	The *intense* heat has melted the iron.	強烈、激烈的 extreme acute	tens(stretch)
intend v. ɪnˈtɛnd	What do you *intend* to do now?	意欲、計劃 plan propose	tend(stretch)
intoxicate* v. ɪnˈtɑksəˌket	The men were *intoxicated* with dreams of fortune.	使陶醉、使興 奮 make drunk excite	toxic(poison)

單字·音標·詞類	例　　　句	中譯·同義字	字源分析
intricate a. 'ɪntrəkɪt	The system of civil courts is rather *intricate*.	複雜的 complex complicated	tric(vexation)
intrigue v. ɪn'trig	The book has *intrigued* my attention and tightly gripped my fancy.	吸引、激起興趣、使困惑 excite beguile	tric(vexation)
n.	The royal palace was filled with *intrigue*.	陰謀 conspiracy scheme	
intrude v. ɪn'trud	I hope I am not *intruding*.	打擾、侵襲 infringe trespass	**trud**(thrust)
intuition n. ˌɪntu'ɪʃən	She trusts *intuitions* rather than reasoned conclusions.	直覺知識、直覺 instinct perception	tui(watch)
inundation* n. ˌɪnən'deʃən	His tears were not drops but a little *inundation* down his cheeks.	狂流、洪水 flood deluge	und(wave)
inure* v. ɪn'jʊr	Being stationed at an arctic base *inures* a man to cold.	使慣於 accustom habituate	ure(practice)
invade v. ɪn'ved	The *invading* paratroopers were soon wiped out.	侵犯 attack aggress	vad(go)
inveigle* v. ɪn'vigl	With patience and diplomacy, she can eventually *inveigle* him into marrying her.	誘騙、誘惑 delude beguile	veigle(blind)

單字·音標·詞類	例　　　　句	中譯·同義字	字源分析
invent v. ɪnˈvɛnt	This polymer was *invented* in England and is an outgrowth of earlier research.	發明、虛構 discover fabricate	**vent**(come)
inventory n. ˈɪnvənˌtorɪ	This book provides a complete *inventory* of the ideas which are afloat among the young.	目錄、存貨 store stock	**vent**(come)
invest v. ɪnˈvɛst	He has *invested* his savings in stocks, bonds, and real estate.	投資、賦與 place commit	**vest**(dress)
invigorate v. ɪnˈvɪgəˌret	His writings are tonic and *invigorating* to those who stand in need of inspiration.	鼓舞、使強壯 、使充滿生氣 strengthen animate	**vigor**
invoke v. ɪnˈvok	The condemned criminal *invoked* the judge's mercy.	懇求 entreat beseech	**vok**(voice)
involve v. ɪnˈvɑlv	I hate to get myself *involved* in affairs of this kind.	使陷於、牽累 、影響 entangle affect	**volv**(roll)
inward a. ˈɪnwəd	The scholar lives an *inward* and unmaterial life.	內部、心靈、 內心的 internal spiritual	
inwards adv. ˈɪnwədz	The sides of the hole seemed to slope *inwards* till they met.	向內、向內 部地 internally	

EPI

upon, toward

在上●朝向

　　字首 epi 源自希臘文副詞與介系詞 $\dot{\epsilon}\pi\iota$ (epi)，原在希臘文是一個十分重要的字首，組成的單字非常多，但這些單字引進英文的却不多，因此英文的 epi，與本書其他字首比較起來，似乎略有遜色。epi 的拼法也可變化為 ep，一般視後接的字根第一個音而定：字根第一個音若是母音或 h 子音，拼作 ep，否則一律拼作 epi。例如下文列舉的 epoch n.「紀元、時期」（希臘文 $\dot{\epsilon}\pi o\chi\eta$ [epochē]，拉丁文 epocha），及 ephemeral a.「短暫的」（希臘文 $\dot{\epsilon}\varphi\eta\mu\epsilon\rho o\varsigma$ [ephēmeros]），均是如此情形。epoch 的字根 ech「保有」原作 $\dot{\epsilon}\chi\omega$ (echō)，與字首結合而成 $\dot{\epsilon}\pi\epsilon\chi\omega$ (epechō)，原為動詞，有「保持、延遲」的意思，再變成名詞的 $\dot{\epsilon}\pi o\chi\eta$ (epochē)，便引申而成「延緩的時間」，也就是「紀元、時期」。ephemeral 的名詞為 ephemera，有「生命短暫之物」的意思，照字首字根推斷，ep 為 upon，hemera 為 day ($\dot{\eta}\mu\epsilon\rho a$ n.f.)，"upon a day"，生命只在朝夕之間，自然非常短暫。

單字·音標·詞類	例　　　句	中譯·同義字	字源分析
ephemeral* a. əˈfɛmərəl	Some people think that jazz is perishable and *ephemeral*.	短暫的 temporary transient	hemera(day)
epidemic a. ˌɛpəˈdɛmɪk	Many children died that winter of *epidemic* fevers.	流行、傳染性的 infectious prevalent	dem(people)
n.	The ugly *epidemic* of rioting flared clear across the nation.	流行、傳染病 contagious disease	
epigram n. ˈɛpəˌgræm	His conversation was a cascade of wit, *epigram*, and poetic images.	雋語、短而機智之妙語 witty saying	gram(write)
epilogue n. ˈɛpəˌlɔg	The *epilogue* of this play is poorly written.	結尾、收場白 conclusion afterword	log(speak)
episode n. ˈɛpəˌsod	His novels are like a series of *episodes* resembling beads on a string.	插曲 event scene	eisod(entrance)
epistle* n. ɪˈpɪsḷ	Pope Gelasius in his *epistle* mentioned a legend which was well-known in his time.	書信 letter missive	stell(send)
epitaph* n. ˈɛpəˌtæf	This is a book of *epitaphs* on the death of the great knight.	墓誌銘體的詩文、墓誌銘 inscription	taph(tomb)

單字‧音標‧詞類	例 句		字源分析
epithet* n. ˈɛpəˌθɛt	Richard I is more familiarly identified by his *epithet* as Richard the Lionhearted.	附加於人名後之描述詞 name appelation	thet(put)
epitome n. ɪˈpɪtəmɪ	The British monarchy itself is an *epitome* of tradition.	典型、縮影 abridgment embodiment	tom(cut)
epoch n. ˈɛpək	Dante's work initiated a new *epoch* in literature.	紀元、時期、時代 period era	ech(hold)

FORE

before

在 前

　　fore 源自古英文 (Old English) 副詞 fore，與希臘、拉丁文毫無關係。英文「土產」的字首字根不多，這是其中比較重要的一個。這個字首除了fore 之外，偶爾也拼作 for ，如下文的 forward「向前」便是一個例子。此外，for 除了有上述 before的用法外，尚有「分離、除外」的意思，例字不多，因此本書並未列入「最重要的 **30 個字首**」的範圍。在此謹列出 for「分離、除外」組成的幾個重要單字，以供參考：forbid v.「禁止」、 forgo v.「拋棄」、forlorn a.「孤寂、可憐的」、 forswear v.「戒絕、放棄」。

單字‧音標‧詞類	例　　句	中譯‧同義字	字源分析
aforementioned a. əˈforˈmɛnʃənd a.	The *aforementioned* material has been sent to your company.	前述的 aforesaid aforenamed	mentioned
aforesaid a. əˈforˌsɛd	We have not seen the *aforesaid* book.	前述、上述的 aforementioned aforenamed	said
fore a. for	At such a distance we could only see the *fore* body of the whale.	前面、在前部的 forward former	
forebear* n. ˈforˌbɛr	The people on the island worship their ancient *forebears.*	祖先 forefather ancestor	be
forebode* v. forˈbod	Such heavy air *forebodes* a storm.	預示、預言 foretell presage	bode
forecast v. forˈkæst	It should be possible to *forecast* accurately any swings in the business cycle.	預測、預見 foreknow predict	cast
n. ˈforˌkæst	They are waiting for the noon weather *forecast.*	預測、先見之明 prediction forethought	
foredoom v. forˈdum	It was an attempt that was *foredoomed* to failure.	事先註定 doom in advance	doom

單字·音標·詞類	例　　　句	中譯·同義字	字源分析
forefather n. ˈforˌfɑðɚ	The *forefathers* of the American people came mostly from Europe.	祖先 ancestor forebear	father
forefront n. ˈforˌfrʌnt	These tribes had lived in the *forefront* of cultural civilization.	最重要的地方、最前鋒之位置 vanguard foremost part	front
foregoing a. forˈgo·ɪŋ	The *foregoing* paragraphs have already been revised twice.	前面、前述的 preceding antecedent	go
foregone a. forˈgɔn	The old lady kept having nostalgic dreams of *foregone* years.	過去、先前的 past previous	go
foreground n. ˈforˌgraʊnd	The candidate has always been kept in the *foreground* since the campaign began.	最引人注意之地位 forefront prominence	ground
foreknow v. forˈno	Who could have *foreknown* that such a disaster might happen?	預知 foretell predict	know
foreman n. ˈformən	The old-time ranch *foreman* had all the responsibilities and few of the benefits of ownership.	工頭、領班 leader head	man
foremost a. ˈforˌmost	He is unquestionably the *foremost* figure among the artists of this country.	首要、第一的 first preeminent	most

單字·音標·詞類	例 句	中譯·同義字	字源分析
forerunner n. for'rʌnɚ	Blustery March days are usually *forerunners* of spring.	前鋒、先驅 harbinger predecessor	runner
foresee v. for'si	Surely you can *foresee* what will happen next.	預知 foretell predict	see
foreshadow v. for'ʃædo	Those dark clouds *foreshadow* a storm.	預示、預兆 forebode presage	shadow
foresight n. 'for,saɪt	The philospher is a man of *foresight*.	遠見、先見之明 prescience foreknowledge	sight
forestall* v. for'stɔl	The mayor *forestalled* a riot by having the police ready.	預先阻止 prevent in advance	**forestall** (ambush)
foretell v. for'tɛl	Eclipses are *foretold* with marvelous exactness.	預測 predict forecast	tell
forethought n. 'for,θɔt	This was no spontaneous crime but a product of careful *forethought*.	預謀、預籌 premeditation prudence	thought
forewarn v. for'wɔrn	We were *forewarned* to expect you before dark.	預先警告 warn in advance	warn
foreword n. 'for,wɝd	He has not written the *foreword* of the book yet.	序、前言、引言 preface introduction	word

forward a.
ˈfɔrwəd

Baggage is carried in the *forward* cars.

前面、前方的
front
advanced

　　　　adv.

The people blocking the entrance were told to move *forward*.

向前
ahead
onward

　　　　v.

His good work should *forward* him in rank.

提昇、促進
advance
promote

15

INTER

between, among

居中

字首 inter 源自拉丁文介系詞 inter，原已有 between, among 的意思。下文例字比較特別的，有 interdict v.「禁止」、interest n.「興趣、利益」二字。單照字首字根推斷，似乎不足以了解為何有「禁止」和「興趣、利益」的意思。interdict 來自拉丁文 interdīcere，其中 dīcere 本為動詞「說話」的意思，加上 inter 之後，由「以言語插入」轉為「判決」的意思，最後又變成現代英文習用的「禁止」。interest 出自拉丁文 interesse 一字，字根部分的 esse 為拉丁文 be 動詞，因此原義為「在其中」，後又引申出「互異」、「參與」、「利害相關」等字義。esse 的第三人稱單數現在式形態為 est，interesse 因而以 interest 的拼法，在十五世紀進入英文，成為「興趣、利益」的意思。

單字・音標・詞類	例　　句	中譯・同義字	字源分析
interaction n. ˌɪntɚˈækʃǝɴ	This book deals with the *interaction* of an individual with his social environment.	交相影響、交互作用 interplay	action
intercede v. ˌɪntɚˈsid	The governments would *intercede* in behalf of the people.	說項、調停 mediate intervene	cede(go)
intercept v. ˌɪntɚˈsɛpt	The letter was *intercepted* by her parents.	中途攔截、中途逮捕 arrest seize	cept(receive)
interchange v. ˌɪntɚˈtʃendʒ	The two boys had a quarrel and started to *interchange* blows.	交換、交替 exchange alternate	change
intercourse n. ˈɪntɚˌkors	Diffidence rendered him inapt for social *intercourse*.	交際、交通 communication dealings	course
interdict * v. ˈɪntɚˌdɪkt	Trade with that foreign country was *interdicted*.	禁止 prohibit proscribe	dict(say)
interest n. ˈɪntərɪst	She does not have much *interest* in physics.	興趣、關心 concern attention	est(be)
n.	The *interests* of the nation should not be ignored.	利益 benefit advantage	
v.	I don't believe my remarks did not *interest* you.	使感興趣 attract affect	

interfere v.
ˌɪntɚˈfɪr

The young men who were robbing the woman told the man not to *interfere*.

干涉、干預
meddle
intrude

fer(strike)

interim* n.
ˈɪntərɪm

The wounded must be treated in the *interim* between the phases of the battle.

中間時期、過渡時期
interval
meantime

interior a.
ɪnˈtɪrɪɚ

No outsider has been to the *interior* recesses of the castle.

內部、內在的
internal
intrinsic

n.

What is the *interior* of the house like?

內部
inside

interject * v.
ˌɪntɚˈdʒɝkt

Every now and then the speaker *interjected* a witty remark.

挿入
interpose
interpolate

ject(throw)

interlace v.
ˌɪntɚˈles

The narrative is *interlaced* with many interesting anecdotes.

使組合、使交織
interweave
mix

lace

interlude* n.
ˈɪntɚˌlud

There were only a few *interludes* of fair weather during the rainy season.

間隔的時間、挿曲
interval
episode

lud(play)

intermediary a.
ˌɪntɚˈmidɪˌɛrɪ

The government was most concerned about importing and other *intermediary* trades.

中間的
intermediate

medi(middle)

單字·音標·詞類	例　　句	中譯·同義字	字源分析
intermediate a. ˌɪntɚˈmidɪɪt	We made a few *intermediate* stops on the journey.	中間的 intervening interposed	medi(middle)
intermingle v. ˌɪntɚˈmɪŋgl̩	Fact and fiction are *intermingled* in his narration.	混合、攙雜 blend commix	mingle
intermission n. ˌɪntɚˈmɪʃən	There is an *intermission* between the acts of the play.	休息時間、中斷 break interruption	miss(send)
intermittent a. ˌɪntɚˈmɪtn̩t	We have had *intermittent* rains since yesterday.	間歇、斷續的 periodic recurring	mit(send)
internal a. ɪnˈtɝnl̩	He suffered *internal* injuries in the accident.	內在、內部的 inner interior	
international a. ˌɪntɚˈnæʃənl̩	*International* trade has slumped slightly this year.	國際的 between or 　among nations	nation
interplay n. ˈɪntɚˌple	Bureaucratic controls are usually imposed upon an *interplay* of private interest.	相互影響、交互作用 interaction	play
interpolate* v. ɪnˈtɝpəˌlet	Editorial comment was *interpolated* in the article.	添進、插入字句 introduce insert	pol(polish)

單字・音標・詞類	例　句	中譯・同義字	字源分析
interpose* v. ˌɪntɚˈpoz	The dense forests *interpose* an almost impassable barrier.	置於中間、挿入、仲裁 insert intervene	**pos**(place)
interrogate v. ɪnˈtɛrəˌget	The suspect is now being *interrogated* by the police.	訊問、質問 question investigate	rog(ask)
interrupt v. ˌɪntəˈrʌpt	It is impolite to *interrupt* when other people are talking.	打斷、妨礙 interfere disturb	rupt(break)
intersect v. ˌɪntɚˈsɛkt	Any two diameters of a circle *intersect* each other.	相交、貫穿 cut divide	sect(cut)
intersperse* v. ˌɪntɚˈspɝs	There are many pictures *interspersed* in the book.	散置、點綴 scatter interlard	spers(scatter)
interstice* n. ɪnˈtɝstɪs	We can clearly see the *interstices* of the wall.	裂縫、空隙 crack crevice	sist(stand)
intertwine v. ˌɪntɚˈtwaɪn	The sex impulse is closely *intertwined* with the life impulse.	交纏、糾纏 intertwist entangle	twine
interval n. ˈɪntɚvl	The father wanted the boy to count the *interval* between a lightning flash and the following thunder.	間隔時間、間隔 gap interlude	val(wall)

單字・音標・詞類	例　　　　句	中譯・同義字	字源分析
intervene v. ˌɪntəˈvin	Business seldom follows any projected course, because unforeseeable developments *intervene*.	挿入、干擾 interfere intrude	**ven**(come)

16

MAL

bad

惡劣

mal 源自拉丁文形容詞 malus 和副詞 male ，原義即為 bad 。例字中的 malediction n.「詛咒」(maledictiō, n. f.)、malefactor n.「作惡者」(malefactor, n.m.)、malevolent a.「惡毒、惡意的」(malevolentia, n.f.) ，便是由 male 的形態變成，其他字則拼作 mal 。下文例字其實不盡由拉丁文轉來，有部分應該說是出自法文的。古法文源自拉丁文，字彙也大多源自拉丁文，如拉丁文的 male habitus 「病態、身體不適」，到了法文搖身一變，便成了 mala-die n.「疾病」，而在十三世紀登陸英格蘭，進入英文，逐漸拼成現今的 malady n.「疾病」。另外，malaise n.「不舒服」也是如此：字根部分的 aise 現今仍是法文名詞，意義相當於英文的 ease 或 com-fort 。拉丁文 malus 的比較級、最高級，分別為 pēior 、pessimus ，由這兩個字變出的英文單字，也可附帶一提。pēior 有 worse 的意思，因此其衍生字 pejorative a. 和 pejoration n. ，便分別有「輕蔑的」和「惡化」的意思。pessimus 相當於英文的 worst ，因此 pessimistic a. 和 pessimism n. 便有「悲觀的」和「悲觀、悲觀論」的意思。

單字·音標·詞類	例　　句	中譯·同義字	字源分析
maladjusted a. ˌmæləˈdʒʌstɪd	The doctor knows how to deal with *maladjusted* children.	失調、不能適應環境的 poorly adjusted	**adjusted**
maladroit a. ˌmæləˈdrɔɪt	A *maladroit* move of my hand caused the car to swerve.	笨拙的 awkward inept	**adroit**
malady n. ˈmælədɪ	He told his physicians that he had a fatal *malady*.	疾病 sickness ailment	habit(have)
malaise* n. mæˈlez	Marked *malaise* and prostration are not features of the common cold in adults.	不適、不舒服 sense of 　ill-being	aise(comfort)
malcontent a. ˈmælkənˌtɛnt	A *malcontent* group of political exiles was conspiring against the regime.	反抗、不滿的 discontented dissatisfied	**content**
malediction* n. ˌmæləˈdɪkʃən	The witch's remains were guarded by a vicious *malediction*.	詛咒 curse execration	dict(say)
malefactor* n. ˌmæləˈfæktɚ	The sinister *malefactor* was soon put into prison.	作惡者、罪犯 criminal evildoer	fact(do)
malevolent* a. məˈlɛvələnt	Mrs. Simpson is a gossipy *malevolent* old woman.	惡毒、惡意的 evil-minded malicious	vol(wish)

單字·音標·詞類	例　　　　句	中譯·同義字	字源分析
malfeasance* n. ˌmælˈfizn̩s	The *malfeasance* of the official was condemned.	瀆職、惡行 misconduct wrongdoing	feas(do)
malform v. mælˈfɔrm	They have found the virus that *malforms* tobacco leaves.	使畸形 cause to be 　badly formed	form
malfunction n. mælˈfʌŋkʃən	Three *malfunctions* have been reported and rectified before the rocket was launched.	故障 bad function	function
malice n. ˈmælɪs	In spite of all he has had to put up with from them, he bears them no *malice*.	怨恨、惡意 spite malevolence	
malicious a. məˈlɪʃəs	Her *malicious* remark enraged him.	懷惡意的 bitter malignant	**malice**
malign a. məˈlaɪn	The offended man gave him a *malign* look.	怨恨、懷惡意 、邪惡的 evil malevolent	gen(bear)
malignant a. məˈlɪgnənt	Many astrologists believe in the *malignant* power of the stars.	有害、惡毒的 spiteful malicious	**malign**
malnourished a. ˈmælˈnɝɪʃt	The *malnourished* baby was rushed to the hospital as its condition worsened.	營養不足的 undernourished	nourish

單字·音標·詞類	例　　　　句	中譯·同義字	字源分析
malnutrition n. ˌmælnjuˈtrɪʃən	Improper food can cause *malnutrition*.	營養不足 poor 　　nourishment	nutrition
maltreat v. mælˈtrit	Only insane people could *maltreat* animals.	虐待 harm abuse	treat

17

MON·MONO

one

獨一

字首 mon、mono 出自希臘文形容詞 μονος (monos)，原有「單獨、唯一」的意思。後接的字根部分第一個音如果是母音，拼作 mon；如果是子音，則拼作 mono。下文的 monastery n.「修道院」，最初起源自希臘文的 μοναστηριον (monastērion)「獨居」，後經拉丁文的 monastērium 轉借入中古英文 (Middle English)，而於十五世紀出現 monastery 的拼法。由 mon、mono 組成的單字，部分過於偏難，本書並未列入，僅在此概略一提，供讀者參考：monad n.「單細胞生物」、monadism n.「單子論」、monandrous a.「一夫制的」、monochrome n.「單色畫法」、monocle n.「單眼鏡」、monocracy n.「獨裁政治」、monocyte n.「單核細胞血球」、monogamy n.「一夫一妻制」、monolatry n.「單神崇拜」、monolingual a.「僅用一種語言的」、monosyllable n.「單音節字」、monotheism n.「一神論」等等。

單字·音標·詞類	例　句	中譯·同義字	字源分析
monarch n. ˈmɑnɚk	The live oak is the *monarch* of the Texas low forests.	王、君主、帝王 king emperor	arch(rule)
monarchy n. ˈmɑnɚkɪ	Morocco is a sovereign independent *monarchy*.	君主政體 state headed 　by a monarch	monarch
monastery* n. ˈmɑnəsˌtɛrɪ	The King does not allow foreign tourists to enter the *monasteries* of the country.	修道院 convent cloister	
monograph n. ˈmɑnəˌgræf	He has written a *monograph* on the cultural transmission between India and China.	專文、專論 discourse dissertation	graph(write)
monolog(ue) n. ˈmɑnḷˌɔg	Early poems are some-times the *monologues* of a young man very isolated in his genius.	獨白 soliloquy	**log**(speak)
monopoly n. məˈnɑpḷɪ	No country has a *monopoly* on morality or truth.	獨占、壟斷 exclusive 　possession	pol(sell)
monotonous a. məˈnɑtṇəs	An owl usually gives a faint *monotonous* hooting.	單調、因單調令人厭煩的 uniform tedious	tone
monotony n. məˈnɑtṇɪ	She always had the desire for a relief from the *monotony* of everyday life.	單調、令人厭煩的單調 dullness uniformity	tone

18

OB

toward, against, over

相對 ● 反對 ● 全面

　　字首ob源自拉丁文介系詞ob，原即有 toward、against、over 的意思。除了 ob 的拼法之外，尚有 oc 、of 、op 與 o 的形態。字根部分的第一個字母為 c、f、p 時，分別拼成 oc、of、op ，如下文的 occult a.「深奧的」、offend v.「觸怒」、opportune a.「合時宜的」等等均是。o 的形態則僅在 omit v.「遺漏」一字中可見到。事實上，omit來自拉丁文 omittere v.「遺棄、放鬆」，原也有 obmittere 的拼法。十五、十六世紀時，英文本有 omit 和 obmit 兩種寫法，後來 obmit 遭到淘汰，便留下今日習見的 omit 。原因是 b、m 兩個子音均是雙唇音，發音部位一樣，兩音相連，久而久之極容易同化成一個音，obmit 自然就被淘汰掉了。

單字・音標・詞類	例　　　　句	中譯・同義字	字源分析
obdurate＊a. ˈɑbdjərɪt	The woman remained *obdurate* to her husband's advances.	冷酷、無情、執拗的 obstinate callous	dur(hard)
obey v. əˈbe	The child does not want to *obey* his father.	服從、遵奉、順從 follow comply	aud(hear)
obfuscate＊ v. ɑbˈfʌsket	The small facts could not be ignored without *obfuscating* the main dramatic purpose.	使模糊、使迷亂 confuse obscure	fusc(dark)
object v. əbˈdʒɛkt	We do not *object* to your proposition.	反對 oppose contravene	ject(throw)
n. ˈɑbdʒɪkt	Can you tell me the name of the *object* in my hand?	物體、物件 thing article	
n.	The attainment of wealth was the *object* of his every effort.	目標、目的 intention goal	
objective n. əbˈdʒɛktɪv	They had different views about the chief *objective* of their plot.	目標、目的 intention end	object
objurgate＊ v. ˈɑbdʒɚˌget	The poet had *objurgated* the custom of garnishing poems with archaisms.	痛罵、嚴責 decry execrate	jur(swear)

單字·音標·詞類	例 句	中譯·同義字	字源分析
obligation n. ˌɑblə'geʃən	I don't have any *obligation* to fulfill.	義務、職責 duty responsibility	lig(bind)
obligatory a. ə'blɪgəˌtorɪ	Obedience is *obligatory* on a soldier.	強制的 compulsory peremptory	lig(bind)
oblige v. ə'blaɪdʒ	The law *obliges* everyone to pay his taxes.	強制、使受束縛 bind coerce	lig(bind)
oblique a. ə'blik	Her *oblique* glances made the boy feel uneasy.	不直接、斜的 indirect slanting	liqu(awry)
a.	She made an *oblique* reference to her illness to avoid any misunderstanding.	間接、迂曲的 devious circuitous	
obliterate v. ə'blɪtəˌret	A successful love affair alone seemed to *obliterate* all his failures.	消滅、擦掉 erase eradicate	liter(letter)
oblong* a. 'ɑblɔŋ	She found an *oblong* sheet of paper in her book.	長方形的 rectangular	long
obnoxious* a. əb'nɑkʃəs	His *obnoxious* manner annoyed all his associates.	可憎、令人討厭的 offensive odious	nox(harm)

單字·音標·詞類		例　　　句	中譯·同義字	字源分析
obscene	a.	The dance in this place is often *obscene* and provocative.	淫穢、猥褻的 filthy indecent	scen(filth)
əbˈsin				
obscure	a.	She could not tolerate the *obscure* dusk of the shuttered room.	昏暗的 dim gloomy	scur(cover)
əbˈskjʊr				
	a.	This *obscure* cottage used to house an unnoticed genius.	幽僻、微賤的 humble inconspicuous	
	v.	Good writing is often *obscured* by age and mildew.	隱藏 hide shade	
observe	v.	We *observed* nothing queer in her behavior.	看到、發覺 detect perceive	serv(keep)
əbˈzɝv				
	v.	The students were told to *observe* the rules.	遵守 obey follow	
obsess	v.	He was too *obsessed* by details.	使心神困擾 preoccupy haunt	sess(sit)
əbˈsɛs				
obsolete	a.	After half a century the theory has become *obsolete*.	過時、已廢的 outdated antiquated	sol(be accustomed)
ˈɑbsəˌlit				
obstacle	n.	He believes he can overcome any *obstacle* in his life.	障礙 barrier hindrance	sta(stand)
ˈɑbstəkl̩				

單字・音標・詞類	例　　　句	中譯・同義字	字源分析
obstinate a. ˈɑbstənɪt	A man so *obstinate* as to resist the strongest arguments can never be brought to repentance.	固執、不屈服的 pertinacious perverse	**sti**(stand)
obstruct v. əbˈstrʌkt	Constant interruptions had *obstructed* our progress.	妨礙 hinder hamper	**struct**(build)
obtain v. əbˈten	The information could not be *obtained* easily.	獲得 acquire attain	**tain**(hold)
obtrude* v. əbˈtrud	We were forced to *obtrude* ourselves into their party.	闖入 trespass infringe	**trud**(thrust)
obtuse* a. əbˈtus	He never gets along well with an *obtuse* dull person.	鈍、愚鈍、遲鈍的 blunt stolid	tus(beat)
occasion n. əˈkeʒən	On what kind of *occasion* did you first meet her?	時機、場合、特殊之大事 event occurrence	cas(fall)
occult a. əˈkʌlt	To him nuclear physics and radiation effects are *occult* matters.	深奧、難解的 abstruse recondite	cul(cover)
occupy v. ˈɑkjəˌpaɪ	The army has *occupied* the town.	占據 seize capture	**cup**(take)

單字・音標・詞類	例　　句	中譯・同義字	字源分析
occur v. əˈkɝ	Successful marriages do not *occur* but are created.	發生 happen appear	**cur**(run)
offend v. əˈfɛnd	You are going to *offend* the teacher if you keep saying that.	觸怒、傷…感情 insult affront	**fend**(strike)
offensive n. əˈfɛnsɪv	The *offensive* was aimed at the enemy's capital.	攻擊 attack invasion	**fens**(strike)
offer v. ˈɔfɚ	Did you *offer* him any good ideas?	提供 give provide	**fer**(carry)
omit v. oˈmɪt	He does not wish to *omit* this valuable book from his reading.	遺漏 exclude eliminate	**mit**(send)
opponent n. əˈponənt	His political *opponents* have been abusing him for years.	對手、敵手 rival adversary	**pon**(place)
opportune a. ˌapɚˈtjun	He was waiting to make his bid for power at an *opportune* moment.	合時宜的 timely appropriate	**port**(port)
opportunity n. ˌapɚˈtjunətɪ	Would I have any *opportunity* to see you again?	機會 chance convenience	**opportune**
oppose v. əˈpoz	They do not feel like *opposing* the chairman's new plan.	反對、對抗、使相對 counter contradict	**pos**(place)

單字·音標·詞類	例　　　　句	中譯·同義字	字源分析
opposite a. ˈɑpəzɪt	They were going in *opposite* directions.	相反、反對的 differing adverse	**oppose**
n.	Though twins, they were complete *opposites* in temperament.	相反的人或物 something 　opposed	
oppress v. əˈprɛs	A ruler should never *oppress* his people.	壓迫、壓制 suppress persecute	**press**(press)

19

PARA

beside, beyond

並列 ● 超越

---

para 源自希臘文副詞與介系詞 παρα (para)，原有 beside、near、beyond 的意思。在希臘文已視作字首，用以組成單字，下文的例字原即全數由希臘文借入英文。除了本書收列的托福字彙，由這個字首組成的英文單字尚有不少。這些單字不屬常用字彙範圍，但是平常仍然可能見到，僅列出於下，以供參考：parabola n.「拋物線」、parallax n.「視差」、parallelogram n.「平行四邊形」、paramilitary a.「輔助正規軍的」、paranoia n.「偏執狂」、paranormal a.「超過正常的」、parasite n.「寄生動物」等。para 除了有 beside、beyond 的意思之外，尚有「防避」的意義，字源為法文，與上述的 para 不同，因此意義也不同。拉丁文動詞 parāre「準備」，到了法文轉成了字首 para，而演變出「防避」的意思。因此，「防避太陽」便成了 parasol n.「陽傘」（字根 sol「太陽」），「降落的防避裝置」成了 parachute n.「降落傘」（字根 chute「降落」），而後又由 parachute 衍生出 paratroops n.「傘兵部隊」、paratrooper n.「傘兵」等字。

單字·音標·詞類	例　　句	中譯·同義字	字源分析
parable n. ˈpærəbl̩	Jesus taught in *parables*.	寓言、譬語 allegory	ball(throw)
paradigm* n. ˈpærəˌdɪm	Many people regard science as the *paradigm* of true knowledge.	模範 example model	digm(example)
paradox n. ˈpærəˌdɑks	The man was a *paradox* — he was a well-known secret agent.	充滿矛盾的人或物、矛盾的話 absurdity contradiction	dox(opinion)
paragon* n. ˈpærəˌgɑn	The attractive lady is a *paragon* of beauty.	模範、典型 model pattern	gon(sharpen)
paragraph n. ˈpærəˌgræf	How many *paragraphs* do you have in your article?	段、節 section of 　writing	graph(write)
parallel a. ˈpærəˌlɛl	The standing committee systems in the two Houses are reasonably *parallel*.	相同、相似的 similar analogous	allel(one 　another)
n.	The situation of modern man has no *parallel* in the past.	相似之物、相同之物 resemblance analogy	
v.	This is a piece of fiction *paralleling* a historical incident.	與…相同或相似 match correspond to	

單字・音標・詞類	例　　　句	中譯・同義字	字源分析
paralyze v. ˈpærəˌlaɪz	The general strike has *paralyzed* the industry.	使無能力 make powerless unnerve	ly(loose)
paraphrase* v. ˈpærəˌfrez	His chief work as writer is to *paraphrase* the obscure into the com-prehensible.	解述意義、意譯 interpret translate	phras(say)

20 PER

through, thoroughly

穿過 ● 完全

字首 per 源自拉丁文介系詞 per，本即有 through, throughout 的意思。在拉丁文原已視作字首，用以組字，下文列舉的英文單字，便泰半借自已成形的拉丁字，如 percolate v.「過濾」出自拉丁文 percōlāre，perennial a.「永久的」出自 perennis，perforate v.「穿孔」出自 perforāre 等均是。下文的 perspire v.，字根 spir 有「呼吸」的意思，與字首 per 組合成「透過呼吸」，却轉成了「流汗」的意思。原來上古拉丁文(Ancient Latin)的 perspīrāre 本僅有 breathe、blow constantly 的字義，但後來傳入英文，到了十七世紀，却引申為「透過細孔而成氣體」或「蒸發」，最後在十八世紀初，開始轉成「流汗」的意思。因此，現代英文的 perspire 已和「呼吸」、「氣體」毫無關係，而僅有「流汗」的用法。此外，必須附帶一提的是，per 也可引申成 away entirely、to destruction「離異、毀壞」的意思，不過這種用法組成的單字不多，下文只有 peremptory a.「絕對、強制的」、perfidy n.「背信」、perish v.「腐壞、死」、perverse a.「倔強的」、pervert v.「引入邪路」各字，有此情況。

單字·音標·詞類	例　　句	中譯·同義字	字源分析
perceive v. pɚˈsiv	Through touching we can *perceive* roughness and smoothness.	感覺 notice observe	ceiv(receive)
v.	They surrendered after *perceiving* the uselessness of further resistance.	理解、發覺 understand discern	
percolate* v. ˈpɝkəˌlet	She is waiting for the coffee to *percolate*.	過濾、滲出 filter exude	col(strain)
percussion n. pɚˈkʌʃən	A drum is played by *percussion*.	敲打 blow impact	cus(shake)
perdurable a. pɚˈdjʊrəbl̩	Our literature is going to be our most *perdurable* claim on man's remembrance.	持久、不朽的 durable eternal	dur(hard)
peremptory* a. pəˈrɛmptərɪ	A mathematician's conclusions ought to be *peremptory* and grounded in infallible evidence.	絕對、強制的 absolute imperative	empt(acquire)
perennial a. pəˈrɛnɪəl	The family and the church have become *perennial* in the experience of man.	永久的 permanent eternal	enn(year)
perfect a. ˈpɝfɪkt	Everybody knows that she can do a *perfect* job.	無缺點、全然的 entire faultless	fect(do)

v. pɚˈfɛkt	Laboratory methods for examining foods must still be further *perfected*.	改進、完成 elaborate consummate	
perfidy* n. ˈpɝˌfədɪ	The name of Judas has become a byword of covetousness and *perfidy*.	背信、不義 deceit treachery	**fid**(faith)
perforate v. ˈpɝˌfəˌret	The little boy *perforated* the jar top to give the captured butterfly air.	穿孔、鑿孔 bore puncture	**for**(bore)
perfunctory* a. pɚˈfʌŋktərɪ	The girl gave a *perfunctory* smile and was again immersed in the book.	敷衍、表面、不關心的 mechanical indifferent	**funct**(perform)
perish v. ˈpɛrɪʃ	Window frames cannot be left bare of paint indefinitely without the woodwork *perishing*.	腐壞、死 expire decay	**is**(go)
permanent a. ˈpɝmənənt	She wishes to find a *permanent* job.	固定不變、永久的 constant perennial	**man**(remain)
permeate v. ˈpɝmɪˌet	An atmosphere of distrust has been allowed to *permeate* the government.	瀰漫、充滿、滲透 penetrate pervade	**me**(glide)
permit v. pɚˈmɪt	Please *permit* me to explain.	允許、許可 allow authorize	**mit**(send)

單字·音標·詞類	例　句	中譯·同義字	字源分析
pernicious a. pɚˈnɪʃəs	The old man had a *pernicious* influence on the children.	有害的 harmful detrimental	nic(kill)
perpendicular a. ˌpɝpənˈdɪkjələ	These two lines are *perpendicular* to each other.	成直角、垂直的 vertical	**pend**(hang)
perpetrate v. ˈpɝpəˌtret	The committee will find out who *perpetrated* the massacre.	為(非)、犯(罪) do commit	petr(effect)
perpetual a. pɚˈpɛtʃʊəl	The maiden had dedicated herself to a life of *perpetual* virginity.	永久、終身的 eternal unceasing	pet(seek)
perplex v. pɚˈplɛks	She looked *perplexed* when she heard the question.	使困惑、使迷惑 puzzle mystify	plex(twist)
persecute v. ˈpɝsɪˌkjut	Christians were once *persecuted*.	迫害、煩擾 wrong harass	secu(follow)
persevere v. ˌpɝsəˈvɪr	The man stood to his post and *persevered* in accordance with his duty.	堅持、堅忍 persist endure	severe
persist v. pɚˈzɪst	Despite his previous failures, he *persisted* in trying.	堅持、持久 endure persevere	sist(stand)

單字·音標·詞類	例　　句	中譯·同義字	字源分析
perspective n. pɚˈspɛktɪv	Many happenings in the past seem less important when viewed in *perspective*.	正確眼光、景色 view panorama	spect(watch)
perspicacious* a. ˌpɝspɪˈkeʃəs	The writer has been well-known for being *perspicacious*.	明察、穎悟的 sharp-sighted shrewd	spic(watch)
perspicuous* a. pɚˈspɪkjʊəs	Their arguments are *perspicuous* in meaning.	明白、明顯的 lucid intelligible	spic(watch)
perspire v. pɚˈspaɪr	Beads of moisture *perspire* through the porous walls of the clay water jug.	流汗 sweat emit	spir(breathe)
persuade v. pɚˈswed	He *persuaded* us to admit that we were wrong.	說服、使相信 convince advise	suad(urge)
pertain v. pɚˈten	Destruction and havoc *pertain* to war.	屬於、適於 belong befit	tain(hold)
pertinacious a. ˌpɝtṇˈeʃəs	A *pertinacious* opponent could be quite a nuisance.	執拗、固執的 stubborn obdurate	tin(hold)
pertinent a. ˈpɝtṇənt	The message of the book is as *pertinent* today as at the time it was written.	適當、有關的 appropriate relevant	tin(hold)
perturb v. pɚˈtɝb	They were obviously *perturbed* by the news.	使心煩意亂、擾亂 disquiet vex	turb(disturb)

單字‧音標‧詞類	例　　　句	中譯‧同義字	字源分析
peruse v. pəˈruz	All applicants should *peruse* the lists carefully.	讀、閱讀 read study	use
pervade v. pɚˈved	All railway waiting rooms seem to be *pervaded* by a heavy, musty odor.	瀰漫、遍布 overspread permeate	vad(go)
perverse a. pɚˈvɝs	The *perverse* girl did just what the elders told her not to do.	倔強、剛愎的 wayward intractable	**vers**(turn)
pervert v. pɚˈvɝt	The pornographers were accused of *perverting* young men.	敗壞、引入邪路 misdirect corrupt	**vert**(turn)

POST

after, behind

在後

post源自拉丁文副詞與介系詞 post，原即有 after、behind 的意思。拉丁文有句諺語 "Post proelium, paremium"（"After the battle, the reward."），其中便有 post 一字作 after 的用法。post 組成的單字部分較偏，本書雖未收錄，但仍在此附帶一提，供讀者參考：postbellum a.「戰後的」、postdate v.「填上事後的日期」、postern n.「後門」、postglacial a.「冰河期之後的」、postgraduate n.「研究生」、postlude n.「終曲」、postprandial a.「正餐後的」等等。

單字·音標·詞類	例　　　句	中譯·同義字	字源分析
posterior a. pɑsˈtɪrɪə	The article discusses the various events that happened *posterior* to the end of the war.	時間上在後、較遲的 following subsequent	
posterity n. pɑsˈtɛrətɪ	We must try to secure the blessings of liberty to ourselves and our *posterity*.	子孫、後裔 descendents offspring	
posthumous a. ˈpɑstʃʊməs	The writer's *posthumous* fame came too late.	死後的 following death	hum(earth)
post-mortem* a. postˈmɔrtəm	The cases have to be examined *post-mortem*.	死後的 after death	mort(death)
postpone v. postˈpoɳ	The meeting was *postponed* because of a dispute among the participants.	延期、延擱 delay defer	**pon**(place)
postscript n. ˈpos·skrɪpt	The writer has added a *postscript* to the manuscript.	附加的資料、附錄 appendix supplement	**scrip**(write)
postwar a. ˈpostˈwɔr	He wrote a book on the *postwar* revival of the theater.	戰後的 after a war	war

PRE

before

在前

字首 pre 源自拉丁文副詞與介系詞 prae，原已有 before 的意思。下文例字 preach v.「宣講」原拉丁文作 praedicāre，字根 dic 有「說話」的意思，後受古法文影響，而轉變成 preach 的拼法。predicament n.「困境」字根 dic 也是「說話」，原在拉丁文有「斷定出來的範疇」的意思（參見 predicate v.「斷定」），目前現代英文仍然保有這個字義，但已不很常用。進入英文之後，到了十六世紀，已逐漸演變成「事先斷定却無法達成」的意思，而成為現代習用的「困境」。pretend v.「假裝」來自拉丁文 praetendere「向前展開、托故推辭」，字根 tend 有 stretch「伸展」的意思，「向前伸展」，擺出姿態，自然不難聯想到「假裝」的意思。preposterous a.「荒謬的」是一個十分有趣的單字，源出於拉丁文形容詞 praeposterus「顛倒、錯亂的」，字首 pre「在前」加上另一字首 post「在後」，「既前又後」，次序錯亂，不「荒謬」也不行！

單字·音標·詞類	例　句	中譯·同義字	字源分析
preach v. pritʃ	The minister has been *preaching* the gospel for years.	宣講、倡導 discourse inculcate	**dic**(say)
precaution n. prɪˈkɔʃən	Proper *precaution* is prudent.	預防、防備 foresight wariness	caution
precede v. priˈsid	There are countries that *precede* ours in per capita contributions.	高於、優於 lead head	**cede**(go)
precedent n. ˈprɛsədənt	*Precedents* would seem to show that the reduction of armaments is conducive to war.	前例、先例 instance antecedent	**precede**
precept n. ˈprisɛpt	Example is better than *precept*.	教訓、箴言 instruction commandment	**cept**(receive)
precinct n. ˈprisɪŋkt	A municipal experiment in planning a whole business *precinct* of offices and shops is under way.	區域、區、範圍 district domain	**cinct**(surround)
precipitate v. prɪˈsɪpəˌtet	The completion of the railway *precipitated* the extinction of waterborne commerce.	催促其發生、加速 hasten accelerate	capit(head)
precipitous a. prɪˈsɪpətəs	The car had fallen down the *precipitous* cliff.	陡峭的 steep sheer	capit(head)

單字·音標·詞類	例　　　　　句	中譯·同義字	字源分析
precise a. prɪˈsaɪs	Her answer was so *precise* that no one else could find any fault with it.	精確、正確的 exact accurate	cis(cut)
preclude v. prɪˈklud	The adoption of one choice often necessarily *precludes* the use of another.	使不能、妨礙、阻止 hinder inhibit	clud(close)
precocious* a. prɪˈkoʃəs	At the *precocious* age of 25 he had written a masterpiece.	早熟、過早的 over-forward premature	coc(cook)
precursor* n. prɪˈkɝsɚ	Greek mathematics was the *precursor* to modern mathematics.	先驅、前輩 forerunner predecessor	curs(run)
predecessor n. ˈprɛdɪˌsɛsɚ	John Adams was Thomas Jefferson's *predecessor* as President.	前任、祖先 forerunner ancestor	decess(decease)
predicament n. prɪˈdɪkəmənt	Mary was in an awful *predicament* after she said that to John.	困境 dilemma quandary	dic(say)
predict v. prɪˈdɪkt	No one could *predict* which team was going to win.	預測、預知 foretell prophesy	dict(say)
predispose v. ˌpridɪsˈpoz	His early training *predisposed* him to a life of adventure.	使傾向於、使偏向於 incline bend	dispose

predominant a. prɪˈdɑmənənt	In rural areas the town and the school district are the *predominant* governmental units.	支配、優勢的 controlling prevailing	dominant
predominate v. prɪˈdɑməˌnet	Moral and humane tendencies normally *predominate* over the sadistic strain in human nature.	支配、佔優勢 rule prevail	dominate
preeminent a. prɪˈɛmənənt	This cuisine is *preeminent* for its seafood.	卓越、超群的 outstanding paramount	eminent
preface n. ˈprɛfɪs	Our defeat and dismay may be the *preface* to our successor's victory.	開端、序言 foreword preliminary	face(speak)
prefer v. prɪˈfɝ	She *preferred* not to go.	寧愛、較喜歡 desire choose	fer(carry)
prejudice n. ˈprɛdʒədɪs	*Prejudice* has rendered her helpless on many occasions.	偏見、成見 partiality bias	jud(judge)
preliminary a. prɪˈlɪməˌnɛrɪ	The members of the meeting were asked to read the *preliminary* articles of the treaty.	序言、預備、 在前的 introductory precedent	limin(threshold)
prelude* n. ˈprɛljud	The woman seemed to enjoy the organ *prelude* to the church service.	序曲、序言 introduction preamble	lud(play)

單字・音標・詞類	例　句	中譯・同義字	字源分析
premature a. ˌprimə'tjʊr	Everybody was surprised by the *premature* fall of snow.	太早的 early untimely	mature
premium n. 'primɪəm	After the war a new car could only be obtained by paying a considerable *premium.*	額外費用、報酬、獎金 reward bonus	em(take)
premonition* n. ˌprimə'nɪʃən	The falling leaves gave a *premonition* of the coming winter.	預先警告、預兆 forewarning portent	mon(warn)
preoccupy v. pri'akjə,paɪ	His mind was *pre-occupied* by the notion all day long.	盤據（心頭）、使凝神於 engage engross	**occupy**
preponderate v. prɪ'pandə,ret	Surplus energy could accumulate in such bulk as to *preponderate* over productive energy.	重量超過、占優勢 outweigh predominate	**ponder**(weigh)
preposterous a. prɪ'pastrəs	The clown wore a false nose and *preposterous* spectacles on his face.	荒謬、反理性的 absurd irrational	**poster**(after)
prerequisite n. pri'rɛkwəzɪt	Payment of the tax is usually considered a *prerequisite* for voting.	必備之事物 something required beforehand	**requisite**
prerogative* n. prɪ'ragətɪv	Cruelty remains the special *prerogative* of men.	特權 claim privilege	rog(ask)

單字・音標・詞類	例　　　句	中譯・同義字	字源分析
presage v. prɪˈsedʒ	A dog crossing a hunter's path is usually thought to *presage* evil luck.	預示 forebode betoken	sag(perceive)
n. ˈpresɪdʒ	The coming of the swallow is a *presage* of the spring.	預兆 omen augury	
prescience* n. ˈprɛʃɪəns	A mother always seems to have an acute phatic *prescience* where her child is concerned.	預知、先見 foresight omniscience	sci(know)
prescribe v. prɪˈskraɪb	A culture often *prescribes* a code of behavior for child training.	規定、命令 impose decree	**scrib**(write)
presence n. ˈprɛzn̩s	Her awesome *presence* usually intimidated the people around her.	存在、儀容 appearance bearing	esse(be)
present a. ˈprɛzn̩t	Juanita was not *present* today and the teacher was quite angry.	出席、在場的 here ready	esse(be)
a.	No one knows what to do with the *present* situation.	現在的 current existing	
v. prɪˈzɛnt	The students *presented* the teacher their work.	提出、呈遞、呈現出 show exhibit	

單字・音標・詞類	例　　句	中譯・同義字	字源分析
presentiment* n. prɪˈzɛntəmənt	I have a strong *presentiment* it will prove a success.	預感 anticipation apprehension	**sentiment**
preserve v. prɪˈzɝv	Ice helps to *preserve* food.	保藏、保存、 保持 save maintain	**serv**(keep)
preside v. prɪˈzaɪd	The minister was asked to *preside* over the funeral service.	主持、管理 direct officiate	**sid**(sit)
presume v. prɪˈzum	The law *presumes* innocence until guilt is proved.	假定、推測 presuppose surmise	**sum**(take)
presumptuous a. prɪˈzʌmptʃʊəs	The nurse enforced the doctor's orders in a way which seemed to him loud and *presumptuous*.	自大、傲慢的 arrogant insolent	**presume**
presuppose v. ˌprisəˈpoz	Let us *presuppose* that he wants more money.	假定、推測 presume conjecture	**suppose**
pretend v. prɪˈtɛnd	She *pretended* not to recognize the man.	假裝 affect simulate	**tend**(stretch)
pretentious a. prɪˈtɛnʃəs	The poem is written in a *pretentious* style.	矯飾、傲慢的 affected conceited	**pretend**
pretext n. ˈpritɛkst	He used his sore throat as a *pretext* for not going to school.	藉口 excuse subterfuge	**text**(weave)

單字·音標·詞類	例　　句	中譯·同義字	字源分析
prevail v. prɪˈvel	The rite of passage is a custom that still *prevails* in certain cultures.	盛行、流行、 占優勢 predominate preponderate	**vail**(strong)
prevalent a. ˈprɛvələnt	Malaria is *prevalent* in these areas.	流行、盛行的 widespread prevailing	**prevail**
prevent v. prɪˈvɛnt	Can't you *prevent* her from entering the hall?	阻止、妨礙 stop impede	**vent**(come)
previous a. ˈprivɪəs	Your *previous* report was not so well prepared as this one.	先前、在前的 former earlier	**via**(way)

23

PRO·PUR

forward, before

向前 ● 在前

　　字首 pro、pur 源出希臘文副詞與介系詞 προ (pro)，和拉丁文介繫詞 prō，本即有 forward、before 的意思。pur 的拼法出自古法文（現代法文作 pour），組成的單字數量極小，遠不如 pro。下文例字中的 profane a.「世俗的」，源自拉丁文 profānus，字根 fan 有「廟宇」的意思（拉丁文作 fānum n.m.），原指「在廟前」，也作「在廟外」，因此而有「世俗」的意思。prohibit v.「禁止」拉丁文作 prohibēre，字根 hib 有 have 的意思（拉丁文 habēre），原義為 hold before，後來引申為 keep away「遠離」，最後而有「制止、禁止」的意思。proscribe v.「禁止」拉丁文作 prōscrībere，字根 scrib 有「寫」的意思，原義為「佈告」。古代官方公布帖文，目的不是要沒收某某人的財產，就是要流放某某人，禁止百姓做某事，因此十六世紀已引申為「放逐」，十七世紀終於又添加了「禁止」的意思。 prostitute n.「妓女」源出 prōstituere v.「置於前」，字根 stitute 有 stand 的意思，後來 prōstituere 引申又成「使拋頭露面」，而至於「賣淫」，因此英文的 prostitute 便有了「妓女」的意思。

單字·音標·詞類	例　　　句	中譯·同義字	字源分析
portend v. porˈtɛnd	In Ireland it is believed that the appearance of a black pig *portends* trouble.	預示、預兆 augur foreshadow	tend(stretch)
portentous a. porˈtɛntəs	The old man gave him a *portentous* wink.	奇特、不祥的 ominous monstrous	**portend**
portray v. porˈtre	The painter has *portrayed* with sure but sparing brush strokes an unforgettable face.	畫像、描繪 paint depict	tray(draw)
proceed v. prəˈsid	Please *proceed* with what you were doing.	繼續、進行 continue advance	ceed(go)
process n. ˈprosɛs	Many questions are in *process* of discussion.	進行、過程 operation proceeding	cess(go)
proclaim v. proˈklem	The newspaper *proclaimed* its adherence to the government's policy.	正式宣稱 declare promulgate	claim(cry)
proclivity* n. proˈklɪvətɪ	They do not like to be forced into social activities for which they have no *proclivity*.	傾向、癖性 inclination propensity	cliv(slope)
procreate* v. ˈprokrɪˌet	The gossipy people keep *procreating* one rumor after another.	製造、生產 produce generate	create

單字・音標・詞類	例　　句	中譯・同義字	字源分析
procure v. prəˈkjʊr	The judicial qualities he developed *procured* for him universal confidence and respect.	取得 obtain secure	**cur**(attend)
prodigal* a. ˈprɑdɪg!	He had been *prodigal* with his money.	揮霍、奢侈、浪費的 extravagant lavish	**ag**(act)
produce v. prəˈdjus	The rains *produced* a quick-growing and lush herbage.	產生、製造、引起 create engender	**duc**(lead)
profane* a. prəˈfen	Jeremiah has been likened to several characters in *profane* history.	世俗的 secular temporal	**fan**(temple)
profess v. prəˈfɛs	They had become what they *professed* to scorn.	偽稱、聲稱 purport avow	**fess**(confess)
profession n. prəˈfɛʃən	What is your father's *profession*?	職業 calling vocation	**profess**
proffer v. ˈprɑfɚ	The hero was *proffered* the leadership but declined it.	提供、提出 offer tender	**offer**
proficient a. prəˈfɪʃənt	The experienced young man is *proficient* in his job.	精通、熟諳的 skilled adroit	**fic**(do)

單字‧音標‧詞類	例　　　句	中譯‧同義字	字源分析
profile n. ˈprofaɪl	His face was presented to us in *profile*.	側面像、輪廓 contour outline	fil(draw)
profligate* a. ˈprɑfləgɪt	The people could not tolerate the *profligate* profusion with which the officials carried on bribery.	恣意、放蕩的 corrupt dissolute	flig(drive)
profound a. prəˈfaʊnd	I have a *profound* sympathy with you and your family.	深深感覺、極深、奧妙的 deep subtle	found(bottom)
profuse a. prəˈfjus	The young man was so *profuse* with his money that he squandered it all.	浪費的 extravagant lavish	fus(pour)
progenitor* n. proˈdʒɛnətɚ	He wrote an article to discuss the *progenitors* of socialist ideas.	起源、祖先、前輩 forefather precursor	gen(bear)
progeny n. ˈprɑdʒənɪ	They have examined one by one the marvelous *progeny* of the workman's art.	成果、子孫、產品 children product	gen(bear)
prognosis* n. prɑgˈnosɪs	The *prognosis* is always unfavorable when after a certain time much fever comes on.	病狀之預斷 foretelling forecast	gno(know)

單字・音標・詞類	例　　句	中譯・同義字	字源分析
prognosticate* v. prɑɡˈnɑstɪˌket	The article has *prognosticated* the future relations between the two countries.	預測、預言 predict forecast	gno(know)
program n. ˈproɡræm	The entire concert *program* is delightful.	節目、計畫、節目單 plan schedule	gram(write)
progress n. ˈprɑɡrɛs	The students are not making much *progress*.	進步、改進 advance improvement	**gress**(go)
prohibit v. proˈhɪbɪt	Smoking is *prohibited* here.	禁止 ban proscribe	hib(have)
project v. prəˈdʒɛkt	The light was *projected* on the window pane.	投影於 throw cast	**ject**(throw)
v.	The new machine is being *projected*.	設計、計畫 plan devise	
n. ˈprɑdʒɛkt	How is your new *project* going?	計畫、設計 design scheme	
prolix* a. proˈlɪks	This is a sprawling book, with discursive and *prolix* paragraphs.	冗長的 verbose diffuse	lix(fluid)

單字·音標·詞類	例　　　句	中譯·同義字	字源分析
prologue n. ˈprolɔg	The audience did not seem to like the *prologue* to the play.	開場白、序言 prelude preamble	**log**(speak)
prolong v. prəˈlɔŋ	The meeting was *prolonged* because an important issue was still being discussed.	延長 lengthen extend	long
prominent a. ˈprɑmənənt	A single tree in a field is *prominent.*	顯著的 conspicuous remarkable	min(protrude)
promiscuous* a. prəˈmɪskjuəs	The guests wished to see her *promiscuous* collection of curios.	各式各樣、雜亂的 disordered miscellaneous	misc(mix)
promise v. ˈprɑmɪs	Anne has *promised* to show me her photo albums.	答應、允諾 assure pledge	**mis**(send)
promote v. prəˈmot	He was *promoted* for outstanding performance in his job.	擢升、促進 advance forward	**mot**(move)
prompt a. prɑmpt	The boss needs a *prompt* answer from you.	迅速、立刻的 quick early	em(take)
v.	The boys were *prompted* by curiosity to open the closet.	驅使、激起 stimulate induce	
promulgate* v. prəˈmʌlget	The king has *promulgated* a decree.	頒布、公布 pronounce proclaim	vulg(people)

單字‧音標‧詞類	例　　　句	中譯‧同義字	字源分析
pronounce v. prəˈnaʊns	Doctors *pronounced* him fit to resume his duties.	斷言、宣稱、清楚地發音 announce articulate	**nounc** 　(announce)
propel v. prəˈpɛl	The locomotive is *propelled* by electricity.	推動、驅使 drive urge	**pel**(push)
propensity n. prəˈpɛnsətɪ	The function of the wife is sometimes to curb the roving *propensities* of the male.	傾向 inclination tendency	**pens**(hang)
prophecy n. ˈprɑfəsɪ	The man has the gift of *prophecy*.	預言 prediction augury	**phan**(speak)
prophesy v. ˈprɑfəˌsaɪ	No one could have *prophesied* a fall in commodity prices.	預言 predict foretell	**phan**(speak)
propitiate* v. prəˈpɪʃɪˌet	The ancients *propitiated* their gods when a disaster was believed to be taking place.	使息怒、撫慰 pacify appease	**pet**(seek)
propitious a. prəˈpɪʃəs	We may succeed if the gods are *propitious*.	慈悲、有利、吉利的 favorable auspicious	**pet**(seek)
proportion n. prəˈpɔrʃən	The *proportions* of local, domestic, governmental, and foreign news had never been set in this news agency.	比例、均衡 ratio balance	portion

單字·音標·詞類	例　　句	中譯·同義字	字源分析
propose v. prə'poz	Have you got anything to *propose* to this committee?	提議 present tender	**pos**(place)
proposition n. ˌprɑpə'zɪʃən	This is a *proposition* that needs no further discussion.	意見、提議 proposal recommendation	**propose**
propound v. prə'paʊnd	The chemist *propounded* a hypothesis in the convention.	提出 proposal tender	**pound**(place)
propulsion n. prə'pʌlʃən	The student raised several questions about rocket *propulsion.*	推進 ejection expulsion	**puls**(push)
proscribe* v. pro'skraɪb	Lasting pacts *proscribing* warfare exist between the two primitive societies.	禁止 interdict ban	**scrib**(write)
prosecute v. 'prɑsɪ,kjut	The policemen were determined to *prosecute* the investigation.	進行、實行 follow pursue	**secu**(follow)
v.	The politicians were *prosecuted* for fraud.	告發、控告、起訴 sue indict	
prospect n. 'prɑspɛkt	I see no *prospect* of his recovery.	希望、展望、景色 outlook anticipation	**spect**(watch)

單字·音標·詞類	例　句	中譯·同義字	字源分析
prospective a. prəˈspɛktɪv	The terms of the *prospective* deal are acceptable.	預期的 expected forthcoming	**prospect**
prosper v. ˈprɑspɚ	After years of poverty the family began to *prosper*.	旺盛、興隆 thrive flourish	sper(hope)
prostitute n. ˈprɑstəˌtjut	The woman has written articles about child *prostitutes*.	娼妓 whore harlot	stitute(stand)
prostrate* v. ˈprɑstret	The captives *prostrated* themselves before the conqueror.	俯臥、臥倒、使衰弱 lay overcome	strat(stretch)
protect v. prəˈtɛkt	The knights rushed forward to *protect* the lady from the fiery dragon.	保護 guard escort	tect(cover)
protest v. prəˈtɛst	The workers are *protesting* against the boss's decision to fire the foreman.	反對、抗議 complain demur	test
n. ˈprotɛst	They could not but yield to the fierce *protests* of other countries.	抗議、反對 complaint disapproval	
protract v. proˈtrækt	The war was *protracted* because of the failed peace negotiation.	延長 lengthen prolong	tract(draw)

單字·音標·詞類	例　　　句	中譯·同義字	字源分析
protrude v. prə'trud	The little girl refused and *protruded* her tongue.	伸出、突出 project jut	**trud**(thrust)
proverb n. 'pravɜ·b	Her relatives all referred her to the *proverb* "marry in haste, repent at leisure."	格言 dictum maxim	verb(word)
provide v. prə'vaɪd	Sheep *provide* us with wool.	供給 supply furnish	**vid**(see)
provident* a. 'pravədənt	Wild squirrels are *provident*.	顧念將來、節約的 considerate frugal	**provide**
providential* a. ˌpravə'dɛnʃəl	It seemed *providential* that he should arrive at just that moment.	幸運的 lucky miraculous	**provide**
provisional a. prə'vɪʒənḷ	A *provisional* government was set up in the territory freed from enemy control.	臨時的 temporary tentative	**provide**
provoke v. prə'vok	An insult can *provoke* a person to anger.	刺激、引起 incite instigate	**vok**(voice)
purport v. pɚ'port	The journalist received a letter that *purports* to express public opinion.	聲稱 claim profess	**port**(carry)

單字·音標·詞類	例　　　句	中譯·同義字	字源分析
purpose n. ˈpɝpəs	What is your *purpose* in doing this?	用意、目的 goal end	**pos**(place)
pursue v. pɚˈsu	The hounds *pursued* the stag.	追捕、追逐 chase seek	**sue**(follow)

RE

back, again

反向 ● 再次

　　re是英文最常用的字首之一，源自拉丁文字首 re- ，本卽有
back 或 again 的意思。由這個字首組成的英文單字，有部分直接
借自拉丁文，部分間接受法文影響，部分乃英國「土製」而成。這
個字首在拉丁文發展初期，除了有re的形態外，另可拼成 red ，後
接字根的第一個音若是母音或 h 子音，便用 red，否則便一律拼作
re。red 的形態到了英文，仍保存在少數單字上，如下文例字的
redeem v.「救贖、補償」(redēmptāre) 、 redound v.「增加」、
redundant a.「很多、過剩的」(後兩字均源自拉丁文 redundāre v.
「泛濫」) 均是。下文 redress v.「匡正、補救」中，dress 原義爲
「整頓」(源出古法文 dresser)，後來引申而成「整頓衣裝、穿衣
」的意思，因此 redress 一字旣是「匡正、補救」，也是「重新穿
衣」。relish n.「美味」的字源也相當特別，原出自古法文名詞
reles, 有「剩餘物」的意思，後來可指吃過食物後「口齒留香」，
而演變出「美味」的意思。

單字·音標·詞類	例　　　句	中譯·同義字	字源分析
react v. rɪˈækt	She *reacted* to the insult with instinctive indignation.	反應 act in response	act
rebate* v. riˈbet	They are going to *rebate* all their prices.	減價 lessen diminish	bat(beat)
rebel v. rɪˈbɛl	The minority people *rebelled* against the government and declared their autonomy.	反叛 revolt	
n. ˈrɛbl̩	The scholar declared himself a *rebel* against the conventions of education.	反抗者、叛徒 revolutionary insurgent	
rebound v. rɪˈbaʊnd	The ball *rebounded* from the wall.	彈回 spring recoil	bound
rebuke v. rɪˈbjuk	The children were *rebuked* when they became too restless.	叱責、指責 chide reprimand	buke(beat)
rebut v. rɪˈbʌt	She *rebuts* the long-accepted dictum that Africa is a continent without a history.	反駁、證明為偽 refute confute	but(push)
recalcitrant* a. rɪˈkælsɪtrənt	The general called forth the forces of the Union to coerce *recalcitrant* states.	頑強反抗、不服從的 unmanageable unruly	calcitr(kick)

單字·音標·詞類	例　　　句	中譯·同義字	字源分析
recall v. rɪˈkɔl	She still *recalls* the events and episodes of her past years.	憶起 remember recollect	call
v.	The general had to *recall* his order when he was under pressure.	取消 revoke repeal	
recant* v. rɪˈkænt	They *recanted* all opinions which differed from those proclaimed by the central leadership.	取消、撤回 revoke retract	cant(sing)
recapitulate v. ˌrikəˈpɪtʃəˌlet	So much for the detailed argument; I will now *recapitulate*.	簡述要旨 summarize epitomize	capit(head)
recede v. ˌriˈsid	The tide, having risen to its highest, is now *receding*.	後退 retreat withdraw	cede(go)
receive v. rɪˈsiv	When did she *receive* the letter you wrote?	接到、接受 get acquire	ceiv(receive)
recess n. rɪˈsɛs	The philosopher enjoys exploring the *recesses* of the mind.	深幽處 privacy corner	cess(go)
n.	Most members of Congress took advantage of the Easter *recess* to go back to their home districts.	休會期、休假期 vacation interval	

單字·音標·詞類	例　　句	中譯·同義字	字源分析
reciprocal* a. rɪˈsɪprəkḷ	The two countries agree to extend *reciprocal* privileges to each other's citizens.	相互、交互的 mutual correlative	proc(forward)
recite v. rɪˈsaɪt	The poet is often asked to *recite* ballads in public.	背誦、詳述 repeat recount	**cite**
reclaim v. rɪˈklem	His wife has *reclaimed* him from a life of drunkenness.	糾正、改正、 拯救 recover reform	**claim**
recline v. rɪˈklaɪn	When I was talking to her, the little girl *reclined* her head on the pillow.	斜倚、橫臥、 依賴 lie repose	clin(lean)
recluse n. ˈrɛklus	His life as a *recluse* is quiet and pleasant.	隱士、遁世者 hermit solitary	clus(close)
recognize v. ˈrɛkəɡˌnaɪz	He had changed so much that we could hardly *recognize* him.	認得、認出、 注意 identify notice	cogn(know)
recoil v. ˌriˈkɔɪl	The troops *recoiled* before the savage onslaught of the enemy.	退却、退縮 shrink flinch	coil(buttocks)
recollect v. ˌrɛkəˈlɛkt	I *recollected* having seen her somewhere.	憶起 remember remind	**collect**

單字·音標·詞類	例　　　句	中譯·同義字	字源分析
recommend v. ˌrɛkəˈmɛnd	They have *recommended* several people to the governor for appointment.	推薦、勸告 advise counsel	commend
reconcile v. ˈrɛkənˌsaɪl	Sooner or later we would have to *reconcile* our ideals with practical reality.	使一致、使和諧、使滿足 appease adjust	conciliate
recondite* a. ˈrɛkənˌdaɪt	The student found the subject somewhat too *recondite*.	深奧、難解的 deep abstruse	cond(hide)
reconnaissance n. rɪˈkɑnəsəns	The air force has sent three *reconnaissance* planes on a mission.	偵察、勘察 survey investigation	connais(know)
recover v. rɪˈkʌvɚ	The army has *recovered* the lost lands.	復得、恢復 restore retrieve	cover
v.	She has not *recovered* from her illness.	使痊癒、使復元 heal recuperate	
recreation n. ˌrɛkrɪˈeʃən	To sit in the sun is one of the family's country *recreations*.	消遣、娛樂 play diversion	create
recruit v. rɪˈkrut	There are times when a nation must suddenly *recuit* a maximal armed force.	招募（新兵） raise muster	cru(grow)

單字‧音標‧詞類	例 句	中譯‧同義字	字源分析
recumbent* a. rɪˈkʌmbənt	The pulse may be as rapid in the *recumbent* as in the standing posture.	橫臥、斜倚的 resting leaning	cumb(lie)
recuperate* v. rɪˈkjupəˌret	The sick animals would not *recuperate* until they got water.	恢復（健康） recover heal	cuper(cover)
recur v. rɪˈkɝ	We all knew that the difficulties would *recur*.	再發生、重現 return reappear	**cur**(run)
redeem v. rɪˈdim	A yearly tribute *redeemed* the borough from all claims.	償還、救贖、補償 liberate compensate	em(get)
redound* v. rɪˈdaʊnd	A conscientious man will always *redound* to his own honor and self-sacrifice.	增加、有助於、促成 contribute conduce	und(wave)
redress v. rɪˈdrɛs	The king tried to *redress* wrongs in his kingdom.	匡正、補救 remedy rectify	dress
reduce v. rɪˈdjus	The car had *reduced* its speed after a few turns.	減低、減少 lessen abate	**duc**(lead)
redundant* a. rɪˈdʌndənt	In recent years skirts became somewhat shorter and less *redundant*.	很多、過剩的 copious superfluous	und(wave)
refer v. rɪˈfɝ	These asterisks *refer* the reader to the foot-notes.	指示、相關 direct pertain	**fer**(carry)

單字·音標·詞類	例　　　　句	中譯·同義字	字源分析
refine v. rɪˈfaɪn	Reading good books helps to *refine* a person's writing.	使文雅、精美、使純、改進 cleanse improve	**fine**
refined a. ˈriˈfaɪnd	She spoke in a painfully *refined* accent.	文雅、高尚、精確的 exact cultivated	**refine**
reflect v. rɪˈflɛkt	The man's internal stresses *reflected* a dry bitterness upon the world.	反映、照出 mirror image	**flect**(bend)
v.	Take time to *reflect* before doing anything important.	考慮、思考 ponder meditate	
reform v. rɪˈfɔrm	The educational system of the country must be *reformed*.	改革、改造、改進 reconstruct ameliorate	**form**
n.	The intellectuals of the country are mostly against the ruler's social *reform*.	改革、改善 betterment amelioration	
refrain v. rɪˈfren	It is hard for him to *refrain* from making a lot of noises.	抑制、禁止 withhold abstain	**frain**(curb)
refresh v. rɪˈfrɛʃ	He *refreshed* himself with a cold shower and rubdown.	使恢復疲勞、使提起精神 renovate enliven	**fresh**

單字・音標・詞類	例　　　句	中譯・同義字	字源分析
refuge n. ˈrɛfjudʒ	A couple had taken *refuge* in the cellar during the war.	安全、保護 protection shelter	fug(flee)
refurbish v. riˈfɝbɪʃ	The Wilsons have *refurbished* their antique table.	刷新、整修 repolish renovate	furbish
refuse v. rɪˈfjuz	He has *refused* to answer any of my letters.	拒絕 decline repel	**fus(pour)**
refute v. rɪˈfjut	The worker had *refuted* the foreman's charge of laziness by working hard.	反駁、駁斥 disprove confute	fut(beat)
regale* v. rɪˈgel	She *regaled* her guests with the best of everything.	款待 entertain feast	gale(joy)
regard v. rɪˈgard	He was *regarded* as a savage brute.	視為、當作 consider estimate	gard(guard)
v.	She *regards* her parents' wishes and stops going out with the boy.	敬重 respect revere	
v.	The President made a brief statement *regarding* the relation between the two nations.	關於 concern respect	

單字·音標·詞類	例　　　　句	中譯·同義字	字源分析
regenerate v. rɪˈdʒɛnəˌret	There are certain forces that will *regenerate* even a corrupt society.	使重獲新生、 使改過自新 restore renovate	**generate**
rehabilitate v. ˌriəˈbɪləˌtet	The nuns attempt to *rehabilitate* the prostitute.	精神重建、恢 復 renew reinstate	hab(have)
rehash* v. riˈhæʃ	The politician's opponent has *rehashed* all his propaganda charges.	舊事新彈、改 成新形式 go over again	hash
rehearse v. rɪˈhɝs	The chorus is scheduled to *rehearse* on Monday.	預演、演習、 詳述 practice recite	hears(harrow)
reimburse v. ˌriɪmˈbɝs	Government employees are usually *reimbursed* for travel expenses.	償還、退款、 補償 refund compensate	imburse(pay)
reinforce v. ˌriɪnˈfors	The atmosphere *reinforced* by candle fumes was stifling.	加強 strengthen augment	**enforce**
reinstate v. ˌriɪnˈstet	The sheriff was finally able to *reinstate* law and order.	使恢復 restore revive	in state
reiterate* v. riˈɪtəˌret	The information was *reiterated* day after day by every organ of publicity.	反復地說、反 復地做 repeat iterate	iterate

單字‧音標‧詞類	例 句	中譯‧同義字	字源分析
reject v. rɪˈdʒɛkt	Her proposal was *rejected* by the chairman of the board.	拒絕、不受、丟棄 decline discard	ject(throw)
rejuvenate* v. rɪˈdʒuvəˌnet	It is said that this magical juice *rejuvenates* even the most decrepit old men.	使返老還童、使充滿活力 reinvigorate	juven(young)
relapse v. rɪˈlæps	He *relapsed* when allowed out of bed.	復發、故態復萌 backslide lapse	lapse
relate v. rɪˈlet	It is difficult to *relate* these results with any known cause.	使有關係 concern refer	lat(carry)
v.	They wanted the traveler to *relate* his adventures.	敍述、說 report narrate	
relax v. rɪˈlæks	Just *relax*; nobody is going to hurt you.	放鬆 ease rest	lax
v.	Discipline is *relaxed* on the last day of school.	鬆懈、放寬 slacken abate	
release v. rɪˈlis	The prisoners of war were finally *released* when the war was over.	釋放 free liberate	lease(loosen)

單字·音標·詞類	例　　　句	中譯·同義字	字源分析
relent v. rɪˈlɛnt	The wind blast would *relent* in a few hours.	變溫和 slacken abate	lent(plaint)
relevant a. ˈrɛləvənt	He began work on the problem by reading all the *relevant* literature.	有關、中肯的 pertinent appropriate	lev(raise)
relic n. ˈrɛlɪk	The book contains pictures of precious *relics* of antiquity.	遺物、紀念物 remains memento	lic(leave)
relieve v. rɪˈliv	Aspirin *relieves* headaches.	減輕 alleviate soothe	liev(raise)
relinquish v. rɪˈlɪŋkwɪʃ	The government was forced to *relinquish* the plan of reform.	放棄 desert forsake	linqu(leave)
relish n. ˈrɛlɪʃ	Hunger gives *relish* to simple food.	美味 taste savor	lish(loosen)
v.	He did not *relish* the prospect of staying after school.	愛好、喜好 enjoy appreciate	
relocate v. riˈloket	The government will *relocate* families forced out by floods.	徙置於另一地方 move reestablish	locate
reluctant a. rɪˈlʌktənt	He is very *reluctant* to give his money away.	不願、勉強的 unwilling disinclined	luct(struggle)

單字・音標・詞類	例　　　句	中譯・同義字	字源分析
rely v. rɪˈlaɪ	*Rely* on your own efforts.	依賴 depend lean	ly(bind)
remain v. rɪˈmen	He *remained* poor all his life.	繼續、停留、居住 stay abide	man(remain)
remark n. rɪˈmɑrk	The chairman wishes to make a few *remarks*.	短語 utterance statement	mark
n.	I did not notice anything worthy of *remark*.	注意 attention heed	
remarkable a. rɪˈmɑrkəbl̩	The scenery here has been praised for its *remarkable* beauty.	出眾、顯著、不平常的 conspicuous extraordinary	remark
remember v. rɪˈmɛmbɚ	Do you still *remember* the day you proposed to me?	記得、憶起 recall recollect	mem(re-member)
remind v. rɪˈmaɪnd	What he just said *reminds* me of a story.	使想起、使憶起 cause to remember	mind
reminiscence* n. ˌrɛməˈnɪsn̩s	In his book the writer describes his *reminiscences* of the war.	令人回憶的事物、回憶 memory recollection	minisc(re-member)

單字·音標·詞類	例　　　句	中譯·同義字	字源分析
remit v. rɪˈmɪt	We *remitted* our efforts after we had rowed the boat into calm water.	緩和、減輕 slacken abate	mit(send)
v.	He has not *remitted* to me the money he promised to send.	滙寄 send forward	
remnant n. ˈrɛmnənt	Her rather sweet expression was the only *remnant* of a former prettiness.	遺跡、殘餘 remainder residue	remain
remonstrate* v. rɪˈmɑnstret	The father *remonstrated* with the child regarding his bad habits.	規勸、抗議 protest expostulate	monstr(show)
remorse n. rɪˈmɔrs	The man is already feeling *remorse* for what he has done.	懊悔 regret repentance	mors(bite)
remote a. rɪˈmot	The city is *remote* from the mountains.	遙遠、隱蔽的 distant secluded	mot(move)
remove v. rɪˈmuv	Jack *removed* his jacket and sat down on the desk.	脫去、遷移、開除 displace dismiss	move
renaissance* n. ˌrɛnəˈzɑns	The transcendental movement marked the full flowering of the New England *renaissance*.	復興、復活 rebirth revival	nais(bear)

單字・音標・詞類	例　　句	中譯・同義字	字源分析
renegade* n. ˈrɛnɪˌged	A *renegade* can utter vicious words about his former believes and associates.	叛徒 traitor turncoat	neg(deny)
renew v. rɪˈnju	The enemy will soon *renew* his attack.	再始、恢復、更新 restore renovate	new
renounce v. rɪˈnaʊns	He has *renounced* his claim to the house.	放棄、否認 disown disclaim	**nounc(announce)**
renovate v. ˈrɛnəˌvet	They are going to *renovate* their old house.	修理、更新 renew repair	nov(new)
renown n. rɪˈnaʊn	Everybody is satisfied with the increasing *renown* of the university.	名聲、名望 fame celebrity	nown(name)
renowned a. rɪˈnaʊnd	He is one of the most *renowned* writers in this country.	著名的 celebrated illustrious	renown
repair v. rɪˈpɛr	We asked Mr. McGovern to *repair* the TV set for us.	修理、修補、改正 fix mend	pair(prepare)
repast* n. rɪˈpæst	The millionaire preferred to be alone during his evening *repast*.	餐 meal	past(feed)

單字·音標·詞類	例　　句	中譯·同義字	字源分析
repatriate* v. rɪˈpetrɪˌet	All prisoners of war should be *repatriated* as quickly as they could be processed.	遣返、歸國 return to the country of birth	patr(father-land)
repeal v. rɪˈpil	The grant that she needed was *repealed*.	撤消、廢止 revoke abolish	peal(call)
repeat v. rɪˈpit	Could you please *repeat* what you just said?	重說、再述 reiterate recapitulate	pet(seek)
repel v. rɪˈpɛl	The brave chieftain had led the people to *repel* onslaughts by starveling barbarians.	逐退、拒絕、驅逐 reject resist	**pel**(drive)
repent v. rɪˈpɛnt	He had *repented* his decision to give up the study of medicine.	懊悔 regret atone	pent(repent)
replace v. rɪˈples	The inept staff member was soon *replaced*.	接替、代替 substitute supersede	place
replenish v. rɪˈplɛnɪʃ	His glass was kept *replenished* by the hostess.	再加滿、補充 refill furnish	plen(full)
replete a. rɪˈplit	He had led a life *replete* with charm.	充滿、充分供應的 well-provided abounding	plet(fill)

單字·音標·詞類	例 句	中譯·同義字	字源分析
replica n. ˈrɛplɪkə	A legislative body should not be merely a *replica* of the lower house.	複製品、複製 reproduction duplicate	**plic**(fold)
reply n. rɪˈplaɪ	Her *reply* to us is not satisfactory.	答覆、反應 answer response	**ply**(fold)
report v. rɪˈport	He has *reported* what he saw.	敍述、公布 describe announce	**port**(carry)
repose v. rɪˈpoz	She has been *reposing* on that couch for hours.	休息、睡眠 recline sleep	**pos**(place)
reprehend* v. ˌrɛprɪˈhɛnd	He was severely *reprehended* for what he had done.	譴責、申斥 reprimand reprove	prehend(take)
represent v. ˌrɛprɪˈzɛnt	Phonetic signs *represent* sounds.	表示、代表 designate denote	**present**
repress v. rɪˈprɛs	She could not *repress* her emotions for too long.	抑制、鎮壓 curb quell	**press**(press)
reprieve* v. rɪˈpriv	The prisoner condemned to death was *reprieved*.	緩刑 postpone respite	priev(take)
reprimand v. ˈrɛprəˌmænd	The child had done something naughty and knew that she was going to be *reprimanded*.	申斥 reproach chide	prim(press)

單字·音標·詞類	例　　句	中譯·同義字	字源分析
reprisal* n. rɪˈpraɪzl̩	The enemy troops will make *reprisals* once they occupy the cities.	報復、報復之行爲 injury done by 　　injury received	pris(take)
reproach v. rɪˈprotʃ	She was *reproached* for being late.	責備、申斥 reprove reprehend	proach(near)
reprobate* v. ˈrɛprəˌbet	Every scheme recommended by one of them was *reprobated* by the other.	拒絕 reject exclude	prob(prove)
reproduce v. ˌriprəˈdjus	Actors *reproduce* the sounds of running horses by pounding pillows.	複製、倣造 repeat copy	**produce**
reprove v. rɪˈpruv	It is embarrassing to hear the children being so sternly *reproved*.	責罵、譴責 chide reprimand	prove
repugnant* a. rɪˈpʌgnənt	They have found the idea thoroughly *repugnant*.	令人厭棄的 repulsive loathsome	pugn(fight)
repulse v. rɪˈpʌls	The tourists were *repulsed* by the sight of the dead crocodile.	使厭惡、拒絕、逐退 reject repel	**puls(push)**
repute n. rɪˈpjut	Only a general of *repute* could get recruits.	美名、名聲、高位 status distinction	put(think)

單字・音標・詞類	例　　　句	中譯・同義字	字源分析
request n. rɪˈkwɛst	The storekeeper said this was a book in great *request*.	需要 demand desire	quest(ask)
v.	The managers have *requested* the board for an opinion.	要求 ask demand	
require v. rɪˈkwaɪr	Growing children *require* more food.	需要、要求 need beseech	quir(ask)
requisite a. ˈrɛkwəzɪt	We need everything *requisite* for the long journey.	需要、必要的 needful indispensable	quis(ask)
requite v. rɪˈkwaɪt	The traitor was *requited* with death.	回報、報酬、報復 reward retaliate	quite(quit)
rescind* v. rɪˈsɪnd	The commander refused to *rescind* his harsh order.	撤銷、廢除 repeal revoke	scind(cut)
rescue v. ˈrɛskju	The men in the fire were *rescued* by the firemen.	解救 save extricate	ex(out) cue(shake)
n.	His brave *rescue* of the cat on the tree was applauded by the neighbors.	解救 liberation deliverance	
research n. ˈrisɝtʃ	His *research* has been a great failure.	研究、調查 study investigation	search

單字‧音標‧詞類	例　　　　句	中譯‧同義字	字源分析
resemble v. rɪˈzɛmbļ	These sisters *resemble* one another.	相似 be similar to	semble(similar)
resent v. rɪˈzɛnt	The dog seems to *resent* seeing anyone standing in front of it.	厭惡、憎惡 dislike hate	**sent**(feel)
reserve v. rɪˈzɝv	*Reserve* enough money for your fare home.	儲備、保留 keep retain	serv(keep)
residual a. rɪˈzɪdʒʊəl	A *residual* quantity of the insecticide on vegetables might cause harm.	殘餘、剩餘的 remaining additional	**residue**
residue n. ˈrɛzəˌdju	The syrup had dried up, leaving a sticky *residue*.	渣滓、剩餘 remainder surplus	**sid**(sit)
resign v. rɪˈzaɪn	They have *resigned* all their rights in the property.	放棄 relinquish renounce	sign
v.	The actress had finally *resigned* herself to playing a minor role.	順從 yield submit	
resilient* a. rɪˈzɪlɪənt	They enjoy watching the *resilient* bodies of the gymnasts.	有彈力、有彈性的 springy elastic	**sil**(leap)
resist v. rɪˈzɪst	A monk must be able to *resist* any worldly temptation.	抵抗、對抗 confront thwart	**sist**(stand)

單字・音標・詞類	例　　　句	中譯・同義字	字源分析
resolute a. ˈrɛzəˌlut	A commander must be *resolute* in giving out orders.	堅決、果斷的 determined persevering	solu(loosen)
resolve v. rɪˈzɑlv	He *resolved* to do better work even when he had failed.	決心 intend purpose	solv(loosen)
v.	Water can be *resolved* into oxygen and hydrogen.	分解 melt resolve	
v.	They have tried to *resolve* all their doubts and difficulties.	解決 settle disentangle	
resonant a. ˈrɛzṇənt	The *resonant* beauty of the writer's prose is greatly relished.	回響、宏亮的 resounding reverberating	son(sound)
resort v. rɪˈzɔrt	Should all other means fail, we shall *resort* to force.	訴諸 go turn	sort(leave)
n.	An appeal to his uncle seemed to be his last *resort*.	手段、憑藉 resource expedient	
n.	A park is a place of popular *resort* in good weather.	常去之處 haunt retreat	
resound v. rɪˈzaʊnd	The room *resounded* with the children's shouts.	充滿聲音、回響 echo reverberate	sound

單字·音標·詞類	例　　　句	中譯·同義字	字源分析
resource n. rɪˈsors	This country has rich natural *resources*.	資源、富源 means wealth	
n.	Her usual *resource* on such occasions was confession.	(應變的)手段、權宜之計、策略 expedient stratagem	
respect n. rɪˈspɛkt	She doesn't have much *respect* for her parents.	尊敬 regard reverence	**spect**(watch)
n.	What you have done is wrong in every *respect*.	方面、細事 particular detail	
respite n. ˈrɛspɪt	The slaves toiled without any *respite*.	休息、中止 rest cessation	**spite**(watch)
resplendent* a. rɪˈsplɛndənt	She looks *resplendent* in her evening gown.	華麗、輝煌的 glorious gleaming	**splend**(shine)
respond v. rɪˈspɑnd	How did she *respond* to your marriage proposal?	回答 answer reply	**spond**(pledge)
responsible a. rɪˈspɑnsəbl̩	I am not *responsible* for anything she says.	負責任的 answerable liable	**spons**(pledge)
restitution* n. ˌrɛstəˈtjuʃən	It is only fair that those who do the damage should make *restitution*.	賠償 reparation amends	**stitut**(stand)

單字·音標·詞類	例　　句	中譯·同義字	字源分析
restore v. rɪˈstor	Harmony was finally *restored* among the foes.	恢復、重建 recover reconstruct	**sta**(stand)
restrain v. rɪˈstren	She could not *restrain* her curiosity and opened the closet.	抑制、約束 repress bridle	**strain**(stretch)
restrict v. rɪˈstrɪkt	Our club membership is *restricted* to twenty.	限制 limit confine	**strict**(stretch)
result n. rɪˈzʌlt	Have you seen the baseball *results*?	結果 outcome consequence	**sult**(leap)
resume v. rɪˈzum	It is sad to see him already *resuming* his old habits.	重拾、重開始 restart recommence	**sum**(take)
resurgent * a. rɪˈsɝdʒənt	Nationalism is a powerful, even a *resurgent* force.	復活、再起的 rising again	**surg**(rise)
resurrection * n. ˌrɛzəˈrɛkʃən	The *resurrection* of hope was soon re-pressed.	復活、復興 revival resurgence	**surg**(rise)
retain v. rɪˈten	Modern mammals *retain* the egg within the body after fertilization.	保留 preserve withhold	**tain**(hold)
retaliate v. rɪˈtælɪˌet	They will *retaliate* if we insult them.	報復 avenge requite	**tali**(talion)

單字・音標・詞類	例　　　　句	中譯・同義字	字源分析
retard v. rɪˈtɑrd	Language can either help or *retard* us in our exploration of experience.	阻礙 hamper stunt	trad(late)
reticent * a. ˈrɛtəsn̩t	Her relatives all remained *reticent* on what had happened.	沈默寡言的 silent taciturn	tic(silent)
retire v. rɪˈtaɪr	He *retired* at the age of sixty-five.	退休 depart withdraw	tir(draw)
v.	You could either remain at table or *retire* to the library with the host.	告退、離去 recede retreat	
retort v. rɪˈtɔrt	She *retorted* her brother's question by another question.	回答 respond rejoin	**tort**(twist)
v.	There exists in animals the impulse to *retort* upon offenders.	報復、回報 answer retaliate	
retract v. rɪˈtrækt	A cat can *retract* its claws.	縮回 withdraw	**tract**(draw)
v.	They *retracted* everything they had previously said.	收回 revoke rescind	
retreat n. rɪˈtrit	The army was in full *retreat*.	撤退 departure withdrawal	**treat**(draw)

單字·音標·詞類	例　　　句	中譯·同義字	字源分析
v.	The enemy *retreated* after we had counter-attacked.	撤退 retire withdraw	
retrench v. rɪˈtrɛntʃ	They have *retrenched* their annual expenses.	節省、減少 reduce curtail	trench(cut)
retribution* n. ˌrɛtrəˈbjuʃən	It is not right to interpret justice in terms of *retribution*.	報應、報復 retaliation requital	tribu(pay)
retrieve v. rɪˈtriv	A Greek sculpture *retrieved* from the ruins of Roman Carthage is on display.	救出、重獲、恢復 regain restore	trieve(find)
return v. rɪˈtɝn	Her memories of the past kept *returning* to her.	再回到、重新浮現 recur remit	turn
reunion n. riˈjunjən	The parted friends all anticipated a *reunion*.	聚會、重聚 meeting get-together	**union**
reveal v. rɪˈvil	The rising curtain *revealed* a street scene.	顯現、揭露 disclose unveil	veal(veil)
revel v. ˈrɛvl	The townspeople celebrated and *reveled* the night away.	狂歡 make merry	bel(war)
revenge n. rɪˈvɛndʒ	The wronged man has been determined to have his *revenge*.	報仇、復仇 reprisal retaliation	veng(claim)

單字・音標・詞類	例　　　句	中譯・同義字	字源分析
v.	The boy had *revenged* his father's murder.	報復、報仇 avenge vindicate	
revenue n. ˈrɛvəˌnju	The government gets *revenue* from taxes.	國家之歲入、所得 income profits	**ven**(come)
reverberate v. rɪˈvɝbəˌret	The glaring light was *reverberated* by the mirror.	反射、回響 reflect resound	verber(beat)
revere v. rɪˈvɪr	The graduate students have been taught to *revere* those academic idols.	尊敬、尊崇 respect worship	vere(fear)
reverse v. rɪˈvɝs	Their positions are now *reversed*.	反轉、調換 alter transpose	**vers**(turn)
revert v. rɪˈvɝt	After the settlers left, the natives *reverted* to their savage customs.	重返、回想 return recur	**vert**(turn)
review v. rɪˈvju	The members of the committee will have to *review* the situation.	細察、觀察 reconsider scrutinize	**view**
n.	He writes book *reviews* for a newspaper.	評論 re-examination critique	

單字・音標・詞類	例　　　句	中譯・同義字	字源分析
revise v. rɪˈvaɪz	The manuscript must be *revised*.	校正 correct amend	**vis**(see)
revive v. rɪˈvaɪv	Old customs sometimes could *revive*.	再興、甦醒、使重現 awaken restore	**viv**(life)
revoke v. rɪˈvok	His licence was *revoked*.	取消、廢除 cancel repeal	**vok**(voice)
revolt v. rɪˈvolt	The peasants *revolted* against the corrupt regime.	反叛 rise rebel	**volt**(roll)
revolve v. rɪˈvɑlv	The idea continued to *revolve* in his mind.	沈思、旋轉 rotate meditate	**volv**(roll)
revulsion n. rɪˈvʌlʃən	When I knew of his cruelty, my feeling toward my new friend underwent a *revulsion*.	劇變、厭惡 reversal repulsion	**vuls**(pull)
reward n. rɪˈwɔrd	He did not receive much *reward* for what he had done.	報酬、賞金 bounty premium	ward(guard)
v.	The man was handsomely *rewarded* for informing the authorities of the conspiracy.	酬報 pay remunerate	

25

SE

away, separate

分離

字首 se 源出古拉丁文 (Old Latin) 副詞與介系詞 sē、sēd，原即有 away、separate 的意思。以這個字首組成的英文單字，幾盡直接由拉丁文借來，如 secede v.「脫離」出自 sēcēdere，seclude v.「使隔絕」出自 sēclūdere，secret a.「秘密的」出自 sēcrētus 等等。後接字根部分第一個音若是母音或 h 子音，則拼作 sed，否則一律拼成 se。但是，由 sed 組成的字並不多，下文例字內僅有 sedition n.「叛亂」一字，屬於這種情況。本節所收各例字，以 sever v.「切斷、分隔」較為特別。sever 與 separate v.「分離」同源，兩字均出自拉丁文 sēparāre。拉丁文的 sēparāre 進入古法文後，轉成 sevrer 和 severer 的形態，再於十四世紀借入英文，而成目前的 sever。這個轉變過程中，有 p 與 v 兩個子音的轉音現象。這種現象在很多語言裡都可見到，英文自不例外，如 recover v.「恢復、痊癒」與 recuperate v.「恢復、使恢復健康」，poverty n.「貧窮」與 pauper n.「貧民、窮人」等等，均是如此。

單字・音標・詞類	例　　　　句	中譯・同義字	字源分析
secede v. sɪˈsid	About ten more members have *seceded* from the political party.	脫離、退出 retire withdraw	**cede**(go)
seclude v. sɪˈklud	The lake is a *secluded* spot frequented by those interested in fishing.	使隔絕、使隔離 isolate segregate	**clud**(close)
secret a. ˈsikrɪt	The men have been out on a *secret* mission.	秘密、暗中的 covert clandestine	**cret**(sift)
secrete v. sɪˈkrit	The burglar has *secreted* the stolen goods.	隱藏 hide conceal	**cret**(sift)
v.	Glands in the mouth *secrete* saliva.	分泌 release discharge	
secure v. sɪˈkjʊr	The city *secured* itself against flood by strengthening the river banks.	保護、使安全 guard safeguard	**cur**(care)
v.	The traveler finally *secured* an inside room on one of the largest steamers.	獲得 obtain procure	
a.	The refugees were looking for a *secure* hiding place.	安全的 safe sheltered	

單字・音標・詞類	例　　　句	中譯・同義字	字源分析
sedition n. sɪˈdɪʃən	The cities were filled with *sedition* because of certain inequalities.	叛亂、暴動 revolt insurrection	it(go)
seduce v. sɪˈdjus	He was so rich that women always tried to *seduce* him.	勾引、誘惑 allure entice	duc(lead)
segregate v. ˈsɛgrɪ‚get	Municipal ordinances meant to *segregate* races were declared void.	隔離 separate dissociate	greg(group)
select v. səˈlɛkt	He was *selected* for the job.	挑選、選擇 choose option	lect(choose)
separate v. ˈsɛpə‚ret	Let's go and *separate* those two boys who are fighting.	分開、分離 disunite split	par(arrange)
a. ˈsɛpərɪt	Their children sleep in *separate* beds.	各別、分開、分離的 detached distinct	
sever v. ˈsɛvɚ	The theologian thinks that theology should be *severed* from philosophy.	區別、切斷、分隔 cleave sunder	separate

26

SUB·SUS

under

在下

sub、sus 也是相當重要的字首，出自拉丁文介系詞 sub，本即有 under 的意思。美國麻塞諸塞州 (Massachusetts)建州箴言 "Ēnse Petīt Placidam sub Lībertāte Quiētem" ("With the Sword She Seeks Quiet Peace Under Liberty")中，「在自由之下」sub Lībertāte這句話裏，便有介系詞 sub。後接的字根第一個字母若是 c、p、t 之一，經常拼成 sus 的形態，如下文的 susceptible a.「易受影響的」、suspend v.「懸掛、停止」、sustain v.「支持、忍受」等均是。此外，字根的第一個字母如果是 c、f、g、m、p、r，則經常同化成 suc、suf、sug、sum、sup、sur，如 succinct a.「簡明的」、suffice v.「足夠」、suggest v.「提議」、summon v.「召喚」、supple a.「柔軟的」、surrogate n.「代理者」等等皆是。其中尤須留意 sur 的拼法。sur 的形態組成的單字極少，但是另一字首 super「在上、超越」，却也有個「雙胞胎兄弟」sur（源出法文），拼法一模一樣，組成的單字却比上述的 sur「在下」多。尤須注意的是，兩個 sur 的意義「一上一下」，全然不同，極易看錯（請參閱本書「最重要的 30 個字首」27. super·sur）。

單字·音標·詞類	例　　　句	中譯·同義字	字源分析
subdivide v. ˌsʌbdəˈvaɪd	Bulkheads *subdivide* the ship into watertight compartments.	再分、細分 further divide	**divide**
subdue v. səbˈdju	The English forces were *subdued* by the Norman troops.	征服 conquer vanquish	**duc**(lead)
subject v. səbˈdʒɛkt	The primitive tribes were *subjected* to colonial rule.	使隸屬、使服從 dominate subjugate	**ject**(throw)
n. ˈsʌbdʒɪkt	The king and queen were kind and fair to their *subjects*.	臣民、在他人力量支配之下的人 dependent subordinate	
n.	The students were dicussing the *subject* of their essays.	主題、題目 topic theme	
subjoin* v. səbˈdʒɔɪn	Let me *subjoin* another example.	添加 annex append	**join**
subjugate* v. ˈsʌbdʒəˌget	The colonial powers *subjugated* the native tribes.	征服、抑制 overcome subdue	**jug**(yoke)
sublime a. səˈblaɪm	The maidens died in a *sublime* spirit of sacrifice.	崇高的 majestic exalted	**lim**(lintel)

單字·音標·詞類	例 句	中譯·同義字	字源分析
submarine a. ˌsʌbməˈrin	The botanist has been studying *submarine* plants for two decades.	海底的 undersea	marine
submerge v. səbˈmɝdʒ	The stream overflowed and *submerged* the suburban areas of the city.	淹沒、浸入水中 dip inundate	merge
submit v. səbˈmɪt	We shall never *submit* to slavery.	屈服、甘受 yield surrender	mit(send)
v.	The manager has *submitted* his plan to the chairman of the board.	提出 propose tender	
subordinate v. səˈbɔrdn̩ˌet	A polite host *subordinates* his wishes to those of his guests.	使居次要地位 、使服從 make subject 　or subservient	ordin(order)
a. səˈbɔrdn̩ɪt	In the army, captains are always *subordinate* to majors.	地位低於、下 級的 junior inferior	
n. səˈbɔrdn̩ɪt	The boss never trusts his *subordinates*.	屬下、部下 junior inferior	
subscribe v. səbˈskraɪb	He *subscribed* his name to the document.	簽名 sign	scrib(write)
v.	We found it impossible to *subscribe* to his unfair plan.	同意、贊同 assent consent	

單字·音標·詞類	例　　　　　句	中譯·同義字	字源分析
subsequent a. ˈsʌbsɪˌkwɛnt	Things had greatly improved in the period *subsequent* to the war.	隨後、繼起的 following ensuing	sequ(follow)
subservient* a. səbˈsɝvɪənt	The obstinate journalist was soon dismissed and replaced by a *subservient* one.	卑屈、阿諛的 subordinate servile	serve
subside v. səbˈsaɪd	The child's fever has *subsided*.	平息、消退 drop diminish	sid(sit)
subsidize v. ˈsʌbsəˌdaɪz	The steamship line was once *subsidized* by the government.	資助 support assist	sid(sit)
subsist v. səbˈsɪst	The town *subsisted* on the remaining mining activities.	賴…爲生、生存 exist endure	sist(stand)
substance n. ˈsʌbstəns	Ice and water are the same *substance* in different forms.	物質 material stuff	sta(stand)
n.	The professor's lecture lacked *substance*.	內容 meaning significance	
substantial a. səbˈstænʃəl	The stories told by the two different boys were in *substantial* agreement.	大體上、實質、眞實的 actual existent	substance

a.	The sick child has made *substantial* progress today.	重大、相當大、堅實的 massive solid	
substantiate v. səbˈstænʃɪˌet	Nobody would believe your charge unless it is *substantiated.*	證實、加強 confirm corroborate	**substance**
substitute v. ˈsʌbstəˌtjut	The lazy worker was finally *substituted.*	代替 replace change	**stitut**(stand)
n.	She couldn't find any sugar, so she used honey as a *substitute.*	代替物、代替者 replacement makeshift	
subsume* v. səbˈsum	Newtonian physics has not been overthrown so much as *subsumed* into a more embracing scheme.	包括 include summarize	**sum**(take)
subterfuge n. ˈsʌbtɚˌfjudʒ	She is always good at employing *subterfuges* to get her own way.	詭計、藉口 excuse pretext	**fug**(run)
subterraneous a. ˌsʌbtəˈrenɪəs	A *subterraneous* passage led from the castle to a brook.	地下的 underground	**terr**(earth)
subtract v. səbˈtrækt	*Subtract* 5 from 9 and you will have 4.	減去 remove deduct	**tract**(draw)

單字·音標·詞類	例　　　句	中譯·同義字	字源分析
suburb n. ˈsʌbɝb	The Nicholsons live in the *suburbs*.	城郊之住宅區、市郊 outskirts	urb(city)
subvert v. səbˈvɝt	These savage politicians have tried to *subvert* our form of government into a tyranny.	破壞、顛覆 overturn demolish	**vert**(turn)
succeed v. səkˈsid	They young prince *succeeded* his father as king.	繼位、繼承、跟著…而來 follow ensue	**ceed**(go)
v.	I didn't think that Laura would *succeed*.	成功 prosper flourish	
succinct a. səkˈsɪŋkt	The lady gave the young man a very *succinct* refusal.	簡明、簡潔的 concise laconic	cinct(gird)
succor * v. ˈsʌkɚ	An escort vessel was sent to *succor* the three vessels attacked by a submarine.	援助、幫助 help aid	**cur**(run)
succumb v. səˈkʌm	A free economic system may *succumb* to the strains of war.	屈服 yield submit	cumb(lie)
suffer v. ˈsʌfɚ	The man had *suffered* a year's imprisonment before being put to death.	遭受、忍受 undergo tolerate	**fer**(carry)

單字·音標·詞類	例　　句	中譯·同義字	字源分析
suffice v. səˈfaɪs	Ten bombs *sufficed* to destroy the fort.	足夠、使滿足 be enough content	**fic**(do)
sufficient a. səˈfɪʃənt	The efforts you make will never be *sufficient*.	足夠、充分的 enough adequate	**fic**(do)
suffocate v. ˈsʌfəˌket	She was *suffocating* in the hot little kitchen.	窒悶、窒息 choke stifle	foc(throat)
suffuse v. səˈfjuz	Her eyes were *suffused* with lovely tears.	充盈、布滿 fill flush	**fus**(pour)
suggest v. səgˈdʒɛst	Did you *suggest* anything to the boss?	提議 propose recommend	gest(carry)
summon v. ˈsʌmən	*Summoning* all his strength, he rose to speak.	召喚、鼓起 call rouse	mon(warn)
supplant v. səˈplænt	The pretty young wife found herself *supplanted* by a brisk, unlovely woman.	取而代之、代替 replace supersede	plant
supple a. ˈsʌpl	The artist's paintings are remarkably *supple* in line and pattern.	易曲、柔軟、流暢的 bending pliable	**plic**(fold)

| | a. | Her *supple* spirit is hidden under an external directness and rough assertion. | 善於適應、順從的
yielding
submissive | |

supplement n.
ˈsʌpləmənt

The encyclopedia was issued in fourteen volumes and subsequently kept up to date by annual *supplements*.

附刊、補遺
addition
appendix

supply

supplicate v.
ˈsʌplɪˌket

The slave fell on his knees and *supplicated* the master.

懇求
entreat
solicit

plic(fold)

supply v.
səˈplaɪ

The government *supplies* books for the school children.

供給
afford
furnish

ple(fill)

support v.
səˈport

Hope can always *support* a person in trouble.

幫助、支持
assist
uphold

port(carry)

suppose v.
səˈpoz

I don't *suppose* she will be able to come.

認為、假定
believe
assume

pos(place)

suppress v.
səˈprɛs

The uprising of the peasants has been completely *suppressed*.

平定、抑制
check
quell

press(press)

surrogate* n.
ˈsɝəgɪt

College presidents or their *surrogates* have appealed for a revival of idealism.

代理者
deputy
delegate

rog(elect)

單字・音標・詞類	例 句	中譯・同義字	字源分析
susceptible a. səˈsɛptəbḷ	He became *susceptible* to the influence of his brothers and sisters.	易受影響、敏感、易感的 sensitive impressionable	cep(receive)
suspect v. səˈspɛkt	We *suspected* that she was not telling the truth.	懷疑、猜想 doubt surmise	spect(watch)
suspend v. səˈspɛnd	A medallion was *suspending* from the man's neck.	懸掛、吊 hang attach	pend(hang)
v.	The bus service was *suspended* for two days because of the strike.	停止 cease arrest	
suspense n. səˈspɛns	For a few weeks matters still hung in *suspense*.	懸而未決 stop cessation	pens(hang)
n.	We waited in great *suspense* for the physician's opinion.	焦慮 anxiety apprehension	
suspicious a. səˈspɪʃəs	I seemed to see a *suspicious* look on her face as she turned to bid me good night.	表示懷疑、懷疑的 doubt skeptical	spic(watch)
sustain v. səˈsten	They had behind them none of those great organizations to *sustain* them.	支持 support uphold	

v.	The teacher wondered whether he could *sustain* another year's teaching.	忍受 tolerate endure	

SUPER·SUR

over, above

在上 • 超越

super 源自拉丁文副詞與介系詞 super ，sur 出自法文介系詞 sur（最早也是源自拉丁文的 super），均有 over、above 的意思。super 所組成的單字，部分借自拉丁文，部分在十七世紀之後，才被英國人以現成的字根或單字拼湊而成。sur 組成的單字，則幾盡從法文傳入，例如下文 sur 的例字中，直接由拉丁文借入的，只有 surreptitious a. 「秘密的」一字（拉丁文作 surruptīcius 或 surreptīcius）。super 組成的單字，不少是比較偏難少見的字彙，本節並未收錄，僅在此列出一些，供讀者參考：superaddition n. 「追加」、superannuation n. 「退休金」、superconductive a. 「超傳導現象的」、 supercool v. 「超低冷却」、 superego n. 「超自我」、superexcellent a. 「優秀的」、 superfine a. 「極細的」、supernormal a. 「超乎尋常的」、 superscribe v. 「題名」等等。

單字·音標·詞類	例　　　　　句	中譯·同義字	字源分析
superabundant a. ˌsupərəˈbʌndənt	The farmers did not know what to do with their *superabundant* crops.	過剩、過多的 excessive inordinate	**abundant**
superb a. suˈpɝb	He knows how to enjoy the *superb* masculinity of good Spanish dancing.	威嚴、宏偉、絕佳的 splendid magnificent	
supercilious a. ˌsupɚˈsɪlɪəs	His lips curled in a *supercilious* smile.	輕蔑、傲慢的 haughty disdainful	cili(eyelid)
superficial a. ˌsupɚˈfɪʃəl	Light can penetrate the *superficial* layers of water.	表面的 surface	fic(face)
a.	The newspapers' *superficial* reports never gave the true picture.	膚淺的 shallow merely apparent	
superfluous a. suˈpɝfluəs	In writing telegrams, it is important to omit *superfluous* words.	不必要、過多的 excessive redundant	flu(flow)
superimpose＊ v. ˌsupərɪmˈpoz	He has *superimposed* new habits upon his old ones.	置於他物之上、附加 overlay attach	impose
superintend v. ˌsuprɪnˈtɛnd	They have formed a committee on finance to *superintend* all appropriations.	管理、監督 supervise inspect	intend

單字·音標·詞類	例　　　句	中譯·同義字	字源分析
superior a. sə'pɪrɪə	The wisdom derived from experience is usually *superior*.	較高、較好的 better higher	
superlative* a. sə'pɝlətɪv	These young artists are men of *superlative* talent and character.	最高、無上的 excellent peerless	lat(carry)
supernal* a. su'pɝnḷ	The plague was interpreted as a *supernal* punishment from heaven for men's sins.	天上、神聖的 heavenly celestial	
supernatural a. ˌsupɚ'nætʃrəl	Nobody could quite understand the *supernatural* character of the soul.	超自然、神奇的 miraculous occult	natural
supersede v. ˌsupɚ'sid	This brief account is intended to *supersede* the necessity of a long and minute detail.	取代、替代 replace substitute	sed(sit)
superstition n. ˌsupɚ'stɪʃən	It is a *superstition* to believe a black cat crossing one's path portends bad luck.	迷信 irrational 　belief	stitut(stand)
supervene* v. ˌsupɚ'vin	What generaly spoils long novels is the untimely *supervening* creative fatigue.	接著來、繼起 、隨著發生 follow come unexpectedly	ven(come)
supervise v. ˌsupɚ'vaɪz	The government sent a man to *supervise* the newspaper's domestic correspondents.	監督、管理 inspect superintend	vis(see)

單字・音標・詞類	例　句	中譯・同義字	字源分析
supremacy n. səˈprɛməsɪ	The fleets have gained the naval *supremacy* in this region of the ocean.	霸權、至高權力 domination sovereignty	**supreme**
supreme a. səˈprim	The soldiers were urged to make the *supreme* sacrifice in the field of battle.	極大、至高的 foremost paramount	
surcharge n. ˈsɝˌtʃɑrdʒ	There is no *surcharge* for the jet airplane service.	額外的索價 extra charge	charge
surface n. ˈsɝfɪs	The men have been staring at the *surface* of the water for hours.	表面 face exterior	face
surfeit n. ˈsɝfɪt	The old man died of a *surfeit* of sprats.	飲食過度、過量 excess superfluity	**feit**(do)
v.	The writer thought the public was already *surfeited* with non-sensical anecdotes.	使生厭、使饜足 cram gorge	
surmise v. sɝˈmaɪz	He *surmised* that this was the true situation.	臆測、猜度 guess conjecture	**mis**(send)
surmount v. sɝˈmaʊnt	We must always learn how to *surmount* an obstacle.	克服、勝過 overcome surpass	mount

單字·音標·詞類	例　　　句	中譯·同義字	字源分析
surname n. ˈsɝˌnem	Do you know Janet's *surname*?	姓 family name	name
surpass v. sɚˈpæs	The reality *surpassed* all expectations.	超越、勝過 surmount transcend	pass
surplus n. ˈsɝplʌs	We had a budget *surplus* this year.	盈餘、剩餘、 過剩 residue surfeit	plus
surprise v. səˈpraɪz	I was not *surprised* to see you here at all.	使驚奇、使吃 驚 stun astonish	pris(take)
surrender v. səˈrɛndɚ	The bandits finally *surrendered* to the police.	投降、降服 submit succumb	render
surreptitious* a. ˌsɝəpˈtɪʃəs	The abbot had made a *surreptitious* copy of the text.	秘密、偷盜的 furtive clandestine	rap(seize)
surround v. səˈraʊnd	The resisting force was *surrounded* by enemy troops swarming from all sides.	包圍 environ besiege	round
surroundings n. səˌraʊndɪŋz pl.	The young man is extraordinarily un-interested in his physical *surroundings*.	環境 environment	**surround**

單字・音標・詞類	例　　　　　句	中譯・同義字	字源分析
surveillance n. səˈveləns	The suspected person was placed under police *surveillance.*	監視、看守 inspection vigilance	veill(watch)
survey n. ˈsɝve	The commissioner shall make a *survey* of the situation.	調查、審度 inspection scrutiny	vey(see)
v. sɝˈve	The critic has *surveyed* almost the whole mass of contemporary literature.	通盤考慮、逐點說明 examine scan	
survive v. səˈvaɪv	Only one of his sons *survived* him.	生命較…爲長 outlast outlive	viv(life)
v.	The secret agents are men trained to *survive* under severe conditions.	繼續生存 last endure	

SYM·SYN

with, together

一起 • 共同

字首 sym、syn 源出希臘文副詞與介系詞 συν (syn)，原義即爲 with、together。除了上述 sym、syn 的拼法，也可拼作 sy、syl。後接字根的第一個字母若是 p、b、m 三個雙唇音之一，拼作 sym，以雙唇音連接雙唇音，方便發音，如下文的 sympathy n.「同情」、symposium n.「座談會」等便是如此。字根的第一個字母若是 s，則拼作 sy，如 system n.「制度」便是；若是 l，則同化成 syl，如 syllabus n.「大綱」。其餘情況均作 syn。不過，sy、syl 的形態並不多見，因此仍然以 sym 和 syn 較爲重要。下文例字的 symposium 出自拉丁文 symposium，拉丁文又出自希臘文 συμποσιον (symposion)，字根 pos (ποσις [posis] n.) 有「飲酒」的意思，因此原希臘、拉丁文都作「酒宴」。英文除有「酒宴」的意思之外，十八世紀以後，更引申而成「座談會」（可把酒言歡的場合）。這個字首組成的單字，除了下文所列的字彙外，尚有 syllable n.「音節」、symphony n.「交響樂」、synonym n.「同義字」、symbiosis n.「共棲」、syncretize v.「使融合」、synod n.「宗教會議」、syntax n.「構句法」等等。

單字・音標・詞類	例　　　句	中譯・同義字	字源分析
syllabus* n. ˈsɪləbəs	The guide has prepared a complete historical *syllabus* for each tour.	大要、大綱 summary of 　outline	labus(book 　label)
symbol n. ˈsɪmb!	The dove is a *symbol* of peace.	象徵 sign token	bol(throw)
symmetry n. ˈsɪmɪtrɪ	A swollen cheek spoiled the *symmetry* of his face.	勻稱、對稱 balance proportion	metr(measure)
sympathy n. ˌsɪmpəθɪ	Please have some *sympathy* for me, sir.	同情 pity compassion	**path**(feeling)
symposium* n. sɪmˈpozɪəm	The department is going to hold a *symposium* on the topic.	座談會 meeting discussion	pos(drinking)
symptom n. ˈsɪmptəm	What are the *symptoms* of AIDS?	徵候、表徵 sign indication	ptom(fall)
synchronize* v. ˈsɪŋkrəˌnaɪz	Action and sound must *synchronize* perfectly.	同時發生 happen 　simultaneously	chron(time)
synchronous* a. ˈsɪŋkrənəs	His recovery was *synchronous* with the therapy.	同時發生的 simultaneous contemporary	chron(time)
syndicate n. ˈsɪndɪkɪt	The real estate men formed a *syndicate* to buy an office building.	企業組合 business group cartel	

單字·音標·詞類	例　　句	中譯·同義字	字源分析
syndrome n. ˈsɪndrəˌmɪ	Schizophrenia is a *syndrome* related to a variety of etiological factors.	綜合病徵 group of 　symptoms	drom(run)
synopsis * n. sɪˈnɑpsɪs	The bilologist is told to make a *synopsis* of his report.	綱領、要略 abridgment abstract	ops(see)
synthesis n. ˈsɪnθəsɪs	A summa is a *synthesis* of the philosophy of an age.	綜合 combination mixture	the(place)
synthetic a. sɪnˈθɛtɪk	She wrote a book on natural and *synthetic* dyes.	人造的 man-made artificial	**synthesis**
system n. ˈsɪstəm	The ministry has long decided to reform the educational *system*.	制度、組織、系統 organism network	histan(set)

TRANS

across, through, over

橫跨 ● 貫通 ● 轉變

trans 源自拉丁文介系詞 trāns，原義即爲 across、through、over。除了 trans 的拼法之外，另有 tran、tra、tres 三種形態。後面所接的字根第一個字母若是 s，拼作 tran，使兩個 s 子音同化成一個 s，如下文的 transcend v.「超越」、transpire v.「蒸發」等均是。字根的第一個字母如果是 v，則拼作 tra，如 traverse v.「橫越」、travesty n.「諧謔化」均是。其餘情況均拼作 trans 的形態。tres 的拼法相當特別。拉丁文的 trans 在古法文作 tres（現代法文作 très adv.，已引申爲「非常」的意思），古法文的 trespasser v.「橫越」進入英文，便搖身變成了 trespass。下文例字中的 travesty，原由法文借入，字根 vest 有「穿衣」的意思（拉丁文作 vestīre），最初指「刻意裝扮以引來嘲笑」，後來轉成了「諧謔、使滑稽」的意思。

transact v. træns'ækt	He *transacts* with stores all over the country.	處理、交易 conduct negotiate	**act**
transcend v. træn'sɛnd	To possess by self-mastery the sources of love and hate is to *transcend* good and evil.	超越、勝過 outstrip eclipse	**scend**(climb)
transcribe v. træn'skraɪb	His entire speech was *transcribed* in the newspaper.	刊印、抄寫 copy summarize	**scrib**(write)
transfer v. træns'fɝ	He was *transferred* to another department.	調職、遷移、移轉 displace shift	**fer**(carry)
n. 'trænsfɝ	He wanted a *transfer* to a better college.	遷移、調職 change advance	
transfix v. træns'fɪks	He *transfixed* the boar with his spear.	刺穿、刺住 pierce impale	**fix**(fix)
transform v. træns'fɔrm	For a moment the smile *transformed* his once stern face.	改變 alter convert	**form**
transfuse v. træns'fjuz	The philosopher seeks to *transfuse* his ideas throughout the land.	灌輸 transmit instill	**fus**(pour)

單字・音標・詞類	例　　　　　句	中譯・同義字	字源分析
transgress* v. trænsˈgrɛs	These exotic birds can migrate and *transgress* their natural climatic barriers.	踰越、違反、 違背 trespass infringe	**gress**(go)
transient a. ˈtrænʃənt	The hotel accommodates only *transient* guests.	過路、短暫的 temporary transitory	**it**(go)
transit v. ˈtrænsɪt	They expect the planet to *transit* shortly after midnight.	通過、經過 cross traverse	**it**(go)
n.	He wrote an article on the *transit* of radio signals from the earth to the moon and back.	通過、變遷 passage change	
transitory a. ˈtrænsəˌtorɪ	Thoughts are illusive, *transitory,* thin shadows of reality.	短暫、一時的 fleeting ephemeral	**it**(go)
translate v. trænsˈlet	The schoolboys had learned to *translate* Latin.	翻譯、解說 render paraphrase	**lat**(carry)
transliterate* v. trænsˈlɪtəˌret	The scholar could *transliterate* Sanskrit words with Roman letters.	音譯 write in the 　letters of another 　alphabet	**liter**(letter)
translucent* a. trænsˈlusn̩t	She was amused by the *translucent* rays of the morning sun.	半透明的 penetrating transparent	**luc**(light)

單字·音標·詞類	例　　　　句	中譯·同義字	字源分析
transmit v. træns'mɪt	Rats *transmit* disease.	傳播、傳達 transfer convey	**mit**(send)
transmute * v. træns'mjut	Energy converts into matter as naturally as matter *transmutes* into energy.	使變化 transform convert	mut(change)
transparent a. træns'pɛrənt	This plastic is more *transparent* than even high-quality plate glass.	透明、明晰的 sheer pellucid	par(appear)
transpire v. træn'spaɪr	A plant *transpires* more freely on a hot dry day.	發散水分、蒸發 exhale evaporate	spir(breathe)
transplant v. træns'plænt	He reported that cancer tissues can be *transplanted* from man to other animals.	移植、使遷徙 transfer transport	plant
transport v. træns'port	Wheat is *transported* from the farms to the mills.	運送 remove transfer	**port**(carry)
transpose v. træns'poz	The letters were *transposed* to change the spelling.	置換、改換位置 interchange shift	**pos**(place)
traverse v. 'trævɚs	They were walking the streets they had *traversed* two nights before.	橫越 cross pass	**vers**(turn)

單字‧音標‧詞類	例　　　　句	中譯‧同義字	字源分析
v.	I accept nobody's precepts *traversing* my own moral freedom.	妨礙、反對 contravene thwart	
travesty n. ˈtrævɪstɪ	To me the trial was a *travesty* of justice.	歪曲、諧謔化 mockery parody	vest(dress)
v.	To *travesty* human nature without cruelty is a great and wonder act.	使滑稽化 disguise parody	
trespass v. ˈtrɛspəs	The farmers were bothered by hunters *trespassing* on their fields.	侵入、侵犯 encroach infringe	pass

30

UNI

one

單一

　　字首uni 源自拉丁文形容詞ūnus，原義即為 one 。uni 的拼法原在拉丁文，已視作字首；後面所接的字根第一個音若是母音，則改拼成un，如下文列舉的unanimous a.「意見一致的」便是一例。下文例字中的 universe n.「宇宙」（拉丁文作 ūniversitās n.f. ），字根 vers 有「轉」的意思，「將萬物轉成一體」，自然變成「宇宙」的意思；形容詞universal指「萬物皆適用」，因而便有了「共同、普遍」的意思。由 uni 組成的單字尚有一些不屬常用字彙範圍，下文例字內不收，僅在此列出，供讀者參考： unicorn n.「獨角獸」、 unifoliate a.「單葉的」、unilingual a.「只用一個語言的」、unipolar a.「單極的」等 。　　　　　　　　　　　　。

單字・音標・詞類	例　　　句	中譯・同義字	字源分析
unanimous a. jʊˈnænəməs	The members of the council were *unanimous* in their approval of the report.	一致、意見 一致的 agreeing consentient	**anim**(mind)
uniform a. ˈjunəˌfɔrm	Great Russia has many dialects, but for so widespread a language it is still remarkably *uniform*.	一致、相同的 regular consistent	form
unify v. ˈjunəˌfaɪ	It would be impossible to *unify* the world and abolish war.	統一 integrate consolidate	
union n. ˈjunjən	The *union* between the two countries will be effected in the future.	聯合、同盟 combination alliance	
unique a. juˈnik	The painter was famous for his *unique* style.	獨特的 unusual exceptional	
unison* n. ˈjunəzn̩	The members of the chorus sang in perfect *unison*.	同音、一致、 和諧 harmony concord	son(sound)
unit n. ˈjunɪt	The family is a social *unit*.	單位、一個 one basic quantity	
unite v. jʊˈnaɪt	A dirt road *unites* the farm road with the main highway.	連接、結合、 聯合 connect coalesce	

單字·音標·詞類	例　　　句	中譯·同義字	字源分析
unity n. ˈjunətɪ	The father tried to make his sons understand the strength that lied in *unity*.	和諧、統一 oneness harmony	
universal a. ˌjunəˈvɝsḷ	Food is a *universal* need of living beings.	共同、普遍的 general all-embracing	vers(turn)
universe n. ˈjunəˌvɝs	Our world is only a small part of the *universe*.	宇宙 cosmos	vers(turn)

最重要的70個字根

ACT·AG·IG

act, drive

行動 ● 推動

　　字根 act、ag、ig源出拉丁文動詞agere，原即有 act、drive 的意思。act 的拼法出自 agere 的過去分詞 āctus 與名詞 āctiō，ig 則是加字首組字時的變體，下文例字中僅有exigency n.「緊急情況」、exigent a.「緊急的」、prodigal a.「揮霍、奢侈的」三個字，以ig組成。agenda n.「議程」源自拉丁文 agendum，有 things to be done 的意思，進入英文後曾有 agend 的拼法，但現今已作廢。cogent a.「使人信服的」，源出拉丁文動詞 cōgere「推進、逼迫」，字首 co「一起」與字根配合，便形成「強迫相信」的意思。prodigal 源自拉丁文形容詞 prōdigus，本即有「揮霍、奢侈」的意思，字首prod 是 pro「向前」比較早期的拼法（參見本書「最重要的30個字首」**23. pro·pur**)，因此配合字根之後，「向前不斷推動」，花錢如流水般，自然浪費了。

單字・音標・詞類	例　　　　句	中譯・同義字	字源分析
act n. æk t	He admitted that he had conducted an *act* of folly.	行爲 performance deed	
v.	One must think carefully before *acting*.	行動 do enact	
v.	She began *acting* as a child of eight.	扮演 perform personate	
action n. ˈækʃən	The machine has been in *action* for days.	動作、行動 activity operation	act
activate v. ˈæktə͵vet	His work was not final, yet it attracted and *activated* others.	使活動、使活躍 make active	active
active a. ˈæktɪv	Mr. Hughes is an *active* member of our club.	活躍、活潑、有力的 energetic vigorous	
activity n. ækˈtɪvətɪ	She did not care much for social *activities*.	活動 action	active
actual a. ˈæktʃʊəl	What is the *actual* situation of the country now?	實際、眞實的 genuine substantial	
actualize v. ˈæktʃʊəl͵aɪz	He was placed in a position calculated to *actualize* his worst potentialities.	實現、實行 make realistic	actual

單字·音標·詞類	例 句	中譯·同義字	字源分析
actuate v. ˈæktʃʊˌet	What are the motives that have *actuated* these religious fanatics?	驅使、激勵 incite animate	
agenda n. əˈdʒɛndə	He sent out an *agenda* before each meeting.	議程 items to be 　　acted upon	
agent n. ˈedʒənt	Chromic acid is an oxidizing *agent*.	代理人、作用 物 actor performer	
n.	He is our company's *agent* in Los Angeles.	代表 representive promoter	
agile a. ˈædʒəl	I saw her bounding down the rocky slope like some wild, *agile* creature.	動作敏捷、輕 快的 nimble brisk	
agitate v. ˈædʒəˌtet	They carried on a discussion which could *agitate* many thinkers on earth.	擾亂、激動、 鼓動 stir rouse	
cogent* a. ˈkodʒənt	The man is able to write *cogent* and expert briefs.	中肯、使人信 服的 convincing compelling	co(together)
counteract v. ˌkaʊntəˈækt	The effect of his preaching was *counteracted* by the looseness of his behavior.	抵消、抵制 check offset	**counter** (against)

單字·音標·詞類	例　　　　句	中譯·同義字	字源分析
enact v. ɪnˈækt	This scene will be *enacted* in a court room.	演出、扮演 act perform	en(in)
exact v. ɪgˈzækt	A task so delicate as this might *exact* the scholar and the philosopher.	需要、強索 extort wring	ex(out)
a.	What was her *exact* response to Tom's proposal?	精確、正確的 precise faithful	
exacting a. ɪgˈzæktɪŋ	It is difficult to get along well with an *exacting* employer.	嚴厲的 strict severe	exact
exigency* n. ˈɛksədʒənsɪ	The president is the sole judge of the *exigency* demanding the use of federal troops.	緊急情況 urgency juncture	ex(out)
exigent* a. ˈɛksədʒənt	The critic regarded literary questions as *exigent* and momentous.	緊急、急需的 pressing exacting	ex(out)
inaction n. ɪnˈækʃən	The writer showed his utmost impatience with the hypocrisy and *inaction* of the bureaucrats.	不活動、怠惰 idleness lethargy	in(not)
inactive a. ɪnˈæktɪv	The citizens are not satisfied with the *inactive* police chief.	不活動、懶惰的 idle inert	in(not)

單字·音標·詞類	例　句	中譯·同義字	字源分析
interact v. ˌɪntɚˈækt	Such discoveries and inventions were made by many generations of *interacting* human beings.	交互作用、相互影響 have reciprocal effect	**inter**(between)
prodigal* a. ˈprɑdɪg‖	The millionaire's son had been too *prodigal* with his money.	揮霍、奢侈的 extravagant lavish	**pro**(forward)
react v. rɪˈækt	Dogs *react* to kindness by showing affection.	反應 respond	**re**(back)
transact v. trænsˈækt	Such business must be solely *transacted* by experts.	處理、執行 perform execute	**trans**(through)

2

ANIM

breath, mind

氣息 ● 心

　　anim 源出拉丁文兩個名詞 anima「呼吸」和 animus「心、精神」，因此有兩種不同的解釋。美國南卡羅萊納州(South Carolina)的建州箴言 "Animīs Opībusque Parātī" ("Prepared in Spirit and Wealth")中，便有 animus「精神」的格變化 animīs。下文例字中的 animus n.「仇恨」，形態與上述拉丁文 animus 相同，原即借自拉丁文，於十九世紀左右已有「仇恨」的字義。另一字 animosity n.「怨恨」，意思雖然與 animus 相似，字源却是法文的 animosité，十五世紀時已進入英文。unanimous a.「意見一致的」組合的方式比較特別。字首看似 un「否定」，其實却是 uni「一」，因此才有「心一致」，以至於「意見一致」的意思（請參閱本書「最重要的 30個字首」**30. uni** 部分）。由 anim 組成的單字，有些不屬常用字彙範圍，僅列出如下以供參考：animal n.「動物」、animism n.「萬物有靈論」、animalcule n.「微生動物」等。

單字・音標・詞類	例　句	中譯・同義字	字源分析
animate v. ˈænəˌmet	What is the mysterious vital force that *animates* the cells of the body?	使有生命、使活潑 enliven vivify	
a. ˈænəmɪt	The swiftly flowing river was the only thing *animate* in the valley.	有生命、活的 living moving	
animosity n. ˌænəˈmɑsətɪ	Only the most bitter people would show growling, snarling *animosity* towards anyone.	憎惡、怨恨 enmity acrimony	
animus* n. ˈænəməs	The wronged woman said these words calmly and without *animus*.	仇恨、敵意 hostility animosity	
equanimity* n. ˌikwəˈnɪmətɪ	In the inner life the rational soul may cultivate *equanimity* in defiance of all outward circumstances.	鎮定、平靜 composure serenity	**equ**(equal)
inanimate a. ɪnˈænəmɪt	Her movement is *inanimate* on the stage.	無生氣、單調的 lifeless dull	**animate**
magnanimity* n. ˌmægnəˈnɪmətɪ	Nothing pays richer dividends than *magnanimity*.	慷慨、高尚 nobleness generosity of mind	**magn**(great)

單字·音標·詞類	例　　句	中譯·同義字	字源分析
magnanimous* a. mæg¹nænəməs	Even his enemies admitted that he was *magnanimous* to the point of knight-errantry.	心地高尚、度量寬大的 forgiving noble	**magn**(great)
pusillanimous* a. ͵pjusl¹ænəməs	The committee's policy of watchful waiting was denounced as *pusillanimous.*	懦弱、膽怯的 cowardly timid	pusill(tiny)
unanimous a. jʊ¹nænəməs	The assembly was *unanimous.*	意見一致、全體一致的 one-minded concordant	**uni**(one)

3

CAD·CAS·CID

fall

降落 ● 降臨

　　字根 cad、cas 、cid 源出拉丁文動詞 cadere，本即有 fall 的意思。cas 的拼法來自 cadere 的過去分詞 casūrus，cid 則來自過去簡單式的 cecidī。由這個字根組成的單字，小部分帶有「降落」的意義，如 cascade n.「小瀑布」和 decadence n.「墮落」，大部分則含有「命運臨頭」的隱義，如 accident n.「意外之事」、case n.「狀況」、casual a.「隨便、偶然的」等均是。 cadence n.「韻律」的形態源自法文的 cadence，指「樂音的滑落」，因此不難想出有「韻律」的意思。 decay v.「衰微」的拼法在各例字中比較特別。 decay 源出古法文 decair（現代法文作 déchoir ），因此字源雖然仍是拉丁文的字首 de 與動詞 cadere，但形態已和其他單字略有不同。

單字·音標·詞類	例　　　句	中譯·同義字	字源分析
accident n. ˈæksədənt	Their parents both died in the traffic *accident*.	意外之事、災害 misfortune calamity	ac(to)
accidental a. ˌæksəˈdɛntl̩	Our meeting was quite *accidental*.	偶然、無意、附屬的 unpredicted contingent	accident
cadence* n. ˈkedn̩s	His magnificent style lies in the grand *cadence* of his poetry.	韻律 flow of rhythm	
cascade* n. kæsˈked	A *cascade* is a fall of water over steeply slanting rocks.	小瀑布 waterfall	
v.	The water *cascaded* a flight of steps and spilled into the street.	像瀑布般落下 fall	
case n. kes	I will not agree in any *case*.	狀況、場合 situation circumstance	
casual a. ˈkæʒʊəl	I want a clear, definite answer, not a *casual* one.	隨便、偶然的 random haphazard	
casualty n. ˈkæʒʊəltɪ	We had *casualties* at sea during the storm.	死傷(人數)、災禍 disaster mishap	casual

單字‧音標‧詞類	例　　　句	中譯‧同義字	字源分析
coincide v. ˌko·ɪnˈsaɪd	The fall of Granada *coincided* with the discovery of America.	時間上相合、一致、符合 concur correspond	**co**(together) **in**(on)
coincidence n. koˈɪnsədəns	It was a *coincidence* that they released two versions of the work simultaneously.	一致、相合、巧合之事 accidental 　occurrence	**coincide**
decadence n. dɪˈkedn̩s	The *decadence* of morals is bad for a nation.	墮落、衰落 decline degeneration	**de**(away)
decay v. dɪˈke	What made the Roman Empire *decay*?	衰微、衰弱 decline degenerate	**de**(away)
n.	The puritans saw a rapid *decay* of moral standards.	衰敗、衰弱 falling deterioration	
deciduous * a. dɪˈsɪdʒʊəs	The antlers of deers are *deciduous*.	(按季節或生長期) 脫落的 falling off at a 　certain season	**de**(away)
incidence * n. ˈɪnsədəns	In an epidemic the *incidence* of a disease is widespread.	影響範圍 range of effect	**in**(on)
incident n. ˈɪnsədənt	Conflict is an inevitable *incident* in any active system of cooperation.	事件 happening occurrence	**in**(on)

單字・音標・詞類	例　　　句	中譯・同義字	字源分析
incidental a. ˌɪnsəˈdɛntl̩	He was allowed a few dollars extra for *incidental* expenses.	臨時、偶然的 casual fortuitous	**incident**
occasion n. əˈkeʒən	This is a great *occasion* for my wife and me.	時機、事件 opportunity occurrence	**ob**(toward)
occasional a. əˈkeʒənl̩	Things like that are quite *occasional*.	偶然、偶爾的 uncommon infrequent	**occasion**

4

CAP·CEIV·CEP·CEPT·CIP· CUP

receive, take

接受 ● 拿取

這是英文相當重要的字根，源自拉丁文動詞 capere，原義卽爲 receive、take。這個字根的各種不同拼法，大多來自拉丁文的動詞變化，小部分則受過法文影響，其中如形態比較特殊的 ceiv，便借自法文（請參閱本書「最重要的30個字首」25. se 中介紹 p ↔ v 變音部分）。下文例字中的 capable a.「能幹的」，原有「能夠接納、容納」的意思，後來在十六、十七世紀之間，轉成了「能幹」。caption n.「標題」十四世紀出現時，原有「捉拿、抓取」的意思，到了十九世紀，美國人開始用這個字來「捉拿」文章的內容，因此便轉爲新聞報導或書中章節的「標題」。 inception n.「開始」源出拉丁文動詞 incipere「開始」，最初有 take in hand 的意思，後來卽引申爲「著手、開始」。precept n.「教訓、箴言」來自拉丁文動詞 praecipere 的變化型，原義爲「事先拿取」，後來在拉丁文再引申爲「預先指導」，而成可用以教導人的「教訓、箴言」。

單字‧音標‧詞類	例　　　句	中譯‧同義字	字源分析
accept v. əkˈsɛpt	I will not *accept* your offer.	接受、同意 receive assent	**ac**(to)
anticipate v. ænˈtɪsəˌpet	He has *anticipated* all my needs.	預爲準備、預期 expect foresee	ante(before)
capable a. ˈkepəbl̩	She is a *capable* secretary.	能幹的 able competent	
capacious a. kəˈpeʃəs	We will need a *capacious* box to put in these books.	寬大的 vast comprehensive	
capacitate v. kəˈpæsəˌtet	Only by this instruction can we be *capacitated* to observe those errors.	使能、授以資格 qualify empower	
capacity n. kəˈpæsətɪ	This bottle has a *capacity* of three quarts.	容量 volume amplitude	
caption* n. ˈkæpʃən	A *caption* is the heading or title of an article.	標題 title heading	
captivate v. ˈkæptəˌvet	Every charm of his *captivates* the women around him.	迷惑 charm enchant	captive

captive n. ˈkæptɪv	A *captive* to love may be the happiest person on earth.	被(美色等所) 迷困者、俘虜 prisoner	
capture n. ˈkæptʃɚ	The *capture* of the town by the enemy was astonishing.	占領、捕獲 seizure apprehension	
v.	The enemy chief was *captured* as he tried to escape.	虜獲、抓住、 占據 seize arrest	
conceive v. kənˈsiv	Nobody could have *conceived* a better idea.	設想、想 think contrive	con(together)
concept n. ˈkɑnsɛpt	The teacher has explained to the students the basic *concept* of the atom.	概念、觀念 idea notion	con(together)
conception n. kənˈsɛpʃən	His *conception* is on the grand scale but he lacks skill and determination needed to make it real.	計畫、觀念、 概念 idea concept	con(together)
deceive v. dɪˈsiv	A foolish woman like that could be easily *deceived*.	欺騙 dupe cozen	de(away)
deceit n. dɪˈsit	Politics is an art of *deceit*.	欺騙 duplicity artifice	deceive

單字·音標·詞類	例　　　句	中譯·同義字	字源分析
deceptive a. dɪˈsɛptɪv	Her *deceptive* innocence and naivety has fooled a lot of people.	虛偽、使人誤解的 misleading illusive	**deceive**
emancipate v. ɪˈmænsəˌpet	The slaves were all *emancipated* on the day of liberation.	解放 free liberate	**e**(out) **man**(hand)
except v. ɪkˈsɛpt	It is desirable to *except* all first-calf heifers in determining butterfat production average.	把…除外 exclude reject	**ex**(out)
prep.	Everyone was present *except* Lucy and Sophia.	除…之外 excluding	
exceptional a. ɪkˈsɛpʃənḷ	There has been an *exceptional* number of rainy days this year.	罕有、異常的 unusual anomalous	**except**
inception n. ɪnˈsɛpʃən	The *inception* of the plan was due to him.	開始、開端 commencement initiation	**in**(on)
intercept v. ˌɪntɚˈsɛpt	They have *intercepted* the telegram sent by the secret agent.	中途攔截、阻止 seize obstruct	**inter**(between)
participate v. pɚˈtɪsəˌpet	Residents of this district often *participate* in barn dances.	參與、分享 partake share	**part**
perceive v. pɚˈsiv	She is so used to the dogs around her that she hardly *perceives* them.	覺察、看出 note observe	**per**(through)

v.	They surrendered because they had *perceived* the uselessness of further resistance.	了解 realize discern	
perceptible a. pɚˈsɛptəbḷ	Something strange was in the air, *perceptible* to the little boy but utterly beyond his understanding.	可感覺到、可 察覺的 sensitive discernible	‧perceive
precept n. ˈprisɛpt	There are times when *precepts* would not be of much help.	教訓、箴言 rule maxim	**pre**(before)
receive v. rɪˈsiv	She has *received* a huge sum of money from her uncle.	收到、接受 accept obtain	**re**(back)
receptacle* n. rɪˈsɛptəkḷ	The poet's mind is in fact a *receptacle* for seizing and storing up numberless feelings.	容器 container repository	**receive**
reception n. rɪˈsɛpʃən	The world has been ready for the *reception* of new ideas.	接受、承認 acceptance admission	**receive**
recipient n. rɪˈsɪpɪənt	Who are the *recipients* of the honorary degrees this year?	接受者 receiver	**receive**
susceptible a. səˈsɛptəbḷ	Though married, he is still *susceptible* to the attractions of other women.	易受影響、易 感的 sensitive impressionable	**sus**(under)

5

CEDE·CEED·CESS

go, yield

行進 ● 退讓

　　cede、ceed、cess 是英文極為重要的字根，來自拉丁文動詞 cēdere，原即有 go、yield 的意思。cess 的拼法源自 cēdere 的過去分詞 cēssus。而 ceed 所組成的單字，如 exceed v.「超過」、proceed v.「前進、發出」、 succeed v.「繼承、成功」，原在拉丁文作 excēdere、prōcēdere、succēdere，後來進入英文，到了十六世紀才逐漸轉成 ceed 的形態。下文的 succeed，字首 suc 為 sub「在下」的變音（參見本書「最重要的 30 個字首」26. sub·sus），原拉丁文 succēdere 有「下降、臨近」的意思，引申又成「繼承」，最後並可指「順利進行」，而有「成功」的意思。凱撒（Julius Caesar，102 或 100 –· 44 B.C.）的著作中，便有 "quod rēs nūlla succēsserat"（「因為一事無成」）一句話，內中 succēsserat 即為 succēdere 的第三人稱單數過去完成式。

單字·音標·詞類	例　　　句	中譯·同義字	字源分析
accede v. æk¹sid	The girl was ready to *accede* to the man's proposal.	同意 assent consent	ac(to)
access n. ¹æksɛs	Professors have free *access* to the library.	使用或接近的 權利、接近、 通路 approach entrance	ac(to)
accessible a. æk¹sɛsəb]	A telephone should be put where it will be *accessible*.	容易取得、可 接近的 approachable available	access
accessory a. æk¹sɛsərɪ	What are the *accessory* functions of the tongue?	附屬、附加的 additional supplementary	access
n.	We will need some house-hold *accessories* such as small tables and lamps.	附屬品、附件 object of secondary 　　importance	
antecede* v. ˌæntə¹sid	The book discusses those thinkers who *anteceded* the rise of capitalism.	在…之先、先 行、居先 precede forego	ante(before)
antecedent* a. ˌæntə¹sidn̩t	That was *antecedent* to this event.	在先、在前的 prior preceding	antecede
cede v. sid	The territory of Louisiana was *ceded* to the U.S. by France.	割讓、轉讓、 讓步 transfer yield	

單字・音標・詞類	例　　　　句	中譯・同義字	字源分析
cession n. ˈsɛʃən	They could envisage no future territorial *cessions* in the west.	讓與、放棄 abandonment concession	cede
concede v. kənˈsid	She *conceded* to her father that she had gone out with the young man.	承認 confess admit	con(together)
v.	Even his enemies *conceded* him courage.	承認、給與、容許 grant allow	
exceed v. ɪkˈsid	The mercy of God *exceeds* our finite minds.	超過 surpass surmount	ex(out)
excess n. ɪkˈsɛs	There was an *excess* of 10 bushels over what was needed to fill the bin.	過多之量、過多、過剩 superabundance surfeit	ex(out)
a.	He came to have *excess* property on hand after the contract ended.	過多、超過的 inordinate exorbitant	
excessive a. ɪkˈsɛsɪv	He was almost driven mad by her *excessive* demands.	過多、過度的 intemperate inordinate	excess
intercede v. ˌɪntɚˈsid	She *interceded* for the old woman with her uncle.	說情、調停 plead intervene	inter(between)
precede v. prɪˈsid	Military penetration usually *precedes* settlement.	在前、先行 come before antecede	pre(before)

單字·音標·詞類	例　句	中譯·同義字	字源分析
precedent n. ˈprɛsəˌdɛnt	The founder of the company also set a *precedent* of only paying himself a salary.	先例 example antecedent	**precede**
procedure n. prəˈsidʒɚ	One of his first *procedures* was to investigate the report.	程序、措施、 步驟 step measure	**proceed**
proceed v. prəˈsid	The pilgrims *proceeded* from one city to another.	前進 progress advance	**pro**(forward)
v.	His lips began to form some words, though no sound *proceeded* from them.	發出、生出 issue emanate	
process n. ˈprɑsɛs	The job is not finished but is still in *process*.	進行 practice operation	**pro**(forward)
v.	Milk is *processed* by pasteurization.	加工、處理 prepare	
procession n. prəˈsɛʃən	The janitor liked to watch the constant *procession* of people passing by the building.	行列、前進 march parade	**proceed**
predecessor n. ˌprɛdɪˈsɛsɚ	He could not do a better job than his *predecessors*.	前任 one that precedes	**pre**(before) **de**(away)

單字·音標·詞類	例　　句	中譯·同義字	字源分析
recede v. rɪˈsid	Having risen to its highest, the tide was *receding*.	後退 retire retreat	**re**(back)
recess n. rɪˈsɛs	The philosopher sought to lay bare the *recesses* of his own soul.	深幽處 corner retreat	**re**(back)
n.	The justices adjourned for their summer *recess*.	休會期、休假期 vacation respite	
retrocede* v. ˌrɛtroˈsid	The island was *retroceded* after a war between the two countries.	歸還 cede back reassign	**retro**(backward)
secede v. sɪˈsid	After a series of disputes they *seceded* from the church.	脫離、退出 separate withdraw	**se**(separate)
succeed v. səkˈsid	No woman could *succeed* to the throne.	繼承、繼續 follow ensue	**suc**(under)
v.	Nobody thought that she would *succeed*.	成功 prosper thrive	
success n. səkˈsɛs	His book was published and was a great *success*.	成功、成功之事物或人 prosperity hit	**succeed**

單字·音標·詞類	例　句	中譯·同義字	字源分析
successive a. səkˈsɛsɪv	This ingenious invention is the product of the *successive* labors of innumerable men.	繼續、連續的 consecutive	**succeed**

6

CID·CIS

cut, kill

切割 ● 殺

　　字根 cid 、cis 源自拉丁文動詞 caedere ，原義即爲 cut, kill
。cid 和 cis 的拼法原在拉丁文已形成，如下文例字的 decide v.「
決定」、concise a.「簡明的」、precise a.「精確的」，原拉丁文便
分別作 dēcīdere v.、concīsus a.、praecīsus a.。例字中的 decide 字
首 de 有 away 的意思，因此拉丁文原義爲「割斷」，後來才引申
而成「解決、決定」。precise 源出拉丁文形容詞 praecīsus，praecī-
sus 又出自動詞 praecīdere ，字首 prae（即 pre ）有 before 的意思
，因此拉丁文原解釋作「截斷、中斷」，經截斷的事物往往比較精
簡，所以又引申而成「精確的」。

單字·音標·詞類	例　　　句	中譯·同義字	字源分析
concise a. kən'saɪs	He gave a *concise* report of the business trip.	簡明的 compact succinct	**con**(together)
decide v. dɪ'saɪd	Have you *decided* what to do about it?	決定、決心 determine resolve	**de**(away)
decisive a. dɪ'saɪsɪv	We shall win a complete and *decisive* victory over the forces of evil.	決定性、確定的 unquestionable conclusive	**decide**
excise v. ɪk'saɪz	The patient's tumor must be *excised*.	切去、除去 eradicate extirpate	**ex**(out)
homicide* n. 'hɑmə͵saɪd	The man was charged with drunken driving and vehicle *homicide*.	殺人 manslaughter	**hom**(human)
incise v. ɪn'saɪz	The sculptor has *incised* an inscription on the monument.	刻、雕、切 carve engrave	**in**(in)
incisive a. ɪn'saɪsɪv	The cut was sharp and *incisive* as the stroke of a fang.	鋒利、尖刻、敏銳的 sharp acute	**incise**
precise a. pre'saɪs	We were demanded to be *precise* when we presented our descriptions of the event.	精確、正確的 exact correct	**pre**(before)

單字・音標・詞類	例　　　　句	中譯・同義字	字源分析
scission* n. ˈsɪʒən	A *scission* is an act of cutting, dividing, or splitting.	切斷、分裂 division schism	
suicide n. ˈsuəˌsaɪd	The girl wanted to commit *suicide* but was too afraid to cut herself.	自殺、自毀 self-destruction	sui(oneself)
v.	The unfortunate man has *suicided*.	自殺 kill oneself	

7

CIT

excite, call

激起 ● 喚起

　　字根 cit 源出拉丁文動詞 citāre ，本即有 excite、call 的意思。下文例字以 solicit v.「懇求」的意義比較特別。 solicit 源自拉丁文動詞 sollīcitāre ，前半部係形容詞 sollus「全體的」的變音，原義為「搖撼、擾亂」，引申而有「催迫、勸誘」的意思，最後自然可再推而為「懇求」。另外，solicitous a.「關心、渴望的」與 solicit 同源，原拉丁文 sollicitus a.本即有「搖動、焦慮的」的意思，也不難以同樣方式推出「關心、渴望」的字義。

單字·音標·詞類	例　　　句	中譯·同義字	字源分析
cite v. saɪt	She kept *citing* passages from Dante when speaking.	引用、舉例 quote adduce	
excite v. ɪkˈsaɪt	The boys are already feeling *excited* about the trip to the seaside.	使興奮、引起 arouse animate	**ex**(out)
incite v. ɪnˈsaɪt	Such behavior is likely to *incite* retaliation.	引起、鼓動 rouse spur	**in**(on)
recital n. rɪˈsaɪtḷ	The poet gave a *recital* of his own poems before a large and attentive audience.	吟誦、述說 repetition narration	**recite**
recite v. rɪˈsaɪt	The poet *recited* his poems from a manuscript.	背誦、朗讀、詳述 repeat reiterate	**re**(again) **cite**
solicit v. səˈlɪsɪt	The peasants *solicited* the king for relief.	懇求 plead supplicate	**sol**(whole)
solicitous a. səˈlɪsɪtəs	The young college graduate is *solicitous* about his future.	懸慮、關心的 concerned apprehensive	**solicit**
a.	The businessman was *solicitous* to get all the benefits.	渴望、熱望的 eager desirous	
solicitude n. səˈlɪsəˌtjud	Having few wants, he had little cause for *solicitude.*	焦慮、掛慮 anxiety disquietude	**solicit**

8

CLAIM·CLAM

cry out

呼叫

　　字根 claim、clam 源自拉丁文動詞 clāmāre，原即有cry out 的意思。clam 的拼法直接借自拉丁文，而 claim 則來自古法文。下文例字中，以 acclaim v.「稱讚」的意義較爲特別。acclaim 源出拉丁文動詞 acclāmāre，字首ac 爲 ad「向」的變音（參見本書「最重要的30個字首」2. **ad**），原拉丁文的字義爲「歡呼」，因此 acclaim 本也有「歡呼」的意思，後來引申成「歡呼以表示贊同」，而有「稱讚」的字義。

單字·音標·詞類	例　　　　句	中譯·同義字	字源分析
acclaim v. ə'klem	This is a book widely *acclaimed* by critics all over the country.	稱讚 praise commend	**ac**(to)
n.	The author deserves the *acclaim* he has received.	稱讚 praise laudation	
claim v. klem	He *claimed* to everyone that he saw a ghost.	宣稱 maintain hold	
v.	Public health must *claim* everyone's attention.	需要 require call for	
n.	The official has his *claim* to be called Europe's leading spokesman.	要求的權利 right privilege	
n.	The present age makes great *claims* upon the world.	要求 demand requirement	
clamor n. 'klæmɚ	Finches and flickers gave out a dissonant and reedy *clamor*.	喧鬧 din tumult	
v.	The subordinate threatened him with impeachment and *clamored* for the suppression of his command.	叫囂 roar loudly demand	

單字・音標・詞類	例　句	中譯・同義字	字源分析
clamorous a. ˈklæmərəs	She stood there watching him walk to and fro on the *clamorous* street.	吵鬧、叫喊的 uproarious vociferous	**clamor**
declaim* v. dɪˈklem	He was often asked to *declaim* on public occasions.	演說、叱責 speak loudly harangue	**de**(complete)
disclaim v. dɪsˈklem	He *disclaimed* the charge that he received financial backing from that company.	否認、拒絕承認 renounce disavow	**dis**(away)
exclaim v. ɪkˈsklem	The children *exclaimed* in delight as the father brought in a puppy.	大叫、呼喊 cry shout	**ex**(out)
proclaim v. proˈklem	Mr. Hart *proclaimed* that he would be a presidential candidate.	宣布 announce promulgate	**pro**(forward)
v.	His accent *proclaimed* him an Irishman.	顯示 show reveal	
reclaim v. rɪˈklem	The man has wanted to *reclaim* lost property.	取回 regain recover	**re**(back)
v.	The most arid area in the country can be *reclaimed* from the desert by irrigation.	開拓 restore reinstate	
v.	There is still hope to *reclaim* him from drunkenness.	糾正 improve reform	

CLUD·CLUS

close

關閉

---

　　clud、clus 源出拉丁文動詞 claudere 或 clūdere，原即有 close 的意思。clud 的拼法來自拉丁文 clūdere ，而 clus 則來自其過去分詞 clūsus。英文的 close a.「關閉的」直接借自法文的 clos a.「關閉的」（動詞作 clore ），而法文的 clos 或 clore 也是源自拉丁文的 claudere 。這個字根除了上述兩種拼法外，另有 claus 和 clois兩種拼法。claus 出自 claudere 的過去分詞 clausus, clois 則出自古法文 cloistre (現代法文作 clore)。這兩種拼法組成的單字不多，也不屬一般常用字彙範圍，因此僅略述如下以供參考：clause n.「子句、條款」、 claustrophobia n.「對幽閉的場所容易產生恐懼的心理疾病」（ phobia n.「恐懼」）、claustral a.「修道的」、 cloister n.「修道院」等。

單字・音標・詞類	例　　　句	中譯・同義字	字源分析
conclude v. kənˈklud	The preacher *concluded* the speech by praising God.	結束 finish terminate	con(together)
v.	He *concluded* that the plan was not workable.	決定、斷定 resolve deduce	
conclusive a. kənˈklusɪv	The man was convicted because of the *conclusive* evidence presented by the prosecutor.	決定性、確定、最後的 definite ultimate	conclude
exclude v. ɪkˈsklud	That request must be *excluded* from further consideration.	排除、拒絕、逐出 bar interdict	ex(out)
exclusive a. ɪkˈsklusɪv	He is our *exclusive* agent in Washington, D.C.	唯一、獨有的 only sole	exclude
a.	The president gave the question his *exclusive* attention.	完全的 whole undivided	
include v. ɪnˈklud	There are ten of us in the house, *including* the three servants.	包含、包括 contain comprise	in(in)
occlude* v. əˈklud	The navy has sunk a lot of ships to *occlude* the harbor.	封閉、遮斷 close obstruct	oc(against)

單字·音標·詞類	例　　句	中譯·同義字	字源分析
preclude v. prɪˈklud	The adoption of one choice often necessarily *precludes* the use of another.	妨礙、阻止 hinder impede	**pre**(before)
recluse* n. ˈrɛklus	The life of a *recluse* is peaceful and inspiring.	隱士、遁世者 hermit anchorite	**re**(back)
reclusive* a. rɪˈklusɪv	The old man enjoyed sitting in the *reclusive* calm of the acacia tree.	隱遁、幽寂的 solitary desolate	**recluse**
seclude v. sɪˈklud	A quiet man sometimes likes to *seclude* himself in isolation.	隔絕、隔離 hide isolate	**se**(separate)
secluded a. sɪˈkludɪd	It might not be easy to find the *secluded* valley where his uncle lives.	隔絕的 isolated remote	**seclude**

10

COR·CORD·COUR

heart, courage

心 ● 勇氣

字根 cor, cord, cour 源出拉丁文名詞 cor「心」。cord 的拼法出自 cor 的屬格 (genitive) 變化 cordis；cour 則出自法文，只有 courage n.「勇氣」一字有這種拼法（古法文作 corage 或 curage，現代法文 courage）。cor 在拉丁文原可引申為「心思、心意」的意思，因此字根加上字首 con「一起、共同」，便成 concord v.「和諧」；加上 dis「分離」，則成 discord n.「不一致、不調和」。希臘文和拉丁文同屬印歐語系 (Indo-European language family)，因此希臘文的 καρδιᾱ (kardiā) n.f.「心」，也與本節所談的字根同源。由希臘文 καρδιᾱ 轉成的英文單字極少，均屬醫學用語，如 cardiac a.「心臟、心臟病的」、cardiogram n.「心電圖」、cardiology n.「心臟學」、carditis n.「心臟炎」等均是。

單字·音標·詞類	例　　　句	中譯·同義字	字源分析
accord v. əˈkɔrd	The scientists' con- clusions seem con- tradictory but can be *accorded* by calm reasoning.	一致、相合 harmonize reconcile	**ac**(to)
v.	The President *accorded* him an honorary title.	給與 allow grant	
n.	There is a persuasive *accord* in his arguments.	協調、和諧 harmony proportion	
n.	The two nations have reached a peace *accord*.	協定、條約 agreement treaty	
accordingly adv. əˈkɔədɪŋlɪ	Later the club also accepted amateurs and *accordingly* changed its name.	於是 consequently correspondently	**accord**
concord v. ˈkɑnkɔrd	The stars move in harmony and *concord*.	和諧、協調、 一致 agreement harmony	**con**(together)
concordant a. kɑnˈkɔrdn̩t	The scholar has expressed views *concordant* with his background and training.	和諧、一致的 harmonious consonant	**concord**
cordial a. ˈkɔrdʒəl	The host has shown a *cordial* regard for his visitor's comfort.	真誠、友善的 hearty gracious	

core n. kor	The *core* of this book is an attempt to comprehend the nature of total war.	中心、最重要部分、要旨 center essence	
courage n. 'kɜɪdʒ	It takes a great deal of *courage* to solve the problem.	勇氣 bravery fortitude	
discord n. 'dɪskɔrd	There is a *discord* between the idealist and materialist philosophies.	不一致、不調和 difference dissention	**dis**(away)
discordant a. dɪs'kɔrdn̩t	These are views *discordant* with present-day ideas.	不一致、不調和的 disagreeing antagonistic	**discord**
	a.	They could hear the *discordant* crowd shouting and laughing.	嘈雜、不悅耳、不和諧的 harsh jarring	
discourage v. dɪs'kɜɪdʒ	She was *discouraged* by one failure after another.	使氣餒、使沮喪 dishearten dismay	**courage**
	v.	Fear that war might break out *discouraged* the family from going abroad.	妨礙、阻礙 dissuade deter	
encourage v. ɪn'kɜɪd	The employer *encouraged* his employees to work harder.	鼓勵 hearten incite	**courage**

High prices for farm
products *encourage*
farming.

促進、助長
aid
　promote

11

CORP·CORPOR

body

身體 • 團體

corp、corpor 源出拉丁文名詞corpus，原義即為 body。corp 的拼法出自 corpus，corpor 則來自其屬格變化 corporis。下文例字意義衍變比較特別的，只有 corporation n.「公司」一字。corporation與另一字 corporate a.「結合成一個團體的」有關，原指「法人團體」，後再推衍而有「有限公司」的意思。此外，例字中尤須注意 corps n.「團體」和 corpse n.「屍體」兩字的發音。 corps 借自法文的 corps n.「身體、團體」，到了十八世紀左右，讀法逐漸與法文相同，p 和 s 均不發音，因此不僅字形和 corpse 略有出入，語音也不同。

corporal a.
ˈkɔrpərəl

Whipping and other *corporal* punishments are absolutely prohibited here.

身體、肉體的
bodily
physical

corporate a.
ˈkɔrpərɪt

The yeomen were a *corporate* society like the country gentry.

結合成一個團體的
combined
cohesive

corporation n.
ˌkɔrpəˈreʃən

A *corporation* is an association of employers and employees in a basic industry.

公司
group of people
　in business

corporeal* a.
kɔrˈpɔrɪəl

The *corporeal* eye sees not all.

肉體的
bodily
physical

　　　　　a.

Her *corporeal* hereditaments include land and large savings.

有形、具體的
material
substantial

corps n.
kor

They have trained a *corps* of lifeguards.

團體、團
body
company

corpse n.
kɔrps

A *corpse* was found in the backyard of the house.

屍體
body
carcass

corpulent* a.
ˈkɔrpjələnt

He was a *corpulent* giant, over six feet in height, and as big round as a hogshead.

肥大、肥胖的
massive
obese

單字・音標・詞類	例 句	中譯・同義字	字源分析

corpus* n.
ˈkɔrpəs

The *corpus* of their fiery dispute was some trivial question.

任何事物的主體
main body

n.

One should not judge the *corpus* of the American literature in the light of these standards.

全集
whole body of
　writings

incorporate v.
ɪnˈkɔrpəˌret

The committee recommended that we *incorporate* several new rules into the bylaws.

編入、併入、合併
combine
blend

in(in)

v.

His thoughts were *incorporated* in the article.

具體表現
embody
incarnate

12

COURS·CUR·CURS

run

跑動

　　字根 cours 、cur 、curs 出自拉丁文動詞 currere，原即有「跑動」的意思。cur 的形態來自 currere，curs 來自其過去分詞 cursus，而 cours 則來自法文。下文例字 discourse n.「談話、論文」源自法文 discours ，法文的 discours 則又來自拉丁文 discursus，字首 dis 為 away 的意思，因此原在拉丁文有「奔馳、四散」的意思，後來又引申成「討論」，指話匣子一打開，便上自天文下至地理，「四方奔馳」的談起來。另一字 succor n./v.「幫助」形態有些特別，也可附帶一提。事實上，下文所列的 succor 是美國英文的拼法，英國英文原本拼作 succour ，由此當不難看出字源：字首 suc 為 sub 「在下」的變體（請參閱本書「最重要的 30 個字首」26. sub·sus 部分），原拉丁文 succurrere v. 本有「馳向、馳援」的意思，後又引申而成「救援、幫助」。

單字・音標・詞類	例　　句	中譯・同義字	字源分析
concourse* n. 'kɑnkors	The fort was built at the *concourse* of the two rivers.	會流處、合流 conjunction confluence	**con**(together)
n.	A mighty *concourse* of people gathered in front of the palace.	羣集 gathering throng	
concur v. kən'kɝ	Leisure and opportunity do not always *concur*.	同時發生 coincide converge	**con**(together)
v.	Those who did not *concur* with his opinion were slaughtered on the spot.	同意 agree accede	
concurrent a. kən'kɝənt	The Germans launched an invasion with the *concurrent* occupation of other towns.	同時發生的 occuring at the same time	**concur**
courier n. 'kʊrɪɚ	*Couriers* who carry official dispatches possess the right of inviolability.	信差 messenger herald	
course n. kors	In the *course* of the year the boy grew much stronger and taller.	過程 progress order	
n.	He showed me the *courses* of the rivers on the map.	所經之路 way route	
n.	He gave a *course* of lectures on medieval paintings.	連續的事物 continuity sequence	

currency n.
ˈkɝənsɪ

This new word is in common *currency*.

通用
circulation
transmission

n.

In Africa beads were used as minor *currency*.

貨幣
money
paper money

current a.
ˈkɝənt

Nobody knows what to do with the *current* crisis.

現在、目下的
present
prevailing

n.

The violent *current* of the mountain stream causes the rocks to collapse.

水流、氣流
flow
flux

n.

None of the officials could resist the strong currents of public opinion.

趨勢
tendency
trend

currently adv.
ˈkɝəntlɪ

His father is *currently* engaged in scientific research.

目前、眼前地　current
presently
at present

cursory a.
ˈkɝsɔrɪ

The committee has issued either no report at all or only extremely *cursory* ones.

匆促、草率的
hasty
careless

discourse n.
dɪˈskors

His *discourses* with his colleagues were witty and inspiring.

談話、會話　dis(away)
talk
conversation

單字・音標・詞類	例　　　句	中譯・同義字	字源分析
n.	This lecture is an acute and suggestive *discourse* upon an intriguing subject.	演講、論文 thesis dissertation	
excursion n. ɪk'skɝʃən	The railway ran Sunday *excursions* to the city.	旅行、遠足 journey trip	ex(out)
excursive* a. ɪk'skɝsɪv	The writer discusses the topic in an amusingly *excursive* style.	散漫、離題的 digressive rambling	ex(out)
incur v. ɪn'kɝ	They had *incurred* large debts to educate their children.	陷於、惹起 bring acquire	in(in)
incursion n. ɪn'kɝʒən	No one can stop the inevitable *incursion* of new techniques into the industry.	進入、入侵、襲擊 invasion aggression	in(in)
intercourse n. 'ɪntɚ͵kors	Shyness renders me inapt for social *intercourse*.	交際、交通 communication converse	inter(between)
n.	The fanatic believed he had direct *intercourse* with the Deity.	靈交、(思想、感情等)交流 exchange communion	
occur v. ə'kɝ	When did the mishap *occur*?	發生 happen appear	oc(toward)

	v.	It never *occurred* to me that she was sick.	被想起 come to mind	
precursor prɪˈkɝsɚ	n.	Greek mathematics was the *precursor* to modern mathematics.	先進、先驅 forerunner harbinger	**pre**(before)
recourse* ˈrikors	n.	They had to handle their own difficulties without *recourse* to outside help.	求助 resort reference	**re**(back)
recur rɪˈkɝ	v.	Should the occasion *recur,* I would not let it happen again.	重現、再回到 reappear return	**re**(again)
recurrent rɪˈkɝənt	a.	Food is the urgent and *recurrent* need of individuals.	頻頻發生、重現、周期性的 returning again and again	**recur**
succor* ˈsʌkɚ	n.	Religion was their chief *succor*.	幫助、援助 aid assistance	**suc**(under)
	v.	The man attempted to *succor* the various distresses of his people.	幫助、援助 help relieve	

CRED

believe

信賴

cred源出拉丁文動詞 crēdere，本即有「信賴」的意思。這個字根除了cred的拼法外，另在下文例字 creed n.「信條」與miscreant n.「惡棍」之中，也可見到兩種變體。 creed 出自拉丁文 crēdere的第一人稱單數現在式 crēdo （英文譯作 I believe），中古英文時期拼作 creda 或 crede，其後到了十七世紀，才逐漸轉成 creed 的形態。miscreant 直接借自古法文的 mescreant （現代法文作 mécréant），字首 mis 有「錯誤、否定」的意思，配上字根，而成「不信之人、異教徒」的原義，到了十六世紀以後，方才變成了「惡棍」。

單字·音標·詞類	例　　　　句	中譯·同義字	字源分析

accredit v.
əˈkrɛdɪt

Only a few counties in this state have been *accredited* with reference to tuberculosis in cattle.

承認合格、授權
empower
authorize

credit

v.

The invention of the telephone was *accredited* to Alexander Graham Bell.

認為…屬於、歸因
ascribe
attribute

credence* n.
ˈkridn̩s

She gave little *credence* to tne rumor, knowing it was probably false.

相信、可信賴
trust
reliance

credentials n. pl.
krɪˈdɛnʃəlz

His *credentials* showed that he had had considerable experience.

證件、介紹信
certificate
voucher

credible a.
ˈkrɛdəbl̩

He gave a *credible* explanation for his tardiness.

可信、可靠的
believable
reliable

credit n.
ˈkrɛdɪt

His *credit* is not very good.

信用
standing
reputation

n.

Don't place too much *credit* in what they said.

信任
belief
trust

v.

She did not *credit* anything he said at all.

相信
believe
accept

v.

They *credit* the invention to him.

歸功於
ascribe
attribute

— 292 —

creditable a.
ˈkrɛdɪtəbḷ

Her *creditable* performance has impressed everyone in the office.

值得稱讚、可稱譽的
reputable
respectable

credit

creditor n.
ˈkrɛdɪtɚ

She did not know how to cope with her *creditor* who had proposed to marry her.

債主
one to whom money is owed

credit

credo n.
ˈkrido

The poor businessman could never understand what an artist's *credo* is.

信條
tenet
doctrine

credulity n.
krəˈdulətɪ

Her *credulity* made her an easy prey for anyone with a hard luck story.

易信、輕信
simplicity
gullibility

credulous a.
ˈkrɛdʒələs

Only a *credulous* person would be taken in by such ads.

輕信的
believing
gullible

creed n.
krid

He accepted the *creed* of his church.

信條
belief
dogma

discredit n.
dɪsˈkrɛdɪt

A number of contradictions cast *discredit* on his testimony.

不信任、懷疑
disbelief
doubt

dis(away)
credit

v.

His careful researches *discredited* the claims of his predecessors.

使失去權威性
cause disbelief

v.

He was thoroughly *discredited* by his role in the recent police scandals.

玷辱
disgrace
taint

單字·音標·詞類	例　句	中譯·同義字	字源分析
incredible a. ɪnˈkrɛdəbḷ	The amount of work she could do in an hour was *incredible*.	不可信、難以置信的 unbelievable improbable	in(not) **credible**
incredulous a. ɪnˈkrɛdʒələs	She was *incredulous* when she heard she had won the first prize.	不相信、懷疑的 unbelieving skeptical	in(not) **credulous**
incredulity n. ˌɪnkrəˈdulətɪ	His *incredulity* was obvious as he listened to her excuses.	不信、懷疑 disbelief skepticism	in(not) **credulity**
miscreant* n. ˈmɪskrɪənt	The police were trying to round up the *miscreants*.	惡棍 evildoer criminal	mis(bad)

CUR

care, cure

照料 ● 治療 ● 懸念

　　字根 cur 源自拉丁文動詞 cūrāre，原即有 care、cure、manage 的意思。下文例字 accurate a.「準確的」源出拉丁文形容詞accūrā-tus，原義即爲「準確的」，指事情能掛念照料得很好，自然不至有所偏誤。 curious a.「好奇、奇怪的」出自拉丁文形容詞 cūriōsus，原有「小心、注意的」的意思，引申而成「好奇的」。另一字 curio n.「古玩」從拼法可知是 curiosity n.「好奇」簡寫而成，十九世紀之後才出現在英文中，一般特指中國、日本等遠東地區的古物。procure v.「取得」出自拉丁文動詞 prōcūrāre，字首 pro 有「向前」的意思，因此原有「管理、代理」的字義，但是進入英文之後，到了十三、十四世紀逐漸衍生出「盡力成就」的意思，而又轉成了「（費力）取得」。

單字·音標·詞類	例　　　句	中譯·同義字	字源分析
accurate a. ˈækjərɪt	His report was dry, factual, and painstaking- ly *accurate*.	準確的 precise exact	ac(to)
curator＊ n. kjʊˈretɚ	Her father has been *curator* of the university library for thirty years.	館長 overseer manager	
cure v. kjʊr	That man claimed he could *cure* any disease.	治療 heal remedy	
n.	There is no *cure* for that disease.	治療的藥物、 方法 healing remedy	
curio n. ˈkjʊrɪˌo	The room was adorned with priceless paintings, tapestries, and *curios*.	古玩、珍品 unusual article	curiosity
curiosity n. ˌkjʊrɪˈɑsətɪ	He cannot bear to see anyone lacking intellectual *curiosity*.	好奇、求知慾 interest inquisitiveness	
curious a. ˈkjʊrɪəs	A man, like a cat, is *curious* about his environment and keeps investigating it.	好奇、好問、 好窺探的 inquisitive prying	
a.	Whatever we are thoroughly unfamiliar with is apt to seem *curious* to us.	奇怪、古怪的 strange odd	

單字·音標·詞類	例　　　　句	中譯·同義字	字源分析
procure v. proˈkjʊr	The man has *procured* enormous wealth by such dealings.	取得 acquire gain	**pro**(forward)
secure v. sɪˈkjʊr	They urged their countrymen to *secure* themselves against brutality.	保護 guard protect	**se**(separate)
v.	In most countries, the good and rare things are usually *secured* by the few.	獲得 obtain procure	
a.	The animal will be *secure* from harm if it stays in the bush.	安全、無受害之虞的 safe sheltered	
security n. sɪˈkjʊrətɪ	The family lived in peace and *security*.	安全 safety protection	**secure**

15

DIC·DICT

say

說話

字根 dic, dict 源出拉丁文動詞 dicāre，原即有「說話」的意思。dict 的拼法出自dicāre 的過去分詞 dictus。下文例字 addict v.「使熱中、專心於」源自拉丁文動詞 addīcere 與形容詞 addictus。字首 ad 有 to 的意思（參見本書「最重要的30個字首」2. ad 部分），addīcere 因而有「贊同、判決」的意思，引申又成「讓與」，而 addictus 由前述動詞「讓與」的意義，便衍生出「獻與、致力於」的解釋，因此 addict 才有「使熱中、專心於」的意思。predicament n.「困境」字源與另一例字 predicate v.「宣稱、斷定」有關，本書「最重要的30個字首」22. pre 部分有詳盡解說，請自行參閱。syndicate n.「企業組合」出自中古拉丁文 (Medieval Latin) 的 syndicatus，但直接的字源卻是法文的 syndicat。字首 syn 出自希臘文，有 with、together 的意思（參見「最重要的30個字首」28. sym·syn），原與字根組合成 syndicat n.「評議員、理事」（不屬托福字彙範圍），後又形成 syndicate，用以指「評議團、評審會」，到了十九世紀，工商業發達，才開始引申成「企業組合」。

單字·音標·詞類	例　　句	中譯·同義字	字源分析
abdicate v. ˈæbdəˌket	The ruler *abdicated* himself from the government.	讓(位)、放棄 renounce disown	**ab**(from)
addict v. əˈdɪkt	Would-be scholars like him should *addict* themselves to history or science.	使熱中、專心於 devote habituate	**ad**(toward)
benediction* n. ˌbɛnəˈdɪkʃən	The young departed with their parents' *benediction*.	祝福、恩賜 blessing beatitude	**bene**(good)
contradict v. ˌkɑntrəˈdɪkt	No truth can *contradict* another truth.	相反、反對、否定 challenge contravene	**contra**(against)
contradictious* a. ˌkɑntrəˈdɪkʃəs	The man is of a *contradictious* nature because he never agrees with anyone on anything.	矛盾、好反駁的 contrary adverse	**contra**(against)
dedicate v. ˈdɛdəˌket	She has *dedicated* her life to her husband's comfort.	獻身、委身 devote submit	**de**(complete)
dictate v. ˈdɪktet	Businessmen often *dictate* their letters.	口授令人筆錄 speak for a person to write down	
v.	A stern father and husband always *dictates* to his family.	命令 prescribe ordain	

單字・音標・詞類	例　　句	中譯・同義字	字源分析
dictator n. ˈdɪkteɾɚ	The secretary general was actually the *dictator* of the political party.	獨裁者 tyrant despot	**dictate**
dictatorial a. ˌdɪktəˈtorɪəl	The staff was not happy under such a *dictatorial* leader.	獨裁、專橫的 domineering oppressive	**dictator**
diction n. ˈdɪkʃən	The poet has created a new *diction* for poetry.	用字遣詞、詞藻、語法 language phraseology	
dictum* n. ˈdɪktəm	A would-be professor must heed the *dictum* "Publish or perish."	格言 saying maxim	
edict* n. ˈidɪkt	The *Edict* of Nantes was issued by Henry IV of France.	詔書、敕令 ordinance mandate	**e(out)**
indicate v. ˈɪndəˌket	Their laughter *indicated* their happiness.	顯示 show demonstrate	**in(in)**
indict v. ɪnˈdaɪt	The man was *indicted* for murder.	控告 accuse prosecute	**in(against)**
interdict* v. ˌɪntɚˈdɪkt	Trade with the Arabian countries was *interdicted* by the government.	禁止 prohibit debar	**inter(between)**
jurisdiction* n. ˌdʒʊrɪsˈdɪkʃən	This territory is subject to the *jurisdiction* of the U.S.	管轄權、司法權 legal power	**juris(law)**

單字・音標・詞類	例　　　　　　句	中譯・同義字	字源分析
malediction* n. ˌmælə'dɪkʃən	The saint's remains were guarded by a *malediction*.	詛咒 curse execration	**mal**(bad)
predicament n. prɪ'dɪkəmənt	She was in an awkward *predicament* after she had said that to him.	困境 dilemma quandary	**pre**(before)
predicate* v. 'prɛdɪˌket	Most religions *predicate* life after death.	宣稱、斷定 declare proclaim	**pre**(before)
v.	Any code of ethics must be *predicated* upon the basic principles of truth and honesty.	使有根據 base found	
predict v. prɪ'dɪkt	Who could have *predicted* what was going to happen?	預測、預知、預言 foresee prophesy	**pre**(before)
syndicate n. 'sɪndɪkɪt	Twelve real estate men formed a *syndicate* to buy the office building.	企業組合 association cartel	**syn**(together)
valediction* n. ˌvælə'dɪkʃən	He was chosen to present the *valediction* at the commencement.	告別辭、告別 leave-taking farewell	**vale**(farewell)
verdict n. 'vɝdɪkt	The popular *verdict* was that it served him right.	判斷、判決 decision judgment	**ver**(true)
vindicate* v. 'vɪndəˌket	He had to stand out to *vindicate* his honesty.	辯明、保護 maintain preserve	**vin**(force)

16

DUC·DUCT

lead

導引

　　duc, duct 出自拉丁文動詞 dūcere，原義即爲 lead ，其中 duct的拼法來自dūcere 的過去分詞 ductus。這個字根除了上述兩種拼法外，並有subdue v. 「使服從、征服」一字的變體。subdue的字源至今一般字源學家仍未有定論，有人認爲係拉丁文動詞subdū-cere「拖、抽取、結算」轉義而成，有人則認爲由拉丁文 subdere v.「置放、抑制、征服」變形而成，莫衷一是。因此，本書將sub-due 收入字根 duc, duct 一節，只是權宜之便，是否眞正源自 duc, duct ，並無法確定。

單字‧音標‧詞類	例　　句	中譯‧同義字	字源分析
abduct v. æbˈdʌkt	His children were *abducted* yesterday.	拐走、綁架 carry off kidnap	**ab**(away)
adduce* v. əˈdjus	Let me *adduce* more pleasing evidence.	舉出、引證 quote cite	**ad**(to)
adduct* v. əˈdʌkt	The doctor told the patient to *adduct* his fingers for a test.	併攏 draw together	**ad**(to)
aqueduct* n. ˈækwɪ͵dʌkt	An *aqueduct* carries a large quantity of water.	水道、溝渠 conduit channel	aqu(water)
conduce v. kənˈdjus	A man like him does not need the qualities that *conduce* to worldly success.	助成、貢獻、引起 contribute effect	**con**(together)
conduct v. kənˈdʌkt	The shepherds were *conducting* the sheep across the stream.	引導 lead guide	**con**(together)
v.	We need an able person to *conduct* this scientific experiment.	管理、指揮 run direct	
n. ˈkandʌkt	This is a *conduct* unbecoming to a gentleman.	行為、舉動 behavior demeanor	
deduce v. dɪˈdjus	He will be able to *deduce* a logical result from the various problems.	推論、演繹 draw infer	**de**(down)

單字·音標·詞類	例　句	中譯·同義字	字源分析
deduct v. dɪˈdʌkt	The tax has already been *deducted* from the paycheck.	扣除、減除 remove subtract	de(away)
duct* n. dʌkt	A *duct* is a channel by which a substance is conveyed.	管、輸送管 pipe tube	
ductile* a. ˈdʌktl̩	We must find a *ductile* metal for this experiment.	可延展、柔軟的 malleable pliant	
educate v. ˈɛdʒəˌket	She wanted her children to be well *educated*.	教育、培育 instruct cultivate	e(out)
educe v. ɪˈdjus	They want to *educe* and cultivate what is best and noblest in themselves.	引出、令顯出 elicit extract	e(out)
induce v. ɪnˈdjus	What *induced* you to do such a foolish thing?	引誘、誘使 influence actuate	in(in)
v.	His illness was *induced* by overwork.	引起 produce effect	
induct* v. ɪnˈdʌkt	Dr. Hoggard was *inducted* as president of the college.	使正式就職 install inaugurate	in(in)
introduce v. ˌɪntrəˈdjus	Tobacco was *introduced* into Europe from America.	引進 bring conduct	intro(in)

單字・音標・詞類	例　　　句	中譯・同義字	字源分析
v.	Tomorrow I will *introduce* a friend of mine to you.	介紹、介紹認識 present acquaint	
produce v. prə'djus	You must *produce* some proof to make people believe you.	提出 exhibit demonstrate	**pro**(forward)
v.	This factory *produces* fabric.	生產 yield generate	
product n. 'pradəkt	What *products* do you import from Southeast Asia?	產物、生產品、結果 yield outgrowth	**produce**
reduce v. rɪ'djus	They have launched a safety campaign to *reduce* forest fires.	減少、減低 lessen abate	**re**(back)
seduce v. sɪ'djus	The employers have tried to *seduce* union leaders with rewards of money.	引誘 allure entice	**se**(separate)
subdue v. səb'dju	It is not easy to try to *subdue* a wilful child.	使服從、征服、抑制 vanquish subjugate	**sub**(under)

17

EQU

equal

均等

　　字根 equ 源出拉丁文形容詞 aequus，原義即為 equal。下文例
字 adequate a.「適量、足夠的」出自拉丁文形容詞adaequātus，字
首 ad 為 to 的意思（參見本書「最重要的30個字首」2. ad），因
此原解釋為「均平、相等的」。借入英文之後，十七世紀時已由「
相等、等量」的原義，衍變成「適量、足夠的」；其反義字 inade-
quate，因此也有了「不充分的」的意思。以 equ 組成的單字有些
比較偏難，不屬托福字彙範圍，僅列出如下以供參考：equation n.
「方程式」、equator n.「赤道」、equiangular a.「等角的」、
equilateral a.「等邊的」、equinox n.「春分、秋分」、equipol-
lent a.「力量相等的」、equivoque n.「雙關語、諧語」等等。英
文另有一字根 equ「馬」，拼法與本節的 equ「均等」相同，須特
別注意。equ「馬」源出拉丁文名詞 equus「馬」（原拉丁文拼法
本與前述的 aequus「均等的」不同），組成的英文單字數量較少，
而且絕多不屬常用字彙範圍：equestrian a.「馬術的」、equine a.
「馬的」、equitation n.「騎術」等。

單字‧音標‧詞類	例　句	中譯‧同義字	字源分析
adequate a. ˈædəkwɪt	This solution is not *adequate* to the problem.	適量、足夠的 sufficient requisite	**ad**(to)
equable a. ˈɛkwəbḷ	For rest and recreation a warm, *equable* climate is doubtless most delightful.	穩定、平靜的 steady temperate	
equal a. ˈikwəl	Premature babies eventually become *equal* to children born after a normal time.	相等、同樣的 alike equivalent	
equality n. ɪˈkwɑlətɪ	Most people believe in the *equality* of men.	平等、相等 sameness equivalence	**equal**
equanimity* n. ˌikwəˈnɪmətɪ	Rest restores the strained muscles to physical *equanimity*.	平靜、鎮定 evenness balance	**anim**(mind)
equate v. ɪˈkwet	The two different quantities must be *equated*.	使相等 make equal	
equilibrate* v. ˌikwəˈlaɪbret	The status of men and women in this aboriginal society tends to be *equilibrated* by a special relationship.	使平衡、使相稱 balance counterpoise	**libr**(balance)
equilibrium n. ˌikwəˈlɪbrɪəm	Scales are in *equilibrium* when weights on each side are equal.	平衡、均衡 balance equipoise	**libr**(balance)

equipoise* n. ˈɛkwəˌpɔɪz	In medieval times the aristocracy served as an *equipoise* to the clergy.	平衡、均衡 balance counterbalance	**poise**
v.	He has made an effort to *equipoise* the opposing interests of the two groups.	使平衡 balance adjust	
equitable a. ˈɛkwɪtəbḷ	Paying a person what he has earned is *equitable*.	公平、公正的 reasonable impartial	
equity n. ˈɛkwətɪ	The tax has to be further adjusted for the sake of *equity*.	公平、公正 impartiality rectitude	
equivalent a. ɪˈkwɪvələnt	The new TV film series has the *equivalent* footage of 12 feature pictures.	相等、等量的 commensurate tantamount	**val**(strong)
n.	This Swahili word has no *equivalent* in English.	相等物 counterpart	
equivocal a. ɪˈkwɪvəkḷ	Her statement was too *equivocal* to convince the board.	模稜兩可、可疑的 dubious ambiguous	**voc**(voice)
inadequate a. ɪnˈædəkwɪt	They could hardly achieve anything in their laboratory with *inadequate* equipment.	不充分的 deficient insufficient	**adequate**

單字‧音標‧詞類	例　　　　句	中譯‧同義字	字源分析
iniquitous* a. ɪˈnɪkwətəs	He was very displeased with the *iniquitous* bargain made previously under pressure.	不公平的 unjust unrighteous	**iniquity**
a.	All his friends disliked him for his *iniquitous* deeds.	邪惡、不法的 vicious nefarious	
iniquity* n. ɪˈnɪkwətɪ	They asked God to forgive their *iniquities*.	邪惡、不義之 行為 sin wickedness	in(not)

18

FAC·FACT·FAIR·FEAT·FECT FEIT·FIC·FICT·FIT

do, make

作●造

　　這是英文形態最複雜，組成單字最多的字根，源自拉丁文動詞 facere，本即有 do、make的意思。各種拼法中，fac, fact, fect, fic, fict 源出拉丁文 facer 的種種動、名詞變化，fair 直接借自法文，而 feat, feit, fit 則間接受 過法文影響。這個字根除了上述九種形態，尚可轉成一個動詞字尾 fy，意思也是 do 或 make。fy 是個異常重要的字尾，組成的重要字彙非常多，在此無法盡述，只列出較常考的一些，供讀者參考：

amplify v.「放大」	ratify v.「批准」
beatify v. 「祝福」	rectify v. 「修正」
diversify v.「使變化」	signify v. 「表示」
edify v. 「教化」	simplify v.「簡化」
fortify v. 「加強」	stupefy v.「使驚愕」
identify v.「認明」	terrify v. 「驚嚇」
justify v. 「辯護」	testify v.「作證」
personify v. 「擬人化」	unify v.「統一」
purify v. 「淨化」	verify v.「證明爲眞」
putrefy v. 「使腐朽」	

單字・音標・詞類	例　　　　　句	中譯・同義字	字源分析
affair n. əˈfɛr	That is my private *affair* which has nothing to do with you.	事情 matter business	af(to)
affect v. əˈfɛkt	Rainfall *affects* plant growth.	影響 influence sway	af(to)
v.	Her speech deeply *affected* the audience.	感動 move overcome	
v.	Youthfulness is something she has to *affect*.	假裝 pretend feign	
affectation n. ˌæfɪkˈteʃən	His love of music was mere *affectation*.	假裝、虛飾行為 assumed manners unnatural imitation	**affect**
affection n. əˈfɛkʃən	The children need love and *affection*.	愛、情感 amity attachment	**affect**
affectionate a. əˈfɛkʃənɪt	She flung an *affectionate* arm around Dick's neck.	摯愛的 loving devoted	**affection**
artifact n. ˈɑrtɪˌfækt	The archeologists have unearthed flints, arrowheads, and other *artifacts* of stone.	人工製品 man-made 　object	art(skill)
artifice* n. ˈɑrtəfɪs	The shrewd merchant had been known as a master of *aritifice*.	策略、詭計 cunning artfulness	art(skill)

單字·音標·詞類	例　　　句	中譯·同義字	字源分析
artificial a. ˌɑrtəˈfɪʃəl	*Artificial* flowers last much longer than natural ones.	人造、虛偽的 man-made fictitious	art(skill)
benefaction* n. ˌbɛnəˈfækʃən	The church received frequent *benefactions* from the wealthy people.	捐助 grant donation	**bene**(good)
beneficent* a. bəˈnɛfəsn̩t	A *beneficent* king is loved by all his subjects.	仁慈的 charitable benevolent	**bene**(good)
beneficial a. ˌbɛnəˈfɪʃəl	Moist, cool summers are not *beneficial* to such crops as maize.	有益的 profitable advantageous	**benefit**
beneficiary n. ˌbɛnəˈfɪʃərɪ	She was the sole *beneficiary* of her father's will.	受惠者 person receiving benefit	**bene**(good)
benefit n. ˈbɛnəfɪt	One can easily affirm the *benefits* of political democracy.	益處、裨益 advantage profit	**bene**(good)
v.	There are a great number of medicines that *benefit* mankind.	有益於 aid advance	
confection* n. kənˈfɛkʃən	The dramatist has presented an amusing *confection* with several charming melodies but with no real substance.	混合、調製 mixture preparation	**con**(together)

單字·音標·詞類	例　句	中譯·同義字	字源分析
counterfeit v. ˈkaʊntɚfɪt	The gang of outlaws has been *counterfeiting* $100 bills for months.	偽造、偽裝 forge simulate	**counter** (against)
a.	This is a *counterfeit* diamond made of paste which is worthless.	假、偽造的 spurious bogus	
defeat n. dɪˈfit	Our soldiers inflicted a severe *defeat* on the enemy troops.	失敗、征服 vanquishment rout	**de**(away)
v.	He *defeated* the opposing candidate by a large margin.	擊敗 beat overpower	
defect n. dɪˈfɛkt	They have carefully examined the timber for *defects*.	缺點 disadvantage shortcoming	**de**(away)
v.	The Russian general *defected* to the West in 1987.	投奔敵方、變 節、叛變 desert rebel	
deficient a. dɪˈfɪʃənt	A mentally *deficient* person is one who is weak-minded.	有缺點、缺乏 的 insufficient defective	**de**(away)
difficult a. ˈdɪfəˌkʌlt	I never enjoy facing such *difficult* situations.	困難、費力的 hard arduous	**dif**(not)

單字·音標·詞類	例　句	中譯·同義字	字源分析
difficulty n. ˈdɪfəˌkʌltɪ	Financial *difficulties* have given him much trouble.	經濟之困難、困難、障礙 hardship impediment	difficult
n.	Her *difficulty* is quite understandable.	困境 predicament dilemma	
effect n. əˈfɛkt	The *effect* of morphine is to produce sleep.	效力、結果 outcome consequence	ef(out)
n.	The *effect* of wind in changing tide levels is immense.	影響 influence power	
n.	The sculptor has achieved amazing *effects* with his woodcuts.	印象、意義 impression significance	
v.	With superb political skill, the Romans *effected* the unification of Italy.	實現 perform achieve	
effective a. əˈfɛktɪv	His arm was too badly injured to deliver an *effective* blow.	有力的 forcible potent	effect
effectual a. əˈfɛktʃʊəl	To the artist painting is but another less *effectual* way of writing dramas or history.	有效的 effective actual	effect

effectuate v. əˈfɛktʃʊˌet	They strove successfully to *effectuate* a settlement not by force but by reason.	使實現、實踐 accomplish execute	**effect**
efficacious a. ˌɛfəˈkeʃəs	Vaccination for smallpox is *efficacious*.	有效的 effective competent	**effect**
efficient a. əˈfɪʃənt	The *efficient* housewife takes the best possible care of her utensils.	有能力、有效的 effective capable	**effect**
facile a. ˈfæsl	The report proved to be surprisingly *facile* reading.	輕而易舉的 easy manageable	
a.	Her *facile* nature adapted itself to any company.	隨和的 docile compliant	
facilitate v. fəˈsɪləˌtet	Certain measures must be taken to *facilitate* the execution of the task.	使容易 ease expedite	**facile**
facility n. fəˈsɪlətɪ	Practice gives a wonderful *facility*.	熟練、靈巧 dexterity adroitness	**facile**
n.	There are in this university excellent *facilities* for graduate studies.	設備 means resource	

facsimile n.
fæk'sɪməlɪ

They have made a *facsimile* record of the man's statements.

複製
reproduction
copy

simile(like)

fact n.
fækt

A *fact* is something that we know to be true.

事實
reality
occurrence

faction n.
'fækʃən

The party had split into several *factions*.

小派系、小組織
group
clique

factious a.
fæk'tɪʃəs

We do not welcome *factious* political analyses like that.

黨派性、喜傾軋的
refractory
seditious

faction

factitious* a.
fæk'tɪʃəs

A clever politician may exploit the *factitious* popular enthusiasm in a totalitarian state.

虛假的
unreal
artful

factor n.
'fæktɚ

Rain and heat are *factors* in growing plants.

原動力、因素
condition
requirement

factory n.
'fæktərɪ

This *factory* produces cars.

工廠
building where things are manufactured

faculty n.
'fækltɪ

The members of the medical *faculty* of the university are required to submit a joint report.

全體教師
teaching staff

單字‧音標‧詞類	例　句	中譯‧同義字	字源分析
n.	He has a *faculty* for saying the right thing.	能力 aptitude knack	
feasible a. ˈfizəb]	I do not think this is a *feasible* plan.	切實可行的 achievable attainable	**feat**
feat n. fit	These stories are about the amazing *feats* of ordinary foot soldiers.	功績、偉業 accomplishment exploit	
feature n. ˈfitʃɚ	A *feature* of English grammar is the number of periphrastic forms.	組成要素 element constituent	
n.	Sparse pine growth is a *feature* of this landscape.	特色、特徵、特性 characteristic peculiarity	
forfeit* v. ˈfɔrfɪt	He *forfeited* his property by the crime he had committed.	喪失 lose renounce	for(outside)
imperfect a. ɪmˈpɝfɪkt	He had only an *imperfect* understanding of his task.	不完全、有缺點的 incomplete defective	**perfect**
infect v. ɪnˈfɛkt	He *infected* everyone with his zeal for nature.	影響、使受感染、傳染 affect contaminate	**in**(in)

單字·音標·詞類	例　　　句	中譯·同義字	字源分析
infectious a. ɪnˈfɛkʃəs	Measles is an *infectious* disease.	有傳染性的 epidemic pestilent	**infect**
magnificence n. mægˈnɪfəsn̩s	The guests were easily impressed by the *magnificence* of the hall.	富麗堂皇 splendor grandeur	**magn**(great)
magnificent a. mægˈnɪfəsn̩t	The pavilion is *magnificent* with painted ceilings and extravagant chandeliers.	壯麗、華麗的 grand extravagant	**magn**(great)
malefaction* n. ˌmæləˈfækʃən	A *malefaction* as such would be condemned by all men.	罪行、犯罪 crime offense	**mal**(bad)
manufacture n. ˌmænjəˈfæktʃɚ	The families engaged in domestic *manufacture* often live and work in one room.	製造 production creation	**manu**(hand)
v.	These factories *manufacture* beautiful jewelry of gold, silver, and precious stones.	製造 make produce	
perfect a. ˈpɝfɪkt	He has done a *perfect* job.	完美、全然的 complete immaculate	**per**(through)
v. pɚˈfɛkt	Art must be selective; nature must be *perfected*.	使完美無瑕、改進 improve refine	

單字・音標・詞類	例　　句	中譯・同義字	字源分析
proficiency n. prə'fɪʃənsɪ	These courses are aimed at giving the students a certain *proficiency*.	熟練、精通 expertness adeptness	**proficient**
proficient a. prə'fɪʃənt	The scholar is *proficient* in mathematics and philosophy.	精通、熟諳的 skilled adept	**pro**(forward)
profit n. 'prɑfɪt	He has made a *profit* on everything he sells.	利潤、收益、利益 gain benefit	**pro**(forward)
v.	Everyone should get as much liberal education as he can absorb and *profit* by.	獲利 gain benefit	
sacrifice n. 'sækrə,faɪs	Sometimes the *sacrifices* made by parents for their children are enormous.	犧牲的行為、損失、犧牲 loss immolation	sacr(sacred)
v.	They are willing to *sacrifice* their lives for the sake of freedom.	犧牲、獻祭 offer forgo	
suffice v. sə'faɪs	Just ten bombs would *suffice* to destroy the enemy's fort.	足夠、使滿足 be enough satisfy	**suf**(under)
sufficient a. sə'fɪʃənt	They have not had *sufficient* information to state the exact damage.	足夠、充分的 adequate ample	**suffice**

單字・音標・詞類	例　　　句	中譯・同義字	字源分析
surfeit v. ˈsɝfɪt	A large and corpulent gourmand is always *surfeited* with good eating.	使饜足、使飲食過度 overfeed cram	sur(over)
n.	A *surfeit* of advice annoys one.	過度、過量 excess superabundance	

19

FER

carry, bear

攜帶 ● 承負

　　字根 fer 源出拉丁文動詞 ferre，原即有 carry, bear 的意思。下文例字以 defer v. 比較特別，旣可作「延緩」，也可作「順從」，乍看之下，兩種字義彷彿相去甚遠。事實上，兩種字義在英文雖共用 defer 一個字，但是字源却不盡相同。 defer 作「延緩」源自拉丁文動詞 differre，字首 dif （ 英文則拼作 de ）有 away 的意思；作「順從」解釋的 defer 則源自 dēferre ，字首可作 down 的意思（ 這兩種字首用法請參閱本書「最重要的30個字首」 **8. de** 與 **9. de‧di‧dis** 兩節 ）。因此，原拉丁文本分爲兩個字，後進入古法文仍分 différer 和 déférer 兩字，到了英文因拼法、唸法均相似，久而久之方才合而爲今日所見的 defer 。此外，例字中的 indifferent a.「不感興趣、漠不關心的」，雖由否定字首 in 和 different a.「不同的」組合而成，但是字義並不是「相同的」，必須解釋爲「不認爲有任何差異、不在乎」，才能聯想出「不感興趣、漠不關心」的意思。

單字・音標・詞類	例　　　　句	中譯・同義字	字源分析
circumference n. sɚˈkʌmfərəns	The *circumference* of the earth at the equator is about 25,000 miles.	圓周、周圍 boundary perimeter	**circum**(around)
confer v. kənˈfɝ	I have to *confer* with him before I talk to you again.	商議 consult deliberate	**con**(together)
v.	The university *conferred* an honorary degree upon the scholar.	賜予、頒與 grant bestow	
conference n. ˈkɑnfərəns	The peace *conference* will be held in Reykjavik next year.	會議 meeting convention	confer
defer v. dɪˈfɝ	The boss is not happy because the payment of the debt is being *deferred*.	延緩、展期 delay procrastinate	**de**(away)
v.	The court has *deferred* its own opinion to that of the Congress.	順從 yield surrender	**de**(down)
deference n. ˈdɛfərəns	The conquered population should be treated with extreme *deference*.	敬意、尊重 honor respect	defer
deferential a. ˌdɛfəˈrɛnʃəl	The young man listened with *deferential* attention to the professor's talk.	恭順的 respectful reverential	defer

單字・音標・詞類	例　句	中譯・同義字	字源分析
differ v. ˈdɪfɚ	My views always *differ* from hers.	不同、相異 diverge disagree	dif(away)
difference n. ˈdɪfrəns	*Differences* in the manufacturing process result in a wide variety of flavors.	不同、差異 distinction discrepancy	**differ**
different a. ˈdɪfrənt	*Different* people do things differently.	不同、差異的 dissimilar diverse	**differ**
differentiate v. ˌdɪfəˈrɛnʃɪˌet	A botanist is able to *differentiate* varieties of plants.	辨別、使有區別 distinguish discriminate	**different**
ferry n. ˈfɛrɪ	The opening of the new bridge terminated the *ferry* service on the river.	渡船 ferryboat boat	
v.	Supplies must be *ferried* out to the island.	以船渡（人、貨）、用飛機運送 transport convey	
fertile a. ˈfɝtl	On our trip we saw *fertile* fields of ripening corn and oats.	肥沃、多產的 productive prolific	

單字·音標·詞類	例　句	中譯·同義字	字源分析
indifferent a. ɪnˈdɪfrənt	The strange man seemed unaffected and quite *indifferent* in the presence of beauty.	不感興趣、漠不關心的 unmoved apathetic	in(not) **different**
• **infer** v. ɪnˈfɝ	A baby could *infer* the existence of an environment which is not part of itself.	推知 conjecture surmise	in(in)
inference n. ˈɪnfərəns	His reasoning is stronger than some modern *inferences* of science.	推論、結論 conclusion deduction	infer
offer v. ˈɔfɚ	What did he *offer* you for having you back in the company?	提供、提出 propose present	of(toward)
n.	He is now considering job *offers* from several firms.	提供、提議、出價 bid proposition	
prefer v. prɪˈfɝ	What color do you *prefer*, red or silver?	較喜、寧愛 desire choose	pre(before)
proffer v. ˈprɑfɚ	The man was *proffered* the leadership of the union but declined it.	提供、提出 offer propound	pro(forward) offer
n.	We thanked him for his *proffer* of hospitality.	提供、提出 attempt suggestion	

單字·音標·詞類	例　　　句	中譯·同義字	字源分析
refer v. rɪˈfɝ	She often *referred* to me in her lectures.	言及、提到 advert allude	**re**(back)
v.	He *referred* his success to the good education he had had.	歸之於 ascribe attribute	
v.	Let's *refer* this dispute to the umpire.	交給、提交 deliver commit	
referee n. ˌrɛfəˈri	We need a *referee* to settle this dispute.	仲裁者、裁判 judge umpire	**refer**
suffer v. ˈsʌfɚ	We all have to *suffer* some time or another in our lives.	受苦、忍受 tolerate abide	**suf**(under)
transfer v. trænsˈfɝ	He has *transferred* to a better university.	遷移、轉學、調職 move change	**trans**(across)
n. ˈtrænsfɚ	He is going to arrange a *transfer* to another college.	轉學、調職、移轉 removal shift	

FIN

end

界限 • 終結

　　fin 源自拉丁文動詞 fīnīre 「限制、結束」和名詞 fīnis n.f.「界限、結束」。古羅馬詩人奧維德 (Ovid, 43B.C. −? 17A.D.) 作品中，有一句 "Fīnis corōnat opus" ("The end crowns the work")，句中第一個字 fīnis，便有 end 的意思。下文例字 finance n. 「財務、財源」出自古法文名詞 finance ，本義為「結束」，特別是「結束財務糾紛」，十五世紀英文借用之後，仍保有這兩種字義，後來現代法文將 finance 引申成「財務、財源」，英文也隨而引進了現代法文的解釋，而成了「財務、財源」。另一字 fine a.「細緻、美好的」源出古法文形容詞 fin ，原有「結束」的意思，其字義衍變可以藉 finish v. 「完成」一字來解釋。finish 除「完成」的意思之外，並可作「修飾、使完美」，因此不難看出同字源的 fine，何以有「細緻、美好」的意思。此外，finesse n.「細緻、技術」也是源出古法文的 fin ，所以意思和 fine 有互通之處。。

單字·音標·詞類	例　　句	中譯·同義字	字源分析
confine v. kən'faɪn	The dikes could *confine* the flood waters.	控制、限於範圍內 bound enclose	**con**(together)
v.	The man was *confined* in a prison for thirty years.	監禁、幽禁 imprison immure	
n.	Darwin had not moved entirely within the *confines* of the thought of his generation.	範圍、界限 limit bound	
define v. dɪ'faɪn	Can you *define* this word?	闡釋、下定義 explain interpret	**de**(down)
v.	Good manners *define* the gentleman.	為…之特質 distinguish characterize	
definite a. 'dɛfənɪt	I want nothing but a *definite* answer.	明確、正確的 exact explicit	**de**(down)
final a. 'faɪnl	What is your *final* decision?	最後的 eventual ultimate	
finale* n. fɪ'nɑlɪ	The audience did not like the *finale* of the ballet.	最後一幕、結局 concluding part	
finance n. fə'næns	The school had to close for lack of *finances*.	財務、財源 income money resources	

	v.	He has managed to *finance* his son through school.	供以經費 supply money for	
fine faɪn	a.	A pencil usually has a *fine* point.	細緻的 slender sharp	
	a.	He has married a *fine* woman.	美好、卓越的 excellent splendid	
	n.	He was demanded to pay a *fine* of 40 dollars.	罰金 penalty amercement	
finesse* n. fə'nɛs		These wines make up in richness and bigness what they lack in *finesse.*	細緻、技術 craft refinement	
finish v. 'fɪnɪʃ		Have you *finished* your homework yet?	完成、結束 end terminate	
	n.	His novels have a *finish*, a flavor, that the cultivated recognize and relish.	完美 perfection elaboration	
finished a. 'fɪnɪʃt		The texture of his writing is even and *finished.*	完美的 perfected consummate	finish

finite a.
ˈfaɪnaɪt

A universal theory cannot be induced from a *finite* number of facts.

有限的
limited
bounded

indefinite a.
ɪnˈdɛfənɪt

The man was sentenced to an *indefinite* prison term.

無限期、模糊 **definite**
的
undetermined
indistinct

infinite a.
ˈɪnfənɪt

The *infinite* wisdom of the wizard saved the prince's life.

無窮、極大的 **finite**
limitless
boundless

refine v.
rɪˈfaɪn

For years the poet has tried to *refine* his poetic style.

使精美、使文 **re**(again)
雅
purify
polish

refined a.
riˈfaɪnd

I was surprised to see that the man had a sensitive, *refined* face.

文雅、精確的 **refine**
cultivated
fastidious

FLECT·FLEX

bend

彎曲

flect, flex 出自拉丁文動詞 flectere 和名詞 flexiō，兩字都有「彎曲」的本義。以這個字根組成的單字，尚有一些不屬常用字彙範圍，列出如下以供參考：circumflect v.「使彎成圓形」、flexor n.「屈肌」、genuflect v.「屈膝、跪拜」等。

單字・音標・詞類	例　　　句	中譯・同義字	字源分析
deflect v. dɪˈflɛkt	The rays passing through the lens are *deflected*.	使轉向、使偏斜 bend deviate	de(away)
flex* v. flɛks	After sitting a few hours, he had to stretch and *flex* his knees.	彎曲 bend contract	
flexible a. ˈflɛksəbļ	Slim *flexible* birches were bowing in the wind.	易彎、柔順的 pliable supple	flex
a.	He has a *flexible* character, pleasant and cooperative but without strong convictions.	易說服、溫順的 manageable tractable	
flexuous* a. ˈflɛkʃʊəs	*Flexuous* shadows on the wall were making interesting patterns.	動搖不定、彎曲的 zigzag undulating	flex
inflect v. ɪnˈflɛkt	A profound feeling for music has *inflected* all his major work.	改變、轉向、彎曲 bend curve	in(in)
inflexible a. ɪnˈflɛksəbļ	He was a man of upright and *inflexible* temper.	不屈、強硬的 unyielding rigid	in(not) **flexible**
reflect v. rɪˈflɛkt	The sidewalks *reflect* heat on a hot day.	反射、反映 image mirror	re(back)

單字‧音標‧詞類		例　句	中譯‧同義字	字源分析
	v.	Take your time to *reflect* before you make up your mind.	考慮、思考 ponder cogitate	
reflective rɪˈflɛktɪv	a.	The box has a *reflective* surface.	反射、反映的 reflecting	**reflect**
	a.	The woman's *reflective* look amused me.	沈思的 meditative contemplating	
reflex ˈriflɛks	n.	A law should be a *reflex* of the will of the people.	反映、反照 reflection	**reflect**
	a.	Sneezing is a *reflex* act.	不自主、非意志所控制的 reflected	

22

FLU

flow

流動

　　字根 flu 出自拉丁文動詞 fluere，意思即為「流動」。這個字根一般常見的形態，均有其拉丁文字源，如 fluen, fluct, flux 等拼法，在拉丁文原已形成。另外有兩種拼法 flum, fluv，也是源自拉丁文 flu 字根的各類變化，但是組成的單字數量少，程度又偏難，因此本節並未收錄，如 flume n.「峽溝、引水道」（出自古法文 flum 和拉丁文 flūmen「河流」）、fluvial a.「河川的」（出自法文 fluvial 和拉丁文 fluviālis「河川的」）、fluminose a.「河川的」、fluviose a.「暢流的」、fluviology n.「河川學」等均是。

單字·音標·詞類	例　　句	中譯·同義字	字源分析
affluence n. ˈæflʊəns	From the various falls and cataracts there is an *affluence* and variety of iris bows.	豐富 abundance profusion	**af**(to)
n.	The heirs of the millionaire were reduced from *affluence* to destitution.	富裕 wealth riches	
affluent a. ˈæflʊənt	The writer's florid and *affluent* fancy was greatly admired by fellow writers.	豐富的 abundant copious	**af**(to)
a.	People in an *affluent* society are usually more refined.	富裕的 rich wealthy	
confluence* n. ˈkɑnflʊəns	The island has been formed by the *confluence* of two rivers.	滙流（處）、群集 concourse convergence	**con**(together)
effluence* n. ˈɛflʊəns	The politician likes the *effluence* of power rather than the conscious application of it.	流露、流出 emission emanation	**ef**(out)
fluctuate n. ˈflʌktʃʊˌet	Commodity prices *fluctuate* from year to year.	波動、變動 swing vacillate	
fluency n. ˈfluənsɪ	Her *fluency* was like the insistent chatter of a stream.	健言、流暢 smoothness volubility	

單字・音標・詞類	例　句	中譯・同義字	字源分析
fluent a. ˈfluənt	The speaker is *fluent* in Javanese and Malay.	流暢的 glib vocal	
fluid n. ˈfluɪd	The medical students have studied the *fluids* of the human body.	流體、液體 liquid	
a.	The essayist used a *fluid* style in writing his most famous essays.	流暢、易改變的 smooth mobile	
flux* n. flʌks	Language is subject to constant *flux*.	變遷、流動、改變 flow mutation	
influence n. ˈɪnfluəns	She has much *influence* on the children she teaches.	影響 direction sway	in(in)
v.	Her decision not to marry the man was greatly *influenced* by her mother.	影響 sway bias	
influential a. ˌɪnfluˈɛnʃəl	These considerations are *influential* in our decision.	有勢力的 controlling forcible	influence
influx* n. ˈɪnˌflʌks	The country is expecting an *influx* of foreign students.	流入、注入 inflow	in(in) flux

單字·音標·詞類	例　　　　句	中譯·同義字	字源分析
reflux* n. ˈriˌflʌks	We have been watching the flux and *reflux* of the tides for a whole day.	退潮 reflow refluence	**re**(back) **flux**
superfluity n. ˌsupɚˈfluətɪ	This book has a *superfluity* of introductions and summaries.	過多、過量 excess extravagance	**super**(over)
superfluous a. suˈpɝfluəs	The student is asked to eliminate *superfluous* words in his thesis.	不必要、過多的 excessive exorbitant	**super**(over)

23

FOUND·FUS

pour, melt

傾流 ● 鎔鑄

　　字根 found, fus源出拉丁文動詞·fundere ，原即有「傾流、鎔鑄」的不同解釋。found 的拼法出自法文的 fondre v.「鎔鑄」，但最早的字源仍然是拉丁文的 fundere; fus 則來自拉丁文 fundere 的過去分詞 fūsus 。下文例字中，語義衍變比較特別的有 futile a.「徒勞、無效果的」和 refuse v.「拒絕」。futile 來自法文的futile a.「徒勞的」，而法文 futile 又出自拉丁文 futtilis （又拼作 fūtilis），原拉丁文解釋爲「容易流出、洩出的」，後引申而成「靠不住、徒勞、無效果的」。refuse 源自法文 refuser v.「拒絕」，而法文的 refuser 則又出自拉丁文動詞 refundere，字首 re 有 back 的意思（參見本書「最重要的30個字首」**24. re** ），因此本義爲pour back 或 return，引申而有「拒絕」的意思。

單字・音標・詞類	例 句	中譯・同義字	字源分析
circumfuse* v. ˌsɝkəmˈfjuz	The army was *circumfused* on both wings.	展開、散布、圍繞 surround envelop	**circum**(around)
confound v. kɑnˈfaʊnd	I always *confounded* him with his twin brother.	分不清、混淆、使混亂 confuse cause disorder	**con**(together)
v.	Her husband's love affair with the actress stunned and *confounded* her.	使驚訝、使惶惑 astound baffle	
confuse v. kənˈfjuz	They have *confused* the issue in the debate.	使混淆、使混亂 blur disorder	**con**(together)
v.	She felt *confused* when she saw her husband walking hand in hand with another woman on the street.	使困惑、使惶惑不安 perplex confound	
diffuse v. dɪˈfjuz	A state in which power is concentrated will be more bellicose than one in which power is *diffused*.	分散、擴散 spread extend	**dif**(away)
a. dɪˈfjus	A critic could be quite impatient with a *diffuse* writer.	冗長的 verbose copious	

單字·音標·詞類	例　　句	中譯·同義字	字源分析
effuse v. ɛˈfjuz	The drawing room *effused* an atmosphere of unhappiness and discontent.	洋溢、散發、流出 radiate emanate	**ef**(out)
found v. faʊnd	The artisans have been asked to *found* a bell.	鑄造 cast	
fuse v. fjuz	These foundries *fuse* zinc and copper into hard, bright brass.	鎔合、鎔化 melt dissolve	
v.	A writer must know how to *fuse* a clutter of detail into a rich and fascinating narrative.	結合一起、合併 blend amalgamate	
fusion n. ˈfjuʒən	Welds are most commonly seen accompanied by *fusion*.	融解 melting smelting	**fuse**
n.	Cement is a *fusion* formed from exact proportions of shale and limestone.	融合一起的東西、聯合 coalition amalgamation	
futile a. ˈfjutl	She gave up after several *futile* attempts.	徒勞、無效果的 fruitless ineffective	
infuse v. ɪnˈfjuz	An aviation curriculum has been *infused* into some forty university departments.	灌輸 introduce inculcate	**in**(in)

單字·音標·詞類	例　　　　　句	中譯·同義字	字源分析
interfuse* v. ˌɪntɚˈfjuz	These curricular designs would seek to *interfuse* the social sciences and humanities.	使融合、使混合 intermingle commix	**inter**(between)
perfuse v. pɚˈfjuz	The room was suddenly *perfused* with light as she opened the window.	使充滿、撒滿 diffuse suffuse	**per**(through)
profuse a. prəˈfjus	The poor men were *profuse* in their thanks after they had found their money.	很多、浪費的 extravagant bountiful	**pro**(forward)
profusion n. prəˈfjuʒən	The rich couple had been known for their taste, hospitality, *profusion*.	揮霍、浪費 extravagance prodigality	**profuse**
refuse v. riˈfjuz	Please don't *refuse* me or I'll kill myself.	拒絕 reject decline	**re**(back)
suffuse v. səˈfjuz	The sky was *suffused* by colorful fireworks.	布滿、充盈 fill infuse	**suf**(under)
transfuse v. trænsˈfjuz	The statesman has *transfused* his ideas throughout the land.	灌輸 transmit instill	**trans**(across)
v.	Life is not merely an added property of matter but something that *transfuses* and transforms it.	使滲入 pervade permeate	

24

FRACT·FRAG·FRANG·FRING

break

破裂

　　字根 fract, frag, frang, fring 源出拉丁文動詞 frangera，原即有 break 的意思。fract的拼法出自 fractus 的過去分詞fractus，frag 出自 fragilis a.「易碎的」、fragmen n.n.「碎片」、fragor n.m.「破裂聲」等拉丁字，frang 出自上述的 frangere，而 fring 則源出拉丁文本身的字根變化，如拉丁字 infringere v.「撞破、打倒」之中，便可見到如此拼法。此外，拼法比較奇特的，尚有 frail a.「脆弱的」和 frailty n.「脆弱、缺點」。這兩個字分別借自古法文的fraile（或作 frele，現代法文則作 frêle）和fraileté，但是這些古法文，仍然來自拉丁文的fragilis，因此字源追根究底起來，自然還是源頭的拉丁文。下文例字意義衍變比較特別的，有 infract v.「破壞、侵犯」、infringe v.「侵犯、違背」、refract v.「使折射」、refractory a.「難駕御、頑固的」四個字。infract與 infringe 同源，出自前述的拉丁文動詞 infringere，原拉丁文有break 的意思，而英文的 break 可作「侵犯、違反」，因此不難了解這兩字為何有如此解釋。refract和 refractroy 源出拉丁文動詞 refringere，有 break off 「衝破、打斷」的意思，因此若是把光之類的物質「打斷」，便可引申而成「使折射」。 refractory 源出拉丁文形容詞refractā-rius，在拉丁文已由前述動詞 refringere 「衝破、打斷」的意思，引申成「好吵架、喧鬧」，後又轉成「難駕御、頑固」。

單字·音標·詞類	例　句	中譯·同義字	字源分析
fraction n. ˈfrækʃən	The price of the commodity declined only a *fraction*.	微量、部分、片 fragment scrap	
fractional a. ˈfrækʃənļ	They spoke after only a *fractional* pause.	極小、極少的 inconsiderable insignificant	fraction
fracture n. ˈfræktʃɚ	The man died from a *fracture* of the skull.	破裂 break rupture	
v.	The boy fell from the tree and *fractured* his leg.	打斷、破碎 break crack	
fragile a. ˈfrædʒəl	We saw a *fragile*, tottering old man on the street.	虛弱、易碎的 feeble frail	
fragment n. ˈfrægmənt	After centuries only *fragments* of the precious religious manuscript have remained.	斷簡殘篇、破片、片斷 scrap morsel	
v.	The vase fell and *fragmented* into small pieces.	成為碎片、打破 break up	
frail a. frel	In so short a time they could only build a bridge with *frail* construction.	脆弱、不堅實的 feeble infirm	

單字・音標・詞類	例 句	中譯・同義字	字源分析
frailty n. ˈfreltɪ	The minister has declaimed on many occasions against the *frailty* of human flesh.	脆弱 weakness infirmity	**frail**
n.	He loved her in spite of her little *frailties*.	缺點、過失 defect blemish	
frangible a. ˈfrændʒəbḷ	Fire-extinguishing fluid should not be put into such *frangible* containers.	易破、易碎的 breakable brittle	
infract * v. ɪnˈfrækt	Neither of these two nations should *infract* their neutrality.	破壞、侵犯 break infringe	**in**(in)
infrangible a. ɪnˈfrændʒəbḷ	They attributed her success to her *infrangible* resolution.	不能破壞、不可侵犯的 unbreakable inviolable	**in**(not) **frangible**
infringe v. ɪnˈfrɪndʒ	The copyright of this book has been *infringed.*	侵犯、違背 violate transgress	**in**(in)
refract * v. rɪˈfrækt	Water *refracts* light.	使折射 reflect	**re**(back)
refractory * a. rɪˈfræktərɪ	The boy was solitary and *refractory* to all education save that of wide and desultory reading.	難駕御、固執的 stubborn perverse	**refract**

25

GEN

bear, kind, race

產生 ● 種類 ● 種族

字根 gen 源出拉丁文動詞 genere「生育」和名詞 gens n.f.「家族、種族」、genus n.n.「種族、種類」，而且與希臘文的 γενοs (genos) n.m.「出生、親族、性別」也有間接關係。下文例字有不少語義衍變比較奇特，乍看之下可能不易了解。如 general a.「普遍、一般的」，來自古法文 general ，原拉丁文作 generālis，本有「屬於同一種類的」的意思，再引申而成「普遍、一般的」。 generic a.「共有、一般的」出自另一字 genus n.「屬、種類」，原有「屬的」的意思（即生物學分類「界門綱目科屬種」之中的「屬」），後來衍變過程和上述 general 一字相同，也轉成了「共有、一般的」。 generous a.「有雅量、慷慨的」源自拉丁文形容詞 generōsus ，本義為「貴族、出身高貴的」，後來在拉丁文已引申成「高尚、慷慨」，指人作為高尚有雅量，看似出身高貴。 genial a.「暖和、和藹的」源出拉丁文形容詞 geniālis ，原義為「誕辰、婚姻的」，引申又有「歡宴、愉快的」的意思，而宴會慶典正是親朋好友和藹相處，溫情洋溢的地方，因此自然又轉而可作「暖和、和藹的」；由此也不難想像，另一字 congenial a.「令人快樂、適合的」究竟從何而來了。genius n.「天才、才能」借自拉丁文名詞 genius ，原指「庇護人一生命運之神」，引申而有「神仙」的意思，最後將非凡的天賦視如天賜神力，便轉成了「天才、才能」。genuine a.

「眞正的」源出拉丁文形容詞 genuīnus，原有「天生、先天的」的意思，天生的特質是實實在在的東西，所以拉丁文本已引申而成「眞正、實在的」。gentle a.「溫和、輕柔的」借自古法文的 gentil，而古法文 gentil 又源自拉丁文形容詞 gentīlis，原義爲「同一家族的」，後來進入法文、西班牙文、義大利文、葡萄牙文等拉丁文方言，逐漸轉成「出身上等家族的」（gentleman n.「紳士」一字便出自這個字源），最後再轉而描述貴紳的行爲態度，便有了「溫和、輕柔的」的意思。ingenious a.「智巧、靈敏的」源自法文 ingéni-eux 與拉丁文 ingeniōsus，原在拉丁文便作「聰穎的」，字首 in 有「在內」的意思，因此「生來便在其中」，自然指人的天生資質。ingenuous a.「坦白、誠樸的」源出拉丁文形容詞 ingenuus，本義爲「天生、土生的」，後來引申而指生來便是自由人（freeman，享有公民權的古羅馬公民），才又轉爲「坦白、誠樸」，有如高雅的自由人。

單字・音標・詞類	例　句	中譯・同義字	字源分析
congenial* a. kənˈdʒinjəl	The family found the atmosphere of the village *congenial* and settled down there.	令人快樂、適合的 pleasant consonant	con(together) **genial**
congenital* a. kənˈdʒɛnətḷ	The baby was born with *congenital* malformations.	天生的 innate inherent	con(together) **genital**
degenerate v. dɪˈdʒɛnəˌret	The old man's health *degenerated* rapidly.	衰敗、墮落 decay deteriorate	de(away) **generate**
a. dɪˈdʒɛnərɪt	The modern and *degenerate* society has rejected the governance of religion.	墮落、卑賤的 corrupted base	
engender v. ɪnˈdʒɛndɚ	Angry words *engender* strife.	產生、釀成 generate beget	en(in) **gender**
gender n. ˈdʒɛndɚ	The Latin language has three *genders,* masculine, feminine, and neuter.	性、性別 sex	
genealogy* n. ˌdʒinɪˈælədʒɪ	After seeing *Roots,* many people became interested in *genealogy.*	宗譜、家系 lineage pedigree	logy(science)
general a. ˈdʒɛnərəl	A government takes care of the *general* welfare.	普遍、大眾的 common extensive	

	a.	A *general* reader reads different kinds of books.	一般、普通的 ordinary common	
generate v. ˈdʒɛnəˌret		These stories *generate* a great deal of psychological suspense.	引起、產生 produce create	
generation n. ˌdʒɛnəˈreʃən		The *generation* of heat is more obvious in mountain ranges than in low-lying plains.	產生、發生 production formation	**generate**
	n.	The family reunion included members from five *generations*.	一代、子孫、一族 offspring stock	
generic* a. dʒəˈnɛrɪk		The novel has a *generic* habit of reaching out to the extremes of literary expression.	共有、一般的 general universal	**genus**
generous a. ˈdʒɛnərəs		Mrs. Wilson was always *generous* in her judgment of people.	有雅量、慷慨的 kindly benevolent	
genesis* n. ˈdʒɛnəsɪs		No one knows much about the *genesis* of this epidemic disease.	根源、創造 origin creation	
genial a. ˈdʒinjəl		The climate in the region is *genial* with ample rainfall.	暖和、和藹的 mild affable	

genital a.
'dʒɛnətl

The doctor believed
that there was something
wrong with his *genital*
gland.

生殖的
generative

genius n.
'dʒinjəs

Albert Einstein was a
mathematical *genius*.

天才、英才
master
mastermind

n.

He has a *genius* for
acting.

才能、天賦
faculty
gift

genre n.
'ʒɑnrə

Some believe that the
epic is the noblest of
literary *genres*.

類型
kind
category

genteel a.
dʒɛn'til

She spent most of her
declining years in
genteel poverty.

裝做貴族、上
流社會、有教
養的
fashionable
well-bred

gentle a.
'dʒɛntl

The boy has a *gentle*
nature.

溫和、和善的
amiable
meek

a.

She gave him a *gentle*
tap on the shoulder.

輕柔的
slight
light

genuine a.
'dʒɛnjʊɪn

He could tell that it was
a *genuine* vintage wine.

真正的
pure
authentic

單字·音標·詞類	例　句	中譯·同義字	字源分析
genus n. 'dʒinəs	These streams are a *genus* by themselves and are not miniature rivers.	種類、屬 kind class	
homogeneous* a. ˌhoməˈdʒinɪəs	It is difficult to have a *homogeneous* group of students because students are not all the same.	同類、相似的 uniform similar	homo(same)
indigenous* a. ɪnˈdɪdʒənəs	Indians were the *indigenous* inhabitants of America.	土著、土產、天生的 native innate	indi(within)
ingenious a. ɪnˈdʒinjəs	The iron safe built into the wall was made by an *ingenious* locksmith.	智巧、靈敏的 clever resourceful	in(in)
ingenuous a. ɪnˈdʒɛnjʊəs	There are times when he could be astonishingly *ingenuous*.	坦白、誠樸的 simple unwary	in(in)
progenitor n. proˈdʒɛnətɚ	These thinkers are called the *progenitors* of socialist ideas.	前輩、祖先 forefather precursor	pro(forward)
progeny n. 'pradʒənɪ	The artist has examined one by one the marvelous *progeny* of the workman's art.	成果、產品、子孫 children outcome	pro(forward)
regenerate v. rɪˈdʒɛnəˌret	Lizards can *regenerate* lost tails.	再生、重生 re-create revive	re(again) **generate**

26

GRAD·GRESS

go, step

行進 ● 層次

　　grad, gress 源出拉丁文動詞 gradior 「踏步、行走」與名詞 gradus n.m. 「步伐、層次」。兩種拼法中的 gress ，出自 gradior 的過去分詞 gressus。下文意義衍變比較特別的例字，只有 graduate v. 「畢業」。graduate 借自中古拉丁文 (Medieval Latin) 動詞 graduāre ，原義爲「授與大學文憑」，可藉字根「層次」的解釋來引申，所謂「更上一層樓」，自然不難聯想出「畢業」的字義。grad 、gress 組成的單字，尚有一些不屬常用字彙範圍，僅列出如下以供參考： gradient n. 「坡度、升降率」、gradienter n. 「傾斜測定器」、gressorial a. 「適合步行的（指動物）」等。

單字·音標·詞類	例　　句	中譯·同義字	字源分析
aggress v. ə'grɛs	The lions were seeking whom they might *aggress*.	進攻 attack assault	**ag**(to)
aggressive a. ə'grɛsɪv	*Aggressive* and positive in his convictions, he became a zealot in any cause he embraced.	積極、好鬥的 militant assertive	**aggress**
congress n. 'kɑŋgrəs	He is going to attend the *Congress* for Cultural Freedom at Montreal.	會議 convention convocation	**con**(together)
degrade v. dɪ'gred	The officer was *degraded* for disobeying orders.	降級、免職 demote depose	**de**(down) **grade**
v.	Their love for their country was *degraded* into a contempt for all foreigners.	(使)墮落、惡化 corrupt debase	
digress v. də'grɛs	I shall not pursue these points further for fear of *digressing* too far from my main theme.	離開本題 deviate diverge	**di**(away)
egress* n. 'igrɛs	The enemy blocked the narrow pass so that no *egress* was possible for our troops.	出路、出口 exit outlet	**e**(out)
gradation n. gre'deʃən	There are many *gradations* between poverty and wealth.	等級 degree in an 　order	

單字·音標·詞類	例　　　　句	中譯·同義字	字源分析
grade n. gred	Milk is sold in *grades*.	等級、階級 degree rank	
v.	Salt is usually *graded* before it is sold.	分等級、歸類 rank classify	
gradual a. ˈgrædʒʊəl	There is a *gradual* change for the better in the patient's condition.	逐漸的 continuous regular	
graduate v. ˈgrædʒʊˌet	Gill is going to *graduate* from college soon.	畢業 receive a degree	
ingredient n. ɪnˈgridɪənt	Understanding is one of the most important *ingredients* of a successful marriage.	組成分子、因素 element component	in(in)
ingress* n. ˈɪngrɛs	There is a gate providing *ingress* to the meadow.	進入 entrance access	in(in)
progress n. ˈprɑgrɛs	The patient is not making any *progress* today.	進步、改進 advance improvement	pro(forward)
v. prəˈgrɛs	Deductive reasoning had to be combined with the methods of experimentation before science could *progress*.	發展、進步 advance develop	

單字·音標·詞類	例　　句	中譯·同義字	字源分析
regress* n. ˈrigrɛs	The gunboats were sent to the harbor to ensure a free ingress and *regress* of ships.	後退 withdrawal egress	**re**(back)
retrograde* v. ˈrɛtrəˌgred	The army has *retrograded* from the front.	後退 withdraw retreat	retro(back- ward)
a.	The teacher asked the student to give the numbers in a *retrograde* order.	相反、顛倒、後退的 inverse retreating	
retrogressive* a. ˌrɛtrəˈgrɛsɪv	The senses represent to us the course of the planets sometimes as progressive, sometimes as *retrogressive*.	後退的 retreating retrograde	retro(backward)
transgress v. trænsˈgrɛs	Her manners *transgressed* the boundaries of good taste.	踰越、違反 exceed trespass	**trans**(over)

27

IT

going, march

行走 • 行進

字根 it 源出拉丁文名詞 iter n.n.「行路、旅行」與 itio n.f.「往、行」。這個字根在下文例字中，除了拼作 it 外，在 perish v.「毀滅、死亡」、transient a.「短暫、片刻的」兩字中，並可見到不同的形態。perish 出自古法文動詞 perir，字首 per 原義為 through，後可轉為「離異、毀壞」，因此 perish 便有「毀滅、死亡」的意思（請參閱本書「最重要的 30 個字首」**20. per**）。transient 源出拉丁文動詞 transīre「越過、超過」（參見下文例字 transit v./n.「通過」），拼法則借自 transīre 轉成的形容詞 transiens，原有「通過的」的意思，後來到了十七世紀，已引申為「短暫、片刻的」。此外，語義衍變比較特別的例字，有 ambition n.「雄心、熱望」和 initial a.「最初的」、initiate v.「發起、開始」。ambition 直接借自法文的 ambition，但更早的字源則是拉丁文的 ambīre v.「奔走」（字首 ambi 有 around 的意思），ambīre 引申又有「奔走以爭取聲望權勢」的意義，因此 ambition 便成了「雄心、熱望」。另外，initiate 和 initial 則分別來自拉丁文的 initiāre v.「開始」和 initiālis a.「最初的」，字首 in 有「在其中、進入」的意思，配上字根，可引申成「著手進行某事」，因此原本在拉丁文便有「開始、最初」的字義。

單字·音標·詞類	例　　　句	中譯·同義字	字源分析
ambition n. æmˈbɪʃən	A young man with *ambition* will always work hard.	雄心、熱望 aspiration enterprise	ambi(around)
ambitious a. æmˈbɪʃəs	After a series of overwhelming victories, the Romans became more *ambitious*.	有野心、熱望的 aspiring enterprising	**ambition**
circuit n. ˈsɝkɪt	The earth makes a periodic *circuit* around the sun.	環行、周圍 revolution circumference	circu(circle)
circuitous a. sɝˈkjuɪtəs	They have adopted a *circuitous* method of solving the problem.	間接、迂廻的 indirect roundabout	**circuit**
exit n. ˈɛgzɪt	There are usually many taxis waiting at the *exit* of the theater.	出口、離去 outlet departure	ex(out)
initial a. ɪˈnɪʃəl	The *initial* symptoms of the disease have begun to appear.	最初、開始的 first commencing	in(in)
initiate v. ɪˈnɪʃɪˌet	The government has actively *initiated* a new construction program.	發起、開始 commence institute	in(in)
itinerant * a. aɪˈtɪnərənt	The couple had joined an *itinerant* theatrical troupe.	巡廻、流動的 traveling vagrant	
itinerary n. aɪˈtɪnəˌrɛrɪ	The *itinerary* that they planned should take them through Canada.	旅行計畫、旅行路線 route journey	

單字・音標・詞類	例　　　句	中譯・同義字	字源分析
itinerate* v. aɪˈtɪnəˌret	The church sent many *itinerating* missionaries to Africa in the 19th century.	巡廻、遊歷 travel wander	
perish v. ˈpɛrɪʃ	The city *perished* in the eruption of the volcano.	毀滅、死亡 expire decease	**per**(through)
transient a. ˈtrænʃənt	Life is *transient*.	短暫、片刻的 temporary ephemeral	**trans**(over)
transit v. ˈtrænsɪt	Ships use the canal to *transit* to the west.	通過、經過 pass traverse	**trans**(over)
n.	For the Gauls the *transit* of so vast a Roman territory was extremely dangerous.	通行、經過 journey passage	
n.	Movements were organized to bolster morale in the *transit* from war to peace.	變遷、改變 change transition	
transitory a. ˈtrænsəˌtorɪ	The man does not care for the *transitory* pleasures of the world.	短暫、頃刻的 fleeting transient	**transit**

28

JAC·JECT·JET

throw, emit

投擲 • 射出

字根 jac, ject, jet 源出拉丁文動詞 iacere，原即有 throw、emit 的意思。中古時期以前，拉丁文並沒有 j 字母。到了中古時期，拉丁字中如有 i 字母兼半母音 (semivowel) 功能者，則逐漸改寫作 j，以便和表示母音功能的 i 有所區別。因此，目前這個字根的三種拼法，與其拉丁文字源何以有 j、i 的差異，應該不難瞭解。三種拼法中，jac 源出前述拉丁文動詞 iacere, ject 出自拉丁文本身的字根變化（如 rēicere v.「摒棄、拒絕」、dēicere v.「擲下、驅逐」等），而 jet 則受了法文影響（如古法文動詞「投擲」便作 jetter 或 getter，現代法文作 jeter）。

單字·音標·詞類	例　句	中譯·同義字	字源分析
abject* a. æb'dʒɛkt	What these organizers could do was merely an *abject* imitation of foreign ideas.	卑劣、卑屈、可恥的 base dishonorable	**ab**(away)
conjecture n. kən'dʒɛktʃɚ	I am afraid your *conjecture* is mistaken.	推測、猜想 assumption hypothesis	**con**(together)
v.	Washington *conjectured* that at least 300 of the enemy were killed.	推測、猜想 guess surmise	
deject v. dɪ'dʒɛkt	He felt *dejected* when she refused his marriage proposal.	使沮喪 discourage depress	**de**(down)
ejaculate* v. ɪ'dʒækjə,let	The members of the parliament were angrily *ejaculating* unfinished sentences.	射出、喊叫、突然說出 eject exclaim	**e**(out)
eject v. i'dʒɛkt	The volcano has *ejected* lava and ashes.	噴出 emit vomit	**e**(out)
v.	The tenants were *ejected* for not paying the rent.	逐出、罷黜 oust expel	
inject v. ɪn'dʒɛkt	The writer has *injected* both color and humor into his rather formidable subject.	加入、注射 force in introduce	**in**(in)
interjacent* a. ,ɪntɚ'dʒesənt	No one has paid attention to his *interjacent* remarks.	居間、中間的 intervening interpolated	**inter**(between)

單字・音標・詞類	例　　　句	中譯・同義字	字源分析
interject* v. ˌɪntɚˈdʒɔkt	Every now and then the speaker *interjected* some witty remark.	插入 interpose interpolate	**inter**(between)
jettison* n. ˈdʒɛtəsn̩	In the election people witnessed the horrifying *jettison* of convictions, honor, and patriotism.	放棄、拋棄 abandonment surrender	
v.	If a diver does not know how to control his equiment or to *jettison* it in an emergency, he would be courting disaster.	投棄、放棄 abandon discard	
object v. əbˈdʒɛkt	I will not *object* to whatever suggestion you make.	反對 oppose demur	**ob**(against)
n. ˈɑbdʒɪkt	Describe the *object* you have in your hand right now.	物體、物件 thing article	
project v. prəˈdʒɛkt	The fountain *projects* its slender column of water about 85 feet in the air.	射出 throw cast	**pro**(forward)
v.	A road is now *projected* all the way along the ridge of the mountain.	計劃、設計 design contrive	
n. ˈprɑdʒɛkt	Do you have any new *projects* on hand?	計畫 plan scheme	

單字・音標・詞類	例　　　　句	中譯・同義字	字源分析
reject v. rɪˈdʒɛkt	He *rejected* their offer of the new position.	拒絕 refuse decline	re(back)
subject v. səbˈdʒɛkt	A servant should *subject* himself to his master.	使服從、使隸屬 submit subjugate	sub(under)
a. ˈsʌbdʒɪkt	The area is now *subject* to very severe droughts.	易蒙受、服從的 submissive subordinate	
n. ˈsʌbˌdʒɪkt	The king has always been benevolent to his *subjects*.	臣民、臣下 dependent subordinate	
n.	He likes to treat religion as the first and greatest of all *subjects*.	論題、主題 theme topic	

JOIN·JOINT·JUNCT

join, connect

連接

　　字根 join, joint, junct　源出拉丁文動詞 iungere，本義即為「連接」。其中 join 與 joint 的拼法來自古法文 joindre　v.「連接」，junct　則出自上述拉丁文 iungere　的過去分詞 iūnctus　。字根三種拼法與拉丁文原字的 i、　j 語音互換現象，請參閱前一節「最重要的70個字根」**28. jac·ject·jet** 部分。下文例字中，意義衍變比較特別的，有 enjoin v.「命令、禁止」和 injunction n.「命令、禁止」。這兩字均出自拉丁文動詞 injungere，原有「使相連、連結」的意思，引申而成「加給、強令」（意義與英文的 impose　相同），其中 injunction　源出 injungere轉成的名詞　injuctiōnem　，而 enjoin則轉由法文的 enjoindre v.「命令」借入。

單字·音標·詞類	例　　句	中譯·同義字	字源分析
adjoin v. əˈdʒɔɪn	His land *adjoins* the sea.	鄰接 connect attach	**ad**(to)
adjunct* n. ˈædʒʌŋkt	Road building and bridge building some- times are *adjuncts* of warfare.	伴隨、附屬物 appendage supplement	**adjoin**
n.	An *adjunct* is a person associated with another in some duty or service.	助手、副手 associate assistant	
conjoin* v. kənˈdʒɔɪn	A certain complex of conditions *conjoin* to create the economic boom.	結合、聯合 join unite	**con**(together)
conjunct* a. kənˈdʒʌŋkt	A man has to feel himself *conjunct* to a social group.	結合的 joined united	**con**(together)
conjunction n. kənˈdʒʌŋkʃən	These are things not normally seen in *conjunction*.	連合、結合 combination association	**conjoin**
conjuncture n. kənˈdʒʌŋktʃɚ	His work is a rare *conjuncture* of realism with idealism.	結合 union combination	**conjoin**
disjoin v. dɪsˈdʒɔɪn	Bivalents will normally *disjoin*.	分開、拆散 separate sunder	**dis**(away)
disjoint v. dɪsˈdʒɔɪnt	Great Britain, *disjointed* from her colonies, suffered a gradual decline.	斷絕、使分離 、使分裂 disunite sever	**dis**(away)

單字·音標·詞類	例　　　句	中譯·同義字	字源分析
disjunction n. dɪsˈdʒʌŋkʃən	The *disjunction* of soul and body has always been an interesting subject.	分離 separation parting	**disjoin**
enjoin* v. ɪnˈdʒɔɪn	He found himself attacked, yet was *enjoined* by conscience from deliberately taking human life.	命令、禁止 command forbid	**en(in)**
injunction* n. ɪnˈdʒʌŋkʃən	The Hindu religion has no *injunctions* against birth control.	命令、禁令 order prohibition	**enjoin**
join v. dʒɔɪn	The brook *joins* the river.	會合、交接 connect unite	
v.	They have asked him to *join* the club.	加入、參加 participate in	
joint n. dʒɔɪnt	If you use *joints,* you can make these short pipes into a long one.	連接物、連接處 juncture hinge	join
v.	The stones *joint* neatly.	接合 fit unite	
a.	We could have great achievements through our *joint* efforts.	共同、連合的 united combined	

單字·音標·詞類	例　　　　　句	中譯·同義字	字源分析
junction n. ˈdʒʌŋkʃən	A *junction* of the two armies shall help us win the battle.	連合 joining union	
juncture n. ˈdʒʌŋktʃɚ	The poet's works emphasize the *juncture* of poetry and music.	連合 union junction	
n.	At this *juncture* in history no one knew what mishaps would ensue.	時刻、時際 moment point of time	
subjoin* v. səbˈdʒɔɪn	Let me *subjoin* another example.	添加 add attach	sub(under)

30

LECT·LEG·LIG

select, gather, read

選擇 ● 收集 ● 閱讀

　　字根 lect, leg,lig源出拉丁文動詞 legere ，原本便有select, gather, read 等多重意義。各種拼法中，leg 來自原動詞 legere, lect 出自 legere 的過去分詞lēctus ， lig 則出自拉丁文原先的字根變化。下文例字意義衍變較特別的，有 collect v.「使鎮靜」、diligent a.「細心、勤勉的」、elegance n.「優雅」、 elegant a.「優雅的」、sacrilegious a.「褻瀆神明的」。collect 源出拉丁文動詞 colligere的過去分詞 collectus，字首 col 有 together 的意思，因此原義為「收集」，進入英文之後，到了十七世紀初，可指人經過情緒波動後再設法「集中」心神，因而轉成「使鎮靜」的意思。diligent 源出法文 diligent ，但更早的字源則是拉丁文動詞dīligere ，有 choose 或 value highly 的意思。人所珍視的事物挑選起來總是比較細心，因此 dīligere 轉成的形容詞 dīligēns ，原本即有「細心」的意思，後來引申又成了「勤勉的」，進入法文和英文之後，兩種字義便保留了下來。 elegance和 elegant 源出法文的 élégance 和 élégant，最早的字源則是拉丁文動詞ēligere「摘下、揀選」，指「極有技巧地」選擇事物，因此原本在拉丁文已形成的名詞 ēlegantia和形容詞 ēlegans，均已轉成「優雅」的意思，進入法文、英文之後，自然也保留了這層字義。sacrilegious源出拉丁文形容詞 sacrilegus ，由sacr「神聖」、 leg 「收集」兩個字根組成，原指「偷竊教堂中的聖器

」，引申而有「褻瀆神明」的意思（請參考 sacrilege n.「竊取聖物、褻瀆神明」）。

collect v.
kə'lɛkt

She has been *collecting* stamps for years.

收集、集合、積聚
gather
amass

col(together)

v.

They were excited and required time to *collect* themselves.

使(心神)安靜或鎮靜
calm
compose

collected a.
kə'lɛktɪd

He became *collected* after entering the quiet room.

鎮靜、平靜的
composed
sedate

collect

collective a.
kə'lɛktɪv

The *collective* interests of the society should be heeded.

集體、聚集的
aggregated
representative

collect

diligent a.
'dɪlədʒənt

Let's be watchful and *diligent*.

細心的
careful
heedful

di(away)

a.

We need a *diligent* investigator to find out the truth.

勤勉的
industrious
sedulous

elect v.
ɪ'lɛkt

A chairman was *elected* to superintend the operation of business.

選舉、選擇
select
choose

e(out)

elegance n.
'ɛləgəns

Her feminine *elegance* is beyond description.

優雅、文雅
grace
refinement

e(out)

elegant a.
'ɛləgənt

She rendered her poetry in a surprisingly *elegant* style.

優雅的
graceful
refined

e(out)

單字・音標・詞類	例　　　　　句	中譯・同義字	字源分析
eligible a. ˈɛlɪdʒəbḷ	These books are not *eligible* for copyright in this country.	合格的 qualified suitable	elect
illegible a. ɪˈlɛdʒəbḷ	He injured his right hand in football, making his handwriting almost *illegible*.	難讀的 obscure unreadable	legible
intellect n. ˈɪntḷˌɛkt	The *intellect* of the country recognized his superiority.	智識份子、智力 mind brains	inter(between)
intellectual a. ˌɪntḷˈɛktʃʊəl	Satire is an *intellectual* weapon.	理智、需用智慧的 intelligent rational	intellect
n.	An *intellectual* is a person endowed with unusual mental capacity.	智者、知識份子 person with intellectual tastes	
intelligence n. ɪnˈtɛlədʒəns	Some conceive of history as the expression of a divine *intelligence*.	智能、理智、聰明 cleverness sagacity	inter(between)
intelligent a. ɪnˈtɛlədʒənt	The *intelligent* animal is able to benefit from its past experience.	有理解力、理智、聰明的 acute discerning	inter(between)

單字・音標・詞類	例　　　句	中譯・同義字	字源分析
intelligentsia* n. ɪnˌtɛləˈdʒɛntsɪə	This country has an unsteady, rebellious, and bright *intelligentsia*.	知識階級、知識份子 intellectuals	inter(between)
intelligible a. ɪnˈtɛlɪdʒəbl̩	She gave an *intelligible* description of her aspirations.	明白、可理解的 clear comprehensible	inter(between)
lecture n. ˈlɛktʃɚ	There are resources of knowledge in books, exhibits, and *lectures*.	演講、講課 address lesson	
n.	Mother always gave me a *lecture* when I did something wrong.	訓誡、譴責 scolding censure	
legend n. ˈlɛdʒənd	All the well-known families had their grotesque or romantic *legends*.	稗史、故事 story tale	
legible a. ˈlɛdʒəbl̩	Murder swelled in the young man's heart and was *legible* on his face.	可看出、可讀的 distinct readable	
legion* n. ˈlidʒən	His reputation as a spiritual guru has won him a *legion* of devoted followers.	衆多的人或物 host multitude	
neglect v. nɪˈglɛkt	The school has *neglected* the real needs of the students.	忽略、不顧 disregard overlook	neg(not)

單字·音標·詞類	例　　句	中譯·同義字	字源分析
negligent a. ˈnɛglədʒənt	The man was *negligent* about traffic regulations and got himself killed.	疏忽、怠忽的 careless lax	**neglect**
negligible a. ˈnɛglədʒəbḷ	Fortunately, the error involved is *negligible*.	很小的 slight trifling	**neglect**
recollect v. ˌrikəˈlɛkt	I could not *recollect* having seen her anywhere.	憶起、記起 remember recall	**re**(back)
recollection n. ˌrikəˈlɛkʃən	The happy *recollections* of her childhood days have kept her awake all night.	記憶、記起、 回想的事物 memory remembrance	**recollect**
sacrilegious a. ˌsækrɪˈlɪdʒəs	Her *sacrilegious* acts infuriated the priest.	褻瀆神的 desecrating blasphemous	sacr(sacred)
select v. səˈlɛkt	They haven't *selected* their leader yet.	挑選、選擇 choose pick	se(separate)
a.	Only a few *select* officials are admitted to the conference next month.	精選、極好的 choice superior	

31

LOCU·LOG·LOQU

speak

說話

字根 locu, log, loqu 源出希臘文名詞 λογos (logos) 和拉丁文動詞 loquor、名詞 locūtiō，原即有「說話、話語」的意思。下文例字中，語義衍變比較奇特的，有 epilog(ue) n.「收場白、結語」和 logical a.「合邏輯的」。 epilog(ue) 源自希臘文名詞 ἐπιλογos (epilogos)，字首 epi 有「附加於上」的意思，原本便指附加在一段話上的「結語」。logical 源出名詞 logic n.「邏輯」，而 logic 來自中古拉丁文的 logica，logica 則又源自希臘文的 λογικos (logikos)，λογικos 又來自上述的 λογos (logos)。希臘文名詞 λογos 本義為「言語、話語」，後來引申而指「思考、推想」，因此輾轉進入英文的時候，早已經有「邏輯推理」的意思。

單字・音標・詞類	例　　　　句	中譯・同義字	字源分析
allocution* n. ˌælə'kjuʃən	Fifteen years ago, when he was pleading with the Americans for a loan, he delivered a sensational *allocution*.	演講、訓示 address exhortation	al(to)
apologize v. ə'pɑlə͵dʒaɪz	I would like to *apologize* if I have done anything wrong.	道歉 acknowledge an offense	**apology**
apology n. ə'pɑlədʒɪ	I think I owe you an *apology*.	道歉、謝罪 confession reparation	apo(from)
catalog(ue) n. 'kætl͵ɔg	We have a complete *catalog* of our commodities.	目錄 list inventory	cata(down)
circumlocution* ˌsɝkəmlo'kjuʃən n.	The speaker had a preference for *circumlocution* rather than forthrightness.	迂迴累贅的陳述 roundabout way of speaking	circum(around)
colloquial a. kə'lokwɪəl	The letter is written in a *colloquial* style.	口語、會話的 conversational	col(together)
dialog(ue) n. 'daɪə͵lɔg	There are many interesting *dialogs* in this play.	對話 conversation discourse	dia(through)
elocution* n. ˌɛlə'kjuʃən	The speaker is an expert user of *elocution*.	演說術、雄辯術 oratorical delivery	e(out)

eloquence n.
ˈɛləkwəns

The writer of this book praises Plato's *eloquence* and moral fervor.

雄辯
fluency
rhetoric

e(out)

eloquent a.
ˈɛləkwənt

The *eloquent* young senator soon became a well-known figure.

雄辯的
fluent in speech

e(out)

epilog(ue)* n.
ˈɛpəˌlɔg

Shakespeare's plays often end with an *epilogue* spoken by one of the characters.

收場白、結語
conclusive
　　section

epi(upon)

eulogize* v.
ˈjuləˌdʒaɪz

This was one of the rare days of June *eulogized* by poets.

稱讚、頌揚
commend
extol

eulogy

eulogy* n.
ˈjulədʒɪ

His speech was an elaborate mixture of *eulogy* and admonition.

頌揚
laudation
commendation

eu(good)

grandiloquent* a.
grænˈdɪləkwənt

The adventurer made a *grandiloquent* speech about his great expeditions.

誇大的
boastful
pompous

grand

locution* n.
loˈkjuʃən

The people in this region have their own *locutions* which they use every day.

語句、慣用語
peculiarity of
　　phrasing

logical a.
ˈlɑdʒɪkl̩

The conclusion they have drawn is *logical*.

合邏輯、合理
的
coherent
reasonable

logic

單字・音標・詞類	例　　　　句	中譯・同義字	字源分析
loquacious a. loˈkweʃəs	Critics disliked the prolonged and *loquacious* death scene in the play.	嘮叨、喧噪的 noisy wordy	
monolog(ue) n. ˈmɑnlͺɔg	Poems are sometimes the *monologues* of a young man isolated in his genius.	獨白、自言自語 soliloquy	**mono**(one)
prolog(ue)* n. ˈprolɔg	*Romeo and Juliet* begins with a *prologue* that summarizes the story for the audience.	開場白、序言 introduction foreword	**pro**(forward)
soliloquy* n. səˈlɪləkwɪ	A *soliloquy* is a discourse made by a person to himself.	獨白 monologue	**sol**(sole)

32

LUC·LUMIN·LUSTR

light, brightness

亮光

---

　　luc, lumin, lustr 源出拉丁文。luc 的拼法來自拉丁文 lūcēre v.「照耀」，lumin 來自拉丁文名詞 lūmen n.n.「光亮」的屬格變化 lūminis 及形容詞 lūminōsus「光亮的」，而 lustr 則出自 lūstrāre v.「照明」。下文意義衍變比較特殊的例字，只有 illustrate v.「舉例說明、畫插圖」一字。illustrate 源出拉丁文動詞 illustrāre，字首 il 爲 in 的變音（字根的第一個音爲 l，因此 in 便同化爲 il），原有「照耀」的意思，後來引申又成「顯示、表明、使著名」（參見另一例字 illustrious a.「著名的」），進入法文（法文作 illustrer）和英文後，便形成了「舉例說明、闡明」的意思，最後「畫出圖畫藉以說明」，終於又衍變爲「畫插圖」的意思。

單字·音標·詞類	例　句	中譯·同義字	字源分析
elucidate v. ɪˈlusəˌdet	The editors have added many critical notes to *elucidate* the text.	闡明、說明 interpret expound	e(out) **lucid**
illuminate v. ɪˈluməˌnet	The fountains are beautifully *illuminated* at night.	照明 light up brighten	**in**(in)
v.	Historical insights serve to clarify and *illuminate* the critical activity of a period.	闡釋、說明 elucidate enlighten	
illumine* v. ɪˈlumɪn	Electric lights *illumine* our houses.	照亮 brighten light	**in**(in)
illustrate v. ˈɪləstret	The professor *illustrated* the new theory by carefully referring to what was already known.	舉例說明 clarify elucidate	**in**(in)
v.	This book is very well *illustrated*.	畫插圖 decorate	
illustrious a. ɪˈlʌstrɪəs	The people discussed in this book are all *illustrious* heroes of antiquity.	著名的 famous celebrated	**in**(in)
lucent* a. ˈlusn̩t	The tourists can watch the underwater world through the *lucent* glass.	透明、明亮的 clear luminous	

lucid a.
ˈlusɪd

In the *lucid* twilight
the lamps seemed a
little dim.

明亮的
luminous
radiant

a.

The writer's style is
lucid because he always
makes his meaning clear.

清晰、易懂的
clear
intelligible

luculent* a.
ˈlukjʊlənt

Her commentary on
the news was *luculent*.

明晰的
convincing
evident

luminary* n.
ˈlumə͵nɛrɪ

The man claimed to
have seen a huge celestial
luminary in his backyard.

發光體
body that gives
　light

n.

The research group will
consist of the inter-
national *luminaries* in
the field.

大師、名人
celebrity
famous person

luminosity* n.
͵lumə'nɑsətɪ

John Dewey thought
that the mind was a
constant *luminosity*.

發光物、光明　**luminous**
brightness
something luminous

luminous a.
ˈlumənəs

The leaves of the trees
were *luminous* with
the bright sunlight.

發光、光亮的
shining
resplendent

a.

His prose was simple
and *luminous*.

明晰的
plain
lucid

luster n.
ˈlʌstɚ

This pearl has a beautiful
luster.

光澤
sheen
gloss

單字・音標・詞類	例　　　句	中譯・同義字	字源分析
lustrous a. ˈlʌstrəs	Her eyes were luridly *lustrous* in her pale face.	光亮的 luminous gleaming	**luster**
a.	The feminist has set a *lustrous* example for other women to follow.	傑出的 illustrious glamorous	
pellucid* a. pəˈlusɪd	The water in the white glass beaker is clear and *pellucid.*	清澈、透明的 transparent translucent	**per**(through) **lucid**
translucent* a. trænsˈlusn̩t	From the canoe I could watch the colorful fish through the *translucent* water.	半透明的 clear transparent	**trans**(through)
a.	His interpretation of the work is amazingly delicate and *translucent.*	容易了解的 clear lucid	

33

MAGN·MAJ·MAX

great

大

字根 magn, maj, max 源出拉丁文形容詞 magnus「大的」，與其比較級 māior「比較大的」、最高級 maximus「最大的」。其中比較級 māior 與字根 maj 的拼法，有 i、j 兩音互換現象，詳細情形請參閱前述「最重要的 70 個字根」 **28. jac·ject·jet** 部分。天主教耶穌會 (Jesuit Order) 箴言 "Ad māiōrem Deī glōriam" ("To the greater glory of God") 中，便有比較級 māior 的格變化 māiōrem。各例字中語意衍變比較特殊的，只有 maxim n.「座右銘、格言」一字。西元六世紀時，羅馬哲學家 包伊修斯 (Boethius, 480?–?524) 在著作中，首先將 prōpositiō maxima (greatest proposition)，視作「公理、定理」（如英文的 axiom）的意思。到了十二世紀，學者逐漸去掉 prōpositiō ，而直接將 maxima 稱作「公理、定理」。maxima 進入英文之後，到了十六世紀，終於又衍變成今日慣用的「座右銘、格言」，拼法也縮短為 maxim。

單字‧音標‧詞類	例　　句	中譯‧同義字	字源分析
magnanimous* a. mæg'nænəməs	Even his enemies would admit that he was *magnanimous*.	度量寬大、心地高尚的 forgiving noble	**anim**(spirit)
magnate* n. 'mægnet	The syndicate was bought by a Mexican *magnate*.	大企業家、巨擘 very influential 　person	
magnificence n. mæg'nɪfəsn̩s	Her guests were impressed by the *magnificence* of her house.	宏大、堂皇 splendor grandeur	**fic**(do)
magnificent a. mæg'nɪfəsn̩t	He is a heavily built man with a *magnificent* pair of shoulders.	絕美、宏偉、富裕的 splendid extravagant	**fic**(do)
magnify v. 'mægnə,faɪ	Objects can be *magnified* with a microscope.	放大、強調 enlarge intensify	
magnitude n. 'mægnə,tjud	The kings could not wage a war of such *magnitude* without inaugurating a new epoch.	巨大、宏大 vastness grandeur	
majestic a. mə'dʒɛstɪk	The white robe looks *majestic* on her.	宏偉、莊嚴的 imperial grand	**majesty**

majesty n.
ˈmædʒɪstɪ

The luminous band of the Milky Way stretches in quiet *majesty* all around the sky.

威嚴、莊嚴
grandeur
magnificence

major a.
ˈmedʒɚ

He was regarded as one of the *major* poets of his generation.

主要、多數的
superior
principal

majority n.
məˈdʒɔrətɪ

The *majority* of the people on earth prefer peace to war.

多數
most
plurality

major

maxim n.
ˈmæksɪm

A *maxim* is a funda-mental principle of conduct.

座右銘、格言
saying
proverb

maximal a.
ˌmæksəməl

I promise I shall do my job with my *maximal* effort.

最大、最高的
highest
greatest

maximum

maximum n.
ˈmæksəməm

It is not easy to find the *maximum* of efficiency with the minimum of labor.

最大量
greatest
　quantity

a.

The *maximum* score on the test is 100.

最高、最大的
greatest
highest

34

MAIN·MAN

hand

手

字根 main, man 源出拉丁文名詞 manus，原即有「手」的意思；其中 main 的拼法係借自法文（現代法文便以 main 作「手」的意思）。下文例字語義衍變比較特別的，有 manifest a.「明顯的」（v.「顯示」）、manifesto n.「宣言」及 manner n.「方式、舉止、態度」。manifest 源出拉丁文 manifestus，內中 festus 在拉丁文原本有 struck 的意思（動詞不定式原作 fērīre)，所以原指「用手敲擊以明示」，而引申為「明顯的」。manifesto 則源出義大利文的 manifesto，但義大利文源起拉丁文，因此字源也是上述的拉丁文。另外，manner 乃直接借自古法文的 manere（現代法文作 manière），但最早的字源則是拉丁文名詞 manus「手」，原指 mode of handling「處置方式」（注意 handle v.「處置」一字即源出 hand n.「手」），引申而成「方式」，再引申而有「舉止、態度」的意思。

單字·音標·詞類	例　　句	中譯·同義字	字源分析
emancipate v. ɪˈmænsəˌpet	The slaves were *emancipated* on the day when the country was conquered.	解放 free liberate	e(out) **cip**(receive)
maintain v. menˈten	Peace in the world must be *maintained*.	維持 sustain uphold	**tain**(hold)
v.	The radicals *maintained* that the government was untrustworthy.	主張 hold assert	
manacle* n. ˈmænəkḷ	The prisoners of the pirates were wearing *manacles*.	手銬 handcuff	
manage v. ˈmænɪdʒ	She does not like anyone else to tell her how to *manage* her own business.	處理、管理 execute conduct	
v.	We finally *managed* to reach the place by dusk.	達成、完成 succeed in 　accomplishing	
maneuver n. məˈnuvɚ	The grand *maneuvers* will be held tomorrow.	演習、調遣 military 　movement	**euver**(work)
n.	When we refused to adopt his idea, he tried to force it on us by a series of *maneuvers*.	策略 manipulation stratagem	

單字‧音標‧詞類	例　　　句	中譯‧同義字	字源分析
v.	The girl *maneuvered* successfully to get the young man to ask her to the dance.	用計策 scheme plot	
manifest v. ˈmænəˌfɛst	She *manifested* much willingness to go.	顯示 show demonstrate	fest(strike)
a.	Witchcraft has *manifest* and latent functions for the individual and for social groups.	明顯的 obvious conspicuous	
manifesto＊ n. ˌmænəˈfɛsto	The professors signed a *manifesto* repudiating the charges made by the press.	宣言 public 　declaration	**manifest**
manipulate v. məˈnɪpjəˌlet	Nature may be so *manipulated* that mathematical laws may be applied to it.	處理、操作 work handle	pul(fill)
manner n. ˈmænɚ	In what *manner* are you going to do it?	方法、方式、 樣子 way fashion	
n.	Her terrible *manners* have worried her mother.	舉止、態度 bearing demeanor	
manual a. ˈmænjʊəl	One should never despise *manual* labor of whatever form.	手、手工的 done by the 　hands	

n.	Mrs. Perkins has just got her copy of the teacher's *manual*.	手冊 handbook	
manufacture n. ˌmænjəˈfæktʃɚ	Families engaged in domestic *manufacture* often live and work in one room.	製造 production creation	**fact**(do)
v.	This substitute for milk is *manufactured* from the soya bean.	製造 make produce	
manumit* v. ˌmænjəˈmɪt	Four million slaves had been *manumitted* by a stroke of the president's pen.	解放 liberate emancipate	**mit**(send)
manuscript n. ˈmænjəˌskrɪpt	The *manuscript* will go to press early next month.	原稿、手稿 handwritten 　　copy	**scrip**(write)

35

MINI·MINU

small

小

　　字根 mini, minu 源出拉丁文形容詞 parvus「小的」的比較級 minor 或 minus「比較小的」，以及最高級 minimus「最小的」。下文語義衍變比較特別，乍看之下不易瞭解的例字，有 minister n.「牧師、部長」（v.「服事」）和 administer v.「管理、給與」、administration n.「管理」。從拼法可看出 administer, administration，原有「家僕、輔佐、代辦」的意思，更早的字源則為比較級形容詞 minus「比較小的」，因此上述幾種不同的字義，均指「代辦較小事務的人」。後來引申而可作服事神的「牧師」，輔佐元首的「部長」。再加上字首 ad（參見本書「最重要的 30 個字首」2. ad），形成 administer、administration 兩字，便有「管理」的意思。其中 administer 一字，在拉丁文作 administrāre，除有「管理」的意思外，並可引申而成「給與、供應」。

單字・音標・詞類	例　　　　句	中譯・同義字	字源分析
administer v. əd'mɪnəstə	A government that is badly *administered* can never be expected to last long.	管理 mangage govern	**ad**(to) **minister**
v.	The government is going to *administer* relief to the refugees.	給與 dispense execute	
administration n. əd,mɪnə'streʃən	Her father has been engaged in the *administration* of public affairs for years.	管理 direction superintendence	**administer**
diminish v. də'mɪnɪʃ	Losses and desertions sharply *diminished* the forces at General Washington's disposal.	減少 reduce curtail	**di**(away)
diminution n. ˌdɪmə'njuʃən	Though sick, he did not experience any *diminution* of his physical powers.	減少、衰落 decrease degradation	**di**(away)
diminutive a. də'mɪnjətɪv	The funny man from the circus is *diminutive* in stature.	小的 small minuscule	**di**(away)
mince* v. mɪns	The director *minced* up the play.	細分、切割 chop hash	
miniature n. 'mɪnɪətʃə	Paris is France in *miniature*.	縮影、縮圖 small copy	

	a.	The small boy kept staring at the *miniature* railway in the window.	縮小的 small minute
minimal a. ˈmɪnɪml̩		The other party showed a willingness only to accept *minimal* terms.	最低、最小的 extremely 　minute	minimum
minimize v. ˈmɪnəˌmaɪz		Centuries of cultivation have *minimized* the distinction among the various regions.	減至最小程度 、輕視 reduce decry	minimum
minimum n. ˈmɪnəməm		We need economic stabilization with a *minimum* of government regulation.	最小量 smallest 　quantity	
minister n. ˈmɪnɪstɚ		A *minister* was there at the wedding this morning.	牧師 churchman clergyman	
	n.	Canadian *ministers* carry the political responsibility for their departments.	部長 official administrator	
	v.	During the plague he *ministered* to the sick.	服事、看護 serve attend	
minor a. ˈmaɪnɚ		There are only *minor* errors in his composition.	較小、較次要的 unimportant petty	

minority n.
mə'nɔrətɪ

Only a small *minority* of students is majoring in a basic subject.

少數
smaller group

minor

minute a.
mə'njut

They said that irrigation could be applied only to *minute* areas.

小的
tiny
infinitesimal

.

a.

Her father showed so much hospitality that he wanted to explain all the *minute* happenings of the ranch.

細小、瑣屑的
petty
trifling

36

MISS·MIT

send, throw

送出 ● 投射

字根miss,mit 源出拉丁文動詞 mittere 與其過去分詞 missus，原即有 send, throw 的意思。下文例字中，message n.「口信」、messenger n.「報信者」兩字可見到另一種拼法 mess。這種形態的拼法出自法文，message 源出法文的 message, messenger 則由其名詞 messager 轉音而成。此外，omit v.「遺漏、忽略」一字字首為 ob「相對、反對」，但拼法却略去了 b 字母，詳細情形可參閱本書「最重要的30個字首」18. ob 一節。例字中語義衍變比較奇特的，有 surmise v./n.「臆測、猜度」一字。 surmise 源出古法文 surmise，更早的字源則是後期拉丁文 (Late Latin) 動詞 supermittere。字首 sur 或 super 有 upon, over 的意思，因此原在拉丁文、古法文指「將罪過歸在某人身上」（亦即「指控、控訴」charge, accuse）。指控人必須事先將事情想妥，有時甚至得費心推想一番，所以最後又引申而成「臆測、猜度」的意思。

單字·音標·詞類	例　句	中譯·同義字	字源分析
admit v. əd'mɪt	She was not *admitted* to the meeting because she did not carry a pass.	准許進入 allow give access to	**ad**(to)
v.	I *admit* I did something wrong.	承認 confess concede	
commission n. kə'mɪʃən	He executed a *commission* for me while he was in Singapore.	委託代辦的事 errand duty	**commit**
n.	A broker receives a *commission* on each share of stock bought for a customer.	佣金 fee allowance	
n.	A U.N. *commission* was formed to investigate the differences between the two countries.	考察團、代表團 delegation deputation	
v.	Judges are not *commissioned* to make or unmake rules at pleasure.	委任、授權 empower authorize	
commit v. kə'mɪt	The patient was *committed* by the court to the state hospital.	委託、交付 entrust consign	**com**(together)
v.	She *committed* suicide on a rainy night.	作、犯 do perpetrate	

單字·音標·詞類	例　　　句	中譯·同義字	字源分析
compromise n. ˈkɑmprəˌmaɪz	The warring nations have finally reached a satisfactory *compromise.*	和解 settlement concession	**com**(together) **promise**
v.	The union and the employers have agreed to *compromise.*	和解 settle arbitrate	
demise n. dɪˈmaɪz	A regent was appointed at the unexpected *demise* of the crown.	死亡 death decease	**de**(down)
demission* n. dɪˈmɪʃən	He has signed his *demission* in form.	辭職、放棄 dismissal relinquishment	**de**(down)
dismiss v. dɪsˈmɪs	After instructing him, the master *dismissed* the servant.	使告退、解散 disband disperse	**dis**(away)
v.	The writer's latest work has been *dismissed* as utterly frivolous.	摒棄、驅除 refuse to 　consider 　seriously	
emissary n. ˈɛməˌsɛrɪ	The warring countries have sent *emissaries* to discuss possible peace terms.	使者 messenger representative	**e**(out)
emit v. ɪˈmɪt	Fire *emits* heat and smoke.	放出、噴出 discharge eject	**e**(out)

單字·音標·詞類	例　　　句	中譯·同義字	字源分析
v.	In this book she *emits* her inmost thoughts concisely and lucidly.	吐露 express couch	
intermission n. ˌɪntɚˈmɪʃən	Do you feel like going out for a while during the *intermission?*	休息時間、間歇、中斷 cessation interval	**inter**(between)
intermit* v. ˌɪntɚˈmɪt	The poor people prayed to God to *intermit* the horrifying plague.	中止、暫停 discontinue suspend	**inter**(between)
intermittent a. ˌɪntɚˈmɪtənt	The child has been having *intermittent* fever since last night.	間歇、斷續的 irregular recurrent	**intermit**
manumit* v. ˌmænjəˈmɪt	With a stroke of the pen the president *manumitted* millions of slaves.	解放 liberate emancipate	**man**(hand)
message n. ˈmɛsɪdʒ	I want to leave Joanne a *message.*	口信、書信 note word	
messenger n. ˈmɛsn̩dʒɚ	The Romans had sent a *messenger* to announce their victory.	報信者 courier herald	**message**
missile n. ˈmɪsl̩	Spears are still used as *missiles* in some parts of the world.	投射的武器、飛彈 projectile	
mission n. ˈmɪʃən	His father serves on a *mission* to help improve agricultural methods.	負有特殊任務之團體、使節團 delegation deputation	

n.	The special squad is out on a secret *mission*.	任務、使命 duty errand	
missive* n. ˈmɪsɪv	The driver delivered the *missives* at the embassy door every morning.	書信、公文 letter epistle	
omission n. oˈmɪʃən	The police detective was chided for the *omission* of clues essential to the case.	遺漏 neglect oversight	**omit**
omit v. oˈmɪt	This valuable book should not be *omitted* from your reading.	遺漏、忽略、略去 overlook eliminate	**ob**(against)
permit v. pɚˈmɪt	Please *permit* me to offer you my congratulations.	允許、許可 allow consent	**per**(through)
promise v. ˈprɑmɪs	Will you *promise* me never to meet him again?	答應、允諾 assure pledge	**pro**(forward)
n.	She has given me her *promise* never to see the boy again.	諾言、約定 guarantee agreement	
promising a. ˌprɑmɪsɪŋ	Mrs. Harper thought her son-in-law was a *promising* young man.	有希望的 full of hope auspicious	**promise**

單字・音標・詞類	例　　　句	中譯・同義字	字源分析
remiss* a. rɪˈmɪs	I have been very *remiss* in not calling upon you.	疏忽、不小心的 careless negligent	remit
remission* n. rɪˈmɪʃən	*Remission* of sins is promised to those who repent.	赦免、寬恕、免除 forgiveness exoneration	remit
remit v. rɪˈmɪt	I will *remit* the money to my cousin in France.	滙寄 send forward	re(back)
v.	Through God priests have the power to *remit* sins.	赦免 forgive pardon	
v.	After we had rowed the boat into calm water, we *remitted* our efforts.	減輕、鬆懈 relax mitigate	
submit v. səbˈmɪt	The question will be *submitted* to the court.	提出 propose commit	sub(under)
v.	Metal can be *submitted* to high heat and pressure.	使降服、使服從 bend comply	
surmise v. sɚˈmaɪz	She knew at the moment that what she had *surmised* was true.	臆測、猜度 guess conjecture	sur(super)

單字・音標・詞類	例　　　句	中譯・同義字	字源分析
n.	What he expressed as mere *surmise* was transcribed by others as a positive statement.	臆測、猜度 supposition conjecture	
transmit v. træns'mɪt	The telephone *transmits* sound.	傳送、傳達 send communicate	**trans**(across)

37

MOB·MOM·MOT·MOV

move

移動 • 動力

字根 mob, mom, mot, mov 源出拉丁文 mobilis a.「可移動的」、mōmentum n.n.「推動、重要」、mōtus n.m.「行動、變動」、movēre v.「移動、震動」。這個字根除了上述四種拼法外，尚有一種極少見的變體，例字中的 mutiny n./v.「叛變」便有如此拼法。mutiny 借自法文的 mutiny，法文 mutiny 又源出拉丁文俗語 movita，但更早的字源則是前文提過的 movēre。「叛變」指情勢變動，因此應該不難了解何以「移動」的字根，能夠衍變出「叛變」的意義。此外，語義衍變較特別的例字，尚有 moment n.「瞬間、片刻」、momentous a.「重大的」和 motif n.「主題」。moment 與 momentous 均出自上文提過的拉丁文名詞 mōmentum「推動、重要」（並請參見下文例字的 momentum 條），而 mōmentum 原在拉丁文即可引申成「時間變動」，也就是「瞬間、片刻」的意思，因此應該可以了解 moment 與 momentous 兩字，意義為何相去甚遠。另一字 motif 借自法文 motif，更早的字源則是中古拉丁文 (Medieval Latin) 的 mōtīvus，例字中的 motive n.「動機」也是源出於此。不過，motif 最初雖指動機，後來却引申而指文學藝術作品中的「動機、動因」，因而轉成了「主題」的意思。

單字・音標・詞類	例　　句	中譯・同義字	字源分析
commotion n. kə'moʃən	A gang of hooligans was making a *commotion* on the street.	暴動 turmoil tumult	**com**(together) **motion**
demote v. dɪ'mot	The soldier was *demoted* from sergeant to corporal.	降級 reduce	**de**(down)
emotion n. ɪ'moʃən	Love between men and women is such a hot, stupid thing, all *emotion* and no thought.	情感、激情 feeling passion	**e**(out)
immobile a. ɪ'mobl̩	She remained *immobile* no matter how the boy tried to tease her.	不動的 motionless fixed	**mobile**
mob n. mɑb	The *mob* had been dispersed before the police arrived.	羣聚之羣眾 assemblage throng	
mobile a. 'mobl̩	Ether and mercury are *mobile* liquids.	流動、動的 movable	
a.	His *mobile* face mirrors every feeling from bitter sadness to ecstasy.	易變的 changeable mutable	
mobilize v. 'mobl̩‚aɪz	All reserve forces will be *mobilized* for overseas duty.	動員 organize assemble	**mobile**
v.	Ego feeling and ego attitude can *mobilize* hostile feelings toward others.	使運動 develop 　acutely	

單字・音標・詞類	例　　　句	中譯・同義字	字源分析
moment n. 'momənt	It was in my *moments* of solitude that I came to realize my helplessness.	瞬間、片刻 instant flash	
n.	Decisions of *moment* must be made with immense care.	重要 importance consequence	
momentary a. 'momən,tɛrɪ	The life of a recluse makes all human trouble appear but a *momentary* annoyance.	刹那、瞬息的 temporary transitory	**moment**
momentous a. mo'mɛntəs	The economic recession has brought *momentous* changes that affect us all.	重大、極重要的 weighty important	**momentum**
momentum n. mo'mɛntəm	The horse galloped with a velocity and *momentum* continually increasing.	運動量、動力 impetus	
motif* n. mo'tif	Disillusion is an excellent *motif* for his new novel.	主題 central theme	**motive**
motion n. 'moʃən	According to the Copernican scheme, the earth has three *motions*.	運動、移動 movement passing	
n.	Their *motion* has been seconded.	動議、提議 proposal proposition	

單字・音標・詞類	例　　句	中譯・同義字	字源分析
motivate v. 'motə,vet	The novelist has adequately *motivated* his hero.	激發、引起動機 impel incite	motive
motivation n. ,motə'veʃən	Sex has been treated as one of the *motivations* of animal behavior.	刺激、誘導 drive incentive	motivate
motive n. 'motɪv	Their chief *motive* was revenge.	動機 incentive inducement	
move v. muv	If you *move* one more step, I'll kill you.	移動 go budge	
v.	Her sad story did not seem to *move* him.	感動、煽動 touch agitate	
movement n. 'muvmənt	An astronomer studies the *movement* of planets.	移動、動作 motion activity	move
n.	The pope has launched a religous *movement*.	社會運動 organized 　action	
mutiny n. 'mjutn̩ɪ	The colonial *mutinies* were soon quashed.	叛變 rebellion revolt	
v.	The extreme left wing of the party *mutinied* just before the election.	叛變 rebel revolt	

單字·音標·詞類	例 句	中譯·同義字	字源分析
promote v. prə'mot	He was *promoted* colonel.	擢升 elevate exalt	**pro**(forward)
v.	The organization is dedicated to *promoting* international under-standing.	促進、鼓勵 further encourge	
remote a. rɪ'mot	The church was too *remote* for a walking bridal party.	遙遠、隱秘的 distant secluded	**re**(back)
remove v. rɪ'muv	He plans to *remove* his family to the seashore.	遷移 shift transfer	**re**(back)
v.	They advocate *removing* the causes of poverty.	除去 eliminate exterminate	

38

PASS·PATH

feel, suffer

感覺 ● 苦痛

　　字根 pass, path 源出希臘文名詞 $\pi\alpha\theta\eta$ (pathē), $\pi\alpha\theta o\varsigma$ (pathos) 和拉丁文名詞 passio，原本即有「感覺、感情、苦痛」的意思。這個字根除了上述兩種形態，尚有 pat 一種拼法，在下文 compatible a.「相容的」、incompatible a.「不能和諧共存的」、patient a.「堅忍的」、impatient a.「不能忍受的」各字中均可見到。這些單字均借自法文，因此 pat 的拼法乃受法文影響的結果。下文例字中語義衍變比較特別的，有 passive a.「消極、被動的」一字。passive 源出拉丁文形容詞 passīvus，原義為「可受痛苦的」，引申而成「消極、被動的」，指受痛苦而不抵抗的人總是比較被動。此外，例字 empathy n.「神入」意義相當特殊，必須略加解說。empathy 源出希臘文 $\dot{\epsilon}\mu\pi\alpha\theta\epsilon\iota\alpha$ (empatheia)，字首 em 有 in 的意思（參見本書「最重要的30個字首」12. em·en·im·in ），指能設身處地深入體會別人情感的心理能力，一般心理學稱為「神入」。

單字・音標・詞類	例　　句	中譯・同義字	字源分析
antipathetic a. æn͵tɪpə'θɛtɪk	He disliked the chairman who was in every way *antipathetic* to him.	引起憎惡的 abhorrent repugnant	**antipathy**
antipathy n. æn'tɪpəθɪ	She felt *antipathy* for the people who beat up her father.	憎惡、反感 repugnance enmity	**anti**(against)
apathetic a. ͵æpə'θɛtɪk	Some women become active instead of *apathetic* as they grow older.	缺乏興趣、冷淡的 impassive indifferent	**apathy**
apathy n. 'æpəθɪ	She could feel the *apathy* of despair in her heart as she listened to his talk.	缺乏情感、冷淡 impassiveness indifference	**a**(without)
compassion n. kəm'pæʃən	One must have *compassion* on other people.	同情、憐憫 sympathy clemency	**com**(together)
compassionate a. kəm'pæʃənɪt	There was a murmur of commiseration, and the soft and *compassionate* voices of women were conspicuous.	有同情心的 sympathetic pitiable	**compassion**
compatible a. kəm'pætəbļ	Nowadays we no longer regard slavery as *compatible* with high civilization.	相容、一致的 consistent congruous	**com**(together)
empathy* n. 'ɛmpəθɪ	Without *empathy* an artistic emotion is purely intellectual and associative.	神入 sympathy	**em**(in)

單字‧音標‧詞類	例　　句	中譯‧同義字	字源分析
impatient a. ɪmˈpeʃənt	She became *impatient* after three hours of waiting.	不能忍受、不耐煩的 restless impetuous	im(not) **patient**
incompatible a. ˌɪnkəmˈpætəbl̩	*Incompatible* people could never get along well with one another.	不能和諧共存、不調和的 disagreeing incongruous	in(not) **compatible**
passion n. ˈpæʃən	His blue eyes blazed with *passion* as he expounded his favorite theme.	熱情 emotion feeling	
n.	She has a *passion* for chess.	愛好 love enthusiasm	
passionate a. ˈpæʃənɪt	He had a *passionate* and inquestioned faith in the virtue of the cause he served.	熱情、熱烈的 enthusiastic ardent	**passion**
passive a. ˈpæsɪv	She is a *passive* girl, content to remain at home and dream.	消極、被動的 inactive lethargic	
pathetic* a. pəˈθɛtɪk	Seeing the dog hunt for her missing pups was *pathetic*.	令人感傷、可憐的 touching pitiable	
pathos* n. ˈpeθɑs	My sister loves stories full of *pathos*, stories that she can cry over.	動人哀感之性質 quality arousing pity	

單字・音標・詞類	例　句	中譯・同義字	字源分析
patient a. ˈpeʃənt	Love is *patient* and kind.	堅忍的 persistent persevering	
n.	The hospital is equipped to handle 500 *patients*.	病人 invalid sufferer	
sympathetic a. ˌsɪmpəˈθɛtɪk	A good teacher is always *sympathetic*.	同情的 affectionate compassionate	**sympathy**
sympathize v. ˈsɪmpəˌθaɪz	She always *sympathizes* with the poor people.	同情 feel sympathy	**sympathy**
sympathy n. ˈsɪmpəθɪ	The kind little girl has *sympathy* for the poor.	同情、憐憫 pity compassion	**sym**(together)

39

PED

foot

脚

　　字根 ped 源自拉丁文名詞 pēs「脚」的複數變化 pedis 和其字根的變化，如下文例字中的 expedite v.「使加速」、expedition n.「迅速行動、探險」、expeditious a.「迅速的」、impede v.「阻礙」，原來分別出自拉丁文的 expedīre, expedītio, expedītus, impedīre，便可看出 ped 在原拉丁文的應用情形。這個字根除了 ped 的形態，另可拼作 pod 和 pus，字源有拉丁文也有希臘文，但這兩種拼法組成的單字都比較偏難，僅列出如下以供參考：pedal n.「踏板」、pedometer n.「記步器」、quadruped a.「四足的」、centiped n.「蜈蚣」、tripod n.「三脚架」、podium n.「管弦樂隊指揮台」、octopus n.「八爪魚」等。

單字・音標・詞類	例　　句	中譯・同義字	字源分析
expediency n. ɪkˈspidɪənsɪ	The crafty lawyer was influenced more by *expediency* than by the love of justice.	權宜、利害 fitness suitability	**expedite**
expedient a. ɪkˈspidɪənt	The harvest had been bad, and it was found *expedient* to disperse the troops over a broader area.	得當、便利的 suitable advisable	**expedite**
expedite v. ˈɛkspɪˌdaɪt	The administration measure is intended to *expedite* the ship-building program.	使加速 hasten accelerate	**ex**(out)
expedition n. ˌɛkspɪˈdɪʃən	She had put on her clothes with remarkable *expedition* and rushed out of the room.	迅速（的行動） haste speed	**expedite**
n.	The researchers are planning an archeological *expedition*.	探險 journey excursion	
expeditious a. ˌɛkspɪˈdɪʃəs	Where wages are high, we shall always find the workmen more active, diligent, and *expeditious*.	迅速的 speedy fast	**expedite**
impede v. ɪmˈpid	The vessels were *impeded* by the storm.	阻礙 check obstruct	**im**(in)
impediment n. ɪmˈpɛdəmənt	Some *impediment* lay between him and his advancement.	阻礙 obstruction hindrance	**impede**

單字・音標・詞類	例　　　句	中譯・同義字	字源分析
peddle v. ˈpɛdḷ	The man has been *peddling* without a license.	販賣、沿街叫賣 go around selling things	
pedestal n. ˈpɛdɪstḷ	A *pedestal* is the base of an upright structure.	底座、基礎 base bottom	stal(rest)
pedestrian n. pəˈdɛstrɪən	The policeman signaled the traffic to halt to allow *pedestrians* to cross the street.	行人 walker hiker	

40

PEL·PULS

drive, push

推動 • 衝撞

　　字根 pel, puls 源出拉丁文動詞 pellere，原即有「推動、衝撞」的意思；其中 puls 的拼法乃出自 pellere 的過去分詞 pulsus，原在拉丁文已視作字根，用以組合單字。這個字根除了 pel, puls 兩種拼法，並可拼作 peal，但是由這種形態組成的單字不多，下文例字中唯有 appeal v.「哀求、引起興趣」和 repeal v.「撤消、廢止」，有如此情況。appeal 源出古法文動詞 apeler（現代法文作 appeler），最早的字源則是拉丁文動詞 adpellere（或拼作 appellere），字首 ad 或 ap 有 to 的意思（參見本書「最重要的30個字首」**2. ad**），因此拉丁文原指「駛向、使（船）靠岸」。後來，這個拉丁文轉成了 adpellāre（或作 appellāre），意思已變作「催促、呼喚」，指以言語「推動」他人。今日英文 appeal 所說的「哀求、引起興趣」，便由最後的這層意思引申而出。appeal 在十六世紀之前，仍拼成上述的古法文形態，過了十六世紀，才轉成今日習見的拼法。此外，repeal 係由字首 re（參見本書「最重要的30個字首」**24. re**）加上 appeal 而成，字形的變化過程與上述 appeal 有關。appeal 原義作「呼求、懇求」，字首 re 則有 back 的意思，因此「將事情喚回」，自然便可引申成「撤消、廢止」。這種語義衍變情形，與本書所收的另外兩字相同，請參見「最重要的30個字首」**24. re** 中 recall 與 revoke 兩個例字。

單字·音標·詞類	例　　句	中譯·同義字	字源分析
appeal v. əˈpil	At Christmas and New Year, people *appeal* to us to help the poor.	哀求、求助 ask entreat	**ap**(to)
v.	The idea of a European federation has *appealed* to many statesmen.	引起興趣 arouse interest	
n.	The school has made *appeals* for support from its alumni.	懇求 invocation entreaty	
n.	That kind of music does not have much *appeal* for me.	吸引力 attraction	
compel v. kəmˈpɛl	Poverty *compelled* him to work day and night.	迫使、強迫 force coerce	**com**(together)
compulsion n. kəmˈpʌlʃən	He was acting under *compulsion* and not on his own free will.	強迫、強制 force constraint	**compel**
compulsory a. kəmˈpʌlsərɪ	The fees are *compulsory* for all applicants.	強制、強迫的 enforced mandatory	**compel**
dispel v. dɪˈspɛl	I can *dispel* your doubts by ascertaining the facts.	卻除、驅散 scatter dissipate	**dis**(away)
expel v. ɪkˈspɛl	Superstitions become lodged in our mental constitutions and sometimes are *expelled* only with the greatest difficulty.	驅逐、逐出 eject dislodge	**ex**(out)

單字·音標·詞類	例　　　句	中譯·同義字	字源分析
expulse v. ɪkˈspʌls	The country had just *expulsed* the detested invaders.	逐出、驅逐 eject oust	**ex**(out)
expulsion n. ɪkˈspʌlʃən	Their *expulsion* from Germany had cost them their homes and property.	驅逐、逐出 banishment exile	**expulse**
impel v. ɪmˈpɛl	He felt *impelled* to tolerate what he intensely disliked.	驅使、逼迫 urge constrain	**im**(in)
impulse n. ˈɪmpʌls	The writer's more successful stories derive from the same kind of *impulse* as his poetry.	刺激、推動力 impetus thrust	**im**(in)
impulsive a. ɪmˈpʌlsɪv	The woman he had married was *impulsive,* capricious, and touchy.	易衝動的 emotional rash	**impulse**
propel v. prəˈpɛl	Steam could be used to *propel* ships.	推動、驅策 push drive	**pro**(forward)
propulsion n. prəˈpʌlʃən	The students are discussing some problems of rocket *propulsion.*	推進 ejection expulsion	**propel**
pulsate v. ˈpʌlset	The country is alive and *pulsating* with beauty.	悸動、跳動 beat throb	**pulse**

pulse n.
pʌls

One feels the *pulse*
of the village in an
English pub.

跳動
throb
vitality

repeal v.
rɪˈpil

The grant would not
be *repealed* until
1970.

撤消、廢止
renounce
annul

re(back)
appeal

repel v.
rɪˈpɛl

The Gauls *repelled*
the invading Romans.

逐退、拒絕
drive back
repulse

re(back)

v.

In his essays there is a
tendency toward
suspicion and sarcasm
that *repels* me.

使不愉快、使
憎惡
disgust
displease

repulse v.
rɪˈpʌls

The police charging the
plant gates were *repulsed*
at every attempt.

擊退
check
repel

re(back)

v.

He offered to help, but
was *repulsed.*

拒絕
reject
decline

repulsive a.
rɪˈpʌlsɪv

Her manner after the
unpleasant incident
became colder and more
repulsive.

冷淡、排斥的
cold
forbidding

repulse

a.

The young man's
suggestion that they
stay in his room was
utterly *repulsive* to
her.

使人厭惡的
loathsome
odious

41

PEND·PENS·POND

hang, weigh, pay, consider

懸掛 • 重量 • 償付 • 思量

字根 pend, pens, pond 源出拉丁文 pendēre v.「懸掛、（有）重量」、pendere v.「衡量、償付」、pondus n.n.「重量、權威」及 ponderāre v.「衡量、思考」。這個字根的拼法除了上述三種，在下文例字 poise n.「平衡、鎮靜、寧靜」、counterpoise v.「使平衡」上，並可見到一種變體。事實上，poise 雖直接借自古法文 pois n.「重量」（現代法文作 poids），但最早的字源仍是拉丁文。例字中語義衍變比較特別的，有 append v.「附加」、appendix n.「附屬物、補償」、impend v.「迫近」。append字首ap 有 to 的意思（參見本書「最重要的30個字首」 **2. ad** ），因此原指「懸加於某物之上」，而有「附加」的語義。 appendix 則源出 append，複數可作 appendixes，也可作 appendices。另一字 impend 出自拉丁文動詞 impendēre，原有 hang over 的意思，引申而指事情臨頭，因而有「迫近」的語義。

單字·音標·詞類	例　　　句	中譯·同義字	字源分析
append v. ə'pɛnd	A seal was *appended* to the document.	附加 adjunct attach	ap(to)
appendix n. ə'pɛndɪks	The principle of official management was invented as a natural *appendix* to political dictatorship.	附屬物、補遺 supplement addendum	**append**
compendious* a. kəm'pɛndɪəs	Such looseness cannot be afforded in a short and *compendious* book like this one.	簡潔的 concise succinct	**compendium**
compendium* n. kəm'pɛndɪəm	This is a one-volume *compendium* of the multivolume original.	摘要 abridgment abstract	**com**(together)
compensate v. 'kɑmpən‚set	Her vanity and excessive sentimentality were *compensated* by her kindness.	抵補、補償 counterbalance counterpoise	**com**(with)
v.	A worker injured on his job should be *compensated.*	賠償、報酬 recompense remunerate	
counterpoise* v. 'kɑʊntɚ‚pɔɪz	All parts of the sphere were nicely *counter-poised.*	使平衡、使均衡 counterbalance offset	**counter**(against) **poise**
depend v. dɪ'pɛnd	I am *depending* on you to tell me the truth.	依賴 rely count	**de**(down)

單字·音標·詞類	例　　　句	中譯·同義字	字源分析
dependence n. dɪˈpɛndəns	The man has been criticizing the modern age's *dependence* upon luxury goods.	依賴、信賴 reliance trust	**depend**
dispense v. dɪˈspɛns	The family had *dispensed* alms among the poor.	分與、分配 provide distribute	**dis**(away)
v.	She *dispensed* her friend from keeping the promise that he had previously made.	免除、赦免 release exempt	
expend v. ɪkˈspɛnd	Public revenue should be *expended* on certain social services.	花費 spend waste	**ex**(out)
expenditure n. ɪkˈspɛndɪtʃɚ	Only after ten years of practice as physician did his income equal his *expenditures*.	開支、消費 expense disbursement	**expend**
expense n. ɪkˈspɛns	We were told to cut down our monthly *expenses*.	消費、費用 cost expenditure	**expend**
n.	A boy's physique should not be developed at the *expense* of his intelligence.	犧牲、損失 sacrifice loss	
expensive a. ɪkˈspɛnsɪv	She enjoys buying *expensive* clothes.	昂貴的 costly extravagant	**expense**

單字·音標·詞類	例　　　句	中譯·同義字	字源分析
impend v. ɪmˈpɛnd	Trouble *impended* over the entire enterprise.	迫近 threaten menace	**im**(on)
impending a. ɪmˈpɛndɪŋ	Fishermen were warned to be wary of the *impending* storm.	迫近的 threatening imminent	**impend**
indispensable a. ˌɪndɪˈspɛnsəbl̩	Freedom to read is one of the *indispensable* conditions of a democratic society.	絕對必要的 needful requisite	**in**(not) **dispense**
pendant* n. ˈpɛndənt	There is a jeweled *pendant* on the chain.	垂飾 something 　suspended	
pendent* a. ˈpɛndənt	This plant has a *pendent* blossom.	懸垂的 suspended overhanging	
pending a. ˈpɛndɪŋ	The judge canceled his vacation because there were too many *pending* cases.	未決定、待解決的 not yet decided	
pendulous* a. ˈpɛndʒələs	The corpulent old man has flabby, *pendulous* jowls.	懸垂、下垂的 drooping suspended	
pension n. ˈpɛnʃən	A *pension* is a fixed sum of money paid regularly to a person.	津貼、恩俸 regular payment	

單字·音標·詞類	例　　　　句	中譯·同義字	字源分析
pensive a. ˈpɛnsɪv	Her face had the *pensive* mournfulness of a seraph in an old sad painting.	哀思、沈思的 meditative contemplative	
perpendicular a. ˌpɝ·pənˈdɪkjələ·	There has been an almost *perpendicular* rise in share prices since last week.	垂直的 upright vertical	**per**(through)
poise n. pɔɪz	The *poise* between widely divergent impulses helps to develop a better personality.	平衡 balance equilibrium	
n.	Her mother is a woman of *poise* and charm.	鎮靜、泰然自若 composure self-possession	
n.	She left from the front door, without disturbing the *poise* of the drawing room.	寧靜 tranquility serenity	
ponder v. ˈpɑndə·	The events of history may be *pondered* only in retrospect.	沈思 meditate muse	
ponderous a. ˈpɑndərəs	The responsibility you have imposed on him would be a *ponderous* burden.	沈重、笨重的 heavy unwieldy	

單字・音標・詞類	例　　句	中譯・同義字	字源分析
prepense* a. prɪˈpɛns	She killed her cousin of malice *prepense*.	預謀的 premeditated aforethought	**pre**(before)
preponderant* a. prɪˈpɑndrənt	White men in this country are always *preponderant* in influence and power.	佔優勢的 dominant paramount	**preponderate**
preponderate* v. prɪˈpɑndəˌret	State ownership will inevitably *preponderate* in the heavy industries.	佔優勢 predominate prevail	**pre**(before)
propensity* n. prəˈpɛnsətɪ	The function of the wife is to curb the roving *propensities* of the male.	傾向 inclination tendency	**pro**(forward)
recompense* v. ˈrɛkəmˌpɛns	We promised to *recompense* him for all his losses.	賠償、報答 requite remunerate	**re**(back) **com**(with)
spend v. spɛnd	How much money did you *spend* on this mink coat?	花用、耗費 consume expend	
suspend v. səˈspɛnd	The cowboy *suspended* his linen to dry on the frame of the wagon.	懸掛、吊 hang append	sus(under)
v.	The publication of the magazine was *suspended*.	停止 discontinue cease	

單字・音標・詞類	例　　　　句	中譯・同義字	字源分析
suspense n. sə'spɛns	Our next strategic move was still in *suspense*.	懸而未決、中止 indecisiveness cessation	**suspend**
n.	*Suspense* is sometimes more terrible than any certainty.	焦慮、懸念 anxiety apprehension	

42

PLIC·PLEX·PLY

fold, weave

摺疊 ● 編結

　　字根 plic, plex, ply 源出拉丁文動詞 plicāre「摺疊、編結」和名詞 plexus「編織、辮結」; ply 的形態則受過古法文影響。這個字根拼法相當複雜，除了上述三種外，並有四種較爲少見：(1) ploy, ploit, (2) ple, (3) play, (4) plo。其中(1)(2)(3)源自古法文，(4)則借自希臘文。英文的 fold 除了名詞、動詞可作「摺疊」外，當字尾(suffix) 使用，可轉成「倍數」的意思，如 twofold a.「兩倍的」、threefold a.「三倍的」等均是。下文例字中，便有不少是由「倍數」的意義組成的，如 duplicate v.「複製」、duplicity n.「重複、雙重性」、triple a.「三重的」、triplicate a.「一式三份（的文件）之第三份的」、quadruple a.「四倍的」、 multiple a.「多數的」、multiply v.「增加」等，均是這種情形。源自希臘文的例字只有 diploma n.「畢業證書、證書」和 diplomacy n.「外交」，語義衍變頗爲特別，應該略加說明。 diploma 源出希臘文名詞 διπλωμα (diplōma)，字首 di 有 two 的意思（希臘文 double 便作 διπλοος [diploos]），因此原指「摺疊的文件」，引申而有「推薦函、許可狀、特權書」等用法。另一字 diplomacy 便由最後這層意義，再衍生而成「外交」的意思。

單字・音標・詞類	例　　　　　句	中譯・同義字	字源分析
accomplice* n. əˈkɑmplɪs	The police did not find the *accomplice* of the burglar.	同謀者 partner associate	**ac**(to) **com**(together)
appliance n. əˈplaɪəns	The company has purchased some fire-fighting *appliances*.	用具、器具 apparatus implement	**apply**
applicable a. ˈæplɪkəbļ	This basic technique of musical rendition is *applicable* to any piece of music.	適用、適宜的 relevant appropriate	**apply**
apply v. əˈplaɪ	The rules cannot be *applied* to such situations.	應用、引用 utilize employ	**ap**(to)
v.	The businessman has *applied* to a bank for a loan.	申請、請求 appeal entreat	
complex a. ˈkɑmplɛks	This is a *complex* camera with many attachments.	複雜、錯綜的 complicated intricate	**com**(together)
complexion n. kəmˈplɛkʃən	They sell creams for *complexion* cleaning.	皮膚 skin of the face	**complex**
n.	This great victory changed the *complexion* of war.	形勢、外觀 appearance impression	
complicate v. ˈkɑmpləˌket	This is going to *com-plicate* matters.	使複雜 confuse involve	**com**(together)

單字·音標·詞類	例　　句	中譯·同義字	字源分析
complicated a. ˈkɑmpləˌketɪd	Life is so *complicated* that one loses all homogeneity and unity of purpose.	複雜的 complex intricate	**complicate**
complicity* n. kəmˈplɪsətɪ	Knowingly receiving stolen goods is *complicity* in theft.	共謀、串通 partnership in 　wrongdoing	**com**(together)
deploy v. dɪˈplɔɪ	He *deployed* his squad on both sides of the road.	散開、部署、 展開 arrange extend	**de**(away)
diploma n. dɪˈplomə	A *diploma* is a document bearing record of a degree conferred by an educational institution.	畢業證書、證 書 certificate	**di**(two)
diplomacy n. dɪˈploməsɪ	*Diplomacy* is itself a skilled profession.	外交 conducting of 　relations between 　nations	**diploma**
display v. dɪˈsple	They have *displayed* a map on the table.	展開 unfold spread	**dis**(away)
v.	These paintings have been *displayed* throughout Canada.	展覽、展示 exhibit show	
n.	His pictures are on *display* in the art gallery.	展覽、表現 exhibition manifestation	

單字・音標・詞類	例　　　　　句	中譯・同義字	字源分析
duplicate v. ˈdjupləˌket	After decades of experiment, experts were still unable to *duplicate* Attic glazed pottery.	複製 copy simulate	du(two)
n. ˈdjupləˌkɪt	They sell doll carriages that are *duplicates* of real baby carriages.	複製品 copy reproduction	
a. ˈdjupləˌkɪt	The firm always made out *duplicate* invoices, one for its own records and one for the customer.	副本、相同的 copied identical	
duplicity n. djuˈplɪsətɪ	These double stars show a doubling of the spectral lines that must be caused by a *duplicity* in the source of light.	重複、雙重性 doubling	du(two)
employ v. ɪmˈplɔɪ	She has *employed* a pen for sketching.	使用 use utilize	em(in)
v.	They did not *employ* him because he had been a convict.	僱用 hire enlist	
explicate v. ˈɛksplɪˌket	The writer did not *explicate* his techniques but the experience out of which his works were written.	解說、說明 explain interpret	ex(out)

單字·音標·詞類		例　　　　句	中譯·同義字	字源分析
explicit ɪkˈsplɪsɪt	a.	It is impossible to have a clear and *explicit* notion of that which is infinite.	明確的 plain unambiguous	**ex**(out)
exploit ɪkˈsplɔɪt	v.	The artist had *exploited* his distinctive talent for book illustration.	運用、利用 use utilize	**ex**(out)
	v.	The gentleman was struck by the degree in which the peasant was *exploited* by the noble.	剝削 use befool	
	n.	History books often laud the *exploits* of Christopher Columbus.	功蹟 deed feat	
implicate ˈɪmplɪˌket	v.	There is enough evidence *implicating* many high officials involved in the conspiracy against the government.	暗示 imply insinuate	**im**(in)
implicit ɪmˈplɪsɪt	a.	The artistic standards of our time are *implicit* rather than codified.	暗含的 implied inferred	**im**(in)
	a.	A soldier must give *implicit* obedience to his officers.	絕對、毫不懷疑的 absolute unquestioning	
imply ɪmˈplaɪ	v.	There is a philosophy of nature *implied* in Chinese art.	暗示、意含 suggest hint	**im**(in)

單字·音標·詞類	例　句	中譯·同義字	字源分析
multiple a. ˈmʌltəpl̩	They have made *multiple* copies of the speech.	多數、多樣的 many manifold	multi(many)
multiply v. ˈmʌltəˌplaɪ	The original manuscript could only be *multiplied* by handwritten copies.	增加 increase augment	multi(many)
perplex v. pɚˈplɛks	These are the questions that have *perplexed* men since time began.	使困惑、使困窘 puzzle bewilder	per(through)
pliable a. ˈplaɪəbl̩	Willow twigs are *pliable.*	柔軟的 flexible supple	
a.	She has a self-controlled, *pliable* personality.	柔順的 compliant complaisant	
pliant a. ˈplaɪənt	The girl has a slim, *pliant* figure.	易曲、柔軟的 flexible lithe	
a.	The clarinet is a very fluent and *pliant* musical instrument.	柔順、順從的 adaptable yielding	
ply* n. plaɪ	The body of a tire has several *plies* of rubberized fabric.	層 fold layer	
v.	The woman has *plied* a trade of her own.	經營、使用 exercise practice	

單字・音標・詞類	例　　　　句	中譯・同義字	字源分析
v.	The soldiers *plied* the farm woman with embarrassing questions.	強求、追問 urge assail	
quadruple a. ˈkwɑdrʊpl̩	The planet has a size *quadruple* to that of the Mars.	四倍的 fourfold	quadr(four)
replica n. ˈrɛplɪkə	A *replica* is a facsimile of an original work of art.	複製品 reproduction facsimile	**re**(back)
replicate v. ˈrɛplɪˌket	They have decided to *replicate* their experiment.	複製、重複 repeat duplicate	**re**(back)
replication n. ˌrɛpləˈkeʃən	The home is often considered as a *replication* of a medieval castle.	複製品 copy reproduction	**replicate**
reply v. rɪˈplaɪ	How did she *reply* to your letter?	答覆、回答 answer respond	**re**(back)
n.	I hope my *reply* to you is satisfactory.	回答、答覆 answer response	
simple a. ˈsɪmpl̩	His life in the mountains is *simple* and peaceful.	樸實的 uncomplicated unsophisticated	
a.	Children grew up in *simple* beauty in his house.	天眞爛漫的 innocent artless	

單字·音標·詞類	例　　　　句	中譯·同義字	字源分析
simpleton* n. ˈsɪmp!tən	I do not find it amusing to be treated like some *simpleton*.	愚人 fool idiot	**simple**
simplify v. ˈsɪmpləˌfaɪ	The management had decided to *simplify* the manufacturing process of the factory.	簡化 abridge curtail	**simple**
supple a. ˈsʌp!	Leather is usually *supple*.	柔軟、易曲的 flexible pliable	**sup**(under)
a.	Because of her *supple* nature, she gets along well with everyone.	柔順、順從的 compliant submissive	
suppliant a. ˈsʌplɪənt	I have not come here as a *suppliant* sinner seeking forgiveness.	哀懇的 begging imploring	**supplicate**
supplicate v. ˈsʌplɪˌket	The young man fell on his knees and *supplicated* God.	懇求 entreat solicit	**sup**(under)
triple v. ˈtrɪp!	Recreation facilities for children were *tripled*.	使成三倍 treble	**tri**(three)
a.	The arrested Russian had worked as a double or even *triple* agent.	三重的 threefold	
triplicate a. ˈtrɪpləkɪt	The *triplicate* of the document is forwarded to the administrative agency.	一式三份（的文件）之第三份的 one of three 　identical copies	**triple**

43

PON·POS·POUND

place, put

安置 ● 寄放

這是相當重要的字根，源出拉丁文動詞 pōnere「安置、寄放」。pon 的拼法出自 pōnere, pos 出自其過去簡單式 pōsui 和過去分詞 positus（或作 postus），而 pound 則是中古英文時期的變體。下文例字有些語義衍變比較特別，茲說明如下。 apposite a.「適當的」源出拉丁文動詞 adpōnere 的過去分詞 appositus，字首 ad 或 ap 有 to 的意思（參見本書「最重要的 30 個字首」2. ad），因此原指「放置於旁」。並列的事物彼此比較能配合，因此拉丁文的 appositus 轉成形容詞之後，又引申出「適當的」的意思。impose v.「加於、欺騙」源出拉丁文動詞 impōnere，字首 im 有 in, on 的意思（參見「最重要的 30 個字首」12. em·en·im·in），原義指「加於、加給」，後來轉而指加給幻覺，而有「欺騙」的意思。另有兩字 impostor n.「騙子」、imposture n.「欺騙」，也都源出 impose。positive a.「確實、實在的」源自拉丁文形容詞 positīvus，原有「安置、添置的」的意思，安置下來的事物比較穩當，所以引申便成「確實、實在的」。 suppose v.「猜測、假設」源出拉丁文動詞 suppōnere，字首 sup 有 under 的意思（參見「最重要的 30 個字首」26. sub·sus），因此原義為「置於下方」，後來轉義而有「以為不如」的意思，然後又轉成「偽造」，最後再引申而成「假設」。因此，十四世紀 suppose 由古法文 suposer（現代法文作 supposer）借入時，早已可作「猜測、假設」。

單字·音標·詞類	例 句	中譯·同義字	字源分析
apposite* a. ˈæpəzɪt	Her use of anecdotes is *apposite*.	適當的 relevant apt	**ap**(toward)
component a. kəmˈponənt	There are many *component* republics in the Union of Soviet Socialist Republics.	組成的 composing constituent	**compose**
n.	The professor has explained to the students the essential *components* of Kant's philosophy.	成分、構成要素 ingredient constituent	
compose v. kəmˈpoz	The assembly was *composed* of delegates from every state in the union.	組成 make up constitute	**com**(together)
v.	She finished *composing* a ballad last night.	撰寫 write create	
v.	Life moves on and one must *compose* oneself to meet it.	使鎮定、使安靜 calm tranquilize	
composite a. kəmˈpazɪt	The natives in this region belong to a *composite* racial type.	混合成的 compounded mixed	**compose**
compost* n. ˈkampost	The play is sheer melodrama, a *compost* of sex and crime.	混合物 mixture compound	**compose**

單字・音標・詞類	例　　　　句	中譯・同義字	字源分析
compound v. kəm'paʊnd	What he has been advocating is a philosophy *compounded* of action, compassion, and universalism.	組成、構成 combine compose	**com**(together)
n. 'kɑmpaʊnd	The islanders' religion is a *compound* of Christian mysticism and Greek philosophy.	混合物 combination medley	
depose v. dɪ'poz	The governor was *deposed* as unfit to hold office.	革職、廢(王位) displace dethrone	**de**(away)
deposit v. dɪ'pɑzɪt	The maid had *deposited* a huge decanter on the table.	放下、置下 place lay	**de**(down)
n.	Ritual is a slow *deposit* of people's imaginative insight into life.	沉澱(物) precipitation sediment	
dispose v. dɪ'spoz	The troops have been *disposed* for immediate withdrawal.	部署、排列 prepare set	**dis**(away)
v.	They *disposed* of a lot of old clothes by burning them.	去除、放棄 discard relinquish	
disposition n. ˌdɪspə'zɪʃən	The *disposition* of the artillery was shown on the map.	佈置、部署 arrangement grouping	**dispose**

單字·音標·詞類		例　　句	中譯·同義字	字源分析
	n.	Sugar has a *disposition* to dissolve in water.	傾向 inclination tendency	
exponent ɪkˈsponənt	n.	She was the most controversial figure in the modern dance and its most successful *exponent*.	解釋者、說明者 explainer expounder	**expound**
expose ɪkˈspoz	v.	The coast is *exposed* to severe gales.	使暴露於 bare uncover	**ex**(out)
	v.	He took off his shirt, *exposing* a sun-tanned back.	展示 display exhibit	
	v.	The journalists have decided to *expose* the voting fraud.	揭穿 unveil unmask	
exposition ˌɛkspəˈzɪʃən	n.	They have been to the industrial *exposition*.	展覽（會）、陳列 exhibition demonstration	**expose**
	n.	The critic was overawed by her splendid work of *exposition* and advocacy.	說明、解釋 elucidation interpretation	

單字・音標・詞類	例　　　句	中譯・同義字	字源分析
expound v. ɪkˈspaʊnd	The biologist *expounded* with distinguished precision the difference between an extinct and an extirpated bird.	陳述 state present	ex(out)
v.	The veteran spent the rest of his life *expounding* the conflict between Christianity and Communism.	解釋、說明 explain interpret	
impose v. ɪmˈpoz	A tax will be *imposed* on all unmarried men.	課（稅）、加於 levy inflict	im(in)
v.	They have *imposed* on his good nature.	利用、欺騙 deceive dupe	
imposing a. ɪmˈpozɪŋ	She works in an *imposing* building.	堂皇、堂堂的 grand commanding	impose
impostor n. ɪmˈpastɚ	She was so infuriated that she called him a liar and an *impostor*.	騙子 pretender trickster	impose
imposture n. ɪmˈpastʃɚ	The old man made a living by lying and *imposture*.	欺騙 deceit fraud	impose
interpose* v. ˌɪntɚˈpoz	These dense forests *interpose* an almost impassable barrier.	插入、置於中間 introduce insert	inter(between)

	v.	The lady *interposed* between two of her friends who were quarreling.	調停、仲裁 mediate intervene	
opponent n. ə'ponənt		He defeated his *opponent* in the election.	對手、敵手 adversary antagonist	**oppose**
oppose v. ə'poz		The building *opposes* the south.	面向 face confront	**op**(against)
	v.	Swamps *opposed* the advance of the troops.	阻止 obstruct thwart	
	v.	Love is *opposed* to hate.	相對、相反的 contradict counter	
opposite a. 'apəzɪt		These two words have *opposite* meanings.	相反的 contrary contradictory	**oppose**
pose n. poz		Every movement of the model seems to be a *pose*.	姿勢 posture position	
	v.	He *posed* an hour for the portrait.	作姿態 model sit	
	v.	A number of the points were *posed* in an unsatisfactory way.	陳述 present offer	

	v.	These questions might be *posed* by the students themselves.	提出 propose propound
posit* v. ˈpɑzɪt		His glance stayed *posited* on the spot.	放置、安置 fix set
position n. pəˈzɪʃən		They took their *position* at the end of the line.	位置 stand place
	n.	The judge has taken the *position* that the law must be enforced at all costs.	立場、見解、態度 attitude posture
positive a. ˈpɑzətɪv		We have *positive* proof that the man was killed by the woman.	確實、無問題的 definite indisputable
	a.	The people should have a more *positive* voice in government.	實在的 concrete genuine
post n. post		He has a good *post* in the public service.	職位 job position
	n.	There are some signs on the *post*.	柱、支柱 pillar column

單字·音標·詞類	例　　　　句	中譯·同義字	字源分析
v.	The students' grades have been *posted*.	公布、揭示、宣告 placard announce	
postpone v. post'pon	The meeting will be *postponed*.	延期、擱置 delay procrastinate	**post**(after)
posture n. 'pastʃɚ	His sitting *posture* is so poor that after a while it may cause him to have back problems.	姿勢 pose position	
n.	She has assumed a *posture* of moral superiority which offends her rivals in the debate.	態度、心態 attitude disposition	
proposal n. prə'pozḷ	They have made *proposals* for mutual disarmament.	建議、提議 suggestion motion	**propose**
propose v. prə'poz	She is going to India, where she *proposes* to spend some time with her friends.	欲、計畫 intend plan	**pro**(forward)
v.	Do you have anything to *propose* to the committee?	提議 tender propound	
proposition n. ˌprɑpə'zɪʃən	He made a *proposition* to buy out his rival's business.	提議 proposal recommendation	**propose**

單字‧音標‧詞類	例　　　句	中譯‧同義字	字源分析
n.	This is a *proposition* that needs no further discussion.	主張、企業、事情 business affair	
purpose n. ˈpɝˌpəs	His *purpose* was above reproach.	企圖、決心 design resolution	**pur**(forward)
v.	The student has *purposed* to write an account of the tragedy.	意圖 design propound	
repose v. rɪˈpoz	We *repose* complete trust in his honesty.	置、放 place put	**re**(again)
reposit* v. rɪˈpɑzɪt	The buried sedimentary rocks have entrapped the water in which the rocks were originally *reposited*.	貯藏 store deposit	**re**(back)
repository* n. rɪˈpɑzəˌtorɪ	The child's desk is a *repository* for his music papers and other oddments.	貯藏所、容器 container treasury	**reposit**
suppose v. səˈpoz	I *suppose* you don't want to see me any more.	推測、假設 guess conjecture	**sup**(under)

supposition n.
ˌsʌpə'zɪʃən

His theory is based on the *supposition* that language contributes largely to forming man's present society.

假定、推測
surmise
hypothesis

suppose

transpose v.
træns'poz

The student has *transposed* the letters of the word to change the spelling.

改換位置、置換
interchange
alternate

trans(across)

v.

He has *transposed* himself completely from the role of systematic philosopher to that of biblical theologian.

改變(性質)、使變形
transform
transmute

PORT

carry

攜帶 ● 運載

　　字根 port 源出拉丁文動詞 portāre，原即有「攜帶、運載」的意思。下文例字有些語義衍變比較特殊，茲說明如下。deport v.「舉止」源出古法文 deporter 或 desporter（現代法文作 déporter），另一例字 disport v.「娛樂」也是源出於此，兩字字首 de, dis 均有 away 的意思（參見本書「最重要的30個字首」9. de·di·dis），照字首字根組合看來，原有 carry away 的意思。把人從日常工作 carry away，便有「娛樂」的意思；再想人平常如何把自己來來去去的 carry，便可看出「舉止」的意思。import n.「意義、重要性」源出拉丁文動詞 importāre「攜入、引入」，後來引申而指引出結果、表達重要意義，最後終而有「意義、重要性」的意思。一般熟知的 important a.「重要的」，即由這個字轉成。portly a.「肥胖的」是英文自創的單字，十六世紀已經形成，讀者必須聯想到「搬運身體」，才能了解其語義衍變。purport v.「聲稱」指「說出對事的意圖」，因此作名詞有「意義、企圖」的意思。出自古法文 purporter v., purport n.（又作 porporter v., porport n.），字首 pur（或 por）有 forward 的意思（參見「最重要的30個字首」23. pro·pur），因此原指「正式表達出來」，後引申而有「聲稱、意義、企圖」的意思。

單字·音標·詞類	例　句	中譯·同義字	字源分析
comport* v. kəmˈport	His conduct did not *comport* with his high position.	相稱 agree correspond	**com**(together)
v.	The judge *comported* himself with dignity.	舉止、處(身) behave conduct	
deport v. dɪˈport	The grandmother taught the child how to *deport* herself in public.	舉止 conduct demean	**de**(away)
v.	Two hundred miners were forcibly *deported* from their homes.	放逐 transport banish	
deportment n. dɪˈportmənt	He placed his feet, one before the other, with the care of a young woman practicing *deportment*.	舉止、行為 behavior carriage	**deport**
disport* v. dɪˈsport	The young men liked to *disport* themselves in the billiard room.	娛樂 amuse divert	**dis**(away)
export v. ɪksˈport	A country's democratic faith can be *exported* to another country.	輸出、外銷 send to another country	**ex**(out)
n. ˈɛksport	The *export* of tobacco has been banned.	輸出 exportation	

import v.
ɪmˈport

Icelanders *imported* the literature of the Continent and translated it into their own tongue.

輸入、進口　　**im(in)**
bring from a
　　foreign source

v.

His words *imported* that some change in the plans had to be made.

意含
mean
signify

n.
ˈɪmport

The proclamation allowed the *import* of an additional 51 million pounds of peanuts.

輸入、進口
importation

n.

He has tried vainly to fathom the *import* of the speaker's words.

意義、涵義
meaning
purport

n.

The writer is less concerned about the literary value of his books than about their social *import*.

重要性
consequence
significance

important n.
ɪmˈpɔrtn̩t

That was a very *important* day in my life.

重要、重大的　**import**
significant
momentous

portable a.
ˈportəbl̩

Julia has bought a *portable* typewriter.

手提、輕便的
handy
manageable

portage* n.
ˈportɪdʒ

The proud young warriors were forced to do *portage*.

搬運
labor of carrying

porter n. ˈpɔrtɚ	At the entrance of the office block was a *porter* in a red uniform.	脚夫 man who carries 　luggage	
portly a. ˈpɔrtlɪ	The man has a plump figure and a *portly* waist.	肥胖、碩大的 stout burly	
purport v. pɚˈport	The editor in chief received a letter that *purported* to express public opinion.	聲稱 profess impart	**pur**(forward)
n.	The *purport* of her letter was that she could not come to our party.	意義、企圖 substance intention	
report v. rɪˈport	He had *reported* nothing to the committee.	敍述、描述 state relate	**re**(back)
n.	The students were asked to write *reports* on several topics.	報告、報導 description account	
support v. səˈport	Will you *support* me in the election?	支持 sustain back	**sup**(under)
n.	I will need your moral *support* after I talk to the chairman.	支持、援助 assistance sustenance	

單字·音標·詞類	例　　　句	中譯·同義字	字源分析
transport v. træns'port	In the early days copper ore was *transported* in wagons.	運送 move carry	**trans**(across)
v.	His anger *transports* him.	使心神恍惚 inflame enrapture	

PRESS

press

擠壓

　　字根 press 源出拉丁文動詞 pressāre 和名詞 pressus ，原即有「擠壓、收縮」的意思。下文例字中語意衍變比較特別的，只有 express 一字。express 作動詞爲「表達」，作形容詞則有「明確、正確、快速的」的意思。動詞和形容詞分別出自法文的 expresser 和 exprès，更早的字源則是拉丁文動詞 exprimere ，字首 ex 有 out 的意思（參見本書「最重要的 30 個字首」11. e‧ec‧ex‧extra），因此原指「壓出、擠出」，引申而成「說出」，再引申而有「描繪、描述、說明」的意思。 express 作形容詞「快速的」的意思，則是十九世紀以後的事。十九世紀中葉，原以 express train 指「特定列車」，但因爲車行速度極快，久而久之竟轉成「快速」的意思。到了十九世紀末，快郵服務創始時，便直接用這個字加在 mail 之前，而稱爲 express mail 。

單字·音標·詞類	例　　句	中譯·同義字	字源分析
compress v. kəm'prɛs	His lips were *compressed* by thought.	緊壓、縮小 contract restrain	**com**(together)
depress v. dɪ'prɛs	Where the highway goes through a city, you may find a *depressed* street or a bridge overhead.	降低、壓下 lower cause to sink	**de**(down)
v.	The physician is able to *depress* irritability of the heart muscle by the use of drugs.	降低、減少 lessen diminish	
v.	Rainy days always *depressed* me.	使沮喪 discourage dishearten	
depression n. dɪ'prɛʃən	There is a *depression* of mercury in the thermometer this morning.	降低 lowering sinking	**depress**
n.	There was a *depression* in international trade during the worldwide oil crisis.	蕭條、不景氣 reduction diminution	
n.	The doctor has found a physical reaction marked by *depression* and languor.	沮喪 dispiritedness dejection	
express v. ɪk'sprɛs	She has *expressed* her discontent.	表達 utter couch	**ex**(out)

	a.	It is his *express* wish that we should go without him.	明確的 definite explicit	
	a.	He was the *express* image of his father.	正確的 exact precise	
	a.	The bullet-shaped train can travel at *express* speed.	快速的 rapid swift	
expressive a. ɪkˈsprɛsɪv		The actor performed with richly *expressive* gestures.	富有表情、表示的 indicative eloquent	express
impress v. ɪmˈprɛs		His name was *impressed* on the metal strip by machine.	刻印、蓋印 imprint engrave	im(in)
	v.	He *impressed* his friends with the sincerity of his intentions.	使感動 move affect	
impressionable a. ɪmˈprɛʃənəb!		The woman has an *impressionable* heart.	敏感、易受感動的 sensitive susceptible	impression
impressive a. ɪmˈprɛsɪv		The Grand Canyon of the Colorado is one of the world's most *impressive* natural wonders.	給人深刻印象、感人的 moving forcible	impress

單字·音標·詞類	例　　句	中譯·同義字	字源分析
oppress v. ə'prɛs	Rulers that *oppress* the people will sooner or later be overthrown.	壓制、壓迫 suppress persecute	op(against)
v.	She has felt *oppressed* by her sense of failure.	壓抑、使如負重荷 burden harass	
press v. prɛs	*Press* the button to ring the bell.	按、壓、擠 thrust depress	
v.	My host *pressed* me to drink.	逼迫、力勸 urge constrain	
pressing a. 'prɛsɪŋ	He was almost driven crazy by the *pressing* necessity of earning a livelihood.	迫切、急迫的 urgent crying	press
pressure n. 'prɛʃɚ	She could feel the quick *pressure* of her companion's hand.	壓、壓縮 squeezing compression	press
n.	Financial *pressures* have forced the government to take stricter measures.	困難、急迫 urgency exigency	
repress v. rɪ'prɛs	The child had developed psychic interests which were later *repressed* by her parents.	抑制 control curb	re(back)

suppress v.
sə'prɛs

The growth of an apical
bud usually *suppresses*
that of adjacent lateral
buds.

抑制
check
stunt

sup(under)

v.

The incipient uprising
had been completely
suppressed.

平定、鎮壓
subdue
quash

46

QUEST·QUIR·QUIS

ask, seek

詢問 ● 尋求

　　字根 quest, quir, quis源出拉丁文動詞 quaerere「尋求、詢問」和 quaesere「尋求、祈求」；其中 quest 的拼法則來自 quaerere 的過去分詞 quaesītus，及名詞 quaestio「詢問、苛求」。下文例字中，只有 conquer v.「征服」一字的拼法，與前述三種形態不同，這是受古法文影響的結果。拉丁文 conquaerere（或作 conquīrere）原有「尋求、求取」的意思，進入古法文拼作 conquerre（現代法文作 conquérir），轉而有「征服」的意思。例字中語義衍變比較特別的，有 exquisite a.「精美的」和 perquisite n.「額外收入」。exquisite 出自拉丁文動詞 exquīrere 的過去分詞 exquīsītus，字首 ex 有 out 的意思（參見本書「最重要的30個字首」11. e·ec·ex·extra），因此原動詞指「考究、精選」，過去分詞 exquīsītus 轉成形容詞自然有「精美」的意思。perquisite 源出拉丁文動詞 perquīrere 的過去分詞 perquīsītus，字首 per 爲 through 的意思（參見「最重要的30個字首」20. per），動詞因而可作「追究、細求」解釋，遺產等主要收入外「盡力求取的收入」，自然就是「額外收入」。

單字·音標·詞類	例　　句	中譯·同義字	字源分析
acquire v. əˈkwaɪr	He has *acquired* a reputation for dishonesty.	獲得、得 obtain attain	ac(to)
acquisition n. ˌækwəˈzɪʃən	Power often results from the *acquisition* of wealth.	獲得 procurement realization	acquire
acquisitive a. əˈkwɪzətɪv	In an *acquisitive* society the form that selfishness predominantly takes is monetary greed.	貪得、有獲取 之傾向的 grasping covetous	acquire
conquer v. ˈkɑŋkɚ	Our troops will *conquer* the enemy.	征服、克服 overcome vanquish	con(together)
conquest n. ˈkɑnkwɛst	Three years would have sufficed for the *conquest* of the country.	征服、戰勝 defeat subjugation	conquer
disquisition* n. ˌdɪskwəˈzɪʃən	He presented his report with profound *disquisitions* on questions of social economics.	論文 discourse treatise	dis(away)
exquisite a. ˈɛkskwɪzɪt	She has in her possession many Sung vases and *exquisite* lacquers.	精美、精緻的 fine excellent	ex(out)
a.	Mr. Monroe is an *exquisite* gentleman.	高尚的 refined finished	

單字·音標·詞類	例　句	中譯·同義字	字源分析
a.	The night-blooming cereus is an *exquisite* white flower with a spicy fragrance.	（因纖美而）令人愉快的 delightful delectable	
inquire v. ɪnˈkwaɪr	They have *inquired* what the weather is likely to be.	詢問、探問 ask question	**in**(in)
v.	The rash speaker had failed to *inquire* the limits of what could be said.	調查、查究 examine investigate	
inquiry n. ɪnˈkwaɪrɪ	The librarian would not answer my *inquiry*.	詢問 question query	**inquire**
n.	A scholar must have complete freedom of *inquiry*.	探究、調查 research investigation	
inquisition n. ˌɪnkwəˈzɪʃən	The senator proposed a brief *inquisition* into the man's political activities.	調查 inquiry examination	**inquire**
inquisitive a. ɪnˈkwɪzətɪv	When I said that, she was a bit *inquisitive*, as girls usually are.	好奇、好問的 curious prying	**inquire**
perquisite* n. ˈpɝˈkwəzɪt	The *perquisites* of a college president include a car and a house.	額外收入、額外賞賜 casual income gratuity	**per**(through)

單字·音標·詞類	例　　　句	中譯·同義字	字源分析
prerequisite n. priˈrɛkwəzɪt	Before there were anesthetics, speed was one of the *prerequisites* of a surgeon.	必要條件、先決條件 preliminary condition	**pre**(before) **require**
query n. ˈkwɪrɪ	She looked at the man in dazed and inarticulate *query*.	質問、疑問 question inquiry	
v.	The editor has *queried* some eminent authors for advice.	詢問 ask enquire	
quest n. kwɛst	The writer of the books has made a long spiritual *quest* into the past of the Tibetan people.	探求 investigation venture	
v.	The mind of a spirited person *quests* ceaselessly for improvements.	追尋、尋找 seek ask	
question n. ˈkwɛstʃən	Never ask me such silly *questions* again.	問題、詢問、質問 inquiry interrogation	
v.	The chairman has *questioned* the absence of a few club members.	質問、詢問 ask inquire	
v.	Babylonian sages *questioned* the stars in their efforts to measure time.	探究、研究 examine ponder	

| | v. | The honesty of these writers is unimpeachable, however much their competency may be *questioned*. | 懷疑
doubt
dispute | |

questionable a.
ˈkwɛstʃənəb!

| | | Canners sometimes take in any *questionable* type of fruit at top prices. | 有問題、可疑的
doubtful
problematic | question |

request n.
rɪˈkwɛst

| | | This book is in great *request*. | 需要
demand
desire | require |

| | n. | I will marry her, sir, at your *request*. | 請求
entreaty
petition | |

| | v. | I am *requested* to write an essay. | 請求、要求
ask
entreat | |

require v.
rɪˈkwaɪr

| | | Growing children *require* more food. | 需要
want
demand | re(again) |

requisite a.
ˈrɛkwəzɪt

| | | I have made a list of the food *requisite* for the trip. | 需要、必要的
necessary
indispensable | require |

requisition n.
ˌrɛkwəˈzɪʃən

| | | The prisoner had been arrested in England on the *requisition* of the Swiss government. | 要求
request
demand | require |

n.	The *requisitions* for the position will be specified in the announcement.	必備條件 requirement condition	

REG·RIG

rule, king, hard

治理 ● 國王 ● 硬直 ● 嚴厲

字根 reg, rig 源出拉丁文 regimen n.n.「管理、治理」、rēgā-lis a.「國王的」、rigor n.m.「硬直、嚴酷」、rigidus a.「硬直、嚴酷的」等字。這個字根除了上述三種拼法外,在下文例字中也可見到其他形態: (1) realm n.「地域、領域」, (2) royal a.「王室、莊嚴的」, (3) regnal a.「國王的」、regnant a.「占優勢、支配的」, (4) reign n./v.「統治」。其中(1)(2)的拼法借自古法文,(3)出自拉丁文 regnāre v.「爲王、執政」,(4)則是英文借自法文之後的變體。例字中語義衍變比較特別的,只有前文提到過的 realm 一字。realm 借自古法文 reaume(或作 realme),原指「王國」,後來引申而有「地域、領域」的意思;十七世紀前,泰半拼作 reaume ,大約在1600年之後,才逐漸統一拼爲 realm 。

realm n.
rɛlm

The emperor had seized power throughout the whole *realm*.

地域
region
territory

n.

The professor is a newcomer in the *realm* of microbiology.

領域
sphere
domain

regal a.
ˈrigḷ

No one dared challenge the emperor's *regal* power.

帝王、王室的
kingly
royal

a.

He lives in *regal* splendor.

似帝王、華麗
、莊嚴的
splendid
stately

regime n.
rɪˈʒim

The totalitarian *regime* was overthrown by the people.

政制、政治系
統
government
political system

n.

Babys' *regime* includes two naps a day.

生活規律
regular pattern
　of action

regimen* n.
ˈrɛdʒəˌmɛn

Under such a *regimen* you will certainly live very long.

養生法
health plan

regiment* n.
ˈrɛdʒəmənt

The Smithsons have gathered a *regiment* of company for their Sunday dinner.

大群、多數
group
large quantity

region n.
ˈridʒən

These geologists have studied the aquatic *regions* of the earth.

區域、地方
territory
area

n.

The student is interested in the abstract *region* of higher mathematics.

領域
field
sphere

regnal* a.
ˈrɛgnəl

The day of the king's coronation was later called the *regnal* day.

國王、君主的　reign
royal
kingly

regnant* a.
ˈrɛgnənt

The offended lady was filled with a *regnant* determination to defend herself.

占優勢、支配　reign
、流行的
dominant
prevalent

regular a.
ˈrɛgjələ

Six o'clock was his *regular* hour for rising.

通常、正常的
usual
normal

a.

A *regular* customer trades often at the same store.

經常、不變的
constant
steady

regulate v.
ˈrɛgjəˌlet

You must try to *regulate* your habits.

管理、調整
conduct
adjust

regulation n.
ˌrɛgjəˈleʃən

We do business only according to *regulations*.

規則　　　　　regulate
rule
direction

reign n.
ren

The crown prince had assumed active *reign* from his father.

統治、王權
rule
sovereignty

	v.	A king *reigns* over his kingdom.	統治 rule govern	
	v.	A complete silence *reigned* inside the house.	占優勢、盛行 prevail predominate	
rigid a. 'rɪdʒɪd		Metals are not perfectly *rigid* but are elastic.	硬的 hard unpliant	
	a.	The schoolboys all dislike the *rigid* schoolmaster.	嚴格、嚴厲的 stern severe	
rigor n. 'rɪgɚ		Moral *rigor* prohibits such innocent pleasures as dancing at crossroads.	嚴厲 severity strictness	
rigorous a. 'rɪgərəs		The problem of liquor smuggling has vexed governments seeking to maintain a *rigorous* policy of liquor control.	嚴厲的 harsh inexorable	**rigor**
royal a. 'rɔɪəl		The prince and his bride honeymooned on the *royal* yacht.	王室、皇家的 kingly regal	
	a.	There is something *royal* in the stately carriage of a stag's head.	莊嚴、氣派的 magnificent splendid	

48

SCRIB·SCRIP

write

書寫

字根 scrib, scrip 源出拉丁文動詞 scrībere「書寫」，scrip 的形態則來自其過去分詞 scrīptus 和名詞 scrīptum「著作、文字」。下文例字語意衍變比較特殊的，有 conscribe v.「徵服兵役、限制」、proscribe v.「宣告非法、禁止」、subscribe v.「簽署（以表同意）」三字。conscribe 源自拉丁文動詞 conscrībere，字首 con 有 together 的意思（參見本書「最重要的30個字首」**6. co·com·con**），原指將姓名寫在一起，因此可衍變出「徵服兵役、限制」的語義。proscribe 的衍變過程本書已詳述過，請參閱「最重要的30個字首」**23. pro·pur** 一節。subscribe 源出拉丁文動詞 subscrībere，字首 sub 有 under 的意思（參見「最重要的30個字首」**26. sub·sus**），原指「寫在下面、簽字」。西式文件簽名一般在下方或右下方，因此在文件上 subscribe，便有認可同意的意思，再引申自然可成「捐助、認捐」。

單字·音標·詞類	例　句	中譯·同義字	字源分析
ascribe v. əˈskraɪb	These reforms should be *ascribed* to those individuals who sacrificed their lives.	歸於、歸功於 refer attribute	a(to)
circumscribe* v. ˌsɝkəmˈskraɪb	The ship had made a voyage that *circumscribed* the world.	在周圍畫線 draw a line around	circum(around)
v.	A heart patient's activity should be *circumscribed.*	限制 limit bound	
conscribe v. kənˈskraɪb	The government has the power to *conscribe* everybody and everything in case of war.	徵服兵役、強制徵召 enlist forcibly	con(together)
v.	Ill-health *conscribed* the force of his intentions.	限制 limit circumscribe	
conscription n. kənˈskrɪpʃən	*Conscription* was often necessary to provide a large army.	徵兵 enforced 　　military draft	conscribe
describe v. dɪˈskraɪb	In 1886 a surgeon in Boston *described* the condition now called appendicitis.	描寫、敍述 portray delineate	de(down)
inscribe v. ɪnˈskraɪb	The mason *inscribed* the woman's name on the tombstone.	刻銘 carve engrave	in(in)

單字・音標・詞類	例　　　句	中譯・同義字	字源分析
v.	He *inscribed* the new book to an old friend.	呈獻、題獻 dedicate address	
manuscript n. ˈmænjəˌskrɪpt	Medieval *manuscripts* were beautifully decorated by the scribes who copied them.	手稿、原稿 handwritten or typewritten composition	**man**(hand)
nondescript* a. ˈnɑndɪˌskrɪpt	Even though she was wearing a *nondescript* outfit, she was still the most striking person in the room.	莫可名狀、難以分類的 indescribable unclassifiable	**non**(not) **describe**
postscript n. ˈpos·skrɪpt	The author later added a *postscript* to the manuscript.	後記、附筆、附加之資料 addition supplement	**post**(after)
prescribe v. prɪˈskraɪb	Legislatures may *prescribe* qualifications for admission to the bar.	規定、命令 dictate enjoin	**pre**(before)
prescript* n. ˈpriskrɪpt	The judge made this decision according to the *prescripts* of existing law.	規則、法令、命令 regulation ordinance	**prescribe**
proscribe v. proˈskraɪb	Lasting pacts *proscribing* warfare exist among many primitive societies.	宣告非法、禁止 outlaw interdict	**pro**(forward)

單字・音標・詞類	例　　句	中譯・同義字	字源分析
scribble v. **ˈskrɪbl̩**	The kid *scribbled* something hastily on the wall and ran away.	潦草書寫、胡寫 write carelessly	
scribe* n. skraɪb	Two copies of the ancient manuscript had been made by *scribes*.	抄寫員、書記官 copyist penman	
script n. skrɪpt	The message was written in a *script* which consists entirely of consonants.	字母 alphabet	
scripture n. **ˈskrɪptʃɚ**	A primitive man usually has great awe for any *scripture*.	經典、聖典 sacred writing something written	**script**
subscribe v. səbˈskraɪb	They found him unwilling to *subscribe* to the agreement.	簽署(以表同意) agree consent	**sub**(under)
v.	Each person in the office *subscribed* ten dollars.	捐助、認捐 donate offer	
superscribe* v. ˌsupɚˈskraɪb	Each letter is *superscribed* with a number indicating its relative order alphabetically.	寫在上面 write atop	**super**(over)
transcribe trænˈskraɪb	These copies were scrupulously *transcribed* from the surviving manuscripts of the war years.	抄寫、複寫 copy reproduce	**trans**(over)

單字・音標・詞類	例　　　句	中譯・同義字	字源分析
v.	His hobby is *transcribing* books into braille.	譯寫成他種文字（速記符號、外國文字等） transliterate	
transcript n. ˈtrænˌskrɪpt	The scholar has published a book containing *transcripts* from the papyrological collections of a museum.	抄本、副本 written copy reproduction	**transcribe**

SECU·SEQU·SUE

follow

追隨

　　字根 secu, sequ, sue 源自拉丁文動詞 sequor「追隨」和其過去分詞 secūtus；其中 sue 的形態則來自古法文。下文例字語意衍變比較特別的，有 execute v.「處死」、sue v.「控訴、請求」、suit v.「適合」。execute（法文 exécuter，拉丁文 exsequor）字首 ex 有 out 的意思（參見本書「最重要的30個字首」**11. e·ec·ex·extra**），原義為「執行」，後在十五世紀左右轉成「執行死刑」，而衍生出「處死」的意思。sue 借自古法文動詞 suer（現代法文作 suivre），最早的字源則是前文提過的拉丁文動詞 sequor，十三世紀仍作 follow 解釋。請求別人辦事，往往須追隨於後，以言語懇求；上法院告人，一告就得追辦不少訴訟手續。因此，到了十五世紀左右，已經引申成「控訴、請求」的意思。suit 作名詞有「控訴、請求」的意思，便來自 sue。而 suit 作動詞的「適合」，則可由字根 follow 的解釋來推想。可以 follow 在一起的事物，自然彼此能配合得很融洽。由此也不難想到，為什麼 suit 作名詞也有「套、套裝」的意思了。

consecution n.
ˌkɑnsɪˈkjuʃən

He has read each chapter of the book separately, abandoning any search for *consecution* of argument.

連續
succession
series

con(together)

---

consecutive a.
kənˈsɛkjətɪv

The chairman has held office for four *consecutive* terms.

連續、繼續不斷的
successive
continual

consecution

---

consequence n.
ˈkɑnsəˌkwɛns

Do you know the possible *consequence* of doing this?

結果
outcome
event

con(together)

---

consequent a.
ˈkɑnsəˌkwɛnt

The period of tension between the two countries and the *consequent* need for military preparedness may imperil world peace.

因…結果而發生的
resultant
resulting

consequence

---

consequential a.
ˌkɑnsəˈkwɛnʃəl

The French were once the only *consequential* immigrant group in America.

重要的
important
vital

consequent

a.

His loud *consequential* voice annoyed the other members of the board.

自大、自傲的
self-important
arrogant

---

ensue v.
ɛnˈsu

The evils *ensued* from lack of a stable government.

因而發生、隨起
follow
result

en(in)

單字・音標・詞類	例　句	中譯・同義字	字源分析
execute v. ˈɛksɪˌkjut	The provisions of the will shall be *executed* no matter what happens.	執行 conduct perform	**ex**(out)
v.	The man was *executed* as a traitor.	處死 put to death	
executive n. ɪgˈzɛkjʊtɪv	He has served in our company as chief sales *executive* for five years.	經理主管級人員、行政官 officer administrator	**execute**
obsequious* a. əbˈsikwɪəs	The king was greeted by his *obsequious* courtiers.	卑躬、諂媚、逢迎的 flattering fawning	**ob**(toward)
persecute v. ˈpɜsɪˌkjut	Christians were once *persecuted*.	迫害、煩擾 oppress molest	**per**(through)
prosecute v. ˈprɑsɪˌkjut	The generals were ordered to *prosecute* the war with the utmost vigor.	進行、經營 follow pursue	**pro**(forward)
v.	Trespassers will be *prosecuted*.	對…提起公訴 sue indict	
pursue v. pɚˈsu	The cowboys were *pursuing* the fleeing Indians.	追擊、追捕、繼續 chase follow	**pur**(forward)

單字・音標・詞類	例　　　　句	中譯・同義字	字源分析
pursuit n. pəˈsut	The house owner has gone out in *pursuit* of the thief.	追捕、追 following chasing	pursue
sequel n. ˈsikwəl	The hero performs even more astonishing feats in the *sequel* of the play.	續集、繼續、 結果 continuation upshot	
sequence n. ˈsikwəns	The city spreads over a *sequence* of low hills.	連續 succession series	
sequential a. sɪˈkwɛnʃəl	He has set forth the essential facts in a well ordered, *sequential* manner.	連續的 serial consecutive	sequence
subsequent a. ˈsʌbsɪˌkwɛnt	*Subsequent* events proved that he had been right.	後來、繼起的 following succeeding	sub(under)
sue v. su	She has *sued* her husband for divorce.	控訴、起訴 charge indict	
v.	Messengers came *suing* for peace.	請求 plead supplicate	
suit n. sut	He started a *suit* to collect damages for his injuries.	訴訟 action case	sue
n.	His *suit* was granted.	請求 request petition	sue

單字・音標・詞類	例　　　　句	中譯・同義字	字源分析
v.	It is difficult to find a time that *suits* everybody.	適合 fit become	
suite n. **swit**	We had to accommodate him and his *suite* which includes his wife and servants.	一班隨員、一班扈從 attendants retinue	
n.	The millionaire's house contains ten *suites* of three to six rooms.	套房 apartment	

50

SED·SESS·SID

sit, set, live

坐 ● 安置 ● 居住

字根 sed, sess, sid 源自拉丁文動詞 sedēre「坐、安置、居住」和 sīdere「坐、停留」；其中 sess 的拼法，則出自兩字的過去分詞 sessus。這個字根除了上述三種拼法，並有 sieg 一種形態，例字中如 siege n.「圍攻」、besiege v.「包圍」均以這種形態組成。siege 源出古法文 siege（現代法文作 siège），更早的字源則是拉丁文俗語 sedicum，原有「座椅」的意思。現代英文以「放置武力」來解釋 siege，使成「圍攻」的意思；再加上字首 be「全面、圍繞」，便成動詞 besiege。例字中語義衍變比較奇特的，尚有 assess v.「估計」、dissident a.「意見不同的」、dissidence n.「異議」、obsess v.「使心神困擾」、preside v.「主持、管理」、session n.「會議、學期」、subsidy n.「補助金」。assess 在古代指坐在裁決席上，裁奪糾紛，判斷是非高下，引申而有「估計」的意思。dissident, dissidence 的字首 dis 有 away 的意思（參見本書「最重要的30個字首」9. de·di·dis），意見不同的人通常不會坐在一起，因此不難想見為什麼可以指「意見不同」。obsess 源出拉丁文動詞 obsidēre，字首 ob 有 toward, against 的意思（參見「最重要的30個字首」18. ob），因此原義為「坐在對面、坐下」，後來引申而成「佔據、圍困」（請參考前文所提 siege 的語義衍變），最後純指人的心情，而有「使心神困擾」的意思。preside 字首 pre 有 before 的意思（

參見「最重要的30個字首」22. pre ），開會時可以先別人而坐，或是坐在首位的人，自然是個能夠「主持、管理」事務的人物。session 字根有「坐」的意思，開會一般得用坐的，因此不難了解可以作「會議」解釋；大學裏上課也必須坐著，因此到了十八世紀，又轉成了「學期」。subsidy 源出拉丁文名詞 subsidium，字首 sub 有 under 的意思（參見「最重要的30個字首」26. sub·sus ），與字首配合而成「坐在下方待命」，因此拉丁文原即有「救助、支援」的意思，引申而成「補助金」。

單字·音標·詞類	例　　　句	中譯·同義字	字源分析
assess v. əˈsɛs	Damages have to be *assessed* after an accident.	估計 estimate appraise	**as**(to)
assiduous a. əˈsɪdʒuəs	The master often praised his *assiduous* servant.	勤勉、有恒的 sedulous persevering	**as**(to)
besiege v. bɪˈsidʒ	I was *besieged* by four of John's children.	包圍、困惱 beset hem in	**be**(around) **siege**
dissidence n. ˈdɪsədəns	There were people arrested for political *dissidence*.	異議、不一致 disagreement dissent	**dis**(away)
dissident a. ˈdɪsədənt	*Dissident* elements within the Thai navy attempted to overthrow Pibul's regime.	倡異議、意見不同的 dissenting contentious	**dis**(away)
n.	A number of *dissidents* forced the government to announce a reduction in the period of national service.	倡反調者、持異議者 dissenter	
obsess v. əbˈsɛs	Fear that someone might steal her money *obsessed* her.	使心神困擾 haunt besiege	**ob**(against)
possess v. pəˈzɛs	The little girl *possesses* great patience.	有、具有 have own	pos(able)

單字・音標・詞類	例　　句	中譯・同義字	字源分析
v.	She was *possessed* by the desire of getting rich.	支配、控制 control dominate	
possessed a. pə'zɛst	He fought like a man *possessed* by some evil spirit.	被（鬼怪）纏 住、瘋狂 crazed controlled	**possess**
preside v. prɪ'zaɪd	The minister was asked to *preside* over the funeral service.	主持、管理 direct officiate	**pre**(before)
reside v. rɪ'zaɪd	Her relative has *resided* abroad for many years.	居住 live dwell	**re**(back)
resident n. 'rɛzədənt	All *residents* of the city are required to comply with the new law.	居民、居住者 inhabitant dweller	**reside**
residual a. rɪ'zɪdʒʊəl	A *residual* quantity of the spray might endanger human health.	殘餘、剩餘的 remaining additional	**residue**
residue n. 'rɛzə,dju	The syrup has dried up, leaving a sticky *residue*.	殘餘、剩餘 remnant remainder	**re**(back)
sedate a. sɪ'det	I could see the trees stretching ahead in their *sedate* beauty of ruby and brown.	靜肅的 quiet placid	

單字・音標・詞類	例　　　　句	中譯・同義字	字源分析
sedative a. ˈsɛdətɪv	The doctor gave her a *sedative* medicine, after which she slept for eight hours.	鎮定的 allaying lenitive	sedate
sedentary* a. ˈsɛdn̩ˌtɛrɪ	For *sedentary* relaxation he is likely to listen to music.	不動、定居的 settled stationary	
sediment n. ˈsɛdəmənt	When the Nile River overflows, it leaves *sediment* on the surrounding fields.	沖積物、沉澱物 settlings dregs	
sedulous* a. ˈsɛdʒələs	His products have the mark of a *sedulous* craftsmanship.	勤勉、努力不懈、小心仔細的 busy diligent	
sessile* a. ˈsɛsl̩	She is particularly interested in the *sessile* marine animals and plants.	固著的 permanently attached sedentary	
session n. ˈsɛʃən	The secretary will read the letter to the House of Representatives in secret *session*.	會議 meeting	
n.	What plans do you have for the coming summer *session*?	學期 term	

單字·音標·詞類	例　　句	中譯·同義字	字源分析
siege n. sidʒ	The scientists have developed a weapon designed to conduct *siege* operation.	圍攻 besetting beleaguering	
subside v. səb'saɪd	The soil *subsided* over the old dump.	降落 descend decline	sub(under)
v.	The child's fever has *subsided.*	消退、平息 drop abate	
subsidiary a. səb'sɪdɪˌɛrɪ	The farmers have considered planting some *subsidiary* crops.	次要、副的 minor supplementary	subsidy
subsidize v. 'sʌbsəˌdaɪz	The state government has *subsidized* the steamship line.	資助 support aid	subsidy
subsidy n. 'sʌbsəˌdɪ	A *subsidy* is a grant of money made by way of financial aid.	補助金 aid grant	sub(under)
supersede v. ˌsupɚ'sid	The automobile has long *superseded* the horse.	替代 replace overrule	super(over)
v.	The welfare of a child generally *supersedes* judgments rendered by any court.	使成無效、廢除 annul override	

51

SENS·SENT

feel, sense

感覺●意識

字根 sens, sent 源出拉丁文動詞sentīre「感覺、意識」與其過去分詞 sensus，以及名詞 sensus「感官、意識」。下文例字意義衍變比較奇特的，有 sentence v./n.「判決」和 sententious a.「言簡意賅的」。 sentence源出法文 sentence，更早的字源則是拉丁文名詞 sententia，而 sententia又來自上文提到過的 sentīre。拉丁文動詞 sentīre原義爲「感覺、意識」，引申而可指人用意識去「斷定、判斷」事情，因此衍生出名詞 sententia，便有「意見、箴言」的意思。在十四世紀的英文中，sentence 尙保有拉丁文原義的「意見、箴言」，同時却也轉成了「判決」的意思。意見、箴言、判決往往只有一句話而已，因此後來便又衍變出「句子」的意思。另一字 sententious 源出拉丁文形容詞 sententiōsus，原來自上述名詞 sententia「箴言」，因此本即有「意味深長、言簡意賅」的意思。

單字‧音標‧詞類	例　　　　句	中譯‧同義字	字源分析
assent v. əˈsɛnt	He at once *assented* to my wishes.	同意 agree accede	**as**(to)
n.	They had my *assent*.	同意、允許 compliance acquiescence	
consensus n. kənˈsɛnsəs	The *consensus* is against revision.	一般的意見、 一致 general agreement	**con**(together)
consent v. kənˈsɛnt	He has *consented* to shoulder the debt for her.	同意 agree assent	**con**(together)
n.	He did it without our *consent*.	同意 permission acquiescence	
consentaneous * ˌkɑnsɛnˈteniəs a.	His hypothesis might be perfectly *con- sentaneous* with scientific truth.	相合、同意的 agreeing suited	**consent**
consentient * a. kənˈsɛnʃənt	It is good news that so far we have received *consentient* reports on this event.	一致、同意的 agreeing unanimous	**consent**
dissension n. dɪˈsɛnʃən	There is continued *dissension* in the ranks of the party.	意見不合、紛 爭 quarreling discord	**dissent**

單字·音標·詞類	例　　句	中譯·同義字	字源分析
dissent v. dɪˈsɛnt	I *dissent* strongly from what the last speaker has said.	不同意 disagree differ	**dis**(away)
n.	When her friend wished to go abroad, she expressed strong *dissent*.	不同意、異議 disagreement discord	
dissentient* a. dɪˈsɛnʃənt	The act was passed with only one *dissentient* voice.	持異議、不贊成的 disagreeing dissenting	**dissent**
insensate* a. ɪnˈsɛnset	Sometimes I wish I were an *insensate* stone.	無感覺、無生命的 insentient inanimate	**in**(not)
a.	The people hated the tyrant for his *insensate* cruelty.	無情、殘忍的 cruel brutal	
a.	He would never succeed in carrying out that *insensate* project of his.	愚鈍的 foolish fatuous	
insensible a. ɪnˈsɛnsəbl	The man hit by the truck was *insensible* for three hours.	不省人事、昏迷的 unconscious	**in**(not) **sensible**
a.	She has grown *insensible* to fear after being tortured for years.	冷淡、不以為意的 indifferent apathetic	

a.	The room grew cold by *insensible* degrees.	難察覺、微細的 slight imperceptible	
insensitive a. ɪnˈsɛnsətɪv	Her eyes became *insensitive* to light after a few years.	無感覺力、無感覺的 insensible unimpressionable	in(not) **sensitive**
nonsense n. ˈnɑnsɛns	She had said nothing but a lot of *nonsense*.	無意義的話、荒謬的行為或言語 absurdity twaddle	non(not) **sense**
presentiment* n. prɪˈzɛntəmənt	I have a strong *presentiment* that it will prove a success.	預感 anticipation forethought	pre(before)
resent v. rɪˈzɛnt	Our cat seems to *resent* having anyone sit in its chair.	憎惡 feel a bitter 　indignation at	re(back)
scent n. sɛnt	Dogs follow the *scent*.	氣味、香 smell fragrance	
sensate* a. ˈsɛnset	*Sensate* matters are those that are materialistic.	可感覺的 materialistic	sense
sensation n. sɛnˈseʃən	Fire gives a *sensation* of warmth.	感覺 sense feeling	sense

單字·音標·詞類	例　　　　句	中譯·同義字	字源分析
n.	The death of the famous actress created a *sensation*.	大事件、轟動的事物 excitement agitation	
sensational a. sɛnˈseʃən̩l	Her *sensational* private life kept her continually before the public.	轟動、引人注目的 arresting spectacular	sensation
sense n. sɛns	A man acquires most of his knowledge through the five *senses*.	感官、感覺、知覺 feeling sensation	
n.	She does not have much *sense*.	判斷力、見識 judgment sagacity	
n.	We must bring him to his *senses*.	理性、健全心智 mind intellect	
n.	He is a gentleman in every *sense* of the word.	意義 significance import	
v.	I could *sense* that there was something wrong with her.	感知、察覺 notice perceive	
senseless a. ˈsɛnslɪs	She fell *senseless* at the sight of the dead man.	不省人事、無感覺的 unconscious insensible	sense

單字·音標·詞類	例 句	中譯·同義字	字源分析

a. What a *senseless* fool I have been! — 愚蠢、無知的 idiotic inane

sensible a.
ˈsɛnsəbḷ

His distress was *sensible* from his manner. — 可感覺的 perceptible tangible — sense

a. He is too *sensible* to do a foolish thing like that. — 有理性、明智的 rational judicious

sensitive a.
ˈsɛnsətɪv

The eye is *sensitive* to light. — 敏感、易感的 perceptive susceptible — sense

sensory a.
ˈsɛnsərɪ

Man perceives by his *sensory* organs. — 感覺、知覺的 of the senses — sense

sensual a.
ˈsɛnʃʊəl

One must be sensitive to the *sensual* and intellectual pleasures that make life so abundantly worth living. — 官能、肉體上的 bodily voluptuous — sense

sensuous a.
ˈsɛnʃʊəs

Some philosophers maintain that most of the arts are *sensuous*. — 訴諸感官的 perceived by the senses — sense

sentence n.
ˈsɛntəns

The *sentence* of the court was three years in prison. — 宣判、判決 decision condemnation

v.	The man was tried on the charge of inciting to riot and *sentenced* to thirty days in jail.	宣判 doom condemn	
sententious* a. sɛnˈtɛnʃəs	She has tried to push home her ideas on social injustice by *sententious* precept.	言簡意賅的 expressive pithy	sentence
sentient* a. ˈsɛnʃənt	Man is a *sentient* being.	有知覺力的 capable of feeling	sense
a.	Since childhood, he has been a man *sentient* of his surroundings.	意識的 aware conscious	
sentiment n. ˈsɛntəmənt	Since 1925, the poet has written many poems of *sentiment* and reflection.	感情、情緒 emotion sensibility	
sentimental a. ˌsɛntəˈmɛntḷ	He has a sincere *sentimental* love for children.	多感、容易感動的 emotional impressionable	sentiment

SIST·STA·STITUT

stand, place, set

站立 ● 安置 ● 固定

字根 sist, sta, stitut源出希臘文名詞 στασις (stasis)「站立、位置」，以及拉丁文動詞 stāre 「站立、保持、停置」、sistere 「安置、停放、停止」。stitut 的形態則出自拉丁文本身的字根變化，如下文例字中的 constitute v.「構成、組成」、destitute a.「缺乏、窮困的」、institute v.「開始」等，最初便分別借自拉丁文的 constituere, destitūtus a., instituere v. 等字。這是英文非常重要的字根，組成的單字極多，拼法也比較繁複。除了上述三種拼法最為常見之外，尚可見到五種形態：(1) destine v.「命運注定、指定」、obstinate a.「固執的」，(2) superstition n.「迷信」，(3) system n.「制度、系統」，(4) restore v.「交還、恢復、重建」，(5) stead n.「利益、好處」、steady a.「穩定、沈著的」。其中(1)(2)源自拉丁文本身的字根變化，(3)(4)(5)則分別出自希臘文、古法文、古英文。例字中有些語義衍變比較特別，茲說明如下。instant a.「立即的」源出拉丁文動詞 īnstāre，字首 in 有 on 的意思（參見本書「最重要的30個字首」**12. em·en·im·in**），因此最早有「在上、居上臨下」的意義，引申而成「迫近、催促、加緊」；事實上，拉丁文本來便有 īnstāns a.一字，出自 īnstāre 的現在分詞 īnstāntem，意思便是「立即、急迫」。prostitute n.「妓女」一字本書前文已介紹過，請參閱「最重要的30個字根」**23. pro·pur** 。stead n.「利益

、好處」源出古英文 (Old English) stẹde ，原義爲standing still ，引申而有「位置、地產」的意義，再引申可指有利之物或有利之處，而成「利益、好處」。古英文屬於日耳曼語系，而日耳曼語系和希臘、拉丁文同屬印歐語系(Indo-European Family) ，因此這些語言的語彙，部分有互通現象。substance n. 「物質、實質」出自拉丁文名詞 substantia, substantia 又來自動詞 substāre 。字首sub 有 under 的意思，因此 substāre 原指 stand under, stand firm，到了後期又引申爲 be present ，名詞 substantia 便由這個表示存在的意思轉而成「物質、實質」。 superstition n.「迷信」借自古法文，但最早的字源則是拉丁文動詞superstāre 。字首 super 有over 的意思，因此 superstāre 原指 stand over 。後來衍變成 stand over something in awe，指人見到不了解的事物而心生敬畏。於是拉丁文便以super-stitio n.f. 一字，作「迷信」解釋，輾轉而形成今日英文的super-stition。

單字·音標·詞類	例　句	中譯·同義字	字源分析
apostate* n. əˈpɑstet	The Church decree excommunicated as *apostates* all those who professed the materialistic and anti-Christian doctrine.	背教者、變節者 diserter renegade	apo(away)
assist v. əˈsɪst	Do you need anyone to *assist* you in your work?	幫助 aid succor	**as**(to)
assistant a. əˈsɪstənt	She is our teaching *assistant* for this semester.	助教、助手 helper aide	assist
circumstance n. ˈsɝkəmˌstæns	Under no *circumstances* will I agree to let you go.	情況、情勢 condition situation	**circum**(around)
circumstantial a. ˌsɝkəmˈstænʃəl	His memory is exact and *circumstantial*.	詳盡的 detailed particularized	circumstance
	a.	Minor details are *circumstantial* compared with the main fact.	不重要、偶然的 minute incidental	
consist v. kənˈsɪst	Coal *consists* mainly of carbon.	組成、爲…所製 be formed be composed	**con**(together)
	v.	True charity does not *consist* in almsgiving.	在於、存在 exist lie	

單字·音標·詞類	例　　句	中譯·同義字	字源分析
consistent a. kənˈsɪstənt	In art all styles are good provided that they are *consistent* and harmonious within themselves.	一致、相合的 agreeing congruous	consist
constant a. ˈkɑnstənt	The children running in and out of the house were a *constant* annoyance for the old lady.	不斷、持續的 steady incessant	con(together)
constituent n. kənˈstɪtʃʊənt	Society is held together by the mutual needs of its *constituents*.	要素、構成分子 element component	constitute
constitute n. ˈkɑnstəˌtjut	Enumerate the qualities that *constitute* a hero.	構成、組成 form compose	con(together)
v.	They had *constituted* a social club for immigrants.	設立、制定 found enact	
desist v. dɪˈzɪst	He had tried to shave but his hand was so unsteady that he had to *desist*.	停止、斷念 stop discontinue	de(away)
destination n. ˌdɛstəˈneʃən	What is the *destination* of this trip?	目的地 journey's end	destine
destine v. ˈdɛstɪn	The prince was not *destined* to attain the throne.	命運、注定 predetermine doom	de(complete)

	v.	Most of the forces *destined* to invade Normandy were gathered on the southern coast of England.	指定 appoint designate	
destiny n. ˈdɛstənɪ		She had to reconcile herself to *destiny* and marry the man she did not love.	命運 fate doom	**destine**
destitute* a. ˈdɛstəˌtjut		This street is *destitute* of trees.	缺乏的 deficient divested	**de**(down)
	a.	The association has established many homes for the *destitute*.	窮困的 poor needy	
distance n. ˈdɪstəns		The *distance* between the eyes varies with individuals.	距離、時間的距離 interval space	**dis**(away)
distant a. ˈdɪstənt		The ship was headed for *distant* countries.	遙遠的 faraway remote	**dis**(away)
ecstasy n. ˈɛkstəsɪ		The excited crowds were sending their shrill cries of *ecstasy* streaming across the street.	狂喜、心神恍惚 transport rapture	**ec**(out)
ecstatic a. ɪkˈstætɪk		He looked at her with an *ecstatic* stare.	狂喜、出神的 fervent enraptured	**ecstacy**

單字・音標・詞類	例　　　　句	中譯・同義字	字源分析
establish v. əˈstæblɪʃ	It is not easy to *establish* a business.	建立 found inaugurate	e(out) **stable**
estate n. əˈstet	She has an *estate* in the country.	地產、財產 lands property	e(out)
exist v. ɪgˈzɪst	No beings can *exist* without air.	生存、活著 be last	ex(out)
existent a. ɪgˈzɪstənt	Under the *existent* circumstances, there is nothing we can do but wait.	現下、現存的 extant contemporary	**exist**
extant a. ɪkˈstænt	This is a masterpiece among the specimens of graphic art found among *extant* barbaric folk.	現存、殘存的 existant surviving	ex(out)
insist v. ɪnˈsɪst	She *insisted* on going with us to the haunted house.	堅持、力言 demand urge	in(on)
install v. ɪnˈstɔl	A new college president was *installed*.	使就職 induct inaugurate	in(in) **stall**
v.	The electrician has *installed* the new fixtures.	裝設 set up	
instance n. ˈɪnstəns	This is only one *instance* out of many.	實例 example case	in(on)

單字・音標・詞類		例　句	中譯・同義字	字源分析
instant 'ɪnstənt	n.	He paused for an *instant* and continued the speech.	瞬間、頃刻 moment twinkling	**in**(on)
	a.	The rioter was sentenced to *instant* death.	立即的 immediate prompt	
institute 'ɪnstəˌtjut	v.	The famous scholar has *instituted* many reforms in lexicography.	開始、創立 commence inaugurate	**in**(in)
	n.	The foundation had established an *institute* for psychical research.	研究所、學院 school academy	
institution ˌɪnstə'tjuʃən	n.	The *institution* of this custom dates back to the 15th century.	創立、設立 establishment foundation	**institute**
	n.	We need more *institutions* of higher learning.	教育事業機構 school academy	
obstacle 'ɑbstəkl	n.	The poverty of some of the districts in the city is an *obstacle* to good education.	障礙 obstruction block	**ob**(against)
obstinate 'ɑbstənɪt	a.	He was so *obstinate* that it was impossible to get him to do or understand anything.	固執、不屈的 perverse pertinacious	**ob**(toward)

單字·音標·詞類	例　　　句	中譯·同義字	字源分析
persist v. pɚˈzɪst	This is a melody that could *persist* in a person's mind for a long time.	持續、堅持 continue persevere	**per**(through)
prostitute n. ˈprɑstəˌtjut	A *prostitute* is a woman who engages in pro-miscuous sexual intercourse for payment.	娼妓 whore harlot	**pro**(forward)
resist v. rɪˈzɪst	This metal can *resist* acid.	抗拒、抵抗 withstand counteract	**re**(back)
restitution* n. ˌrɛstəˈtjuʃən	It is only fair that those who do the damage should make *restitution*.	賠償 compensation remuneration	**re**(back)
restore v. rɪˈstor	The lost child was *restored* to its parents.	交還 return reinstate	**re**(back)
v.	Harmony was finally *restored* among the rivaling states.	恢復、重建 reconstruct renovate	
stability n. stəˈbɪlətɪ	These metals have a structural *stability* that should ensure long life.	堅固、堅定 firmness steadiness	**stable**
stabilize v. ˈstebḷˌaɪz	The engineers are considering using a chemical treatment to *stabilize* the fabric.	使堅固、使穩定 set steady	**stable**

stable a.
ˈstebl̩

The personnel of the Supreme Court remained relatively *stable*.

穩定的
steady
durable

stage n.
stedʒ

There are different *stages* in the growth and development of a child.

階段、時期
step
phase

v.

The artists' club has *staged* a special art exhibition.

舉行、發起
produce
bring out

stall n.
stɔl

The woman has a candy *stall* at the fair.

攤位
stand
booth

v.

The soldiers were *stalled* here for four days by heavy enemy fire.

使進退維谷、阻礙或停止…的前進
hinder
hamper

stance* n.
stæns

The figure in the picture has a threatening *stance*.

姿勢
posture

state n.
stet

The people were not satisfied with the unsanitary *state* of the building.

情形、狀態
condition
position

n.

For Aristotle the *state* was an association of men for the sake of the best moral life.

國家
nation
commonwealth

v.	The witness *states* the facts very clearly.	陳述 assert narrate	
stately a. ˈstetlɪ	He kept dancing while his wife watched in *stately* aloofness.	有威嚴的 imposing lofty	**state**
statement n. ˈstetmənt	The prisoner has already made his verbal *statement*.	敘述、供述 relation account	**state**
statesman n. ˈstetsmən	Unfortunately the republic was subject to men who were mere demagogues and in no sense *statesmen*.	政治家 politician	**state**
static a. ˈstætɪk	Dynamic modern society can be contrasted with *static* feudal society.	靜止、靜態的 not active dormant	
station n. ˈsteʃən	The policeman took his *station* at the corner.	位置 place position	
v.	The commander has *stationed* his troops on the hill.	安置、配置 set post	
stationary a. ˈsteʃənˌɛrɪ	The population has remained *stationary* for years.	不變、固定、 不動的 stable immobile	**station**

statue n.	There is a bronze	像、雕像	
ˈstætʃʊ	equestrian *statue* in	image	
	front of the library.		

stature n.	Mr. McKinnel is a man	身材、身長	
ˈstætʃɚ	of tall *stature*.	height	
		standing posture	

n.	Tennessee Williams was	卓越	
	a playwright of *stature*.	prestige	
		distinction	

status n.	In his speech the mayor	地位、身份	
ˈstetəs	once referred to the	role	
	city's *status* as a tourist	recognition	
	attraction.		

statute n.	The *statute* of the	規章、法令	
ˈstætʃʊt	university will be	regulation	
	amended by the end of	edict	
	this year.		

stead* n.	This tradition stands	利益、好處	
stɛd	primitive people in good	avail	
	stead.	advantage	

steadfast a.	Benjamin Franklin was	堅定的	steady
ˈstɛdˌfæst	a *steadfast* servant of	firm	fast(fixed)
	his country.	persevering	

steady a.	What shall I do to make	穩定的	
ˈstɛdɪ	the table *steady*?	stable	
		balanced	

a.	My husband has a	沈著、鎮定的	
	steady temper.	calm	
		sedate	

單字・音標・詞類	例　句	中譯・同義字	字源分析
v.	The man tried to *steady* the horse which had been frightened.	使穩定 stabilize compose	
subsist v. səbˈsɪst	Many adult persons can *subsist* on less than half the amount of protein recommended.	生活、存在 live exist	sub(under)
subsistence n. səbˈsɪstəns	His small patrimony was enough for a *subsistence.*	生計 livelihood maintenance	**subsist**
substance n. ˈsʌbstəns	Ice and water are the same *substance* in different forms.	物質 material stuff	sub(under)
n.	Pea soup has more *substance* than water.	實質 essence	
n.	After years of hard working he has become a man of *substance.*	財產、資產 wealth means	
substantial a. səbˈstænʃəl	It is a mere dream, neither *substantial* nor practical.	眞實、實在的 real actual	**substance**
a.	He has given us a rather *substantial* argument.	內容充實的 firm solid	
a.	The student has made some *substantial* improvement.	重大的 important essential	

單字・音標・詞類	例　　　句	中譯・同義字	字源分析
substantiate v. səbˌstænʃɪˈet	The man could not *substantiate* his charge because it was not true.	證實 confirm corroborate	**substance**
substitute v. ˈsʌbstəˌtjut	We have *substituted* a new technique for an old one.	代替 replace change	**sub**(under)
n.	Honey is an excellent *substitute* for sugar in many recipes.	代替物 replacement alternative	
superstition n. ˌsupɚˈstɪʃən	It is a *superstition* to believe that a black cat crossing one's path portends bad luck.	迷信 irrational belief	**super**(over)
system n. ˈsɪstəm	The dissenters are very dissatisfied with the present political *system*.	制度、系統 organism scheme	**sys**(together)

53

SPEC·SPECT·SPIC

watch, look

觀望 ● 瞻望

　　字根spec, spect, spic源出拉丁文名詞species「景象、外觀」和動詞 spectāre 「觀看、瞻望」；spic 的拼法則出自拉丁文本身的字根變化。下文例字中的despise v.「輕視」和 despite prep.「不顧、雖有」，形態比較特別。這兩字均出自拉丁文動詞 dēspicere「輕視」（despite 則來自其過去分詞 dēspectus），後來轉經古法文而進入英文，目前拼法上的些微差異，便是受古法文影響的結果。此外，語義衍變比較奇特的例字，有 auspice n.「前兆」、auspicious a.「吉兆、幸運的」、specter n.「鬼魂、幽靈」。auspice, auspicious 源出拉丁文動詞 auspicor「鳥卜、占卜」，另一字根au有「鳥」（拉丁文作 avis n.f.）的意思。古羅馬時代占卜官以鳥的飛行、進食情形，預卜事情的吉凶，於是「觀看飛鳥」便成了占卜的意思。另一字 specter 借自法文 spectre（目前英式英文仍拼作spectre），最早的字源則是拉丁文名詞spectrum。spectrum 在拉丁文中指眼睛所見到的異象，因此原有「幻景、虛像」的意思，引申而成「鬼魂、幽靈」，十七世紀時已進入英文，但在現代英文中則作「光譜、殘像」等意思。

單字·音標·詞類	例 句	中譯·同義字	字源分析
aspect n. ˈæspɛkt	The fierce *aspect* of the robbers frightened the children.	外貌 appearance countenance	a(to)
n.	A question may have many *aspects*.	方面、觀點 bearing view	
auspice n. ˈɔspɪs	He took her gentle words as an *auspice* of happiness.	前兆、吉兆 omen token	au(bird)
n.	The organization was established under the *auspices* of the United Nations.	贊助、保護 protection support	
auspicious a. ɔˈspɪʃəs	This successful party should be an *auspicious* beginning for our company.	吉兆、幸運的 favorable propitious	**auspice**
circumspect a. ˈsɝkəmˌspɛkt	The wicked people are always alert and *circumspect*.	慎重、小心的 watchful heedful	**circum**(around)
conspectus* n. kənˈspɛktəs	The professor has given a brief *conspectus* on rose diseases and their control.	大綱、概要 outline synopsis	**con**(together)
conspicuous a. kənˈspɪkjʊəs	His intention was *conspicuous* only to his friends.	顯明的 obvious manifest	**con**(together)

單字·音標·詞類	例　　句	中譯·同義字	字源分析
a.	She is a *conspicuous* figure.	引人注目、出眾的 striking eminent	
despicable a. ˈdɛspɪkəbļ	To deceive one's good friend is *despicable*.	可鄙、卑劣的 shameful degrading	**despise**
despise v. dɪˈspaɪz	Boys who tell lies are *despised* by their classmates.	輕視 scorn loathe	**de**(down)
despite prep. dɪˈspaɪt	*Despite* their objection, I will do it just the same.	不顧、雖有 in spite of notwithstanding	**de**(down)
expect v. ɪkˈspɛkt	I didn't *expect* to see you here.	預期 anticipate foreknow	**ex**(out)
inspect v. ɪnˈspɛkt	Let us *inspect* your motives.	檢查 examine scrutinize	**in**(on)
introspect* v. ˌɪntrəˈspɛkt	To *introspect* is to look within one's own mind or psyche.	內省 look within	**intro**(within)
perspective n. pɚˈspɛktɪv	Many happenings of the past would seem less important when viewed in *perspective*.	回顧、遠景 prospect vista	**per**(through)
perspicacious* a. ˌpɝspɪˈkeʃəs	A *perspicacious* person could well discern good from bad.	敏銳、明察的 keen shrewd	**per**(through)

單字・音標・詞類	例　　　　　句	中譯・同義字	字源分析
perspicuous* a. pɚˈspɪkjʊəs	His *perspicuous* argument convinced the people who had been against his proposal.	明晰、顯明的 clear manifest	**per**(through)
prospect n. ˈprɑspɛkt	I see no *prospect* of his recovery.	希望、期望 hope anticipation	**pro**(forward)
n.	The *prospect* from the mountain is wonderful.	景色 view spectacle	
v.	Hundreds of people have *prospected* this region for gold.	探勘、尋找 search explore	
prospective a. prəˈspɛktɪv	The announcement declaring his candidacy is *prospective*.	預期的 foresighted expected	**prospect**
respect v. rɪˈspɛkt	Parents must be *respected*.	尊敬、敬重 revere venerate	**re**(back)
n.	He has no *respect* for his promises.	尊敬、敬重 esteem reverence	
n.	In what *respect* do you think they resemble each other?	方面、顧慮 aspect consideration	
respecting prep. rɪˈspɛktɪŋ	A discussion arose *respecting* the merits of different automobiles.	關於 regarding concerning	**respect**

單字・音標・詞類	例　　　句	中譯・同義字	字源分析
respective a. rɪˈspɛktɪv	They were chosen according to their *respective* merits.	各自、個別的 particular individual	respect
retrospect v. ˈrɛtrəˌspɛkt	She kept *retrospecting* the faces of the people she had known as a child.	回想 reflect re-examine	retro(backward)
n.	The new chapter starts with a *retrospect*.	回顧 review re-examination	
specimen n. ˈspɛsəmən	The detective has compared *specimens* of the two persons' handwriting.	樣品 example sample	
specious* a. ˈspiʃəs	His *specious* reasoning could fool a lot of people.	似是而非、像是眞的、假裝老實的 plausible deceptive	
spectacle n. ˈspɛktək|	The parade this morning was a fine *spectacle*.	景象、壯觀 sight display	
spectacular a. spɛkˈtækjələ	The director has presented a *spectacular* play at the National Theater.	引人注目、壯觀的 wonderful unusual	spectacle
specter* n. ˈspɛktə	A *specter* is a fear-inspiring vision of the imagination.	鬼魂、幽靈 ghost phantasm	

單字·音標·詞類	例　句	中譯·同義字	字源分析
spectral* a. ˈspɛktrəl	He saw the *spectral* form of the headless horseman.	鬼怪、虛幻的 ghostly illusory	**specter**
speculate v. ˈspɛkjə͵let	The weathermen often *speculate* about the chances of rain.	思索、推測 meditate surmise	
v.	I do not like to *speculate* in stocks.	投機 risk hazard	
suspect v. səˈspɛkt	She did not *suspect* that the man had killed her daughter.	懷疑、猜想 doubt conjecture	**sus**(under)
n. ˈsʌspɛkt	The police had questioned the murder *suspect*.	嫌疑犯、被懷疑的人 one who is suspected	
a.	Religion has been academically *suspect*.	令人懷疑、不可信的 distrusted suspected	
suspicion n. səˈspɪʃən	He succeeded in dispelling their *suspicions* and won their confidence.	懷疑 doubt mistrust	**suspect**
suspicious a. səˈspɪʃəs	We haven't seen any *suspicious*-looking strangers around here.	令人懷疑、可疑的 questionable dubious	**suspect**

54

STRAIN·STRESS·STRICT· STRING

draw tight

緊縮 ● 壓榨

strain, stress, strict, string 源出拉丁文動詞 stringere，原即有「緊縮、壓榨」的意思。各種不同拼法中，string 出自上述 stringere 一字，strict 出自其過去分詞 strictus，strain 和 stress 則受過古法文影響。除了這四種拼法之外，下文例字中並可看到比較少見的四種形態：(1) straight a.「直、直接的」，(2) stretch v.「拉緊、伸展」，(3) strangle v.「使窒息、勒死」，(4) strait n.「海峽、困境」。其中(1)(2)源出中古英文 (Middle English) 動詞 strecchen 「拉緊」，(3)出自拉丁文動詞 strangulāre「勒死」，(4)則來自古法文。strait 的語義衍變有些奇特，必須說明一下。最早的字源爲上述拉丁文動詞 stringere「緊縮」，進入古英文之後，原作形容詞用，有「緊縮的」的意思。後來引申指兩大海域間的狹窄通道，而成「海峽」；再指「緊縮的情勢」，而有「困境」的意思。另有一字 district n.「區域」語義衍變也相當特別。district 源出拉丁文動詞 distringere 的過去分詞 districtus，原義爲「約束、束縛」。中古時代開始以 district 指封建領主所轄的地區，尤其指領主法律能夠約束的地區，因而可引申出「區域」的意思。

單字・音標・詞類	例　　　句	中譯・同義字	字源分析
astringent* a. əˈstrɪndʒənt	The air was so *astringent* with pine scent that it tightened the nostrils.	收縮、有收縮性的 contracting constricting	a(to)
astrict* v. əˈstrɪkt	In ancient times peasants were *astricted* to the soil.	限制、約束 limit constrain	a(to)
constrain v. kənˈstren	Hunger *constrained* the prisoner to eat.	強迫 impel coerce	con(together)
v.	He tried to *constrain* his mind not to wander from the task.	抑制、壓制 withhold constrict	
constraint n. kənˈstrent	He did this under *constraint*.	強迫、逼迫 compulsion exigency	constrain
n.	There is a *constraint* between them as if they were strangers.	拘束不安、態度不自然 embarrassment unnatural manner	
constrict v. kənˈstrɪkt	The rock obstruction *constricts* the width of the valley from five miles to one.	壓縮、束緊 squeeze constringe	con(together)
constringe* v. kənˈstrɪndʒ	Cold *constringes* the pores.	收縮、壓縮 contract compress	con(together)

單字·音標·詞類	例　　句	中譯·同義字	字源分析
distrain* v. dɪˈstren	The chattels were *distrained* for non- payment of rent.	扣押 seize confiscate	**dis**(away)
distress n. dɪˈstrɛs	She is in great *distress* because her husband has just died.	悲痛 affliction agony	**dis**(away)
n.	He spent his fortune in relieving *distress* among the poor.	窮困 hardship indigence	
v.	I am much *distressed* to hear the news of your mother's death.	使痛苦、使悲 愁 pain grieve	
district n. ˈdɪstrɪkt	Do you know where the Italian *district* of the city is?	區域、地域 area territory	**dis**(away)
restrain v. rɪˈstren	She could not *restrain* her curiosity and opened the closet.	抑制、約束、 阻止 curb debar	**re**(back)
restraint n. rɪˈstrent	Absolute liberty is absence of *restraint*.	約束、抑制 bridle curb	**restrain**
restrict v. rɪˈstrɪkt	There are countries where literacy is largely *restricted* to the upper classes.	限制、約束 bound confine	**re**(back)

單字‧音標‧詞類		例　　　句	中譯‧同義字　字源分析
straight stret	a.	The stream is unusually *straight*.	直、直立、垂 直的 upright erect
	a.	I want a *straight* answer.	直接、率直的 direct undeviating
	adv.	She went *straight* home after the party.	直接、立即地 directly immediately
strain stren	v.	The rope is *strained* by the weight.	拉緊 stretch tighten
	v.	She often *strains* her eyes to look at things.	竭盡、過份使 用而損傷、扭 傷 exert wrench
	n.	The rope broke under the *strain*.	拉力、拉緊 force sprain
	n.	The *strain* of sleepless nights made her ill.	過勞、壓力 pressure exertion
strait stret	n.	The British warships have just passed the *Strait* of Gibraltar.	海峽 narrow passage

n.	He has been in dire financial *straits* since last year.	困難、窮困、困境 difficulty need
strangle v. ˈstræŋɡl	The bone wedged in her throat and *strangled* her.	使窒息、勒死 choke to death throttle
stress n. strɛs	Under the *stress* of bad weather the ship had to return.	壓迫、壓力 pressure strain
n.	Once in a while you have to lay *stress* on a particular argument.	強調、重要 importance emphasis
v.	In his speech the senator *stressed* the political implication of this affair.	強調 emphasize underscore
stretch v. strɛtʃ	He *stretched* the violin string until it broke.	拉緊 tighten strain
v.	*Stretch* out your arms and hold me.	伸展、伸出 reach extend
n.	The cat woke and gave a *stretch*.	伸開、伸展 extending expanding
n.	We could see *stretches* of fields from where we were standing.	廣大的空間 unbroken length

	n.	He worked for six hours at a *stretch*.	一口氣 (不停地)、一段時間 unbroken period

strict a.
strɪkt

The school we are attending have many *strict* rules.

嚴格、嚴厲的
rigid
severe

a.

She wanted to tell me her secret in *strict* confidence.

完全、絕對的
exact
precise

stricture* n.
'strɪktʃɚ

There has been a *stricture* against the disclosure of classified information.

約束、拘束
restriction
constraint

n.

The young man has not been keen about rousing his mother-in-law's suspicions or *strictures*.

非難、責難
blame
censure

string n.
strɪŋ

I need some paper and a piece of *string*.

繩子、帶、線
cord

n.

The owner of the house returned home with a *string* of fish on his back.

一串、一列、
series
group

v.

The whiskey had *strung* her up to recklessness.

使興奮、使緊張
make tense
key up

單字·音標·詞類	例　　　句	中譯·同義字	字源分析
v.	Merchants *string* their prosperous modern houses along this fairly new business thorough-fare.	成一串列排起、排成一列 stretch in a line	
stringent a. ˈstrɪndʒənt	The P.O.W.s have faced the most *stringent* confinement that can be laid upon a human being.	嚴格的 binding rigorous	

STRU·STRUCT

build

建造

　　stru, struct 源出拉丁文動詞struere與其過去分詞 structus，以及名詞 structio，原即有「建造、構造」的意思。這個字根除了上述兩種拼法，尚有一種極少見的形態： destroy v.「毀壞、毀滅」。這種拼法曾受古法文影響，但最終的形態則是英文本身在十四世紀左右發展出來的。由這個字根組成的單字，尚有少數比較少見，因此僅僅列出如下以供參考：superstructure n.「上層構造」、instrumentalist n.「樂器演奏家」等。

單字・音標・詞類	例　　　　句	中譯・同義字	字源分析
construct v. kən'strʌkt	The engineers are *constructing* a bridge.	建築 build erect	**con**(together)
construe* v. kən'stru	The spokesman's announcement was wrongly *construed*.	解釋、分析 interpret analyse	**con**(together)
destroy v. dɪ'strɔɪ	The town was completely *destroyed* after the bombardment.	毀壞、毀滅 demolish annihilate	**de**(down)
destruction n. dɪ'strʌkʃən	War means *destruction*.	毀滅、毀壞 annihilation devastation	**destroy**
instruct v. ɪn'strʌkt	Nelson was *instructed* to sail for Naples.	下指令與、教 導 teach order	**in**(in)
v.	I have been *instructed* by my agent that you still owe me $50,000.	通知 inform notify	
instrument n. 'ɪnstrəmənt	In the castle we saw many medieval *instruments* of torture.	工具 apparatus implement	**in**(in)
instrumental a. ˌɪnstrə'mɛntļ	This novel was *instrumental* in bringing on open conflict.	有幫助的 helpful conducive	**instrument**
misconstruction* ˌmɪskən'strʌkʃən n.	Our *misconstruction* of his words has made him seem to advocate what he opposes.	誤解、曲解 misinterpretation misunderstanding	**misconstrue**

單字·音標·詞類	例　　　句	中譯·同義字	字源分析
misconstrue* v. ˌmɪskənˈstru	A reader should be on guard against *misconstruing* the intention of a given passage.	誤解 misinterpret misrender	mis(wrong) **construe**
obstruct v. əbˈstrʌkt	The veins have been *obstructed* by clots.	阻隔、妨礙 block impede	**ob**(against)
structure n. ˈstrʌktʃɚ	Doctors study the *structure* of the human body.	構造、結構 formation construction	
n.	Our dormitory is a brick *structure*.	建築物 building erection	

56

TACT·TANG

touch

接觸●毗連

　　tact, tang 源出拉丁文動詞 tangere 與其過去分詞 tāctus，以及名詞 tāctus，原即有「接觸、毗連」的意思。這個字根除了上述兩種拼法外，並有下列五種次要的形態：(1) attain v.「得到、達成」；(2) contagion n.「傳染病」，contagious a.「有傳染性的」；(3) contiguous a.「鄰近的」；(4) contingent a.「偶然、意外的」；(5) integral a.「完整、構成的」，integrate v.「結合成一整體」，integrity n.「完整、正直」。其中(1)受過古法文影響，其餘(2)(3)(4)(5)均出自拉丁文本身的字根變化。下文例字意義衍變比較奇特的，有 contingent a.「偶然、意外的」和 tact n.「機智、圓滑」。contingent 源出拉丁文動詞 contingere，字首 con 有 together 的意思（參見本書「最重要的30個字首」**6. co·com·con**），因此原本作「接觸、鄰近」解釋，後來引申又有「遭遇、遇到」的意思。事情要能接觸在一起，有一番遭遇，也不容易，所以 contingent 便有了「偶然、意外的」的意思。tact 源出前文提過的拉丁文名詞 tāctus，原作「觸感」解釋，後來指用手接觸、處理事務，而引申為處事所需要的「機智、圓滑」。

單字·音標·詞類	例　　句	中譯·同義字	字源分析
attain v. əˈten	After a few years he was able to *attain* a position of great influence.	得到、達成 achieve accomplish	**at**(to)
contact v. ˈkɑntækt	The salesman has *contacted* a few prospects.	接觸 touch reach	**con**(together)
n.	Japan's new *contacts* with Europe had brought enormous changes in her society.	接觸、接近 touch approximation	
contagion n. kənˈtedʒən	War had become a *contagion* attacking neutrals as well as belligerents.	傳染病、有害的影響 epidemic poison	**con**(together)
contagious a. kənˈtedʒəs	Many people are *contagious* long before they are aware of the presence of their disease.	有傳染性的 catching infectious	**contagion**
contiguous a. kənˈtɪgjʊəs	Kentucky and Tennessee are *contiguous* states.	鄰近、鄰接的 bordering adjoining	**con**(together)
contingent* a. kənˈtɪndʒənt	Floods are sometimes *contingent* and un-expected.	偶然、意外的 accidental fortuitous	**con**(together)
intact a. ɪnˈtækt	These ancient houses are largely *intact* even after some 3,500 years.	完整、未受傷的 complete uninjured	**in**(not)

單字·音標·詞類	例 句	中譯·同義字	字源分析
intangible a. ɪnˈtændʒəbḷ	The soul is a subtle and *intangible* thing.	不能觸摸的 imperceptible impalpable	in(not) **tangible**
a.	When he saw the woman standing in front of the door, he had an *intangible* feeling of impending disaster.	模糊、難弄明白的 vague elusive	
integral a. ˈɪntəgrəl	Here a hospital, a medical school, and a laboratory of science are all in one *integral* group.	完整、合成的 complete composite	in(not)
a.	Science has become an *integral* part of the scholar's cultural environment.	構成整體所必須的 constituent inherent	
integrate v. ˈɪntəˌgret	The numerous reports must be *integrated* into a few policy statements.	結合成一整體 constitute combine	in(not)
integrity n. ɪnˈtɛgrətɪ	The invading chieftains had guaranteed the *integrity* of the small kingdom.	完整 completeness entireness	in(not)
n.	A writer of *integrity* has a duty toward his opinions.	正直 righteousness rectitude	

單字·音標·詞類	例 句	中譯·同義字	字源分析
tact n. tækt	It requires *tact* to avoid things likely to be unpleasant to guests.	機智、圓滑 diplomacy adroitness	
tactful a. ˈtæktful	The Secretary of State has shown his *tactful* skill in negotiations.	圓通、機敏的 diplomatic clever	tact
tactics n. ˈtæktɪks	Strategy wins wars; *tactics* wins battles.	戰術、策略 method maneuver	
tactile* a. ˈtæktl̩	One could get *tactile* sensations manipulating these controls.	可感觸到的、觸覺的 tangible tactual	
tactual* a. ˈtæktʃuəl	The blind child is going through a series of *tactual* tests.	觸覺的 touching tactile	
tangent* a. ˈtændʒənt	The straight line is *tangent* to the curve.	相切、接觸的 touching	
a.	Much of his work is chaotic and distorted by *tangent* obsessions.	脫離目的、脫離常軌的 erratic aberrant	
tangible a. ˈtændʒəbl̩	He wished he had had a *tangible* reward for his efforts.	可觸知的 touchable tactile	
a.	The conquest of a territory meant a *tangible* advantage to the conqueror.	實質、真實的 material real	

a.	I have never been in a community where happiness was so *tangible*.	可察覺的 perceptible discernible	

57

TAIN·TEN·TIN

hold, keep

保存 ● 固守 ● 堅持

字根 tain, ten, tin 源出拉丁文動詞 tenēre，原即有 hold, keep 的意思；其中 tain 的拼法受過古法文影響，tin 則主要來自拉丁文本身的字根變化。除了這三種拼法，下文例字中尚可見到一種相當奇特的形態：rein n./v.「箝制、駕馭」。rein 的拼法借自古法文 rene（又拼作 raigne 或 rainne，現代法文則作 rêne），最早的字源則是拉丁文動詞 retinēre「保存、制止」（參見另一例字 retain v.「保留、保持」），形態由拉丁文經古法文進入英文，已經起了極大的變化。例字中語義衍變比較特別的，有 continent n.「大陸」、countenance n.「表情、面貌、贊成」、retinue n.「侍從人員」。 continent 源出拉丁文動詞 continēre，字首 con 有 together 的意思（參見本書「最重要的 30 個字首」6. co·com·con），因此原作「包容、包含」解釋。 continent 的形態由拉丁文經古法文進入英文，原作形容詞「包容的」解釋，到了十六世紀逐漸轉成名詞，指包容廣大的空間，而衍變出今日「大陸」的意思。countenance 的拼法出自古法文，最早的字源則是中古拉丁文的 continēntia，字首 con 與上一字相同，有 together 的意思，因此原作「節制、節操」解釋，指人能約束自己的行為舉止。進入法文之後，已轉成「舉止、態度」（現代法文作 contenance），再進入英文，則又引申而指「表情、面貌」。最後，又可以指人對事顯露出沉著的表情，而衍

變成「贊成」的意思。retinue 源出前文提過的拉丁文動詞 retinēre 「保存、制止」，引申而指將人保留下來，供主人使喚，爲主人辦事，而有「侍從人員」的意思。

單字·音標·詞類	例　　句	中譯·同義字	字源分析
abstain v. əbˈsten	They *abstained* from comment.	棄權、戒絕 refrain forbear	**abs**(from)
abstention n. æbˈstenʃən	*Abstention* from smoking and alcoholic liquors is conducive to health.	節制、自制 withholding forbearance	**abstain**
appertain* v. ˌæpɚˈten	These islands had been determined by the President to *appertain* to the U.S.	屬於 belong befit	**ap**(to) **pertain**
contain v. kənˈten	Books *contain* knowledge.	包含 embrace comprise	**con**(together)
content n. kənˈtɛnt	He emptied his pocket of its *contents*.	所容之物 something 　　contained	**contain**
n.	When a man has nothing to say, sonority without *content* is the smartest effect he can achieve.	內容、要旨 substance subject	
v.	Nobody could have thought that he would *content* himself with those threats.	使滿足、使滿意 please gratify	
a.	The poor man was *content* with any food he could eat.	滿足、滿意的 satisfied gratified	

單字·音標·詞類	例　　句	中譯·同義字	字源分析
continent n. ˈkɑntənənt	A *continent* is a continuous mass of land.	大陸 mainland	con(together)
continual a. kənˈtɪnjʊəl	I have grown tired of this *continual* rain.	不停、連續的 constant ceaseless	**continue**
continue v. kənˈtɪnjʊ	He ate dinner and then *continued* his work.	繼續、擴展 extend persist	con(together)
continuous a. kənˈtɪnjʊəs	The *continuous* flow of the brook formed a ravine.	不斷的 incessant unceasing	**continue**
countenance n. ˈkaʊntənəns	He kept his *countenance* so well that he had the air of having made a fine speech.	表情 expression appearance	coun(together)
n.	He had a pleasant *countenance,* good-looking and gentleman-like.	面貌、容貌 face visage	
n.	He has no support or *countenance* in accepted tradition.	贊成、贊許 approval sanction	
v.	Although militant, he never *countenanced* violence.	贊成、鼓勵 favor abet	
detain v. dɪˈten	The men were *detained* by the police for questioning.	拘留、阻止 arrest hinder	de(away)

單字・音標・詞類	例 句	中譯・同義字	字源分析
detention n. dɪˈtɛnʃən	The schoolmaster has ordered the *detention* of the tardy boy after school hours.	延遲、拘留 delay withholding	**detain**
entertain v. ͵ɛntɚˈten	Mr. Bopp is *entertaining* his in-laws over the weekend.	款待、使娛樂 amuse divert	**enter**(between)
v.	We *entertain* no grievance against her whatsoever.	懷抱 harbor cherish	
impertinent a. ɪmˈpɝtn̩ənt	These students should rigidly exclude courses of study *impertinent* to their central purposes.	不相干、不合的 inapplicable irrelevant	**im**(not) **pertinent**
a.	A child is constantly taught not to make *impertinent* remarks to his elders.	無禮、魯莽的 insolent imprudent	
maintain v. menˈten	One must have sufficient exercise to *maintain* physical and mental vigor.	維持、支持 keep uphold	**main**(hand)
v.	The politician *maintained* that his government was untrustworthy.	主張 hold assert	
maintenance n. ˈmentənəns	The mere *maintenance* of the fences gives much to do.	維持、保養、 支持 support sustenance	**maintain**

單字・音標・詞類	例　　　　句	中譯・同義字	字源分析
n.	The *maintenance* of this belief was not rational.	擁護、主張 defence vindication	
obtain v. əbˈten	Everyone wants to *obtain* the prize.	獲得 gain attain	**ob**(toward)
pertain v. pɚˈten	These are the responsibilities that *pertain* to fatherhood.	屬於、關於 belong concern	**per**(through)
pertinacious a. ˌpɚtn̩ˈeʃəs	There was nothing the adults could do about the child's *pertinacious* curiosity.	固執、執拗的 obstinate obdurate	**per**(through)
pertinent a. ˈpɚtn̩ənt	The message of the book is as *pertinent* today as at the time it was written.	恰當、切題 relevant apt	**pertain**
rein n. ren	His grandmother had wanted to hold him under a tight *rein* in his youth.	拘束、箝制、韁繩 check curb	**re**(back)
v.	We managed to *rein* our conversation round to other topics.	控制、駕馭 control curb	
retain v. rɪˈten	These terms are *retained* today because of constant use.	保留、保持 keep preserve	**re**(back)
retentive a. rɪˈtɛntɪv	These soils are *retentive* of moisture.	有保持力的 able to retain	**retain**

單字・音標・詞類	例　句	中譯・同義字	字源分析
a.	The old woman has a *retentive* memory	記性好的 tenacious persistent	
retinue* n. ˈrɛtṇˌju	During the service we saw two assisting priests and a *retinue* of altar boys.	侍從人員、隨員 suite train	**re**(back)
sustain v. səˈsten	Can this shelf *sustain* all the books?	支撐、支持 support uphold	**sus**(under)
v.	Our expedition force has *sustained* a major defeat.	蒙受 suffer undergo	
sustenance* n. ˈsʌstənəns	It is chiefly through his equipment that man draws *sustenance* from the external world.	生計、食物 living food	**sustain**
sustentation n. ˌsʌstɛnˈteʃən	Taxes are needed for the *sustentation* of a state college.	維持、支持 maintenance preservation	**sustain**
tenable a. ˈtɛnəbḷ	Their position was no longer *tenable* and they retreated to the main line of defense.	可守、可維持的 defensible maintainable	
a.	His theory is *tenable* for the time being.	站得穩、有條有理的 reasonable sound	

tenacious a.
tɪˈneʃəs

The ships of the empire provided a slender, but very *tenacious,* link between East and West.

堅靱、黏性強的
tough
cohesive

　　　　　a.

Men are more *tenacious* dieters than women.

固執的
stubborn
obstinate

tenacity n.
tɪˈnæsətɪ

We will need a clay of the most extraordinary *tenacity.*

黏著（力）
adhesiveness
glutinousness

tenacious

　　　　　n.

The women maintained their convictions with a fearless *tenacity.*

堅持
persistence
determination

tenant* n.
ˈtɛnənt

It is the *tenants* of the upper floors who make all the noise and uproar.

房客
dweller
inhabitant

tenet* n.
ˈtɛnɪt

Observation and deduction are the two great *tenets* of the physical science.

信條、教理、原理
doctrine
dogma

tenor* n.
ˈtɛnɚ

The *tenor* of the book is expressed in the introduction.

要旨、大意
substance
purport

　　　　　n.

The earth and the sun will continue the even *tenor* of their ways for an inconceivably long period.

進程、趨勢
tendency
trend

tenure n.
ˈtɛnjɚ

The mayor spent his
tenure of office fighting
for time to assess facts
and to think.

任期、保有
hold
occupation

58

TEND·TENS·TENT

stretch

伸展 ● 向前

---

　　tend, tens, tent 源出拉丁文動詞 tendere 與其過去分詞tēnsus
或 tentus，原即有「伸展、向前」的意思。下文例字語意衍變比較
奇特的，有 intend v.「意欲」和 portend v.「預示、預兆」。in-
tend源出拉丁文動詞 intendere，字首 in 有at 的意思（參見本書
「最重要的30個字首」 **12. em·en·im·in** ），原拉丁文作「指向、
瞄準」解釋。後來指人心裏的意圖，如同有一定的方向，而引申出
「意欲」的意思。portend 源出拉丁文動詞 portendere，字首 por
係 pro 的變音，有 forward 的意思（參見「最重要的30個字首」**23.
pro·pur** ），與字根組合可作「向前推測事情的動向」解釋，因而
有「預示、預兆」的意思。

單字·音標·詞類	例　　句	中譯·同義字	字源分析
attend v. əˈtɛnd	I have to *attend* a funeral.	參加、出席 be present at	at(to)
v.	I will *attend* you to the mayor's party.	陪伴 accompany escort	
v.	The doctor *attended* his patients regularly.	照顧、侍候 tend serve	
v.	*Attend* to my words.	注意 listen heed	
attendance n. əˈtɛndəns	We need your *attendance* at the meeting.	出席 presence	attend
n.	The king went to the castle with his *attendance* of court officials.	隨從、隨侍 train retinue	
attention n. əˈtɛnʃən	We must call *attention* to this error.	注意、留意 notice consideration	attend
attentive a. əˈtɛntɪv	I hope you would be very *attentive* when Mr. Rigby talks to you.	注意、留意的 heedful observant	attend
contend v. kənˈtɛnd	Many students are *contending* for the scholarship.	競爭 contest compete	con(together)

	v.	He had stubbornly *contended* for what he believed to be the truth.	爭論、辯論 argue debate	
	v.	Many writers *contend* that literature must serve a moral function.	主張 maintain assert	
contention kənˈtɛnʃən	n.	In spite of the violent *contention* among the tribes, the nation was advancing in prosperity.	爭鬥、競爭 strife conflict	**contend**
	n.	This is no time for *contention.*	爭論 squabbling controversy	
	n.	The preacher has supported his *contention* with biblical and mythological evidence.	論點 claim charge	
contentious kənˈtɛnʃəs	a.	The captain has never commanded such a *contentious,* disagreeing crew before.	好爭吵的 quarrelsome belligerent	**contend**
distend dɪˈstɛnd	v.	The bat's body was so *distended* that it appeared spherical.	膨脹、擴大 swell dilate	**dis**(away)
extend ɪkˈstɛnd	v.	Man's knowledge of the universe can be further *extended.*	擴大、延長 advance lengthen	**ex**(out)

單字‧音標‧詞類	例 句	中譯‧同義字	字源分析
v.	Financial aid will be *extended* where needed.	給與 grant proffer	
extensive a. ɪkˈstɛnsɪv	The linguist has an *extensive* knowledge of languages.	廣泛、廣闊的 wide far-reaching	**extend**
extent n. ɪkˈstɛnt	He could exert the full *extent* of his power and rescue the imprisoned man.	範圍 scope compass	**extend**
intend v. ɪnˈtɛnd	Is that what you *intended*?	意欲、設計 aim contrive	**in**(at)
intense a. ɪnˈtɛns	The students listened to the announcement with *intense* attention.	緊張、集中 (心思)的 strained close	**in**(at)
a.	I could see an expression of *intense* anxiety on his face.	非常、劇烈的 extreme acute	
a.	The young man is *intense* in everything he does.	熱心的 ardent earnest	
intensify v. ɪnˈtɛnsəˌfaɪ	The depression of the early thirties *intensified* his dissatisfaction with the capitalist system.	加強 heighten enhance	**intense**

單字·音標·詞類	例　句	中譯·同義字	字源分析
intensive a. ɪnˈʰɛnsɪv	His *intensive* study of conifers has made him famous.	透徹、強烈的 exhaustive zealous	**intense**
intent n. ɪnˈtɛnt	One must use one's leisure time to good *intent.*	目的、意圖 aim object	**intend**
intention n. ɪnˈtɛnʃən	Complete and final victory was his *intention.*	目的 end purpose	**intend**
intentional a. ɪnˈtɛnʃənļ	*Intentional* damage is sometimes difficult to prevent.	有意、故意的 designed intended	**intention**
ostensible* a. ɑsˈtɛnsəbļ	The *ostensible* validity of his predictions regarding the civil war shocked everyone.	顯而易見、表面的 conspicuous specious	**os**(before)
ostentation* n. ˌɑstənˈteʃən	The building is characterized by *ostentaion* and ornamental frills of the Victorian era.	虛飾 pretentiousness floridity	**os**(before)
ostentatious* a. ˌɑstənˈteʃəs	The architects went ahead with their plans to build an *ostentatious* skyscraper.	華美、引人注 目、誇示的 conspicuous exaggerated	**os**(before)
portend* v. porˈtɛnd	People in Ireland generally believe that the appearance of black pigs *portends* serious trouble.	預示、預兆 bode forecast	**por**(forward)

單字‧音標‧詞類	例　　　句	中譯‧同義字	字源分析
portent* n. ˈpɔrtɛnt	It is only natural that *portents* should play a large part in the activities of crabbers and fishermen.	預兆、徵兆 sign omen	**portend**
n.	The *portents* of atomic science have been witnessed for a long time.	驚異之事、異常之人或物 wonder prodigy	
portentous* a. pɔrˈtɛntəs	The events under are *portentous*.	前兆、不祥的 ominous inauspicious	**portend**
a.	He was a man of *portentous* abilities.	驚人、異常的 marvelous prodigious	
pretend v. prɪˈtɛnd	It is *pretended* that in a recession workers are generally more idle.	主張 claim assert	**pre**(before)
v.	She *pretended* that she did not see me.	假裝 affect feign	
pretentious a. prɪˈtɛnʃənʃəs	They have a *pretentious* style of entertaining their guests.	矯飾、自負的 showy self-important	**pretend**
superintend v. ˌsuprɪnˈtɛnd	The playwright himself has *superintended* the publication of a score of good plays.	監督、管理 direct supervise	**super**(over) **intend**

單字·音標·詞類	例　句	中譯·同義字	字源分析
superintendent ˌsuprɪnˈtɛndənt n.	A *superintendent* is coming to our school tomorrow.	監督者、管理者 inspector supervisor	**superintend**
tend v. tɛnd	Some painters *tend* to rejoice in the commonplace.	傾向 incline lean	
v.	The association *tended* destitute mothers and children.	看護、服侍、照料 attend keep	
tendency n. ˈtɛndənsɪ	Some regard political economy merely as a science of *tendencies*.	趨勢、傾向、癖性 inclination propensity	**tend**
tender v. ˈtɛndɚ	The staff had *tendered* a banquet to their colleague on retirement.	提供、提出 offer proffer	
tense a. tɛns	The first twelve pages of the book have a *tense* and gripping power.	緊張、拉緊的 rigid exciting	
tensile* a. ˈtɛnsl̩	This implement is made of highly *tensile* steel alloy.	可伸張、可延展的 ductile malleable	
tension n. ˈtɛnʃən	The mechanic has slipped the belt over the pulleys and adjusted its *tension*.	拉力、拉緊 tautness	**tense**

單字・音標・詞類	例　　　　句	中譯・同義字	字源分析
n.	*Tensions* distort personalities.	緊張 stress pressure	

TOR·TORT

twist

扭曲●撚絞

　　字根 tor, tort 源出拉丁文動詞 torquēre 與其過去分詞 tortus，原即有 twist 的意思。下文例字中，字形與語義衍變比較奇特的，只有 torch n.「火炬、知識文明的泉源」一字。torch 的拼法源出晚期拉丁文 (Late Latin) 俗語 torca，但最早的字源仍是前文提過的拉丁文動詞 torquēre。早期的火炬常以粗麻繩搓撚成條，再浸染松脂而成，因此 torch 便有「火炬」的意思。火炬可在暗夜發出煌煌的火光，宛如啓發人智識的明燈，於是再引申便成「知識文明的泉源」（可參考比較 enlighten v.「照耀、教化」一字）。

單字・音標・詞類		例　　　　句	中譯・同義字	字源分析
contort kən¹tɔrt	v.	His face *contorted* in a grimace at the heat.	扭曲 distort deform	**con**(together)
distort dɪs¹tɔrt	v.	His face was *distorted* by pain.	扭曲、使變形 twist deform	
	v.	The journalist *distorted* the news to make it seem sensational.	曲解、歪曲 misrepresent falsify	
extort ɪk¹stɔrt	v.	His intelligence *extorted* the admiration even of his worst enemies.	引出、強取 squeeze extract	**ex**(out)
retort rɪ¹tɔrt	v.	"It is not true," he *retorted*.	反駁、回答 answer rejoin	**re**(back)
torch tɔrtʃ	n.	The men had to carry *torches* in the dark of the night.	火炬、火把 portable flaming 　　light	
	n.	The *torch* of the philosopher's wisdom was handed down the ages.	知識文明的泉源 source of 　　enlightenment	
torment ¹tɔrmɛnt	n.	She did not show any of the bodily *torments* she was suffering.	折磨、拷打、痛苦 affliction torture	

單字‧音標‧詞類	例　句	中譯‧同義字	字源分析
tor'ment tɔr'mɛnt　v.	These are the problems that *torment* men's hearts and warp men's lives.	使苦惱、使痛苦、折磨 rack distress	
torsion* n. 'tɔrʃən	The *torsion* bar is a device which minimizes sidesway and road jolts in automobiles.	扭力、扭 twisting stress	
tortuous a. 'tɔrtʃuəs	The expedition force had begun a *tortuous* climb into the highlands.	彎曲的 circuitous sinuous	
torture n. 'tɔrtʃɚ	The worst *tortures* of ancient times are still used in some countries today.	拷問、折磨 torment rack	
v.	It is not easy to *torture* wooden boards into uncouth shapes.	扭曲 distort warp	
v.	The man set himself to *torture* me as a school-boy would devote a rapturous half hour to watching the agonies of an impaled beetle.	折磨、使受痛苦 agonize torment	
torturous a. 'tɔrtʃərəs	The P.O.W. fell into *torturous* sleep after the painful inter-rogations.	痛苦、扭曲的 painful distorted	**torture**

TRACT·TREAT

draw

抽拉 • 引出 • 劃線

　　tract, treat 源出拉丁文動詞 trahere; tract 的拼法來自 trahere 的過去分詞 tractus，treat 則受過古法文影響。除了這兩種最常見的拼法之外，另也有下列幾種比較少見的形態：(1) portray v.「描寫」，(2) portrait n.「人像、肖像」、trait n.「特性」，(3) trace n.「痕跡」，(4) track n.「足跡、路」，(5) train n.「行列、隨從人員」，(6) trail n.「蹤跡、小徑」，(7) trek n./v.「旅行」。其中(1)至(5)來自古法語，(6)出自北部古法語 (Old North French) 或中古低地德語 (Middle Low German)，而(7)則出自中古荷蘭語。例字中有些語義衍變比較特殊，茲說明如下。trail n.「蹤跡、小徑」原指人移動時，拖曳衣裝留下的痕跡；其他如 trace n.「痕跡」和 track n.「足跡、路」，也是這種衍變方式。另有一字 trek n./v.「旅行」，衍變過程也和上述三字極為類似。trek 源自荷蘭文動詞 trekken，原有 draw, pull 的意思，後指在一空間上拖拉，而有 travel, march 的語義。荷蘭語屬於日耳曼語系，與拉丁文同源於印歐語系，因此 trek也列屬字根 **tract·treat** 一節。treat v.「對待、款待、治療、論述」源出拉丁文動詞 tractāre，原義為「拖拉、引導」，後引申而成「施行、處理」，再引申便有英文現存的各種意義。其中「論述」的語義，又可應用到例字中的 treatise n.「論文」、tract n.「小冊子、論文」、treaty n.「條約」三字；內中 treaty 原在古代也有

「論述、論文」的意思，後來才轉成論述、處理兩國事務的「條約」。前述的 tract 除有「小冊子、論文」的語義，並可作「區域」解釋。要瞭解這層字義，仍須回到字根「抽拉」的意思。tract 作「區域」解釋，源出拉丁文名詞tractus，原義為「拖曳、拉長」，後來指空間延長，便引申出「區域」的意思。trait n.「特性」的意義必須以字根作「劃線」解釋來了解。這個字源出拉丁文名詞 tractus ，除了上述「拉長、區域」的意思，並可作「線條、路線」。人或事物的特性一般總有「脈絡」可尋，因此到了十八世紀，便逐漸發展出「特性」的意思。

單字·音標·詞類		例　　　句	中譯·同義字	字源分析
abstract æb'strækt	v.	In minting baser metal is added or *abstracted*.	抽出 remove separate	**abs**(from)
	v.	His lengthy report should be *abstracted*.	節略、摘要 curtail epitomize	
'æbstrækt	n.	An *abstract* of the book will be appended.	摘要 summary epitome	
'æbstrækt	a.	Sweetness is *abstract;* sugar is concrete.	抽象的 nonsubjective	
	a.	These are *abstract* problems involving judgment and ability to reason.	難以了解的 abstruse recondite	
attract ə'trækt	v.	He shouted to *attract* attention.	吸引、引誘 draw allure	**at**(to)
attractive ə'træktɪv	a.	The big tree is a sanctuary *attractive* to birds.	有引誘力、動人的 inviting alluring	**attract**
contract kən'trækt	v.	The generals *contracted* their armies into one force.	縮小、省略 concentrate abbreviate	**con**(together)
	v.	She *contracted* polio when she was eleven months old.	感染、招致 catch incur	

單字・音標・詞類	例　　　　句	中譯・同義字	字源分析
n. ˈkɑntrækt	They have not signed the *contract* yet.	合約、合成 agreement treaty	
detract* v. dɪˈtrækt	These exaggerated reports tend to *detract* attention from the real issue.	轉移 draw divert	**de**(away)
v.	This affair *detracted* nothing from the credit due to him.	減損、貶抑 belittle derogate	
distract v. dɪˈstrækt	The audience had been irritated and *distracted* by the entrance of the late concertgoers.	分心、轉移 （意向） disturb annoy	**dis**(away)
v.	She was *distracted* by the uncertainty of her future.	使困惑、使困擾 confound harass	
v.	The excursion to the zoo served to *distract* him for at least one afternoon.	使娛樂 amuse divert	
entreat v. ɪnˈtrit	I must *entreat* both the patience and attention of the reader.	懇求 beseech implore	**en**(in)
entreaty n. ɪnˈtritɪ	The robbers paid no attention to her *entreaties* for mercy.	懇求、乞求 appeal supplication	entreat

單字・音標・詞類	例　　　　　句	中譯・同義字	字源分析
extract v. ɪkˈstrækt	The surgeon has *extracted* the bullet from the wound.	取出、抽出 draw take	ex(out)
v.	I have *extracted* out of the pamphlet a few notorious falsehoods.	摘錄、引用 cite quote	
n. ˈɛkstrækt	We will need vanilla *extract* and lemon *extract* for this dish.	濃縮物、精粹 essence concentrate	
n.	An *extract* is a selection from a writing or discourse.	選粹、摘錄、引述 quotation excerpt	
intractable a. ɪnˈtræktəbļ	The small girl has an *intractable* temper.	難駕馭、倔強的 unruly refractory	in(not) **tractable**
maltreat v. mælˈtrit	Only vicious people *maltreat* animals.	虐待 harm abuse	**mal**(bad) **treat**
portrait n. ˈpɔrtret	There are *portraits* of famous personages on the walls of his study.	人像、肖像、描寫 picture portrayal	**portray**
portray v. pɔrˈtre	The novelist *portrays* life the way most of us see it.	描寫 depict delineate	**por**(forward)

單字・音標・詞類	例　　句	中譯・同義字	字源分析
protract v. pro'trækt	The trial must not be *protracted* in duration by anything that is obstructive or dilatory.	延長、拖長 prolong defer	**pro**(forward)
retract v. rɪ'trækt	The hawk flipped out its wings and *retracted* them again.	縮回 draw back pull in	**re**(back)
v.	She *retracted* everything she had previously said.	收回 recall recant	
retreat v. ri'trit	The enemy *retreated*.	撤退、後退 withdraw recede	**re**(back)
n.	The army is in full *retreat*.	撤退 withdrawal retirement	
n.	The old man regarded his hut as a *retreat* and a camp rather than a home.	避難處、安全的地方 shelter asylum	
subtract v. səb'trækt	If 6 is *subtracted* from 9, the answer is 3.	減去 remove deduct	**sub**(under)
v.	That would *substract* nothing from his his merit.	減少、減損 reduce diminish	

trace n. tres	Every *trace* of the crime had been removed.	痕跡、足跡 sign vestige	
v.	In spite of the mist the sailors were able to *trace* the outline of the island.	探出、追蹤、 描繪 delineate pursue	
track n. træk	We saw the *tracks* of a rabbit near a cliff.	足跡、痕跡 trace footprint	
n.	The man seemed to have been stopped by something on the mountain *track*.	路、途徑 way path	
v.	The hunter has been *tracking* a grizzly bear for two weeks.	追踪 follow pursue	
tract n. trækt	The botanist has been to the wooded *tract* between the two rivers.	區域、廣大的 一片 stretch territory	
n.	A *tract* is a pamphlet or booklet issued for propaganda.	小冊子、論文 treatise dissertation	
tractable a. ˈtræktəbḷ	The teacher prefers *tractable* children to those that never stop playing tricks.	溫順的 docile pliant	

traction* n.		The medical student is	牽引(力)
ˈtrækʃən		especially interested in	drawing
		the gravitational	pulling
		traction exerted by	
		abdominal viscera on	
		the diaphragm.	
trail n.		The dogs found the	蹤跡、嗅跡
trel		*trail* of the foxes.	track
			scent
	n.	We found a *trail* in the	小徑
		woods.	path
			road
	v.	The dog *trailed* the man	追蹤、尾隨
		constantly.	follow
			pursue
	v.	Tom's little brother	拖、拉
		trailed his toy cart on	drag
		a piece of string.	haul
train n.		Long *trains* of camels	行列、連串
tren		are common scenes in	chain
		a desert region.	succession
	n.	The king brought a staff	隨從人員、扈從
		of 80 in his *train*.	attendence
			retinue
	v.	When a whale is	拖、拉
		harpooned, he *trains*	drag
		with him the bold little	trail
		creature who has flung	
		the fatal weapon.	

	v.	These soldiers have been *trained* for nine months.	訓練 drill discipline	
trait n. tret		The television was a distinctly new medium with its own *traits*.	特性、特點 feature characteristic	
treat v. trit		She hated the way he had been *treating* her.	對待 handle deal with	
	v.	This evening I shall *treat* myself to a bottle of red wine.	款待、宴饗 entertain feast	
	v.	During his stay at the hospital, he was *treated* with transfusions of blood.	治療 care for medically	
	v.	Literary history has to *treat* problems of intellectual history constantly.	論述 deal with discuss	
treatise n. ˈtritɪs		He is preparing a *treatise* on the natural resouces of the region.	論文 thesis discourse	treat
treaty n. ˈtritɪ		The President has the power to make *treaties*.	條約 pact covenant	

單字・音標・詞類	例 句	中譯・同義字	字源分析
trek n. trɛk	The couple had already made their *trek* to town.	旅行、移居 journey migration	
v.	The cavalryman saw a few desert dwellers *trekking* toward the oasis.	緩慢地旅行 travel slowly	

61

TRUD·TRUS

thrust, push

推擠 • 強迫

　　字根 trud, trus 源出拉丁文動詞 trūdere 與其過去分詞 trūsus，原即有 thrust, push 的意思。這個字根除了上述兩種拼法外，尚有一種形態：threat n. 「威脅」。 threat 出自古英文 (Old English) 名詞 thrēat，但本節例字絕大部分源出拉丁文，字源顯然不同。然而，古英文屬於日耳曼語系，而日耳曼語系和拉丁語系均源出印歐古語，因此 threat 的拼法和本節的拉丁字根，仍可看出有部分相似。何況這些字本即同源，收錄在同一節中，也是極為自然的事情。例字中意義衍變比較特殊的，有 abstruse a. 「深奧的」一字。abstruse 源出拉丁文動詞 abstrūdere，字首 ab 有 from, away 的意思（參見本書「最重要的30個字首」 **1. ab·abs**），因此原指將物件推往他處，而有「隱藏、遮掩」的意思。後來，轉成形容詞 abstrūsus 即作「隱密的」解釋，最後又引申出「深奧的」的意思。

單字·音標·詞類	例　句	中譯·同義字	字源分析
abstruse a. æb'strus	The calculations of mathematicians are sometimes *abstruse*.	深奧、難解、隱藏的 hidden recondite	**abs**(from)
extrude v. ɪk'strud	Plastic material is *extruded* through very small holes to form fibers.	擠出、逼出 eject project	**ex**(out)
intrude v. ɪn'trud	The young man did not want to *intrude* upon her uninvited.	侵擾、闖入 encroach trespass	**in**(in)
intrusive a. ɪn'trusɪv	Her *intrusive* remark annoyed the people at the meeting.	闖入、冒昧的 encroaching impertinent	**intrude**
obtrude* v. əb'trud	The snail slowly *obtruded* its tentacle.	伸出、使突出 extrude intrude	**ob**(toward)
v.	We were forced to *obtrude* ourselves into their party.	強入、闖入 trepass infringe	
obtrusive* a. əb'trusɪv	The propaganda was occasionally *obtrusive*.	強迫、魯莽的 forward impertinent	**obtrude**
protrude v. pro'trud	Memories *protrudes* into his consciousness.	伸出、突出 thrust bulge	**pro**(forward)
protrusive a. pro'trusɪv	He pulled a *protrusive* manuscript from his pocket.	伸出、突出的 protuberant obstrusive	**protrude**

threat n.
θrɛt

The students quieted
at once on the teacher's
threat to keep them in
after school.

威脅
menace

threaten v.
ˈθrɛtn̩

The sign by the gate
threatens trespassers
with arrest.

威脅、恐嚇
warn
menace

threat

v.

The sky *threatens* a
storm.

預示…之兆
portend
menace

thrust v.
θrʌst

He *thrust* his hand into
his pocket.

插入、推
drive
shove

v.

The assassin *thrust* a
dagger into her heart
and slew her.

戮、刺
stab
lunge

n.

Forward *thrusts* in
history have not always
been the product of
universal assent.

推進(力)
drive
push

n.

A bayonet *thrust* in the
abdomen killed the
soldier.

刺、戮
stab
lunge

62

VAC·VAN·VOID

empty

空虛 ● 缺乏 ● 空閒

　　vac, van, void 源自拉丁文動詞 vacāre 和名詞 vānitās，原即有「空虛、缺乏、空閒」的意思；void 的形態乃來自古法文(Old French)的拼法。除了上述三種比較常見的拼法之外，下文例字中，亦可看到 vain a.「空虛、無結果、自負的」一種形態。這種形態也是受古法文影響的結果。vain 最早源自拉丁文形容詞 vānus 「空虛的」，後來進入古法文轉成 vain、vein、veyn 三種拼法，其中 vain 借入英文之後，一直沿用迄今。

avoid v. əˈvɔɪd	We *avoided* driving through big cities on our trip.	避免 shun evade	**a**(to)
avoidance n. əˈvɔɪdn̩s	Some people consider the use of merger agreements a means of tax *avoidance*.	避免、廻避、取消 escape annulment	**avoid**
devoid a. dɪˈvɔɪd	I found her place *devoid* when I woke up.	空、無的 empty vacant	**de**(away)
a.	Her somewhat sallow face was *devoid* of makeup.	缺乏的 lacking wanting	
evacuate v. ɪˈvækjʊˌet	The sick and wounded should be *evacuated* from the combat area.	撤離、撤空 remove empty	**e**(out)
evanesce * v. ˌɛvəˈnɛs	The scarf fell into the air and seemed to *evanesce*.	消失、消散 disappear dissipate	**e**(out)
evanescent * a. ˌɛvəˈnɛsn̩t	Some flowers are *evanescent*.	短暫、迅速凋落的 impermanent fleeting	**evanesce**
a.	His *evanescent* brushwork and psychological clarity have long been lost in modern painting.	極輕盈、薄弱、極纖細、空靈的 unsubstantial fragile	

單字·音標·詞類	例　　句	中譯·同義字	字源分析
vacancy n. ˈvekənsɪ	There was a *vacancy* of sound after the train had left.	空、空虛 barrenness loneliness	vacant
n.	Sometimes little *vacancies* from toil could be very sweet.	空閒、閒暇 leisure vacation	
vacant a. ˈvekənt	Is that seat *vacant*?	空的 empty unoccupied	
a.	After hearing the news, she sat down with a peculiarly *vacant* expression on her face.	茫然的 dull expressionless	
vacate* v. ˈveket	The throne was *vacated* by the exile of the royal family.	使空、取消 empty annul	
vacation n. veˈkeʃən	These students are hired to fill in for workers on *vacation*.	休假、假期 holidays recess	vacate
vacuity* n. væˈkjuətɪ	To some smoking fills the *vacuities* of life.	空虛 emptiness blankness	vacuous
vacuous* a. ˈvækjuəs	These experiments must be performed in *vacuous* spaces.	空、空虛的 empty void	
a.	The young man sat there with a *vacuous* expression.	茫然、愚蠢的 dull inane	

單字・音標・詞類	例 句	中譯・同義字	字源分析
vacuum n. ˈvækjʊəm	The music stopped and the voices rose into the *vacuum* it left.	眞空、空間、空虛 empty space void	
vain a. ven	All he could make was *vain* promises.	空虛的 empty worthless	
a.	The government made a *vain* effort to stop the military coup.	無效、無結果的 fruitless unsuccessful	
a.	He was *vain* of the honor which he had won.	自負、得意的 conceited inflated	
vanish v. ˈvænɪʃ	Many species of animals have *vanished* from the surface of the earth.	消失、消散 disappear dissolve	
vanity n. ˈvænətɪ	She well knew the *vanity* of her own attainments.	空虛、空幻 hollowness worthlessness	**vain**
n.	*Vanity* is a characteristic which all human beings share.	虛榮、自負 conceit arrogance	
void a. vɔɪd	The office has fallen *void.*	空、空虛的 empty vacant	

a.

A woman *void* of
common sense usually
amuses him.

缺乏的
wanting
lacking

n.

The frustrated girl
stood by the door
gazing out into the
void.

真空、空虛、
空處
emptiness
vacancy

n.

The alternation of solid
and *void* is characteristic
of a Japanese house.

空隙、裂縫、
孔洞
opening
gap

63

VAIL·VAL

strong, worth

有力 ● 實價

　　vail, val 源自拉丁文動詞 valēre，原即有 be strong, be worth 的意思；其中 vail 的形態曾受古法文影響。下文例字須特別注意的，有 invalid 一字。invalid 源出拉丁文形容詞 validus「有力、壯健、堅固的」，字首 in 為否定字首，因此可作形容詞「有病、殘廢的」，也可作名詞「病人」。又因原字 valid 作形容詞有「有效、健全的」的意思，所以 invalid 也可作「無效、無價值的」解釋。這一來，invalid 一字便有了不大相同的兩種解釋。因此，為了區別起見，語音便有所不同：重音在第一音節，讀作 ˈɪnvəlɪd 的，是形容詞「有病、殘廢的」或名詞「病人」；重音在第二音節，讀作 ɪnˈvælɪd 的，則是形容詞「無效、無價值的」。

單字·音標·詞類	例　　　句	中譯·同義字	字源分析
avail v. ə'vel	Heroism could not *avail* against the emeny fire.	有用、有益 serve benefit	**a**(to)
n.	His effort was of no *avail.*	有用、利益 use benefit	
available a. ə'veləbḷ	We want only the latest *available* information.	可得、可用的 useful attainable	**avail**
countervail* v. ˌkaʊntɚ'vel	We need *countervailing* military power to fight the enemy.	對抗、抵消 counteract offset	**counter**(against)
equivalent a. ɪ'kwɪvələnt	This vitamin pill is *equivalent* to four oranges.	相等、相當的 same tantamount	**equ**(equal)
n.	This Russian word has no *equivalent* in English.	相等物 match counterpart	
evaluate v. ɪ'væljʊˌet	Trained observers will visit and *evaluate* the teachers in their classrooms.	評估、估計 rate appraise	**e**(out) **value**
invalid a. ɪn'vælɪd	Now that rockets can escape gravity, it is *invalid* to say that what goes up must come down.	無效、無價值的 indefensible unjustified	**in**(not) **valid**

'ɪnvəlɪd	n.	He hired a nurse to care for his *invalid* mother.	有病、殘廢的 sickly disabled	in(not)
'ɪnvəlɪd	n.	The nurse has arranged a bed table for the *invalid*.	病人 sickly person	
invalidate ɪn'vælə͵det	v.	We do not know whether the facts will confirm or *invalidate* his claim.	使無價值、使無效 discredit nullify	**invalid**
invaluable ɪn'væljəb!	a.	A flair for language is *invaluable* to the career diplomat.	無價、非常珍貴的 priceless precious	in(not) **value**
prevail prɪ'vel	v.	A number of curious customs still *prevail* in this region.	盛行、流行 persist become widespread	**pre**(before)
	v.	Truth and honesty will *prevail*.	占優勢、戰勝 predominate preponderate	
prevalent 'prɛvələnt	a.	Malaria is *prevalent* in these countries.	普遍、流行的 widespread extensive	**prevail**
	a.	Law schools with a nominal college affiliation have become *prevalent*.	佔優勢、最具力量的 dominant influential	

valiant a.
ˈvæljənt

The commander who
has testified in the court
has a *valiant* war record.

勇敢的
brave
heroic

valid a.
ˈvælɪd

The attorney's client
has no *valid* ground for
divorce.

有效、健全的
sound
substantial

validate v.
ˈvæləˌdet

Legislation by the whole
Congress is required to
validate the treaty.

使有效、批准　**valid**
support
ratify

v.

True ideas are those
that we can assimilate,
validate, and corroborate.

證實
verify
substantiate

valor n.
ˈvælɚ

The prince admired even
the fortitude and *valor*
of the woman's sons.

勇氣、勇武
courage
bravery

valuable a.
ˈvæljəbl̩

Experience made him a
valuable member of
any committee.

有價值、貴重　**value**
、可估計的
precious
estimable

valuation n.
ˌvæljʊˈeʃən

If the final bid is below
the reserve *valuation* of
the wool, the sale may
be closed.

估價額、估價　**value**
、評價
estimation
appraisal

value n.
ˈvæljʊ

Nowadays people know
the price of everything
and the *value* of nothing.

價值、重要性
worth
importance

v.

The house has been
valued at US $80,000.

估價、評價
rate
appraise

v.	I have always *valued* our friendship.	重視、珍重 prize treasure	

64

VEN·VENT

come

到來

　　字根ven, vent源出拉丁文動詞venīre 與其過去分詞 ventus，原即有「到來」的意思，引申也可作「遭遇、達到、發展出」。戰功彪炳的凱撒講過一句流傳千古的名言："Venī, vidī, vicī" ("I came, I saw, I conquered.")。其中便有 venī (I came) 一字，爲venīre 的第一人稱單數過去簡單式。下文例字有些語義衍變比較特殊，茲說明如下。convenience n. 「方便、便利」和 convenient a.「方便、合適的」源出拉丁文動詞 convenīre ，字首con 有together 的意思（參見本書「最重要的30個字首」 6. co·com·con ），因此原作「同來、會晤、相約」解釋，後又引申而成「相稱、適當」，進入英文之後，於是就有「方便、合適」的意思。inventory n. 「詳細目錄」源出拉丁文名詞 inventārium ，更早的字源則是動詞 invenīre 「找到、尋得、查知」。拉丁文 inventārium原已有「雜物清單」的意思，指清查物品所記錄的目錄，英文的 inventory 至今仍保有這個意思。souvenir n. 「紀念品」源自法文動詞souvenir 「回憶、回想」，更原始的字源則是拉丁文動詞 subvenīre，字首sub 有under 的意思，因此原作「來援、救助」解釋，後來又引申而成「回想」。到外地觀光，總會取一些東西回來，讓日後追憶起來有憑有據，於是便有了「紀念品」的意思。

單字·音標·詞類	例　　　句	中譯·同義字	字源分析
advent n. ˈædvɛnt	The birds and the squirrels could well feel the *advent* of spring.	來臨、到來 coming arrival	**ad**(to)
adventitious* a. ˌædvɛnˈtɪʃəs	In works of imagination and sentiment meter is but *adventitious* to composition.	偶然、外來的 accidental extraneous	**ad**(to)
adventive* a. ædˈvɛntɪv	The botanist has planned to study the *adventive* weeds in this area.	外來、非土生的 immigrant not native	**ad**(to)
adventure n. ədˈvɛntʃɚ	The explorer has gone through many strange *adventures*.	奇遇、冒險 incident hazard	**ad**(to)
adventurous a. ədˈvɛntʃərəs	The king encouraged *adventurous* Portuguese captains to push out into the Atlantic.	愛冒險、膽大的 venturesome daring	**adventure**
avenue n. ˈævəˌnu	There was a traffic accident on the Fifth *Avenue*.	大街、通路 road alley	**a**(to)
circumvent* v. ˌsɝkəmˈvɛnt	The soldiers *circumvented* the town after winning the battle.	繞行 go around encircle	**circum**(around)
v.	The heroine of the melodrama is *circumvented* with perils.	使陷入困難或危險 entrap ensnare	

單字・音標・詞類	例　　　句	中譯・同義字	字源分析
v.	They *circumvented* their enemies by craft and drove them out by force.	用計超過、欺詐、阻遏 beguile thwart	
contravene* v. ˌkɑntrəˈvin	Under no circumstances should you *contravene* the law.	違反、侵犯 disregard infringe	**contra**(against)
v.	This proposition is not likely to be *contravened*.	反駁、否定 dispute contradict	
convene v. kənˈvin	The executive directors *convened* once a week.	集會、集合 convoke assemble	**con**(together)
convenience n. kənˈvinjəns	The scholar has praised the *convenience* of the new alphabet for transcribing spoken English.	方便、便利 advantage efficiency	**con**(together)
convenient a. kənˈvinjənt	These programs are broadcast at the hours that are more *convenient* for housewives.	方便、合適的 appropriate handy	**con**(together)
convention n. kənˈvɛnʃən	The members of the board are planning the next annual sales *convention*.	會議 meeting conference	**convene**
n.	Words express whatever meaning *convention* has attached to them.	習慣、習俗 custom practice	

單字·音標·詞類	例 句	中譯·同義字	字源分析
conventional a. kənˈvɛnʃən|	It has been *conventional* to regard these prehistoric human beings as cave dwellers.	傳統、習慣上的 traditional customary	**convention**
event n. ɪˈvɛnt	We made careful planning and awaited the *event*.	結果 outcome result	e(out)
n.	Such an *event* would shock the conscience of the world.	事件 occurrence happening	
eventful a. ɪˈvɛntfəl	An *eventful* affair brought the two countries to the verge of war.	重大、重要的 momentous critical	**event**
eventual a. ɪˈvɛntʃʊəl	Some philosophers had predicted the *eventual* decay and extinction of the monarchical system.	最後的 last ultimate	**event**
eventuate v. ɪˈvɛntʃʊˌet	His illness *eventuated* in death.	結果為、終歸 result terminate	**event**
intervene v. ˌɪntəˈvin	A week *intervenes* between Christmas and New Year's Day.	介於其間、於 …之間發生 occur befall	**inter**(between)
v.	The elder *intervened* to settle the dispute of the two families.	干涉、調停 interfere intercede	

單字・音標・詞類	例　　句	中譯・同義字	字源分析
intervention n. ˌɪntɚˈvɛnʃən	His *intervention* in the dispute was resented by everyone.	仲裁、干涉 interference intercession	**intervene**
invent v. ɪnˈvɛnt	Who *invented* the light bulb?	發明、創作 devise contrive	**in**(on)
inventory n. ˈɪnvənˌtɔrɪ	The shopkeeper asked the boy to make an *inventory*.	詳細目錄 list record	**invent**
prevent v. prɪˈvɛnt	There was no one who could have *prevented* this from happening.	防止、阻礙 impede hinder	**pre**(before)
preventive a. prɪˌvɛntɪv	The health officials have taken a *preventive* measure against rats.	預防的 precautionary wary	**prevent**
revenue n. ˈrɛvəˌnju	The property is expected to yield an annual *revenue* of 10,000 dollars.	總收入、收益 、收入 profits income	**re**(back)
souvenir n. ˌsuvəˈnɪr	That sword is a *souvenir* brought back from Japan.	紀念品 memorial momento	**sou**(under)
supervene* v. ˌsupɚˈvin	An event *supervened* that brought disaster to my uncle's family.	跟隨、接著來 follow ensue	**super**(over)
venture n. ˈvɛntʃɚ	This *venture* in plain speaking cost us dear.	投機、商業上的冒險 risk speculation	

單字·音標·詞類	例 句	中譯·同義字	字源分析
v.	I am too old to *venture* on a new way of life.	冒險從事 risk tempt	
venturesome a. ˈvɛntʃɚsəm	I hunt, but I am never a *venturesome* hunter.	好冒險、大膽 的 enterprising intrepid	**venture**

VERS·VERT

turn

轉動 ● 轉變

　　字根 vers, vert 源出拉丁文動詞 vertere 及其過去分詞 versus，原義即爲「轉動、轉變」。這是英文非常重要的字根，組成的單字極多。除了上述兩種拼法，下文例字中也可看到一種極少見的形態：divorce v./n.「離婚」。divorce 源出拉丁文名詞 dīvortium「離婚」，進入法文後轉成 divorce，於十四世紀左右開始出現在英文文獻上。由此可知，目前的變體在拉丁文階段已大致形成。例字中有些語義衍變比較特別，茲說明如下。advertise v.「登廣告」源出拉丁文動詞 advertere「轉向、注意到」（參見例字 advert v.「談及、注意到」），advertere 收入法文後轉成 avertir，意思也變作「通知」，後來進入英文，又引申成「通知產品問市」，而有「登廣告」的意思。universe n.「宇宙、世界」和 universal a.「普遍、一般的」兩字源出拉丁文形容詞 ūniversus，字首 uni 有 one 的意思，因此原作「整個、全體的」解釋，後來引申而有「萬有、宇宙」的字義，因此 universe 和 universal 一指宇宙，一指萬般事物皆可應用。verse n.「詩」源自拉丁文名詞 versus，原作「犁溝」解釋，後來暗指詩行排列有如犁溝，寫完一行便須「轉」到下一行，因而衍變出「詩」的意思。vertex n.「最高點、頂點」源出拉丁文名詞 vertex「極端」，原指幾何體「轉」出的端點，而特指與底部相對的「頂端」，如拉丁文的 vertex mōntis，就是「山頂」的意思。

adversary n. ˈædvɚˌsɛrɪ	His powers of sarcasm made him feared as an *adversary*.	對手、仇敵 opponent foe	**adverse**
adverse a. ədˈvɝs	Her feelings were still *adverse* to any man save one.	有敵意、敵對 的 hostile antagonistic	**ad(to)**
a.	These circumstances would be *adverse* to success.	不利的 unfavorable detrimental	
adversity n. ədˈvɝsətɪ	The country has gone through a period marked by *adversities* and misfortunes.	不幸(的事)、 災難 misery calamity	**adverse**
advert v. ədˈvɝt	The couple had *adverted* briefly to the circum- stances of their first meeting.	談及、注意到 refer allude	**ad(to)**
advertise v. ˈædvɚˌtaɪz	They are going to *advertise* the house for rent.	登廣告、公布 announce publish	**advert**
anniversary n. ˌænəˈvɝsərɪ	They celebrate their wedding *anniversary* every year on August 6.	周年紀念 yearly return of a date	**ann(year)**
averse a. əˈvɝs	He is not *averse* to a glass of wine or two with his friends.	反對、不願意 的 opposed disinclined	**a(from)**

單字・音標・詞類	例　　　　句	中譯・同義字	字源分析
aversion n. ə'vɝʒən	She had an *aversion* to work.	嫌惡 dislike abhorrence	**averse**
avert v. ə'vɝt	Some mortar and dust came dropping down, which he *averted* his face to avoid.	移轉、避開 turn away	**a**(from)
v.	Many highway accidents can be *averted* by courtesy.	防止、避免 prevent ward off	
controversial a. ˌkɑntrə'vɝʃəl	Their *controversial* marriage was the biggest event of the year.	引起爭論、爭論的 debatable disputatious	**controversy**
controversy n. 'kɑntrəˌvɝsɪ	The *controversy* was between the labor unions and the environmentalists.	爭論、辯論 dispute wrangle	**contro**(against)
controvert* v. 'kɑntrəˌvɝt	There was an important point which no one had *controverted* in the discussion.	否認、反駁 deny disprove	**contro**(against)
conversant* a. 'kɑnvɚsn̩t	He is not yet *conversant* with the new regulations.	嫻熟、熟識的 familiar acquainted	**con**(together)
conversation n. ˌkɑnvɚ'seʃən	I had a pleasant *conversation* with our new neighbors.	談話、會話 dialogue informal talk	**converse**

單字‧音標‧詞類		例　　　句	中譯‧同義字	字源分析
converse kənˈvɝs	v.	The students were asked to *converse* with each other in French.	談話 talk discourse	con(together)
	a.	They started from the same place in *converse* direction.	相反的 opposite reverse	
ˈkɑnvɝs	n.	"Hot" is the *converse* of "cold."	相反的事物 opposite reverse	
convert kənˈvɝt	v.	The old house was *converted* into a new one.	改變 alter transform	con(together)
	v.	He did not try to *convert* her to his religion.	使改變信仰、意見、使皈依 turn convince	
ˈkɑnvɝt	n.	He was a *convert* to her religion.	（新）皈依者、改變信仰者 disciple neophyte	
diverse dəˈvɝs	a.	The people at the meeting had offered *diverse* judgments on the matter.	不同的 different distinct	di(away)
diversify dəˈvɝsəˌfaɪ	v.	They have *diversified* the educational program by introducing new subjects.	使多樣化、使變化 vary variegate	diverse

單字·音標·詞類	例　　句	中譯·同義字	字源分析
diversion n. dəˈvɝʒən	The writer mars the story by a *diversion* into irrelevant material.	離正題 deviation digression	**divert**
n.	Hiking is a favorite *diversion.*	娛樂、消遣 amusement pastime	
diversity n. dəˈvɝsətɪ	Climatic *diversities* result in a great variety of plant life.	多樣、不同 variety difference	**diverse**
divert v. dəˈvɝt	He was trained as a surgeon, but later *diverted* to diplomacy.	轉向、轉入 deviate digress	**di**(away)
v.	The people *diverted* themselves with games.	消遣、娛樂 entertain amuse	
divorce v. dəˈvors	Mrs. Wilson wanted to *divorce* her husband.	和…離婚、分離、分裂 disunite dissolve	**di**(away)
n.	There were 11 million children of *divorce* in the United States in 1980.	離婚 legal dissolution of a marriage	
extrovert * v. ˈɛkstroˌvɝt	An *extroverted* person is usually active and energetic.	使外向、使外傾 push outward	extro(outside)

單字·音標·詞類		例　　　　句	中譯·同義字	字源分析
	n.	An *extrovert* is predominantly interested in the outside world.	外向之人 one whose interest is more in the outside world	
inadvertent a. ˌɪnəd'vɝtn̩t		Her *inadvertent* remark infuriated her mother.	無意、不注意的 unintentional heedless	in(not) **advert**
introvert* v. ˌɪntrə'vɝt		The *introverted* young man is given to odd moods and uncommunicativeness.	使內向、使內省 turn inward	intro(within)
	n. 'ɪntrəˌvɝt	*Introverts* think about themselves much of the time.	內向者、慣於自省之人 one whose thoughts are directed inward	
inverse* a. ɪn'vɝs		DCBA is the *inverse* order of ABCD.	倒轉、反的 inverted contrary	in(to)
	n.	He had no luck with his experiment, so he tried the *inverse* of this process and got a positive result.	倒轉、相反 opposite reverse	
invert* v. ɪn'vɝt		The gardener *inverts* a bell jar over his rose cutting.	倒轉 overturn overset	in(to)

單字·音標·詞類	例　　　　句	中譯·同義字	字源分析
obverse* n. ˈɑbvɝs	The *obverse* of "all A is B" is "no A is not B."	反換命題、相 對物 converse counterpart	obvert
obvert* v. əbˈvɝt	The wizard asked the king to *obvert* the mirror to the sun.	轉向、使面向 turn to present 　　a different 　　surface of	**ob**(against)
perverse a. pɚˈvɝs	Many people felt it *perverse* that a bondman's son should be made a bishop.	錯誤的 improper incorrect	**per**(through)
a.	The *perverse* girl did just what she was told not to.	固執、倔強的 stubborn intractable	
pervert v. pɚˈvɝt	The bishop was accused of *perverting* youths.	敗壞、使墮落 、引入邪路 corrupt debase	**per**(through)
n.	It is said that the judge has *perverted* some evidence and omitted the rest.	曲解、誤解 misinterpret misconstrue	
n. ˈpɝvɝt	The millionare was accused of being a sex *pervert*.	性變態者 one practicing 　　sexual perversion	
reverse v. rɪˈvɝs	Their positions are now *reversed*.	反轉、顛倒 overturn transpose	**re**(back)

單字·音標·詞類	例　　　　句	中譯·同義字	字源分析
n.	They had hoped for a sunny day but the fact was just the *reverse*.	相反 contrary opposite	
n.	They met with heavy *reverses*.	不幸、惡運 misfortune defeat	
a.	The figures will be given again in *reverse* order.	相反、顚倒的 opposite converse	
revert v. rɪˈvɝt	After the settlers left, the natives *reverted* to savagery.	恢復(原狀)、回到、復歸 return reverse	**re**(back)
subversion n. səbˈvɝʃən	Their *subversion* of the government led to a civil war.	推翻、滅亡 destruction demolition	**subvert**
subvert v. səbˈvɝt	Through history there are maniacs who labor to *subvert* the great pillars of human happiness.	顚覆、破壞、推翻 overturn demolish	**sub**(under)
transverse* a. trænsˈvɝs	The stairway ascends gracefully from the *transverse* hall.	橫向、橫的 extended across	**trans**(across)
traverse v. ˈtrævɚs	The railway *traverses* the country.	橫貫、橫過 cross penetrate	**tra**(through)

單字·音標·詞類	例 句	中譯·同義字	字源分析

	v.	I think they will *traverse* his proposals.	反對、阻止 thwart contravene	
	v.	This period has been thoroughly *traversed* by historians.	仔細檢查 examine survey	
universal ˌjunəˈvɝsḷ	a.	Vanity is a *universal* human weakness.	普遍、一般的 general all-embracing	universe
universe ˈjunəˌvɝs	n.	The earth is a mere speck in the *universe*.	宇宙、世界 cosmos world	uni(one)
versatile ˈvɝsətḷ	a.	The young woman has a *versatile* disposition.	易變的 changeable unsteady	
	a.	He is a *versatile* actor, able to play any role from king to clown.	多才多藝、多方面的 many-sided	
verse vɝs	n.	The professor used some of the poet's *verses* as exercises in one of his textbooks.	詩、詩節 poem stanza	
versify ˈvɝsəˌfaɪ	v.	The old tale has been *versified* through the centuries.	將(散文)改寫成韻文、用韻文記載 compose verses put in verse form	verse

version n.
ˈvɝʒən

The scholar plans to
compare the original
text of the work with
its Arabic *version*.

翻譯（本）
translation

　　　　n.

Each of the three girls
gave her *version* of the
quarrel.

敘述、說明
account
interpretation

vertex* n.
ˈvɝtɛks

There is a monument
on the *vertex* of the
hill.

最高點、頂點
summit
apex

vertical a.
ˈvɝtɪkl̩

She has drawn only a
vertical line on her
paper.

垂直、直立的
upright
perpendicular

vertiginous* a.
vɝˈtɪdʒənəs

The professor is
expounding on the
vertiginous motion
of the earth.

旋轉的
rotary
whirling

vertigo

　　　　a.

She always feels
vertiginous at
great heights.

感覺眩暈、令
人眩暈的
dizzy
giddy

vertigo* n.
ˈvɝtɪˌgo

Vertigo is a disturbance
which is associated with
various known diseases.

眩暈
dizziness
giddiness

66

VEY·VIA·VOY

way

道路 ● 途徑

　　vey, via, voy 源出拉丁文名詞 via「道路、途徑」，其中vey、voy 的拼法曾經受過古法文影響。拉丁文有句格言 "Via trīta via tūta" ("The beaten way is the safe one.")，內中便有 via 一字作 way解釋。下文例字語義衍變比較奇特的，有trivia n. pl.「瑣事」和 trivial a.「微不足道、瑣碎的」。這兩個字同源自拉丁文名詞 trivium，字首 tri 有 three 的意思，因此原拉丁文作「三岔路、通衢」解釋。由「三岔路、通衢」引申出「瑣事」，有兩種十分有趣的解說。一派字源學家認為，古羅馬時代三岔路口等通衢大道，係尋常百姓聚集討論家務事的地方，因此拉丁文本來便有trivialis a. 一字，作「尋常、平凡的」解釋。又有一派學者主張和中古時期歐洲的大學教育有關。中古時代大學必修的七項文理學科中，以文法、修辭、邏輯三科最為瑣碎，因此 trivia 的單數形態 trivium，一直到今天，還可以指這三種學科。無論如何解說，總能讓我們了解「三岔路、通衢」為何變成了「瑣事」。

單字·音標·詞類		例　　　句	中譯·同義字	字源分析
convey v. kənˈve		Words cannot *convey* what is in my heart.	傳達、運送 carry communicate	con(together)
	v.	The pipe is for *conveying* water.	傳導、傳送 transmit conduct	
conveyance n. kənˈveəns		The railways are suited to the *conveyance* of heavy loads at high speed.	運送、運輸 transportation carrying	convey
	n.	Books are for the *conveyance* of ideas.	傳達、傳遞 transmission	
convoy v. kənˈvɔɪ		The man had been *convoyed* by Secret Service agents.	護送、護衛 conduct escort	con(together)
	n. ˈkɑnvɔɪ	Each *convoy* was escorted by seven warships.	被護送之船隊 或車隊、護送 、護衛 escort guide	
deviate v. ˈdivɪˌet		Party principles permit no one to *deviate*.	逸出正軌、離 開本題 digress deflect	de(away)
deviation n. ˌdivɪˈeʃən		He was expelled from the Communist party for *deviation*.	逸出常軌、偏 差 digression aberration	deviate

單字·音標·詞類	例　　句	中譯·同義字	字源分析
devious* a. 'divɪəs	There is a *devious* path along the mountain ridge.	繞道、迂廻的 roundabout circuitous	**de**(away)
a.	Her *devious* arguments have to be corrected.	有偏差、不正直的 astray erring	
envoy n. 'ɛnvɔɪ	The mutineers of the ship sent an *envoy* to deal with the captain.	使者 agent representative	**en**(in)
impervious* a. ɪm'pɝvɪəs	The fabric has been waterproofed so that the coat was *impervious* to rain.	不能透過的 impenetrable impassable	**im**(not) **pervious**
obviate* v. 'ɑbvɪˌet	She has tried to *obviate* the necessity of going to see her parents.	避免 prevent avert	**ob**(against)
obvious a. 'ɑbvɪəs	Her unwillingness to go was quite *obvious*.	明顯的 evident manifest	**ob**(against)
pervious* a. 'pɝvɪəs	This metal is especially *pervious* to heat.	可透過的 penetrable	**per**(through)
previous a. 'privɪəs	The man's face is shown in the photograph on the *previous* page.	在前、先前的 former preceding	**pre**(before)
trivia* n. pl. 'trɪvɪə	Much of our research is wasted on *trivia*.	瑣事 trifles	tri(three)

單字·音標·詞類	例　　　句	中譯·同義字	字源分析
trivial a. ˈtrɪvɪəl	The girls talk only about *trivial* matters.	微不足道、瑣碎的 petty trifling	tri(three)
via prep. ˈvaɪə	We are going from Paris to New Delhi *via* the Suez Canal.	經由 through by	
voyage n. ˈvɔɪ·ɪdʒ	Their families are going on a *voyage*.	旅行 journey trip	

67

VID·VIEW·VIS

see

看見 ● 審視

vid, view, vis 源出拉丁文動詞 vidēre「看見、審視」與其過去分詞 visus; view 的拼法來自中古英文 (Middle English)，但早期曾受古法文影響。下文例字意義衍變比較特別的，有 provide v.「供給」、purvey v.「供給」、providential a.「按天意、由神意的」。provide 源出拉丁文動詞 prōvidēre，字首 pro 有 forward 的意思（參見本書「最重要的30個字首」**23. pro·pur**），因此原拉丁文作「前瞻、先見、預知」，引申又有「慎防、未雨綢繆」的語義。英文「供給」的意思，便出自最後這層語義。purvey 字源和 provide 完全相同，只不過由拉丁文轉入古法文時，拼法已變成 purveier 和 purveeir，再借入英文，便發展出和 provide 大不相同的形態。providential 源自上述拉丁文動詞 prōvidēre 轉成的形容詞 prōvidens 原有「有先見、深謀遠慮的」的意義。後來引申而指能預知未來的神，而衍變出「按天意、由神意的」的意思。下文尚有兩個字變化形態相當奇特，應該說明一下。prudence n.「謹慎、智慮」和 prudent a.「謹慎的」兩字，分別是 providence n.「對將來的顧慮」及 provident a.「有先見之明的」變音而成。（這種變音現象，在 poor a.「貧窮的」和 poverty n.「貧窮」兩字的情形中，也可見到。）原先，拉丁文已有 prūdens a. 和 prūdentia n.f. 兩字，出自動詞 prōvidēre「先見、預知」，因此應該不難想像「謹慎、智慮」的意思從何而來了。

advise v. əd'vaɪz	The doctor *advised* the patient not to drink too much.	忠告、勸告 warn admonish	**ad**(to)
advisement* n. əd'vaɪzmənt	Our boss has taken your application under *advisement*.	考慮、熟思 consideration deliberation	**ad**(to)
envisage v. ɛn'vɪzɪdʒ	Some philosophers *envisage* man simply as the locus of a polytheism.	想像、視 regard view	**en**(in) **visage**
v.	The plan *envisaged* lavish use of mechanical equipment of all kinds.	預見 foresee contemplate	
envision v. ɛn'vɪʒən	One could *envision* the imperfectibility of man through a long process of evolution.	想像、擬想 foresee envisage	**en**(in) **vision**
envy v. 'ɛnvɪ	I don't *envy* people like him.	羨慕、嫉妒 covet begrudge	**en**(in)
n.	I have wild *envy* of the man in the taxi with her.	羨慕、嫉妒 jealousy grudge	
evidence n. 'ɛvədəns	The prosecutor was not able to produce enough *evidence* to prove him guilty.	證據、證詞 proof testimony	**e**(out)

單字·音標·詞類	例　句	中譯·同義字	字源分析
n.	When the ship reached port, it gave abundant *evidence* of the storm.	痕跡、跡象 sign indication	
v.	Her smiles *evidenced* her pleasure.	顯示 demonstrate manifest	
evident a. ˈɛvədənt	It must be *evident* to everybody that someone has been here.	明顯的 manifest palpable	e(out)
improvise v. ˈɪmprəˌvaɪz	The cook hastily *improvised* a supper.	臨時製作、及席作成 imagine extemporize	im(not) **pro**(before)
invidious* a. ɪnˈvɪdɪəs	The four confidential advisers of the crown soon found their positon embarrassing and *invidious*.	招嫉妒、惹人惡感的 envious offensive	envy
invisible a. ɪnˈvɪzəb|	Tourism is becoming the nation's greatest *invisible* export.	看不見、隱形的 unseen intangible	in(not) **visible**
prevision* n. prɪˈvɪʒən	Some *prevision* warned the explorer of trouble ahead.	先見、預知 foresight prognostication	pre(before) **vision**
provide v. prəˈvaɪd	Olives *provide* an important item of food.	供給、供應 afford furnish	pro(forward)

v.	The rules *provide* that dues must be paid monthly.	規定 stipulate	
providence* n. ˈprɑvədəns	The peasants work in their traditional *providence*.	對將來的顧慮 、節約 prudence thrift	**provident**
provident* a. ˈprɑvədənt	Wild squirrels are *provident*.	有先見之明、 節約的 thrifty frugal	**pro**(forward)
providential* a. ˌprɑvəˈdɛnʃəl	Theologians assume that nature operates only according to a *providential* plan.	按天意、由神 意的 decreed by 　divine 　providence	**providence**
provision n. prəˈvɪʒən	We are running out of *provisions*.	供應品 supply stock	**provide**
a.	A *provision* of the lease is that the rent must be paid promptly.	條款、規定 clause stipulation	
provisional a. prəˈvɪʒənḷ	A *provisional* government was set up in the territory just freed from enemy control.	臨時的 conditional tentative	**provision**
prudence n. ˈprudn̩s	The politician has acted with considerable *prudence*.	謹慎、智慮 foresight discretion	**providence**

單字・音標・詞類	例　　　句	中譯・同義字	字源分析
prudent a. **ˈprudn̩t**	A *prudent* businessman never does anything except for a useful end.	謹愼的 cautious discreet	**provident**
a.	She had been a *prudent* wife.	節儉的 frugal thrifty	
purvey v. pɚˈve	These government bulletins *purvey* the information you need.	供給、供應 provide supply	**pur**(forward)
purview* n. **ˈpɚvju**	The problem in Sri Lanka does not fall within the *purview* of the Security Council.	範圍、權界 limit range	**pur**(forward) **view**
review n. rɪˈvju	The writer has taken a *review* of the war in his book.	回顧、檢討 re-examination retrospect	**re**(back) **view**
n.	He writes *reviews* for magazines.	評論 commentary criticism	
v.	The students were told to *review* the lessons.	溫習、再檢查 re-examine revise	
v.	We have to *review* the situations before writing the report.	細察、檢查 inspect scrutinize	
revise v. rɪˈvaɪz	The manuscript has been *revised* twice.	校正、修訂 correct amend	**re**(back)

| | v. | The lecturer has already *revised* his opinions. | 改變
change
alter | |

supervise v.
ˌsupɚˈvaɪzɚ

| | | The president *supervised* the young institution in a paternalistic way. | 監督、管理
oversee
superintend | **super**(over) |

survey v.
sɚˈve

| | | The Secretary has *surveyed* the state universities on the Western Coast. | 視察、考察
examine
inspect | **sur**(over) |

| | v. | Men are *surveying* the land before it is divided into house lots. | 測量
plan
measure | |

ˈsɝve

| | n. | The ministers wish to have a *survey* of the situation before making their decision. | 通盤考慮、審度、檢討
examination
review | |

| | n. | A *survey* showed that the northern boundary was not correct. | 測量
estimating
measuring | |

view n.
vju

| | | The *view* from the top of the mountain is breath-taking. | 景色
sight
scene | |

| | n. | It was our first *view* of the Indian Ocean. | 看、視察
inspection
sight | |

	n.	What are your *views* on this subject?	見解、想法 notion opinion	
	v.	We have to *view* the matter from the taxpayer's standpoint.	觀察、看 behold examine	
	v.	This plan was *viewed* favorably.	認爲、考慮 regard ponder	
visage ˈvɪzɪdʒ	n.	The man had black hair and a rather handsome *visage*.	面貌 face	
	n.	The writer was amused by the gloomy *visage* of the mining town.	外觀 appearance look	
visible ˈvɪzəbḷ	a.	Employees usually look for a *visible* path of advancement.	顯而易見、可見的 noticeable perceptible	
vision ˈvɪʒən	n.	The old man's *vision* is poor.	視力 sight view	
	n.	He had a *vision* of the future.	幻想、夢想 dream illusion	
	n.	The woman claims she could see *visions*.	幻像、幻影 phantom apparition	

visionary a.
ˈvɪʒənˌɛrɪ

Most plans for world peace are *visionary*.

幻想的
imaginary
fanciful

vision

n.

He was ridiculed as a *visionary* when he first proposed the plan.

夢想者、理想主義者
dreamer
enthusiast

visit n.
ˈvɪzɪt

We are going to pay Mrs. Dundy a *visit*.

拜訪、暫居
call
sojourn

v.

They haven't *visited* their new neighbor yet.

拜訪
make a call

v.

Plague and famine *visited* the country.

侵襲、施加（苦痛、罰）
inflict
impose

visitation* n.
ˌvɪzəˈteʃən

The *visitation* of a diocese by a bishop is generally a great event.

訪晤
visit

visit

vista* n.
ˈvɪstə

These galleries are extended into *vistas* by mirrors.

景色、遠景
view

n.

These philosophies open before us an infinite *vista* of human improvement.

展望、遠景
prospect
view

visual a.
ˈvɪʒuəl

So far I have only *visual* impressions of the man.

視覺、可見的
optical
visible

單字·音標·詞類	例　　　句	中譯·同義字	字源分析
visualize v. ˈvɪʒʊəlˌaɪz	People generally *visualize* atomic scientists as bearded old men.	想像 imagine picture	**visual**
v.	The company leader had not *visualized* such an attack from the enemy.	預見、預測 foresee forecast	

68

VIG·VIT·VIV

life

生命 • 精力

字根 vig, vit, viv 源出拉丁文名詞 vigor「精力、活力」、vīta「生命」及動詞 vīvere「生存、生活」。希臘名醫希波克拉底斯 (Hippocrates, 460?–?377B.C.) 有句留傳千古的名言 "Life is short, art long."，以拉丁文寫出，便成 "Vīta brevis are longa"，句中 vīta 一字即爲 life 的意思。這個字根除了上述三種拼法比較常見外，另有兩種拼法如下：vegetate v.「生長」與 victuals n.pl.「食物、食品」。vegetate 源出拉丁文動詞 vegetāre，原即有「生長」的意思。 victuals 則出自上述拉丁文動詞 vīvere「生存、生活」的過去分詞 vīctus，引申作名詞之後，可指生存所需的物品，因此原拉丁文已有「食物、食品」的意思。

單字‧音標‧詞類	例　　　句	中譯‧同義字	字源分析
convivial* a. kən'vɪvɪəl	These were Virginians of the *convivial* sort, lovers of scenery and horses.	友善、愉快的 social mirthful	**con**(together)
invigorate* v. ɪn'vɪgə͵ret	This lotion could *invigorate* the skin.	使充滿生氣與 活力、使強壯 strengthen animate	**in**(in) **vigor**
revival n. rɪ'vaɪvl̩	The townsfolk enjoyed the *revival* of old costume parties.	恢復、復興、 復活 renewal reanimation	**revive**
revive v. rɪ'vaɪv	Our hopes *revived*.	重振、甦醒、 復活 awaken resusciate	**re**(again)
v.	An old play is sometimes *revived* on the stage.	重演、恢復 renew restore	
revivification* n. rɪ'vɪvəfə'keʃən	The return of spring, and the *revivification* of nature, is a period hailed with uncommon delight.	復活、甦醒、 使恢復（氣力） revival reinvigoration	**re**(agan)
survival n. sɚ'vaɪvl̩	One faces problems of *survival* in arctic conditions.	生存 lasting duration	**survive**
survive v. sɚ'vaɪv	She *survived* her husband.	生命較⋯爲長 outlive outlast	**sur**(over)

v.	These men have been trained to *survive* under severe conditions.	繼續生存、繼續存在 last endure
vegetate* v. ˈvɛdʒəˌtet	Algae usually *vegetate* vigorously.	生長 grow sprout
v.	He is perfectly content to *vegetate,* leading a humdrum, uneventful life.	飽食終日無所事事地生活 idle loaf
victuals* n. pl. ˈvɪtlz	They had drinks, cakes, and pastry, but no substantial *victuals.*	食物、食品 food eatables
vigil n. ˈvɪdʒəl	They spent an all-night *vigil* awaiting the arrival of a celebrity.	守夜 watch guard
vigilance n. ˈvɪdʒələns	The health officials have constant *vigilance* against the spread of disease.	注意、警戒、警惕　**vigil** caution circumspection
vigilant a. ˈvɪdʒələnt	A *vigilant* mountain climber is wary of the weather.	警戒、注意的　**vigil** watchful alert
vigor n. ˈvɪgɚ	The plant grows with *vigor.*	生氣、精力 dash stamina

單字·音標·詞類	例 句	中譯·同義字	字源分析
vigorous a. ˈvɪgərəs	The government took *vigorous* measures to stop the practice.	有力、精力充沛的 energetic strenuous	vigor
vital a. ˈvaɪtḷ	Perseverance is *vital* to success.	極需、不可或缺的 essential indispensable	
vitalize v. ˈvaɪtḷˌaɪz	A leader knows how and when to *vitalize* the patriotism of his nation.	賦以生命力 activate energize	vital
vivacious a. vaɪˈveʃəs	In contrast to the orangutan, the chimpanzee is highly active and *vivacious*.	活潑、快活的 lively sprightly	
vivacity n. viˈvæsətɪ	Her life is full of surprising *vivacity*.	充滿生命力、活潑、快活 liveliness animation	
vivid a. ˈvɪvɪd	She is an exuberant, *vivid* girl.	活潑、有生氣的 spirited animated	
a.	He gave a *vivid* description of what he saw during the horrible massacre.	生動、強烈、鮮明的 keen intense	

vivify* v.
ˈvɪvəˌfaɪ

Our imagination can
often *vivify* what is in
our mind.

使生動、賦予
生命
quicken
animate

vivisect* v.
ˌvɪvəˈsɛkt

She doesn't like her
biology teacher because
he often wants the
students to *vivisect*
frogs.

行活體解剖
dissect alive

sect(cut)

69

VOC·VOK

voice, call

聲音 ● 召喚

　　字根voc, vok源出拉丁文名詞 vōx「聲音」的格變化，及動詞
vocāre「召喚」；其中 vok的拼法來自中古英文(Middle English)。
除了上述兩種拼法比較常見，下文例字中並可看到另外兩種形態：
(1) vouch v.「擔保、保證」， avouch v.「承認、斷言」；(2) vow v.
「立誓」， avow v.「公開承認」。這兩種拼法均出自中古英文，
但在轉借過程中，也曾受古法文影響。例字中語義衍變比較奇特的
，有vocation n.「職業」和 avocation n.「副業、嗜好」兩字。a-
vocation源出拉丁文名詞 vocātio「呼喚、恩召」，原指「蒙神召
喚」。中古時代歐洲宗教觀念極盛，認為職業乃神召喚分派的工作
，因此這個字借入古法文之後，已有「職業」的意思，再借入英文
，自然便保有了這個意思。avocation 字首 a 為ab 的變音，有from
、away的意思（參見本書「最重要的30個字首」1. ab·abs，以及「
最重要的70個字根」65. vers·vert 中 averse與 avert 兩字 ），原拉
丁文作 āvocātio n.f.，指將人叫離日常的工作，而作「散心消遣的
行為」解釋。因此，進入英文後，自然也保留了這種意義，而成為
「副業、嗜好」。

單字·音標·詞類	例　句	中譯·同義字	字源分析
advocate v. ˈædvəˌket	They *advocate* building more schools.	主張 urge vindicate	**ad**(to)
n. ˈædvəkɪt	The most enthusiastic *advocates* agree in this with the severest critics.	提倡者、擁護者 supporter promoter	
avocation* n. ˌævəˈkeʃən	He is a lawyer by profession but painting has been his *avocation* for many years.	副業、嗜好 hobby diversion	**a**(away)
avouch* v. əˈvautʃ	They have *avouched* their guilt.	承認、自認 confess accept	**a**(to) **vouch**
v.	Millions of people were ready to *avouch* the exact contrary.	斷言 affirm asseverate	
avow* v. əˈvau	These impoverished people do not have the frankness to *avow* their poverty.	公開承認 acknowledge claim	**a**(to) **vow**
convocation n. ˌkɑnvəˈkeʃən	The Accession Council is the oldest governmental *convocation* in England.	集會 meeting convention	**convoke**
convoke v. kənˈvʊtɪ	The government *convoked* a congress of physicists.	召集 assemble convene	**con**(together)

單字·音標·詞類	例　　　句	中譯·同義字	字源分析
equivocal a. ɪˈkwɪvəkḷ	His *equivocal* argument did not convince anyone.	意義不明顯、模稜兩可的 ambiguous hazy	equ(equal)
a.	The result of the experiment was *equivocal* and proved nothing.	不確定、未決定的 undetermined inconclusive	
equivocate* v. ɪˈkwɪvəˌket	The captured men avoided both persecution and outright lying by *equivocating* with their questioners.	矇混、閃爍其詞、推托 shuffle evade	equ(equal)
evoke v. ɪˈvok	A good joke *evokes* a laugh.	引起 educe elicit	e(out)
invoke v. ɪnˈvok	Spokesmen for the two tribes *invoked* the spirits of departed chiefs to tell them they were now as one.	以法術召（鬼） adjure conjure	in(on)
v.	The condemned criminal *invoked* the judge's mercy.	請求、乞求 entreat implore	
irrevocable a. ɪˈrɛvəkəbḷ	His decision is *irrevocable*.	不能變更、不能取消的 unchangeable irreversible	ir(not) **revoke**

單字・音標・詞類	例　　　句	中譯・同義字	字源分析
provoke v. prəˈvok	Her grotesque behaviors *provoked* laughter.	引起 rouse incite	**pro**(forward)
v.	He was *provoked* beyond endurance.	激怒 incense infuriate	
revoke v. rɪˈvok	The king *revoked* his decree.	取消、撤回 recall recant	**re**(back)
vocabulary n. vəˈkæbjəˌlɛrɪ	He has studied the Latin contributions to the *vocabulary* of English.	字彙 words lexicon	
vocal a. ˈvokḷ	Men are *vocal* beings.	發聲的 capable of making 　oral sounds	
a.	Many of the *vocal* natives on the island have reputations as street-corner orators.	自由發言、滔 滔不絕的 outspoken eloquent	
vocalize v. ˈvokḷˌaɪz	The dog *vocalized* his pain in a series of long howls.	說出、以聲音 表示出 utter voice	**vocal**
vocation n. voˈkeʃən	She chose teaching as her *vocation*.	職業 profession calling	

單字·音標·詞類	例　　句	中譯·同義字	字源分析
vociferate* v. voˈsɪfəˌret	Their prayers were *vociferated* like blasphemies.	吼叫、大聲呼 叫 roar bellow	**fer**(carry)
vociferous a. voˈsɪfəˌrəs	We could well hear the *vociferous* cheers of the people inside the hall.	喧囂、呼喊的 clamorous uproarious	**fer**(carry)
vouch v. vautʃ	No one can *vouch* for his honesty.	擔保、保證、 支持 guarantee uphold	
vow v. vau	He *vowed* that he would be loyal to the king.	立誓 swear pledge	
n.	She wants her husband to make a *vow* never to drink again.	誓言、誓約 pledge oath	

VOLU·VOLV

roll

旋轉 ● 捲繞 ● 轉成

volu, volv 源出拉丁文動詞 volvere 與其過去分詞 volūtum，原即有「旋轉、捲繞、轉成」的意思。下文例字語義衍變比較特別的，有 volume n.「書冊、體積、大量」一字。 volume 源出拉丁文名詞 volūmen（由動詞 volvere 轉成），指「手抄的卷軸」。古代西洋文書典籍以羊皮紙或草紙抄寫成卷，收藏時也習慣捲成筒狀，因此 volume 便可作「書冊」解釋。後來引申又指書卷中包含的大量內容，因而也可以作「體積、大量」的意思。

單字・音標・詞類	例　　　句	中譯・同義字	字源分析
convolve* v. kən'vɑlv	The painter's sweeping brushstrokes *convolved* like thunderclouds.	捲、盤、旋繞 twist roll together	**con**(together)
devolve* v. dɪ'vɑlv	After the general fell, command *devolved* upon the colonel.	移交 transfer convey	**de**(down)
evolution n. ˌɛvə'luʃən	Even in the biological world, *evolution* is not always in the direction of progress.	演化、發展 movement transformation	**evolve**
evolve v. ɪ'vɑlv	Natural cheese *evolves* carbon dioxide during the course of its aging.	發展、放出 develop emit	**e**(out)
v.	From these premises he *evolved* a startling new set of philosophic axioms.	引出、推理 derive educe	
intervolve* v. ˌɪntɚ'vɑlv	These mazes are intricate and *intervolved*.	互捲、捲合 twist within 　one another	**inter**(among)
involute* a. 'ɪnvəˌlut	He was a remarkable man, *involute* and brilliant.	複雜、難解的 intricate abstruse	**involve**
involve v. ɪn'vɑlv	She never had the slightest intention of *involving* herself with him.	牽涉、捲入 connect entangle	**in**(in)

	v.	A tragic opera must *involve* convincing treatment of an elemental conflict.	包括 comprise comprehend	
	v.	Changing these improper attitudes *involves* a task of mass education.	意味著、需要 imply entail	
revolt rɪˈvolt	n.	The fleet was already in *revolt*.	叛亂、背叛 rebellion insurrection	re(back)
	v.	The people of the country *revolted* against the tyrant.	背叛、叛變、叛亂 rebel mutiny	
	v.	His nature *revolts* against such unfair treatment.	嫌惡、起惡感 disgust nauseate	
revolution ˌrɛvəˈluʃən	n.	A bell rings for each *revolution* of the hectograph.	旋轉 circling rotation	revolve
	n.	The king was killed after the bloody *revolution*.	革命 overthrow rebellion	
revolve rɪˈvɑlv	v.	The earth *revolves* round the sun.	周轉、旋轉 rotate gyrate	re(back)
	v.	He *revolved* the story in his mind as he waited.	沈思、考慮 ponder meditate	

voluble* a.
ˈvɑljəbḷ

He, who once had been so *voluble,* became almost inarticulate as he saw the girl approaching.

健言、口若懸河的
fluent
glib

volume n.
ˈvɑljəm

The work was published in five *volumes.*

書冊、書本
tome
book

n.

The *volume* of the sun is 1,200,000 times greater than that of the earth.

體積
body
dimensions

n.

Volumes of smoke pour from the chimneys of the factory.

大量、多量
bulk
mass

voluminous a.
vəˈlumənəs

We have *voluminous* evidence to prove him guilty.

很多、豐富的　volume
full
ample

volute* n.
vəˈlut

Her locks of hair were curled in little flat *volutes.*

渦形
spiral
whorl

volution* n.
vəˈljuʃən

A *volution* is a rolling or revolving motion.

旋轉
twist
convolution

最重要的 70 個字根
［補正］

孫述宇教授

1️⃣ ACT・AG・IG

〔補正〕：應當說拉丁動詞 *agere* 有現在式詞幹（present stem）ag(e)-和過去分詞詞幹（past participle stem）act-。現在式詞幹 ag-與一些詞首或前綴結合時，會發生在拉丁語中常見的音變而成為 ig-。

現在式詞幹 ag(e)-生出現在分詞 *agens*（詞幹為 agent-）和將來分詞 *agendus*（詞幹為 agend-），這些就是英文字 agent 和 agenda 的來源。

2️⃣ ANIM

〔補正〕："呼吸"的原始印歐語詞根是*anə-，它的一個有後綴的詞形在拉丁語中是 anim-，這根產生出名詞 *animus* 和 *anima*。

英文 animosity 的字源，可以從法文 *animosité* 進到拉丁 *animositas*。把拉丁名詞 *animus* 的幹 anim-加上形容詞後綴，就生出形容詞 "敵意的" *animosus*；把它的詞幹 animos-加上抽象名詞後綴就生出抽象名詞 "敵意" *animositas*。

3️⃣ CAD・CAS・CID

〔補正〕：拉丁文 *cadere* "跌落" 的現在式詞幹是 cad(e)-，過去

分詞詞幹是 cas-。cad-與前綴結合時會變成 cid-。

4 CAP・CEIV・CEP・CEPT・CIP・CUP

〔補正〕：拉丁文"捉"*capere* 的現在式詞幹是 cap-，過去分詞詞幹是 capt-；這兩幹在有前綴的情形下都會有音變，於是有 cip-和 cept-等；在古法語那邊它們變成了 ceiv-和 ceit 的模樣。這就是本章字形的基本道理。

但是 capacity、capacitate、capacious 等字不是直接來自動詞 *capere*，而是形容詞 *capax*，它的幹是 capac-。

5 CEDE・CEED・CESS

〔補正〕：拉丁動詞 *cēdere* 的現在式詞幹是 cēd(e)-，過去分詞詞幹是 cess-。由於 cēd-幹中的根元音是個長元音 ē，英文有時用重疊字母來代表長元音（尤其是 e 和 o），所以有 ceed 的寫法。

6 CID・CIS

〔補正〕：拉丁 *caedere* 的現在式詞幹 caed-和過去分詞詞幹 caes-，與前綴結合時會變音成為 cid-和 cis-。

7 CIT

〔補正〕：拉丁動詞 *ciere* 的過去分詞詞幹 cit-構造出重複動詞（frequentative 或 iterative，行動的情狀不是一次而是多次的）*citare*。學界認為英文 cite 來自拉丁 *citare* 的現在式詞幹 cit-，citation 來自它的過去分詞詞幹 citat-；但是 solicit 等字中的 cit-則是來自 *ciere* 的過去分詞詞幹 cit-。

8 CLAIM・CLAM

〔補正〕：拉丁動詞 *clamare* 和名詞 *clamor* 所含的詞根大概是 *clama-；更基本的印歐詞根是*kla-或者*kelə-。*clamare* 的現在式詞幹 clam-經過古法語生出英文的 claim；過去分詞詞幹 clamat-則生出 clamation、acclamation、declamation 等。*clamor* 加上形容詞後綴生出拉丁形容詞 *clamorosus*，那就是英文 clamorous 的來源。

9 CLUD・CLUS

〔補正〕：拉丁動詞 *claudere* 或 *cludere* 的現在式詞幹是 claud-或 clud-，過去分詞詞幹是 claus-或 clus-。

詞幹 claus-加上後綴就生出 "僧院小室" *claustrum*，這是古法文 *cloistre* 和英文 cloister 的來源。由拉丁來的形容詞是 claustral，由法文來的是 cloistral。加上拉丁（源自希臘）的 *phobia*，就有科學上的新拉丁字 claustrophobia。

10 COR・CORD・CORE

〔補正〕："心" 的詞根，在原始印歐語中大概是*kerd-。它的後代，在希臘是 *kardia*，在拉丁是 *cor*（詞幹是 cord-）；在現代英語是 heart（來自古英語 *heorte*），首尾上的 h 與 t 正好與拉丁希臘詞幹上的 k（或 c）與 d 對應。這套對應法則叫做 Grimm's Law。

11 CORP・CORPOR

〔補正〕：拉丁名詞 *corpus* 的詞幹是 corpor-。從這個詞幹產生動詞 *corporare*，它的過去分詞詞幹就是 corporat-，於是有 corporate、corporation 等英文字。

12 COURS · CUR · CURS

〔補正〕：cur-和 curs-分別是拉丁動詞 *currere* 的現在式與過去分詞的詞幹。

13 CRED

〔補正〕：拉丁動詞 *crēdere* 的現在式詞幹是 crēd-，它的元音是長的，英文有一種拼寫方法是用兩個 e 來代表長的 e，因此有 creed 的拼法。這詞幹 cred-所構成的現在分詞（好比英文的 believing）詞幹是 credent-，那就是英文字 credence（〈L *credentia*）和 credential 的來源。

credere 的過去分詞詞幹是 credit-。

14 CUR

〔補正〕：本章的英文字應當以拉丁名詞 *cura* "料理" 爲源頭，因爲學界認爲動詞 *curare* 和形容詞 *curiosus* 都由它而生。英文形容詞 curious 來自 *curiosus*；名詞 cure 來自 *cura*；動詞 cure 則是來自 *curare*。

curare 的過去分詞詞幹是 curat-，那便是教會裡的 curate、curacy 等字的來源。

15 DIC · DICT

〔補正〕：拉丁的 "說" 字，普通動詞是 *dicere*，其現在式詞幹是 dic-，過去分詞詞幹是 dict-；從這兩個詞幹，分別生出語貌較正式的 *dicāre*（過去分詞詞幹是 dicat-），以及重複的 *dictāre*（過去分詞詞幹是 dictat-）。本章英文字的字形須有這幾條詞幹方能充份說明。

至於詞根，應當是 dic-。它來自原始印歐的*deik-。

16 DUC・DUCT

〔補正〕：duc-和 duct-分別是拉丁動詞 *dūcere* 的現在式和過去分詞詞幹。

17 EQU

〔補正〕：在拉丁文，形容詞 *aequus* "平、正" 是最基本的，把它的幹 aequ(o)-加上形容詞後綴-alis 就有了另一個形容詞 "相等" *aequalis*（英文字 equal 的來源）；加上第一類動詞的後綴 āre 就有動詞 "等於" *aequāre*，它的過去分詞詞幹是 aequat-，那就是英文 equate 和 equation 等的來源。

18 FAC・FACT⋯⋯

〔補正〕：拉丁動詞 *facere* 有現在式詞幹 fac-和過去分詞詞幹 fact-，這兩幹上的元音 a 在有前綴的情形下會變為 i 或 e；到了古法語中，這元音又再改變，分詞詞幹上的 c 也會失落而只剩 t，於是有這種種的形態。

這個字讓我們看見許多音變的情形。若要深究詞根，*facere* 和英文動詞 do 竟是同根產物，兩者都源於印歐詞根*dhē-（印歐輔音 dh 會變成拉丁的 f 和日耳曼的 d）。而英文動詞後綴-fy 來自古法語的-fier，相當於拉丁的-facere 或者-ficāre——後者是從 *facere* 所生的形容詞後綴-ficus 生出的。*facere* 的過去分詞詞幹是 fact-，*-ficāre* 的過去分詞詞幹是-ficat-，所以英文的-fy 動詞會有兩種抽象名詞的詞形：-faction（如 satisfy／satisfaction）和-fication（justify／justification）。

19 **FER**

〔補正〕：拉丁動詞 *ferre*（原是 *ferere*）與英文 bear（古英文 *beran*）同源，都來自原始印歐詞根*bher-。

ferre 的詞形有些奇怪，它的過去分詞詞幹是來自另一詞的 lat-。所以字典會說 relate 和 translate 源自 *referre* 和 *transferre*。表示"延緩"的 defer 也與 delay 有字源關係，因為拉丁 *differre* 生出的重複動詞 *dilatāre*，這詞變成古法文的 *delayer*，再變成英文 delay。

20 **FIN**

〔補正〕：基本的是拉丁名詞 *finis*，它生出形容詞 *finalis*（英文 final 的來源）和動詞 *finire*。*finire* 的過去分詞詞幹是 finit-，本章的一些英文字即由此而來。

21 **FLECT · FLEX**

〔補正〕：應當說 flect-和 flex-是動詞 *flectere* 的兩條詞幹。名詞 *flexio*（詞幹是 flexion-）也是來自 flex-，-io（詞幹是-ion-）是羅馬人構造抽象名詞的常用後綴。

22 **FLU**

〔補正〕：原始印歐語有個"漲溢"詞根*bhleu-，在拉丁中變成 flu-，加上種種後綴，生出動詞"流"*fluere*，名詞"河"*fluvius* 和 *flumen*；從名詞又生出形容詞 *fluvialis*、*fluviosus*、*fluminosus* 等。這些詞的詞幹就是本章中英文字的建材。

23 **FOUND · FUS**

〔補正〕：*fundere* 的現在式詞幹是 fund-，過去分詞詞幹是

fus-。這動詞的根並沒有鼻音 n（在原始印歐語中原是*gheu-的形狀），*fundere* 上的 n 是個"鼻音中綴"（nasal infix）。這種語音現象通常只發生在動詞的現在式詞幹上；譬如英語的 stand 有個 n，stood 卻是沒有的。下章中拉丁動詞 *frangere* 的兩幹 frang-／fract-也是例證。

24 **FRACT・FRAG・FRANG・FRING**

〔補正〕：拉丁動詞 *frangere* 的根是*frag-（在原始印歐語中是*bhreg-；英語的動詞 break 也由此而來），而現在式詞幹是frang-，過去分詞詞幹是 fract-。frang-上有個鼻音中綴 n（見廿三章補正），fract-有過去分詞特色的 t，而詞根上的有聲顎音 g 受到這 t 的牽連變爲無聲顎音 c。frang-上的 a 若遇有前綴就會變成 i，於是產生了 fring-。

25 **GEN**

〔補正〕：原始印歐詞根*gen(ə)-是所有這些字的源頭，它產生英語的 kin（古英語 *cyn*）和 kind（古英語 *gecynde*），希臘的 *genos*，拉丁的 *genus* 和 *gens*（詞幹爲 gent-）。這根的零級形狀 gn-生出拉丁動詞"生產"*gignere*（過去分詞詞幹 genit-）和 *(g)nasci*（過去分詞詞幹(g)nat-），從 genitive、progenitor 到 nation、native、nature、cognate（拉丁 co＋*gnatus*）的許多英文字都由此而生出。

拉丁名詞 *genus* 的詞幹是 gener-，與前面第十一章的 *corpus*、corpor-相類。gener-產生動詞 *generare*、generat-，那是英文 generate、generation 等字的來源。

26 **GRAD・GRESS**

〔補正〕：應當說 grad-和 gress-是拉丁動詞 *gradi* 的現在式和

過去分詞詞幹。

　　但本章有些英文字並非來自動詞 *gradi*，而是名詞 *gradus* "級"
以及所產生的形容詞 *gradualis* 和動詞 *gradāre*，gradat-。

27 IT

　　〔補正〕：構詞常用的幹 it-是拉丁動詞 *ire* 的過去分詞詞幹。*ire*
的現在式詞幹 i-也能加上後綴-(e)nt-來構成現在分詞，如 *transire* 的
現在分詞就是 *transiens*、transient-。*ire* 的根應當是 i，來自原始印
歐詞根*ei-"去"。

　　拉丁名詞 *iter* 的詞幹是 itiner-，這可以說明英文字 itinerant 和
itinerary 等的拼寫。

28 JAC・JECT・JET

　　〔補正〕：作者說得對，拉丁的 i 和 j 是同一字母的不同寫法而
已，這字母既代表元音，也代表半元音與輔音。

　　拉丁動詞 "投擲" 的現在式詞幹是 jac-，過去分詞詞幹是
jact-，後者因種種原因會變成 ject-的形狀，到古法語就成了 jet-。
例如加強的拉丁動詞 "投擲" 便是以這詞幹加上後綴-āre 而成的
jectāre，這詞在古法語中變成 *jeter*，來到英語便是 jet。

29 JOIN・JOINT・JUNCT

　　〔補正〕：拉丁動詞 *jungere* 的現在式詞幹是 jung-，過去分詞詞
幹是 junct-；這兩幹在古法語中變爲 join-和 joint-。

30 LECT・LEG・LIG

　　〔補正〕：應當說 leg-和 lect-是動詞 *legere* 的現在式與過去分
詞詞幹。leg-在有前綴及其他情況下變音成 lig-。

31 LOCU・LOG・LOQU

〔補正〕：拉丁動詞 *loqui* 的現在式與過去分詞詞幹分別是 loqu-和 locut-（不是 locu-）。

logic 雖然很像 *loqui*，但並非同根。logic 的詞根是*leg-，與上一章的字相同。

32 LUC・LUMIN・LUSTR

〔補正〕：在原始印歐語中"光照"的詞根是*leuk-，這根在拉丁出現時是 lūc-，它產出動詞 *lūcēre*，名詞 *lūx*、lūc-和形容詞 *lūcidus*。*leuk-加上一個輔音 t 就產生英語的 light（古英語 *leoht*），加上後綴音節就有拉丁的名詞 *lumen*、lumin-和 *luster*、lustr-。

33 MAGN・MAJ・MAX

〔補正〕：這章的基本字根是印歐的*meg-，希臘的"大"*mega* 或 megal-（如"自大狂"megalomania）即由此而來，印度的"大"*maha*（如土邦的"大王"是 *maharaja(h)*，佛教的"大乘"是 *mahayana*）亦然。拉丁的 magn-來自它帶鼻音後綴的根形，maj-和 max-則是比較級和最高級的幹。

34 MAIN・MAN

〔補正〕：拉丁文"手"是 *manus*，詞幹是 man(u)-。*main* 是法文的拼寫。

35 MINI・MINU

〔補正〕：詞根*mei-生出帶鼻音後綴的拉丁形容詞"較小的"*minus* 或 *minor*，和"最小的"*minimus*。

從拉丁來的英文字，minor 是"小的"，major 是"大的"——如音樂上相對的小調和大調，地理上相對的"小亞細亞"（Asia Minor）和"（大）亞細亞"（Asia（Major））。minister 是加上後綴而成，原意是"小人物"，轉意便是"侍僕、牧師（神之僕）、部長或大臣（帝王之僕）"；相對的是 magister "大人物"，這字再變便是"主人" master 和"初級法官" magistrate。

36┃ MISS・MIT

〔補正〕：應當說 mit-和 miss-是 *mittere* 的現在式與過去分詞詞幹。

messenger 來自 message，多了一個鼻音 n，音變的原因不明，但情形與 passenger／passage 一樣。

37┃ MOB・MOM・MOT・MOV

〔補正〕：本章章首列出的四個詞形不是詞根，也不全是詞幹。詞根*meuə-生出拉丁動詞 *movere*，它的現在式詞幹是 mo(v)-，過去分詞詞幹是 mot-。前者產生英文字 move、remove 等；後者產生 motion、motive、motor 等。

現在式詞幹 mo(v)-加上後綴而生出 mobile 和 moment 等詞，這些詞並沒有 mob-或 mom-這樣的根或幹。

38┃ PASS・PATH

〔補正〕：pass-是拉丁動詞 *pati* 的過去分詞詞幹；*pati* 的現在式詞幹是 pat-。*pati* 和 *agere* 是相對立的兩動詞：*agere* 是"做"，它的過去分詞詞幹 act-生出英文形容詞 active "主動的"（〈L *activus*）；*pati* 是"受"，它的過去分詞詞幹 pass-生出 passive "被動的"（〈L *passivus*）。這兩動詞的現在分詞詞幹分別是 agent-和

patient-；在文法上，agent 是"主詞"，patient 是"受詞"。病人叫做 patient 也因爲他是承受著病苦；而 passion 的"苦難"之意也是這樣來的。（宗教音樂與藝術都用 passion 這個字來說耶穌與別的聖徒受難的經過。）

至於 path-則是個希臘詞幹。

39 PED

〔補正〕：拉丁文"腳"是 *pes*，詞幹是 ped-；希臘文"腳"是 *pous*，詞幹是 pod-。它們共同的印歐語詞根是 *ped-，學者用元音替換的術語來說，拉丁的 *pes* 來自這根的平常級或 e 級，希臘的 *pous* 來自它的 o 級。印歐詞根*ped-來到日耳曼語言中，經過規律性音變，終於產生英語的 foot（古英語 *fōt*）和德語的 *fuss*。

拉丁的幹 ped-和希臘的 pod-都產生英文字，後者主要出現在醫學上。

40 PEL · PULS

〔補正〕：拉丁動詞 *pellere* 的詞根大概是 pel-，不過在構造本章各英文字的要素 pel-和 puls-卻都不是詞根，而是 *pellere* 的現在式和過去分詞詞幹。

41 PEND · PENS · POND

〔補正〕：本章的英文字雖或來自同一詞根，但牽涉到幾組詞幹。拉丁動詞 *pendere* 的現在式詞幹 pend-與過去分詞詞幹 pens-是一組，名詞 *pondus* 的幹 ponder-是另一組；從 ponder-生出的動詞 *ponderāre* 又有兩詞幹 ponder-和 ponderat-。

至於 poise 等英文字，則是來自古法語的音變：拉丁的 pens-（*pensum*）失音成了 pes-，再變就是 *pois* 了。

42 PLIC・PLEX・PLY

〔補正〕：本章的英文字，除了 diploma 那組之外，其他都來自拉丁動詞 *plicāre* 和 *plectere*。*plicāre* 的兩詞幹 plic-和 plicat-都能構成新詞，而不定式在古法文中變成 *plier*，終於以-play、-ply、-ploy 等形狀出現在英文裡。*plectere* 的過去分詞詞幹 plex-也產生很多新詞。

但 quadruple、multiple、triple 等字是另一個詞根的產物。

43 PON・POS・POUND

〔補正〕：本章的字源有些混淆。拉丁動詞 *ponere* "放置" 的現在式詞幹是 pon-，過去分詞詞幹是 posit-（有時會失去 i 而成 post-），兩者都能構成新詞。但那些 pose 字卻是在古法語中從另一個拉丁動詞 "停留" *pausāre* 那裡得到詞形的。

至於 compound，來自拉丁 *compōnere*，中古英文拼作 *compounen*，以 ou 代表長 o 音。這字在古法文中多出一個 d，影響所及，今天英文 compound 也多了個 d。

44 PORT

〔補正〕：從拉丁動詞 *portāre* 出來構造新詞的是它的現在式詞幹 port-和過去分詞詞幹 portat-。

45 PRESS

〔補正〕：本章的說明有些錯漏。本章的字，可以追源到印歐詞根*per-，而在拉丁的源頭則是動詞 "擊、壓" *premere*（來自詞根的異體*prem-），它的現在式詞幹是 prem-，過去分詞詞幹是 press-。本章所舉的英文字來自這個過去分詞詞幹，或者由它產生的加強動

詞 *pressāre*。

　　但 *premere* 的現在式詞幹也產生新詞。遇有前綴時，這幹上的根元音 e 會變為 i，如 *imprimere* 或 *exprimere*（過去分詞詞幹是 impress-、express-）。一些重要的英文字，如 print、printing、imprint、imprimatur 等，便是這現在式詞幹產生的，編者都漏收了。

46 QUEST · QUIR · QUIS

〔補正〕：拉丁動詞 *quaerere* 的現在式詞幹 quaer-和過去分詞詞幹 quaesit-，在與前綴結合以及在古法語中起音變，會有 quer-、quir-、quesit-、quisit-，以及縮短成 quest-等形狀。

47 REG · RIG

〔補正〕：拉丁有兩個不同源的動詞，一是 *rēgere* "君臨統治"，一是 *rīgere* "成為硬直"。與 *rēgere* 同根的是 "君王" *rēx*（詞幹 rēg-），這根也產生印度的 *rajah*。

　　rēx 在古法語中變了音，英文因此有 royal 這個字。*rēgere* 的現在式詞幹 rēg-構成現在分詞 *rēgens*、rēgent-，英文字 regent 及 regency 由此而來。

　　與 *rīgere* 同根的是名詞 *rigor* 與形容詞 *rigidus*，它們生出英文的 rigor（或 rigour），rigorous，rigid 等。

48 SCRIB · SCRIP

〔補正〕：本章的字來自拉丁動詞 *scribere* 的現在式詞幹 scrib-和過去分詞詞幹 script-（不是 scrip-）。

49 SECU・SEQU・SUE

〔補正〕：本章的字來自拉丁動詞 *sequi* 的現在式詞幹 sequ-和過去分詞詞幹 secut-（末尾有 t，不只是 secu-）。

50 SED・SESS・SID

〔補正〕：能夠構造新詞的 sed-、sid-、sess-都不是詞根，而分別是拉丁動詞 *sedēre* 和 *sidere* 的現在式詞幹和共同的過去分詞詞幹。

如要追尋詞根，學者認爲這兩個拉丁動詞共同的原始印歐語詞根是*sed-*，它也是英語 set 和 sit 的根。

51 SENS・SENT

〔補正〕：sent-和 sens-是動詞 *sentire* 的現在式與過去分詞的詞幹，不是根。

52 SIST・STA・STITUT

〔補正〕：印歐語言——包括英、法、俄、希臘、梵語等——中表達 "站立、建樹" 的詞類有 st 音的非常多。學者經過比較研究，認爲原始印歐語中有個代表這意思的詞根*sta-*。英語中的 stand、stood、stead 等都是這根的產物。

在拉丁語中，這詞根一方面生出動詞 *stare*，另一方面又生出 *sistere*。（*sistere* 是個 "複音動詞"，它是把詞根*sta-*的開首輔音 s 重複了一下）。*stare* 的現在式詞幹生出一批字（英文的 stay、rest，產生於現在分詞的 constant、instance 等），過去分詞詞幹又生出一批（state、station、status、stature 等）；*sistere* 亦如此，現在式詞幹生出 insist、insistent、persist、persistence 等。*sistere* 和 *stare*

的過去分詞詞幹同是 stat-，從這幹又生出動詞 *statuere*，它的現在式詞幹與一些前綴生出一些現在分詞 constituent、constituency 等，而過去分詞詞幹 statut-也生出一些字，如 constitute、constitution 等等。

53 | SPEC・SPECT・SPIC

〔補正〕：有構造新詞功用的 spec-和 spect-，分別是拉丁動詞 *specere* 的現在式和過去分詞詞幹。從 spect-生出另一個狀貌不同的動詞 *spectāre*，它的過去分詞詞幹是 spectat-。

至於 spic-，那是 spec-在有前綴的情形下變音而成。

54 | STRAIN・STRESS・STRICT・STRING

〔補正〕：拉丁動詞 *stringere* 的現在式與過去分詞詞幹分別是 string-和 strict-。strain-和 stress-是兩者在古法語的後身。strait-也來自 strict-。*stringere* 的詞根是*streig-，在現在式詞幹上多了個"鼻音中綴"n。

至於 straight 和 stretch，都是古英語 *streccan* 的後身。strangle 則來自拉丁動詞 *strangulare*，本身來自希臘，與拉丁的 *stringere* 沒有關係。

55 | STRU・STRUCT

〔補正〕：stru-和 struct-是拉丁動詞 *struere* 的現在式與過去分詞詞幹。名詞 *structiō*、*structiōnis* 是詞幹 struct-加上名詞後綴-iō、-iōnis 而成。

56 | TACT・TANG

〔補正〕：本章的詞類共同的詞根其實是*tag-。tang-與 tact-只

是動詞 *tangere* 的現在式與過去分詞詞幹；名詞 *tactus* 的幹就是 *tangere* 的過去分詞詞幹 tact-。

　　動詞不定式 *tangere* 上顯現現在式詞幹 tang-，這幹是詞根 tag- 加上個鼻音 n 構成。(這種 "鼻音中綴" 的出現，參看前面第廿三章字根的補正)。其他名詞和形容詞，如 contagion、contagious、contiguous 等，都沒有這個中綴。

57 TAIN・TEN・TIN

　　〔補正〕：本章的字源是拉丁動詞 *tenēre*。這動詞的現在式詞幹是 ten-，這幹與前綴結合時會變成 tin-；另外，在進入古法文後變成 tain-。

　　tenēre 的過去分詞詞幹是 tent-，本章的一些字是由它構成的，如 abstention、content 等。過去分詞詞幹較少音變，例如 abstain (tain-是法文現在式詞幹)、abstinence (tin-是拉丁現在式詞幹變了音)、abstention (tent-是過去分詞詞幹)。

58 TEND・TENS・TENT

　　〔補正〕：拉丁 *tendere* 的現在式詞幹是 tend-；過去分詞詞幹在古典時代是 tent-，到中古時代多用 tens-。由於這過去分詞詞幹有兩個形狀，所以像 intend 這樣的動詞就有相關的名詞與形容詞 intent、intention 和 intense、intensive。

　　值得注意的是，*tendere* 和上一章的 *tenēre* 都有過去分詞詞幹 tent-。所以我們要分辨那些-tention 字的來源，例如 intention 來自 *tendere*，retention 則來自 *tenere*，兩字的基本意義自然也就不同。

59 TOR・TORT

　　〔補正〕：拉丁 *torquere* 的現在式詞幹是 torqu-，過去分詞詞幹

是 tort-。在古法語中，torqu-失音而成 tor-。例如 torment，在拉丁原本是 *torqu(e)mentum*。

60 **TRACT · TREAT**

〔補正〕：本章的字，除了一兩個之外，都源於拉丁動詞 *trahere*。它的現在式與過去分詞詞幹分別是 trah-和 tract-；現在式詞幹構成新詞較少，本章的例字只有 portray 一個而已。portray 來自古法語 *portraire*，由拉丁 pro- + *trahere* 變成。

過去分詞詞幹 tract-（以及法語變體 treat）構成的新詞則很多。tract-還產生了一個加強動詞 *tractāre*，它在古法語中變成 *traitier*，英文動詞 treat 由此而生。

61 **TRUD · TRUS**

〔補正〕：trud-和 trus-不是 *trudere* 的根，而是它的現在式和過去分詞詞幹。

至於編者說 *trudere* 與來自古英語的 threat 有字源關係，那是對的。學界認為這兩詞都來自原始印歐詞根*treud-"擠壓"。

62 **VAC · VAN · VOID**

〔補正〕：拉丁 *vacāre* 的現在式詞幹 vac-和過去分詞詞幹 vacat-都產生一些新詞。*vacāre* 和形容詞 *vacuus* 的詞根是 vac-。

詞幹 van-來自形容詞 *vānus*（英文 vain 的前身）。它的詞根是 vano-，學者認為 vano-與 vac-同源，都是由原始印歐詞根*eu-增長而成。

void 是拉丁形容詞 *vacuus* 在古法語中輾轉變成的。

63 | VAIL · VAL

〔補正〕：本章的英文字——以及講說 "病癒康復" 的 convalesce 及 convalescent——都來自拉丁的 *valēre*。這動詞的現在式詞幹 val-很能造詞，過去分詞詞幹 valit-卻很少造詞。

valēre 的印歐詞根是*wal-，牛津拉丁字典說它與古德語 *waltan* "統治" 以及庫車語（所謂吐火羅西支方言，在中國新疆發現的死語言）*walo* "君王" 是同源詞。

64 | VEN · VENT

〔補正〕：ven-與 vent-是拉丁動詞 *venire* 的現在式與過去分詞詞幹。

65 | VERS · VERT

〔補正〕：vert-和 vers-是拉丁動詞 *vertere* 的現在式與過去分詞詞幹。本章英文字的主幹，都出自這兩個詞幹，以及由 vers-產生的重複動詞 *versāre*（自動式 *versari*，過去分詞詞幹 versat-）。

至於 divorce 的詞形，那是因為它的拉丁前身 *divortium*（di-＋vort-＋-ium）是由詞幹 vert-的異體 vort-構成。拉丁動詞 *vertere* 有個異體是 *vortere*，*versāre* 也有 *vorsāre*。

66 | VEY · VIA · VOY

〔補正〕：本章的英文字，編者用拉丁名詞 *via* 來說明來源，頗為合適。由 *via* "道路" 就生出動詞 *viāre* "上路、走"（過去分詞詞幹是 viat-），有些字——如 deviate——須這樣說明。再如 convey（〈OF *conveier*〈L *conviāre*）以及 convoy（〈OF *convoier*，是 *conveier* 的異體）、envoy 等字，也是這個來歷。

編者如果追尋 *via* 的詞根，就能說明更多字的道理。*via*（拉丁的 v 讀作 [w]）的印歐詞根是*wegh-，它在日耳曼語系中生出德文的 *weg* 和英文的 way（古英文 *weg*）；在拉丁中除了 "道路" *via*，又生出 "攜帶" *vehere*（過去分詞詞幹 vect-），於是給英文送來了 vehicle、vector 等字。

67 VID·VIEW·VIS

〔補正〕：vid-和 vis-是拉丁動詞 *vidēre* 的現在式和過去分詞詞幹。view 卻既不是詞根也不是詞幹，而是來自古法文中一個獨立的字。

68 VIG·VIT·VIV

〔補正〕：本章的英文字所採用拉丁詞幹，計來自動詞 *vigēre*（現在式詞幹 vig-）、*vegetāre*（現在式詞幹 veget-，來自另一動詞 *vegēre* 的過去分詞詞幹 veget-）、*vigilāre* 和名詞 *vigil*；以及動詞 *vivere*（現在式詞幹 viv-和過去分詞詞幹 vict-）和名詞 *vita*（詞幹 vit-）。

這幾個詞來自兩條不同的詞根。一是印歐詞根*weg-，它產生 *vigēre*、*vegēre* 和 *vigil*；英語中土生土長的 wake、waken，也由此而來。另一條詞根是*gwei-，*vivere* 和 *vita* 是它的產物，古英語的 *cwic*（quick 的前身）和希臘的 *bios* "生命" 也是。

69 VOC·VOK

〔補正〕：本章的字採用了拉丁名詞 *vōx* 的幹 vōc-和動詞 *vocāre* 的兩幹 voc-和 vocat-。

vok-即是 voc-。（拉丁文雖有字母 k ，但只用來拼寫少數希臘字；拉丁的 [k] 都以字母 c 代表。古英文承受拉丁傳統，以 c 代表 [k]；中古英文才開始選擇性地用字母 k 來拼寫 [k]。[k] 出現在字尾

會用 k 或 ck 拼寫；若不在字尾，則要有前元音 i 或 e 相隨才用 k
拼寫──如 kin 或 keen，否則都用 c。）

70 VOLU・VOLV

〔補正〕：動詞 *volvere* 的現在式詞幹是 volv-，過去分詞詞幹是
volut-（幹末有 t，不只是 volu-而已）。

［附錄一］
英 語 簡 說
源流、結構、聲韻、詞彙、書寫

孫述宇教授

作者簡介

孫述宇，美國耶魯大學英國語言及文學博士
（1963），現任教香港中文大學英文系，曾任台灣
中山大學客座教授，成功大學外文系及中正大學
外文研究所教授，講授「英國文學」、「英語史」
及「古代英語」等課程。

㈠英語與印歐語言

英國和英語的歷史都不算很長久。公元前 55 年，凱撒領着羅馬
遠征軍渡海登上名為不列顛（Britannia）的大島，事後得意洋洋向元
老院作了那篇有名的三字捷報：" *Veni, Vidi, Vici*：我到了，見了，克
了"。他所到的島還不是英國，所敗的土人也不是英人，是說塞爾特
語言（Celtic）的不列顛人（Britons 或 Brythons）。數十年後不列顛成
了羅馬殖民地，羅馬人在島上各地建造的防禦工事和馳道至今歷歷
在目，他們的軍營仍是許多英國城鎮的名字。不列顛人和羅馬統治
者尚能相安，前者納賦稅服勞役，後者治理和保護他們。島上的外
患主要是那些同樣說着塞爾特語言的皮克特人（Picts）和斯各特人

(Scots)；皮克特人來自北部，斯各特人來自愛爾蘭，他們後來移居北部而使蘇格蘭(Scotland)得名。北海上漸漸也有些說日耳曼語言(Germanic)的日耳曼人（又稱條頓人 Teutons）到來擄掠。羅馬駐軍憑着較優良的裝備與訓練，維持這殖民地的秩序與安寧達四百多年。

最後羅馬被迫從不列顛撤軍，原因是歐洲北部的日耳曼蠻族大羣大羣南下，使羅馬帝國本土備受威脅。羅馬駐軍一旦撤離，慣於受保護的不列顛人不能自衛，於是有日耳曼部族從歐洲渡海來到，據地建國。依照貝德主教(The Venerable Bede)所記，日耳曼人是應邀前來救援的，因爲不列顛人覺得皮克特人的欺侮難以忍受。日耳曼人於公元449年由兩個領袖恆依斯特(Hengist)和何沙(Horsa)統率着來到，他們打敗皮克特人後，看見島上物產富饒而居民懦弱，就傳訊到家鄉，叫多派些弟兄過來逐鹿。得訊前來的是盎格利(Angles)、撒克遜(Saxons)和朱特(Jutes)三部的人，他們佔據了島上大部份土地，把土著不列顛人逐到西南隅上。貝德記事於三百年後，細節難保無訛，但大體似乎是正確的。日耳曼人在不列顛建了七個王國，由於其中以盎格利人所建的三國最大，全島也就叫做"盎格利人之國"(Anglaland，後變成 England)，條頓各部所講大同小異的日耳曼語也因而叫做"盎格利語"(Anglisc，後變爲 English)，這就是英國和英語的源始。

經過比較語言學(comparative philology 或 linguistics)的學者從十九世紀開始研究，今人對英語的了解比前人透徹得多。我們知道，第一代英國人所說的英語是遍佈北歐的日耳曼語言之一種，盎格利和別的條頓人渡海建國時把它帶了過來。今天，日耳曼語言是許多互相難以溝通的語言，除英語外，尚有德、荷、比、瑞士、丹、挪、瑞典和冰島的話；但是在從前，這些語言之間的差異很微小。比較語言學者認爲它們有一個共同的祖語，叫做原始日耳曼語

(Proto-Germanic)；這個祖語在歷史上漸漸分化成不同的方言，方言間的差異再增大，就變成不同的語言。倘若再向上回溯，原始日耳曼語當初與許多歐亞古語——拉丁、希臘、古印度的梵語、不列顛語等等——的先祖也顯然是互相講得通的。學者把這一大羣語言合併爲印歐語族(Indo-European Language Family)①。根據族內現存語言以及過去語言的文字記錄，他們運用比較方法把許多並無文物佐證的原始語言一一反推重構出來，包括全個語族的老祖宗原始印歐語(ProtoIndo-European，簡寫作 PIE 或 IE)。從前那些口講著原始印歐語的所謂原始印歐人呢，學者判斷他們約在距今六千年前還聚居在東歐或西亞某處內陸地區，因爲原始印歐語的詞彙與這樣的一個自然環境相脗合。

可是學者根據什麼理由而認爲印歐語族內的語言是親屬，而族外的語言便不是它們的親屬呢？理由主要有二，一是同源的詞彙，一是同源的詞尾或詞形變化(inflexions)。先說詞彙，印歐語言有許多同義的語詞，它們的語音相近，顯見得是同根生的(cognate)；比方名詞中，有些指日月星辰和自然現象的，又有些指動植物種和禽畜農作的，又有些指四肢五官和家庭關係的、以及從一到十等簡單數目字便是。試以數字爲例，我們若把日耳曼系的德語、塞爾特系的威爾殊語、現代的意大利語、古典希臘共同語、以及斯拉夫系的俄羅斯語並列，再比較英語，可以看出它們是如何相像：

	德	威	意	希	俄
<u>one</u>	eins	un	uno	(oinẽ)	odin
<u>two</u>	zwei	dau	due	duo	dva
<u>three</u>	drei	tri	tre	treis	tri
<u>four</u>	vier	pedwar	quattro	tettares	chetyre
<u>five</u>	fünf	pump	cinque	pente	pyat'

	德	威	意	希	俄
<u>six</u>	sechs	chwech	sei	hex	shest'
<u>seven</u>	sieben	saith	sette	hepta	sem'
<u>eight</u>	acht	wyth	otto	oktõ	vosem'
<u>nine</u>	neun	naw	nove	ennea	devyat'
<u>ten</u>	zehn	deg	diece	deka	desyat'

沒有語言學專門知識的人也會覺得這幾行字是有關係的。它們的一字都是以元音開始，後有鼻音；二字是齒音 d 或 t（德語的 z 等於 ts）帶着元音，還有個圓唇音 u,v 或 w；三字是齒音加 r，字內的元音是前方元音。四、五兩字的情形複雜些，說明頗費唇舌，暫且按下；六與七都是以 s 開始（在希臘語中則一同變爲 h ②），六字的後方多有 k 和 s（意語沒有了，但它的祖先拉丁語卻是有的），七的後方可有双唇音 p,b,β,v 和齒音 t 以及鼻音 m,n。八字是元音開始，後有顎音和齒音；九的前方有個鼻音，後方也會有；十是以齒音開始，後方會有顎音和鼻音。例外是存在的，俄語中尤其多；但無可否認，這些語言中同義的數字語音都很相似，而與其他語族的語言——比如漢語或日語——截然不同。

　　相似之中，差異還是有的，學者怎樣面對它們呢？比如上述數目字中的元音，不是前後高低乃至單純複合的差異都有嗎？輔音方面，n 和 r 在各種語言中都很一致，但是那些唇齒顎音不是常有些清濁塞連和吐不吐氣的出入嗎？比較語言學者認爲這都無傷大雅，只要差異自有其一貫性，則那些同義字仍可視爲同源。語言分化，主因就在語音改變，因此分化出來的不同語言自然會以一些不同語音來表達同樣的意思。但在另一方面，語音改變總有某程度的普遍性，所以倘若語音的差異有規律性，就反映出同源的可能。元音的情形太繁，我們且以輔音來說明。在日耳曼語言的歷史上，學者認爲原

始日耳曼語從原始印歐語中分化出來時，輔音 n,m,l,r,s 等保持不變，唇齒顎系列的塞音卻有系統地轉變了，變化的規則就是有名的古里穆聲律(Grimm's Law，那是編纂《格林童話》的大學者 Jacob Grimm 首先整理出來的)。這聲律的項目中，齒音方面有這樣的一條：

IE d → Gmc t

這條的意思是說，在原始印歐語變成原始日耳曼語時，原來的 d 變成了 t；這即是說，在別的印歐語言的語詞出現 d 的地方，日耳曼同義詞就會出現 t。知道有此規律，又看見上段中二字和十字裏頭四種非日耳曼的印歐語言都以 d 開始，我們看見英語這兩個字是 two 和 ten 時，就會有不出所料之感，並且能夠相信這兩個英文字與那八個印歐字是同源的。(比較語源學者以爲在原始印歐語中這兩字的語形大概是 *dwo 和 *dekm。) 事實上，德語以外的日耳曼語差不多都以 t 開始這兩個數目字；德語在這位置上出現 z，是德語另起音變的結果③。這兩重音變在許多同源的字上都反映出來，比方"牙齒"，拉丁的 dens (詞幹是 dent-) 和英語的 tooth (原本在 o 後也有個 n) 之間有 d 與 t 的對換，而德語的 Zahn 又出現 z④。

　　次說詞尾。印歐語族的現代語，詞尾分歧很大；但回溯歷史，這些現代語的前身在愈古的時代，詞尾就愈相近。以動詞現在時態來說，學者推斷在原始印歐語中三人稱的單多兩數詞尾是這樣的：

	我	你	他
單	-ō	-si	-ti
多	-mes	-te	-nti

後來這祖語分化成各種語言，六個詞尾在這些後代語言上起了或多或少的變異，其中梵語保存着最完整的面貌，拉丁希臘等古語改變得稍多。等到古語變成中古語，再變成近代語，這些詞尾變得更多。今天，南歐的西班牙和法語等都還保留着它們的一些影子，德語亦然；但英語的改變就太大了。英語中動詞現在式的六個詞尾是：

$$\begin{array}{ccc} - & - & -s \\ - & - & - \end{array}$$

簡化至此，祖宗輪廓已茫不可見。可是兩三百年前這第三人稱單數的 s 還是 th，依照古里穆聲律它與印歐的 t 是對應的；第二人稱單數的詞尾還是-st，比原始印歐語只多了個 t，而這 t 的由來是可以解釋的。九百年前的古英語，除了第二三人稱單數有 st 和 th 外，第一人稱單數有 e 爲詞尾，那是印歐的 ō 弱化而成的；三個人稱的多數詞尾都是 ath，那應當是印歐第三人稱多數詞尾 nti 變成的：末尾的 i 脫落了，n 也脫落了（英語的這些變化都是規律性的），t 轉變成 th，a 是詞幹上元音變成的。有記錄的日耳曼語言數哥特語（Gothic）最古老，它的這六個詞尾是：

$$\begin{array}{ccc} -a & -st & -th \\ -m & -th & -nd \end{array}$$

把音變考慮在內，我們必須承認它們與原始印歐語的詞尾十分接近。

㈡**古英語與英語文法**

英語史的分期，把五世紀至十一世紀的英語稱爲古英語(Old

English，簡寫 OE）。從前學術界也曾稱古英語爲盎格魯撒克遜語（Anglo-Saxon，簡稱 AS）。

古英語的語音有日耳曼特色，重音差不多一定落在頭一個音節之上，除非這個音節是那些讀得輕的詞首（prefixes）。古英語是綜合度（synthetic）頗高的語言，詞尾變化相當繁複（即所謂 highly inflected）。它的名詞有性別（gender）、種類（declension）、數目（number）和格別（case）；形容詞亦然 ⑤，而且更有日耳曼語言特具的兩套變化。它的動詞有時態（tense）和語態（mood），並分爲強弱兩大類，強的就是今天所謂"不規則動詞"的前身，弱的變化是今天動詞的規則變化。強動詞其實並非不規則，它們是遠古的印歐動詞演變而成，它們的元音遞換（Ablaut, apophony）——如 sing:sang:sung 的 i:a:u 遞換——有一定的模式，但這些道理在這裏不便細說。日耳曼動詞的時態特別簡單，只有過去和現在兩者，現在包含了將來；因此英語的時態語尾比較法國西班牙等語言簡單。近代英語所具有的其他詞類，在古英語中差不多都齊全，而用法與今天有同有異。在重要的當代語言中，古英語與德語最相像，因爲兩種同屬日耳曼語的兩支。

我們且以名詞爲例來窺看一下古英語的複雜結構。古英語名詞的性別有陽（masculine）陰（feminine）中（neuter）三種，與德語相同，比法語多了一種，但今天已消失於無形了。它的文法數目有單數和多數，與現代英語相同。遠古的日耳曼語言，名詞本有單、多和双（dual）三種文法數目，和古典希臘語一樣；動詞也會隨着作這三種數目的變化。可是在不列顛島上，英語的名詞與動詞再也沒有双數了。古英語的代名詞上還遺留着這數目：我們兩人是 *wit*，你們兩人是 *git*。

古英語名詞的格有四，拉丁式文法稱之爲主格（nominative）、屬格（genitive）、予格（dative）、賓格（accusative），各格的詞形多

不相同，而同一格別的單數與多數詞形也互異。以 hound 的前身 *hūnd* 爲例，衆格的形貌是這樣的：

	主	屬	予	賓
單	hūnd	hūndes	hūnde	hūnd
多	hūndas	hūnda	hūndum	hūndas

在八個詞形中都出現的 *hūnd* 含着這個名詞的幹（stem），格的意思存在這裏，後面的尾部是衆格差異所在，叫做格尾（case ending）。格尾的變化這麼多，比較像拉丁希臘等古語，而與現代英語大異其趣。今天 hound 字只有三個寫法（hound, hounds, hound's）與兩個讀法（[haund, haundz]），原因是古英語 *hūnd* 字格尾上的元音 e,a, u 後來都漸漸弱化而終於消失，鼻音 m 也消失了，只餘 s，於是格尾變成只是有無 s（[z]）之別。這 s 除了是單數屬格的格尾 （書寫時加上個 apostrophe 符號），又給推廣成爲多數各格的共同格尾，而終於成了數目而不是格別的表徵。值得注意的是，古英語的名詞原本並無單純表徵數目的詞尾。當格尾這樣接近完全消滅時，英語就轉而倚靠前置詞來幫助達意，屬格主要靠 of，予格靠 to ⑥。

　　古英語的名詞，同種類的格尾相同，不同種類的相異。上段的 *hūnd* 屬於數量最多的一種。下面再列舉數種，以說明今天的所謂"不規則名詞"的由來：

	foot	ox	dēer
單主	fōt	oxa	dēor
屬	fōtes	oxan	dēores
予	fēt	oxan	dēore
賓	fōt	oxan	dēor

多主	fēt	oxan	dēor
屬	fōta	oxena	dēora
予	fōtum	oxum	dēorum
賓	fēt	oxan	dēor

比較他們的單數與多數主格，就可知道為什麼今天 foot 的多數詞形是 feet，ox 的多數是 oxen，而 deer 的多數仍是 deer ⑦。這幾種名詞從前為數頗夥，尤其是像 oxa 那種格尾變化較少的"弱名詞"；可是後來它們漸漸模仿 *hūnd* 那種數衆勢大的種類而作了類比變化（analogical change），終致 *hūnd* 的模式成了規律，名詞都以 s 來表徵多數。

可是名詞的格是什麼東西？有什麼用處？格是印歐語名詞、代名詞和形容詞的一種性質，是印歐語言結構的基本要項。它的一項最主要功用是表達名詞在句中的地位，這也就是拉丁文法給諸格命名的原因。名詞若是句中主詞，就用主格（如說 The hounds bite）；若有主從或衍生關係，就用屬格(The hounds' teeth)；若是句中動詞的間接受詞，就用予格(Give meat to the hounds)；若是直接受詞，就用賓格(Feed the hounds)。現代英語中 hounds 這個字的各格詞形相同，只是屬格多了一個 ' 符號而已；在古英語中，我們在前段曾列出，這些詞形依次是 *hūndas，hūnda, hūndum, hūndas*。

格的用處並不止於此。古代印歐語言，屬、予、賓各格都有兩三樣到八九樣功用。它們的一樣重要功用是作副詞。需要說動作的時間空間時，古語常用時空名詞的某格別來表達。如果要表達行動的時空延袤(duration 和 extent)，多是用賓格；古英語如此，所以今天英語還可以說 The meeting lasted the whole morning 或者 He runs two miles daily，而不須加 for。要表達行動發生之時（所

謂 time　when)，多用予格；若是說發生於某時之內 (time within)，則用屬格。英語的予格副詞很少遺留下來，屬格副詞則相反，今天還用得很多，不僅止於說時間。比如店舖寫着 Open Evenings，這 evenings 中的 s 並非多數的表徵，而是個缺少了' 符號的單數屬格詞尾⑧。我們說 go upstairs 或者 play outdoors，同樣是以名詞的單數屬格做副詞，而並非因為走上許多道樓梯或者在多重門戶外遊戲之故。如果要表達必然或必要性，英語除了可以用形容詞衍生的副詞 necessarily，也可以用名詞屬格 of　necessity 或者 needs（其實是 need's）。廿世紀中葉前的文字裏常可見到 must needs 或 needs　must 兩字連用，令我國學生惶惑不已；較齊備的字典會說明 needs 是個副詞，是名詞 need 的屬格。

　　像其他印歐古語一樣，古英語名詞的屬、予、賓每一格都可作某些動詞的直接受詞。這即是說，動詞的直接受詞並不一定要用賓格，也可能用屬或予。今天許多英語動詞的唯一受詞之前會有個 of 或者 to——如 approve of, listen to, admit of, admit to——就是這個緣故。古語的動詞常藉受詞的不同格別來表達不同的意思；說"聽"的動詞中，希臘的 *akouein* 和拉丁的 *audire* 都會隨着受詞的不同格別而有"聽見""聽信"乃至"使用名字"的意思；古英語的 *gehieran* 也差不多。今天的 hear 是 *gehieran* 的後身，雖然使用予格的"聽信"之意歸了 listen to，它還有使用賓格的"聽見"和使用屬格的"贊同、首肯"之意（如說 They won't hear of that，"這個他們不答應"）。現代英語的動詞常能與不同的前置詞連用而有不同的意思，這個複雜問題與從前受詞的格別問題是一脈相承的。

　　形容詞的受詞同樣可能用予格或屬格，不一定用賓格。常用的 similar，受詞須用予格，所以它總是與 to 連用，比如說 A is similar to B。它的前身是拉丁的 *similis*，這字的受詞是不能用賓格的。與 similar 相似的 like 字又如何？在 A is like B 這樣一句話裏，受詞

B 是什麼格別？《牛津大字典》說 like 的受詞是予格，因爲它的前身 OE *gelic* 的受詞用予格。不過，予格若沒有前置詞 to 來幫助表徵，在現代英語中與賓格無從分辨。過去，like 與 similar 一樣，常與 to 連用。遲至十九世紀，詩人雪萊在悲劇 *Cenci* 中還有 Sweet sleep, were death <u>like to</u> thee 之句。

㈢中古英語與英語詞彙

英語史上，古英語之後的時期叫做中古英語(Middle English，簡稱 ME)。英語這回變質，也有個政治原因，那就是在 1066 年時，由於英國的皇室出了繼承問題，歐陸上諾曼第地方的大公爵威廉(William, Duke of Normandy)以親屬身分渡海前來爭位，他統率的諾曼人(Normans)於一場惡戰中把英國貴族推舉爲君主的哈羅德(Harold)射死，繼而收拾了英國的山河。時爲十一世紀中葉，但鑑於語言變化遲緩，學術界多以世紀的終結來劃分古英語與中古英語。

諾曼人滅了英國 (史稱 the Norman Conquest)給英語造成怎麼樣的變化呢？

一方面是英語結構的簡化進程因而加速。諾曼統治者來到英國，說的是一種法語方言，叫做諾曼法語(Norman French)。諾曼人本是日耳曼蠻族南下的一支，來自丹麥和斯堪的納維亞半島一帶——Norman 即是 Norseman 或 Northman——在故鄉講日耳曼北支的語言，來到原屬羅馬帝國的諾曼第時，就如建立法國的日耳曼部族法蘭克人(Franks)一樣，丟棄了母語而在本地學了一口從拉丁語演變成的法語方言。由於法語與日耳曼語差異頗大，諾曼人登陸英國時，就不如早時直接從北歐來到的丹麥與挪威人那麼容易與英人溝通。但英人這時已淪爲奴僕，勢不能不與主人來往；加以英語又已沒有一個政權和文學傳統來維持規矩，於是就加速簡化。

複雜的語言結構久而久之都會簡化，英語的簡化過程在古英語時期便已開始，但五七百年間變化不大；在中古英語的三四百年內，英語卻變得與前大不相同。十一世紀末的英語，今天的英國人讀起來有如讀一種外國語，與讀德語同樣困難；但是十四世紀末的英語，如喬叟《坎特伯雷故事集》(Chaucer, *Canterbury Tales*) 中的英語，英人今天一讀就會覺得這是英語，只不過非常古老和艱澀而已。在這三百年間，英語的許多日耳曼結構特色都淡化而趨於消失。形容詞的兩類變化劃一起來了，格別消失了，數目也不分了。名詞的格別基本上也消失了，而分辨數目的詞尾出現了。在動詞方面，雖然日耳曼特有的強動詞至今尚存，但數目已大爲減少；弱動詞的幾類也劃一起來而成爲動詞的楷模了；而動詞的人身和數目詞尾，在過去式中劃一了，在現在式中也幾乎劃一了。

另一方面，英語的詞彙成分起了劇變。古英語的詞彙，九成以上是盎格魯撒克遜人固有的詞語，所餘不到一成則來自北歐那些所謂維京人(Vikings)說的日耳曼語（與古英語很相近）、土著的塞爾特語(許多是地名)、和拉丁(因爲拉丁商賈與條頓部族早有交易)。諾曼人到來統治英國，雖然民間仍使用英語，宮廷和政府卻用法語；等到這個諾曼英廷失去了諾曼第並與歐陸斷了連繫，英政府改以英語爲國語之時，英語中就摻進巨量的法語詞。這些法語詞具有統治階層的特色，它們主要出現在政治、軍事、法律，以及精緻文化的範圍裏。現在英美的政治詞語，源自法國的極多，如 people, nation, country, state, govern, parliament, crown, reign, sovereign, realm 等基本詞語都是；封建制度中除了 king, gueen, lord, lady 是英語固有，其他 feudal, fief, vassal, noble, royal 以及 prince, duke, marquis, viscount, baron 諸爵位，都是法語。軍事上的 war, peace, arms, assault, banner, battle, siege, soldier, troop, army, navy 以及軍階 corporal, ensign, sergeant, lieutenant, captain, colonel, admiral 等也都是法語。法律上的法國語詞，有 court, crime, defendant, plaintiff, plea, plead, sue, suit, accuse, attorney, judge, justice, injury, penalty, property, heir 等。說到精緻文化，宗教上的許多語詞，如 religion, saviour, trinity, clergy, friar, preach, pray, sermon, conscience, duty, grace, mercy, cruel, charity, chastity 等，都是法語提供的。在文學、藝術、建築各方面，法語詞比比皆是。小說《薩克遜刼後英雄略》（*Ivanhoe*）中有個下人指出，畜牲在牧養之時都以英語呼喚：ox, cow, calf, swine, sheep, deer；等到宰殺來享用時，肉類的名稱卻是法語：beef, veal, pork, bacon, mutton, venison。烹飪詞語也以法語為主：fry, boil, broil, roast, stew。英文和法文字典裏，許多字是全同或者十分相像的。

現代英語詞彙中外來字的主要來源是法語，其次便要數拉丁和希臘語了。希臘和羅馬是西方文明的源頭，十四世紀的文藝復興運動使千多年來被忽視的古典學術重新受到重視，希臘和拉丁語文也就進入歐洲各國的學校，再從學校來到社會上。拉丁是法語的祖先，英語中許多拉丁系統的語詞和詞素究竟是直接來自拉丁，抑來自法語，或來自拉丁的其他後裔如意大利或西班牙語，是很難確定的；但無論如何，拉丁系統的語言在英語詞彙中的分量，與日耳曼語言對抗是綽綽有餘。英語中許多意思都可以隨意選用日耳曼字或拉丁字來表達，分別不大；譬如 god 與 deity，ghost 與 spirit，end 與 terminal，oversee 與 supervise。在日常生活的範圍，日耳曼詞彙是英語的主體，但隨着智識水準升高，拉丁的比重增加，終於凌駕其上。英國人愛用樸實的日耳曼基本名詞，如 sun, moon, son and daughter, tree, stone, fight，可是與這些名詞相應的形容詞卻多是以拉丁詞幹構成的，如 solar, lunar, filial, arboreal, lapidary, pugnacious 或 belligerent。又如名詞"火"是英語固有的 fire，動詞

"生火"卻是拉丁的 ignite；"法律"是古英語傳下來的 law，"立法"卻是拉丁的 legislate。

希臘語詞除了一小部分早被拉丁吸納而循拉丁途徑進入之外，其餘進入英語字彙的主要途徑是學術。當英國人在文藝復興之後學習閱讀希臘的哲學、歷史學、悲劇和史詩時，希臘字自然就會從柏拉圖、希羅多德、索伏克里斯、和荷馬的書頁上來到英語裏。今天，在哲學範圍內，philosophy 固然是個希臘字，metaphysics, ontology, teleology, epistemology 等無不是希臘字。在文學上，詩歌方面的 poetry, epic, rhythm, ode, iambic 等是希臘字，戲劇方面的 drama, tragedy, comedy, chorus, theater 也是希臘字，連 scene 這個短短的字也源於希臘。上段說到拉丁字供應英語許多形容詞，希臘字也派這種用場。說到戰爭，拉丁供給了 bellicose，希臘供給的是 polemical，用在言語文字的爭戰上；說到石頭，拉丁的 *lapis* 貢獻了 lapidary，希臘的 *lithos* 也貢獻好些 litho-(如 lithograph)和 -lithic(如 neolithic)字。

沒有活人使用的語言叫做死語言，依這定義，希臘和拉丁已經死了，因為今天意大利人已不使用拉丁，希臘人也不用古典希臘語。可是由於文藝復興以來歐洲各國都以希臘文和拉丁文為學術語文，希臘和拉丁語詞繼續流通在各國學術界，它們的詞素更為歐洲現代學術製造新語詞。生物學上的物種都有個拉丁學名，新發現的物種仍循此例得到學術名稱。化學上的元素亦然，像金和鐵的元素符號之所以是 Au 和 Fe，是因為它們的拉丁名字是 *aurum* 和 *ferrum*；氫叫 hydrogen，因為它是"水素"，水的希臘名是 *hydor*；氦(helium)是十九世紀方才以光譜方法從太陽上先發現到的，它絕不是希臘人想得到的東西，卻用希臘文的太陽 *helios* 來命名。這樣，儘管在日常生活上已經死滅，然而在學術上得到了一種奇異的新生命的古典希臘和拉丁語文，叫做"新拉丁"(New Latin，簡寫 NL)。它寄生在現

代語文裏，英文字典收着許多它的字。拉丁文的乳汁是 *lac*，現代科技上與乳汁有關係或相似的物質和概念，以它的詞幹 lact- 來構詞的有 lactam, lactase, lactate, lacteal, lactescent, lactic, lactiferous, lactobacillus, lactoflavin, lactogenic, lactometer, lactone, lactoprene, lactoprotein, lactose 等，這裏頭許多東西都不是羅馬人見過的。

英美學者習慣以一種英語讀音來讀這些新拉丁詞語。在老年科醫學中，gerontology 的兩個 g 都讀成 [dʒ]，不是古典希臘的 [g]。心理學 psychology 的第一音節讀成 [saɪ] 不是 [psy,psü]。

㈣現代英語與語音變動

英語史的最後時期是現代英語(Modern English，簡稱 ModE 或 MnE；又叫 New English, NE)，它的起點是 A.D.1500。有些人主張在十八世紀再劃一道界線把現代英語分出前後期，理由是早年和近年的現代英語之間仍有頗為明顯的差異。早年的作家如斯賓塞(E. Spenser)和莎士比亞，他們的文字今人讀來頗覺陌生，因為除了詞義古舊之外，他們還會分辨 *thou* 和 you (你、您)，他們的動詞較少用輔助動詞和進行式，假設語氣卻用得很強，又有一些於今已廢的詞，如 *methinks* 和 *me seems* (我覺得)，*hight* (名叫) 等等。後來的作家，不論是狄更斯、珍奧斯汀，甚至更早的約翰孫博士和費爾丁，今天讀來都比較自然。

英語進入現代時期，文法結構的改變漸漸塵埃落定，語音上卻還起了一陣劇烈騷動。學者發現，在前後兩百年間，英語的元音紛紛移動了一番。不過在敍述這場語音史上罕見的變動之前，我們可以先把英語語音過去的變化簡略地說一下。

英語史上繁多的音變可以分為結構性的與非結構性的兩大類。結構性的音變，是英語文法的特色，英語的一些詞類是藉此而變化

的；例如單數的 man 變爲多數的 men，名詞 brood 變爲動詞 breed。非結構性的音變則不然，儘管它們的一些結果影響英語文法結構極大，但這類音變並不是有意識的行爲。

非結構性的音變又可再分爲脫落與變換兩類。脫落是指語音的消失，變換是指語音的替代。這兩者都可能發生在語詞的頭部、中部、或尾部。

語音在尾部脫落，叫做 apocope。尾部脫落了元音、輔音、或者兩者構成的整個音節，在英語史上是極普通的事；因爲英語的重音照例落在語詞根上，詞尾讀得輕，尾上的音會自然而然地弱化而終於消失。尾上語音失去，詞尾便會簡化；我們看見像 *hūnd* 這樣的典型名詞在現代英語中變成除了單數屬格外其他格別都無從分辨。古英語的形容詞也有格別，且有強弱兩套變化，但今天只剩下一個詞形；動詞除了第三人身單數現在式之外，今天已無人身的詞尾變化了。現代英語雖仍然算是個"屈折語言"(inflected language)，但與從前相比，已顯得非常簡單，其轉變的主因就是尾部語音脫落。由於詞尾變化少了，英語於是使用代名詞、助動詞和前置詞來補足詞意，用得比古典語言多得多。這樣，它的綜合度減低而分析度增加，整體就日漸遠離希臘拉丁的陣營，而與我們的漢語越來越相像了。

有些奇怪的字，也是由尾部失音造成的。英文字尾上的 gh，是中古英語時期開始採用的拼寫法，古英文只用 h 來代表，讀音原是 [x]（像德人 *Bach* 或 *Fichte* 名字中的 ch），這個 gh 今天倘不是變了 [f]（如 laugh 或 rough），就是失落了（如 high 或 through；而 thought 和 light 等字只有 t 音在尾上）。另外，現代英語中一些極普通的字是由失去了尾上的 n 而成的，例如數目字 a 與人身代名詞 my 和 *thy*，它們在古英語中原是 *an*、*min*、*þin*。這些字末尾的 n 有點兒藕斷絲連的味道，a 有時須是 an（如 an apple），而 my 和 *thy* 在謂語的位置須作 mine 和 *thine*（the apple is mine）。有些時候，

這個尾 n 會落下而連接在一些名詞起始的元音上；莎翁《李爾王》劇中的傻瓜不住叫李爾做 nuncle，那是 uncle 頭上加 n 而成的⑨。另一方面，有些字開首的 n 也因為這種含混不清的情況而失去。現代英語的毒蛇 adder 相當於德語的 *Nadder*，它在古英語和中古英語的前身也都有 n；圍裙 apron 來自古法文 *naperon*，十六世紀的英文還有 *naperon* 和 *napron* 的寫法；橙子 orange 頭上也應有 n，因為它在波斯、阿拉伯、希臘、以及西班牙、意大利語中都有個頭 n。

語詞頭部失音叫做 aphesis。在英語語詞頭部很少發生整個音節的失落⑩，因為英語的重音多落在開頭的音節上，重讀的音節是不會失落的。但是雙輔音的組合若出現在語詞頭上，第一個輔音就可能失去。古英語中不少字是以 hl,hn,hr,hm 開頭的，後來失去 h 音，中古英文也就不再寫出 h 來；今天的 loaf,nut,ring 等字便是這樣來的，what 與 why 等字從前都是 hw 開頭，今雖亦可讀 ［hw-］，但讀 ［w-］ 更為普遍。古史詩中英雄人物 Hrothgar 和 Hrothulf 威風凜凜的大名，演變成今天的 Roger 和 Ralph。現代英文有些 gn- 和 kn- 字，前者如 gnat, gnarl, gnaw，後者如 knave, knee, knight，字頭上的 g 和 k 都失了音，但由於失音在拼寫定型之後，所以在文字上還寫出來。單憑讀音，現代人分不出 knave 和 nave，或者 night 和 knight。英人讀古典拉丁希臘文或者新拉丁時，也是把詞頭的雙輔音簡化，psychiatry 的開首只讀 ［s］，xenophobia 讀 ［z］，pterodactyl 讀 ［t］。

語詞中部失音叫做 syncope。英語有個把長字縮短的習慣，縮短的方法往往是把讀得輕的音略去；例如 history 或 factory 常讀成少了元音 o 而只剩下兩個音節，laboratory 也會失去一個甚至兩個 o，而剩下四甚至三個音節。這縮短習慣在人名和地名上表現尤為突出，如人名 Nicholas 可縮成 Nick，Richard 成 Rick 或 Dick，William 成 Will 或 Bill，他們的後人姓氏可以是 Nicholson,Richardson, Williamson，也可以是 Nixon, Dixon, Wilson。姓氏中，Maugham [mɔːm] 和 Vaughan [vɔːn] 只剩下一個音節，Marjoribanks 剩兩個，Cholmondeley 更有乾脆改寫爲 Chomley 的。地名 Alwalton 原本是 *Aethelwoldingtun*，Alvingham 源於 *Eanwulfingaham*。（怎麼會有這樣長的地名？原來古時條頓好漢喜歡以猛獸自況，尤其樂用豺狼之名，如 *Beowulf, Cynewulf, Hrothulf* 等，*Eanwulf* 便是個這樣的名字；詞尾 -ing 即是子孫，略如日後的 -son；-inga 是 -ing 的多數屬格：*Eanwulfingaham* 便是 Home of the Eanwulfsons，"埃安烏夫子孫聚居地"之意。*Cynewulf* 的後人聚居之處，今天有 Kilvington 或 Killingholme 等有趣的名字。）

有些音特別容易在中部消失。人名和地名中的 h 和 w 便是例子，像 Bonham 或 Chatham 裏的 h，和 Bromwich 或 Greenwich 裏的 w，都是沒有音的。（因此"格林威治天文台"的名字不大妥當，"格林尼治"是較好的音譯）。古英語的音素 /f/ 在語詞中段——這時讀 [v] 或 [w]——也會消失，今天 have 的第三身單數是 has，過去式是 had，都是這種音變的結果。又如 head 在古英文中是 *heafod*，lord 是 *hlaford*，都有這個音素。古今相較，head 勝在簡單，不過，如果我們記得古里穆輔音轉換規律（Grimm's Law），*heafod* 馬上讓我們看出英語和拉丁的"頭"（*caput*）是同源的。同樣，*hlaford* 雖較 lord 冗長，但它的詞形稍加分析——*hlaford* < *hlaf* + *weard*，即如今天說 loaf ward 或 bread keeper——就顯示出這"主人"的語意來源是"（一家子的）麵包保管人"，十分有趣。演變爲 lady 的 *hlafdige*，原意是"麵包搓製人"。

其次講語音的變換替代。英語的輔音在古英語時期已有過一些重要的變換，如 [sk] 變成 [ʃ]，一部份的 [k] 移前變爲 [tʃ]。[ʃ] 在古英文裏寫作 sc，如 *sceap*（羊）、*scip*（舟）、*fisc*（魚）；中古英文改拼作 sh，乃有今天的 sheep、ship、fish。[tʃ] 在古英文裏寫作

c，如 *cese*（酪）、*cild*（兒童）、*cirice*（教堂）；這種 c 後來改寫爲 ch，這些字於是成了 cheese、child、church。到了中古和現代英語的時期，由於英文書寫已漸漸定型，輔音變換後不能把拼寫也作相應的改變，於是文字與讀音常有差異。例如無數的-tion 和-tial 字都沒有 ［t］而有 ［ʃ］，azure 或 pleasure 有 ［ʒ］而沒有 ［z］或 ［s］，就是例子。

元音的變換，從原始印歐語到原始日耳曼語再到古英語，有一段頗繁複的歷史，我們在此不必細述。自從古英語有記錄以來，直至中古英語末期，英語的元音一般都算穩定。少數的變動，如古英語的/a/變成/o/，/y/在不同地區變成/e/、/i/、/u/，由於變動發生在英文拼寫尚未固定之時，新的語音就有新的拼法來代表，於是也不致爲後世製造文字與語音間的混亂⑪。可是到了中古英語的末葉，當文字拼寫已漸次定型後，英語元音所起的一番大規模騷動就造成一片混亂了。這場騷亂叫做"元音大變動"（The Great Vowel Shift，那是 O. Jespersen 所創的稱謂），它發生在十六世紀前後百餘二百年間，在這時期英語元音活像一盤棋子受到震盪，先後紛紛易位。下面的草圖代表一般歐洲現代語言元音在口腔中前後高低的位置，這些也就是英語元音在這番騷動前的位置：

前　i,(y)　u　後
　　e　　　o
　　(æ)　　a

在元音變動時，英語舊有的長 i 一步步變成今天的複元音 ［aɪ］⑫（例如 file 讀［faɪl］），長 u 同樣地變成複元音 ［aʊ］（OE *fūl* 變成的 foul 讀 ［faʊl］）；低一層，長 e 向上移成爲 ［i:］（feed 是 ［fi:d］），長 o 也向上移而成 ［u:］（food 是 ［fu:d］）⑬；再低一層，長 a 先移前再

移向上，成爲複元音 [eɪ]（face 是 [feɪs]）。總言之，長的元音每一個都大大地改變了，共同的趨勢是向上移和複音化。短元音在這時期卻變得不多，e、i、o 事實上可說沒有變，a 和 u 則有時變，有時不變，而即使變動，其情形也有異於長元音。在大變動之前，英語長短元音只有長短之別，音質是一樣的；大變動後就不同了，出現了下面這些典型的長短音質差異：

a-:	grave/gravity	nation/national	[eɪ]/ [æ]
e-:	heal/health	redeem/redemption	[i:]/ [e]
i-:	write/written	revise/revision	[aɪ]/ [ɪ]
o-:	lose/loss	goose/gosling	[u:]/ [ɔ]
	host/hostile	verbose/verbosity	[ou]/ [ɔ]
u-:	profound/profundity	redound/redundant	[au]/ [ʌ]

這系列的長短元音差異，雖然很突出，爲別種語言所無，但是仍然遠遠未能繪出元音大變動的全貌，更未能充分反映英語元音紊亂的實況。以a來說，它今天除了 [eɪ] 和 [æ] 之外，還有許多別的讀音，試看bar,car,par; bare,care,pare; ball,call,pall; ward,wash, watch 這幾組字，可知 a 是很受前後方某些輔音的影響的。此外，英語元音更會發生一些伸長、縮短、升高、降低、合併等變化，發生時又沒有多少規律性，學者有時須引用方言的影響來說明。例如 ou 的讀音很多，雖說它有幾個來源，但若不引用語音的伸縮升降和合併等等觀念便無法解釋。現代英語的元音是個十分麻煩的問題，絕不是三言兩語說得清楚的。

最後講到結構性的元音變動。像其他日耳曼語言一樣，古英語會變動元音來分辨文法上的種類。我們都知道 man 的多數詞形是men，老派的文法書把它歸入"不規則名詞"類中。其實 man/men 的

變化是有規則的；對照著前段的元音位置圖，我們可以看見從 a 變為 e 是向口腔前方移動。他如 foot/feet 或 goose/geese 的數目變動，也是以元音移前來達成；louse 和 mouse（OE　*lūs,*　*mūs*）變成 lice 和 mice（OE　*lȳs,*　*mȳs*）也是元音前移。元音這種"前移變異"（front mutation）也叫做"i/j 變異"（i/j mutation, Umlaut），因為它的起因是古日耳曼語中帶著 i 或 j 的詞尾：尾上有 i 或 j 這種前方元音或半元音，詞根上的後元音 a、o、u 就會因應移前變為前元音。像 men、feet、lice 等字的祖先，在史前古語中都曾有帶 i 的詞尾，只是後來消失了而已。英語形容詞的比較級，從前的詞尾也帶 i，所以從 old 會生出 elder 和 eldest——older 和 oldest 只是後來依照類比原則規律化的詞形。longer 也是類比產物而已，long 的比較級應當是 *lenger*；喬叟的確是寫 *lenger* 的。從 long 生出的抽象名詞"長短"是 length，元音移前了，因為詞尾-th 在遠古時本是 *ipu*。這詞尾也使 strong 生出 strength，以及 foul（<OE *fūl*）生出 filth（<OE *fȳlþ*）。古時從名詞或形容詞產生動詞，用的詞尾是-jan，其中的 j 又是會引致詞根上的後元音向前移的；因此有 blood/bleed、food/feed 以及 full/fill 等出現元音變異的相關字。看了這些例，舉一反三，當可明白為什麼說元音前移是古英語構詞的主要法則。

　　強動詞（所謂"不規則動詞"）如 sing/sang/sung 等等的系列中也有元音變動，這種叫做遞換（gradation, Ablaut），它的性質與"i/j 變異"有別，元音並不是向前移，而且也不能在鄰近語音中找到起因。元音遞換是範圍遍及所有印歐語言的一種語音變化，它與遠古語音的高低和強弱似乎都有關係。學者以它為研究語源的利器，對它的本質仍在積極探討之中。至於英語的強動詞，乍看之下好像類別繁多，可是藉著印歐語元音對應與遞換研究之助，我們今天已能把它們歸併為六七種，而且找到它們共同的級數遞換模式。

㈤代表英語的文字

前面四節講的範圍都是英語，現在我們講講代表英語的文字。

英文的礎石是一套拼音字母。這套字母不是英國人的創製，是往日羅馬人使用來記錄他們的拉丁語的，所以叫做拉丁字母。羅馬人也不能僭冒發明之功，他們只不過借用了希臘字母而酌予增刪修訂而已。希臘字母脫胎於閃族人(Semites)的文字，由於第一個字母叫做 alpha，第二個叫做 beta，全套也就叫做 alphabet。後來拉丁字母乃至其他字母，都叫做 alphabet。希臘字母共廿四個，初時只有大寫，小寫是稍後的產物。字母可以左右反轉來寫，因爲希人初時仿效閃族，行文從右到左，後來才改爲從左到右——中間還有過叫做"牛耕田式"(boustrophedon)的行文方法，那就是向左和向右逐行交替而行，這種方法常可在古碑上見到。

拉丁字母與希臘字母頗爲相似：如果把 U 和 V 分開來計算，拉丁字母也正好是廿四個，其中過半數保存著希臘的原貌。在兩套字母不對應的地方，希臘有三個吐氣音(aspirates, θ、ϕ、x)，一個雙輔音 ψ [ps]，兩個長元音 η（長 E）和 Ω（長 O）；拉丁有 F 和 H，並以 Y、U、V 三個字母來對應希臘的 upsilon（大寫 γ，小寫 υ），以 C、K、Q 對應希臘的 k。拉丁新字母的重複對應，給日後歐洲文字製造些麻煩。

今天，拉丁字母流行全球各地，不但西歐和南北美各國風從，別處的非印歐語言也會採用來拼音——這叫做"拉丁化"(Latinization)或"羅馬化"(Romanization)。但它並沒有達到壟斷的地步，且不言回教與佛教地區各有字母，即使在歐洲來說，希臘至今堅執著本國固有的字母，而俄國等斯拉夫語國家也使用一套接近希臘的西里爾字母（Cyrillic，據說是九世紀僧人 St. Cyril 所創）。不同系統的字母可以依照語音來換寫(transliterate)；比方希臘女神

AθHNA 可用拉丁字母換寫爲 *ATHENA*，俄國河流 *BO$_{HT}$A* 可寫成
VOLGA。若不另加說明，換寫就是以拉丁字母來寫。換寫的一大好
處是便利，因爲依這原理只用一種字母便可寫出多種文字。英美許
多英文字典在說明語詞來源時都會把希臘、斯拉夫、甚至非印歐語
言的字用拉丁字母寫出來。不過，換寫的方法有時並不一致，使別
種語文的字形有出入⑭。

在英國使用拉丁字母之前，條頓古代的巫師爲了作法時故弄玄
虛，曾參考拉丁希臘文字而創製了一套字母，名叫 runes（意謂"秘
密文字"）。這套日耳曼字母在北歐各國有幾種大同小異的字體，以
在英國發現的一種來說，爲首的六個字母的形狀是：

$$\text{ᚠᚢᚦᚨᚱᚲ}$$

這六字可換寫成 F、U、TH、A（或 O）、R、C，因此整套字母也叫
做 futharc 或 futhorc。英國最古老的一些紀錄是以這種文字刻寫
的。等到天主教會到來傳教，僧人用拉丁字母把聖經譯成古英文，
又把口傳的古英語文學用拉丁字母記錄下來，漸漸拉丁字母就風靡
全英，取代了日耳曼字母。

可是廿四個拉丁字母不敷英語之用。早年天主教士譯寫古英文
時，爲了標示 /θ/ 和 /w/，曾經借用日耳曼字母 Þ（叫做 *Thorn*）和
Ƿ（*Wynn*）；其後由兩個 V 合成的新字母 W 出場，Ƿ 就退役了；Þ
則一直使用到中古英語時期，才終於由雙文字母 TH 取代。雙文字母
（digraph）是標音的新術，它不需製造新字母而能標示更多的語音：
普通字母連接時標示的是字母個別的音連接起來（如 tree 中的
tr），但雙文字母標示的並不是字母個別原有的音，而是另一個單音
（如 thee 中的 th）。現代英文拼音的材料就是廿六個字母和一些雙
文字母⑮，其中 CH、SH、TH 所代表的都是單一字母以外的語音。

理想的拼音文字，應當是每個語音都只有一個字母代表，而每個字母也只代表一個語音。缺少這一對一的關係，語音與文字間出現混亂，這種文字就叫做不合語音學原則(unphonetic)。現代英文正是這樣的文字，它的讀音混亂得很。它的 ou 有六七種不同讀法；另一方面，[aɪ] 又有 i、ie、y、ye 以及較少見到的 ae、ai、ay、ei、ey、ui、uy 等拼法。數百年來要求文字改革之聲不絕於耳，本世紀蕭伯納且在遺囑中撥款辦理這件事⑯。

英文讀音混亂的原因很多。上節所說英語語音的種種變動當然是個主因；音變若發生在文字書寫漸趨固定之後，必然會使文字的讀音違反規則，元音大變動是個突出的例子。但字母的沿革也是個重要原因。英文字母中 C 和 G 素稱麻煩，以下我們就以它們兩者以及有關的雙文字母 CH 和 GH 爲例，具體說說文字與語音都有所改變時所造成的後果。

首先，拉丁字母 C 和 G 都是把希臘的第三個字母 Γ 修改而成。羅馬人丟開 Γ 的直線字形而把一個曲線字形修改成 C，先是讓它同時既代表希臘 K 的 [k] 又代表 Γ 的 [g]；後來才又把 C 加多筆劃成爲 G 來代表 [g]，讓 C 只代表 [k]。這樣做，雖然使 C 不致同時代表 [k] 與 [g] 兩音，免了一種混淆，可是仍讓 C 重複 K 的功能，任由兩個字母代表同一個 [k] 音。自此以後，C 與 K 的混同一直在使用拉丁字母的語文中爲患，如人名 Carl 即是 Karl，Catharine 的一些變體卻是用 K 拼寫的，吐火羅語是 *Tocharian* 和 *Tokharian*，塞爾特語是 *Celtic* 和 *Keltic*，日耳曼字母 *futhorc* 也即是 *futhork*，等等，等等。從前拉丁文倒沒有這種煩惱，因爲它的字母 K 是備而不用的。拉丁文字典的 K 部近乎空白；連希臘人名中的 K 也給拉丁換寫成 C，例如蘇格拉底和德謨克利圖原是 *Sokratēs* 和 *Dēmokritos*，經過拉丁換寫，在今天的英文資料裏變成 Socrates 和 Democritus。古英文跟隨拉丁，只用 C 不用 K；今天的 book、back、king，從前是 *bōc*、 *bæc*、*cyng*(*cyning*)。現代英文是 C 和 K 都使用，原則上是在元音之前寫 C，元音之後寫 K 或 CK，視乎元音長短而定；像 cook、cloak 和 cock、clock 就是典型的寫法。只是例外也很多，為了語音問題有時元音前須用 K，如 king、keel 等字便是；而數不清的-ic 字都在元音後寫 C，不寫 CK。

其次，C 和 G 原本代表的 [k] 和 [g] 是上顎後方軟顎的塞音 (velar stops)，這些語音在一些語言中較穩定，在另一些語言的某些歷史時期內，若遇到前元音 [e] 和 [i] 等，就會移前變成上顎前方的硬顎音(palatals)，這叫做硬顎化或前顎化(palatalization)。但前顎化的情形與結果不一，在對於英語大有影響的一種法語方言裏，拉丁的 C 前顎化時，先從 [k] 變為 [ts]，再變為 [s]：這就是英語中所謂"軟 C"的來源。因此，現代英文裏，後元音 a、o、u 之前的 C 都仍然是 [k]，如 cat、cot、cut 或 cake、cool、cow；前元音 e 和 i 之前的 C 則前顎化而讀 [s]，如 cede、accept、cite、city。reciprocal 中的兩 C 一是 [s] 一是 [k]，原因亦可在元音中找到。G 音方面，前顎化同樣產生出"軟 G"，在英語中是 [dʒ]。現代英文中的 G 在 a、o、u 前也仍是硬的 [g]，如 gash、gosh、gush 或 game、good、gown；軟的 [dʒ] 音只會出現在 e 和 i 之前，如 genius、George、gigantic、gist。有時，由於是外來字或別的原因，e 和 i 前的顎音仍是後顎性的，這時 [k] 就會改用 K 來拼寫，如 kite、kitchen、keel、kerchief；[g]就或者用歐式的雙文字母 GH 和 GU，如 ghetto、gherkin 和 guide、guilt、distinguish，或者仍用 G，如 gear、get、give，任由它與 gel 或 gin 中的軟 G 混淆不可分辨。

[k] 的前顎化還有一種情形是產生 [tʃ]。古英語發生過這種音變，古英文的 *cild*、*cese*、*cirice* 等字中的 C 都讀 [tʃ]。法國和別的拉丁國家也有類似的音變，而且早已用雙文字母 CH 來標示這個語音；從中古英語時期開始，英文也效法而行，把 *cild*、*cese*、*cirice* 等

字重拼，終於有今天的 child、cheese、church 等。

可是雙文字母 CH 另有傳統。希臘有三個不吐氣的唇、齒、顎音字母 Π、Τ、Κ，拉丁文換寫為 P、T、C（絕少用 K）；希臘另有三個與它們平行的吐氣字母 φ、θ、Χ，拉丁文換寫為 PH、TH、CH。這雙文字母 CH 代表的語音，在古典希臘語中是［kʰ］，約莫就是英語的［k］，因為英語的這個語音也是強烈吐氣的；後來它在希臘語演變成［x］，仍是顎音，但不是塞音(stop)而是擦音(fricative)。英語由於沒有這個音，就仍用往日的［k］來讀它。所以英語中來自希臘的字，CH 是讀［k］的，如 chord、mechanic、stomach。

總結來說，英文中 C 代表的語音原本是［k］，遇到後元音 a、o、u 時並不改變，仍舊讀［k］；遇到前元音 e 和 i 時就會前顎化而讀［s］。因為別的緣故在 e 和 i 前仍有［k］音的英文字，都會用 K 來拼寫，不致混淆。G 代表的［g］遇到 a、o、u 時也不改變，仍舊讀［g］；遇到 e 和 i 時就會前顎化而讀［dʒ］。可是因他故而在 e 和 i 前仍有［g］音的英文字，除了少數是改用 GH 或 GU 拼寫之外，大多數仍然只用 G 拼寫，於是造成相當的混淆。［k］在英國本土和南歐一些地方前顎化時變為［tʃ］，在文字上以雙文字母 CH 來代表；可是 CH 同時又代表希臘字母 Χ 的［k］。GH 在字頭代表［g］，但在中間和尾上卻代表古英語［x］（古英文用 H 代表）的後身，那就是或者讀［f］（如 tough），或者不讀音（如 though）。

標音的文字，到頭來會影響語音。許多人根據文字的拼寫來讀語詞，讀出並非語詞原有的音來，這叫做 spelling pronunciation。C 和 G 兩字母供給了一個好注腳。當英人看見 C 和 G 帶著 e、i 或 y 時，很自然就要用［s］和［dʒ］來讀，並不理會這個字有沒有前顎化的歷史。字典告訴我們，同一個詞，Keltic 只有［k］一種讀法，Celtic 則有［s］和［k］兩種，而且［s］的更通行，所以中譯是"塞爾特"。羅馬文豪 Cicero 的兩個 C 應該讀［k］，因為那時拉丁文沒

有前顎化，但在英語中唸成［s］，中文也譯爲"西塞羅"；史詩《奧德賽》中把人變豬的女妖，由於拉丁傳統把她換寫成 Circe，英語也就用［s］來唸那兩個 C，其實這名字換寫成 Kirkē 更正確。英語中那些源自希臘的 cy-和 gy-字讀出軟的 C 和 G 音更沒道理，因爲古希臘的［k］和［g］音都沒有前顎化的現象，而這些字的 Y 是換寫希臘的 υ（upsilon），那個元音即使在英語或法語中也不會引起前顎化。英文裏面"婦科"及其他與婦女有關的字，頭一個音節就在軟硬 G 之間搖擺，［gaɪ-］呢？［dʒaɪ-］呢？［dʒɪ-］呢？希臘的"女"字 γυνή 若不換寫成傳統的 gynē，而換寫成學術上通行的 gunē，就不會有這毫無道理的猶豫了。

註　釋

① 　印歐語族至今已發現有十系語言，依次爲：
　　㈠吐火羅（Tokharian）：新疆發現的兩種西域中古語。
　　㈡印度伊朗（Indo-Iranian）：印度和伊朗的許多古今語言。
　　㈢安那托利（Anatolian）：赫梯（Hittite）等古語。
　　㈣亞美尼亞（Armenian）：現代亞美尼亞語和一些古語。
　　㈤波羅的斯拉夫（Balto-Slavic）：波羅的海濱和中東歐斯拉夫國家的古今語。
　　㈥希臘（Hellenic）：希臘古今的方言與共同語。
　　㈦阿爾巴尼亞（Albanian）：現代阿爾巴尼亞語及一些古語。
　　㈧意大利（Italic）：拉丁等古語及其後裔意法西與羅馬尼亞等現代語。
　　㈨塞爾特（Celtic）：愛爾蘭和不列顛系統的古今語言。
　　㈩日耳曼（Germanic）：英國和西北歐多個國家的古今語言。
　十系之中，吐火羅和安那托利是最晚近的發現。

過去學者曾把這語族分為東西兩派，東派最初只有印度和伊朗的語言，其餘從斯拉夫到日耳曼都歸入西派。後來有人提出以"百"字的顎音 k 有無變成 s 為衡量尺度，把上列中的㈡㈣㈤㈦編入東派，並以古伊朗的百字為名，稱之為 *satem* 語言；把㈥㈧㈨㈩編入西派，以拉丁的百字命名，稱之為 *centum* 語言。及至㈠和㈢的研究顯示流行在新疆和土耳其的這兩系東方語言卻是 *centum* 語之時，學界了解到地域與語言的劃分殊難一致，漸漸對分派也不那麼重視了。

②　這是希臘語音的一種規律性改變。在"太陽"、"兒子"、"站立"等常用基本字上頭，別的印歐語言都以 s 開始，希臘語都以 h（亦即字母上的吐氣符號 c）。

③　德語的這些音變是古里穆氏第二套聲律的內容。

④　判斷印歐語言中的同源字時，完全相同的語音反不如規律性的差異有份量。語音全同，學者就要猜疑那是後來輸入的借字(loanword)。比如英語中的 dental，由於它的詞幹與拉丁詞幹完全相同，並無音變，學者即使沒有別的資料印證，也會憑語音斷定它是個借字，不是英語固有的字。

⑤　印歐語族的古語中，形容詞與名詞的詞形變化相近，兩者最初原屬同一詞類。

⑥　英語的前置詞 to 和 of 與法語的 *à* 和 *de* 很相像，也很有關係：to 和 *à* 的受詞都是予格，而本身也成了予格的表徵，那些規定要予格的動詞多與之連用；of 和 *de* 則同樣起類似的屬格作用。《牛津大字典》(*The Oxford English Dictionary*，簡稱 *OED*) 中 of 和 to 兩字之下有詳細說明。

⑦　古英語中的 *fōt* 的元音是長的，後來用兩個 o 來拼寫；*fēt* 的 ē 也同樣改為 ee。*oxa* 的 a 弱化後脫落了，只剩 ox；*oxan* 的 a 弱化成為 ə，寫作 e，於是有 oxen。deer 原不是鹿而是野獸，相當於德語的 *Tier*，希臘的 thēr。

⑧　這個副詞 evenings 等於德文的副詞 *abends*。德文在這裏不會混淆了單數屬格與多數主格，前者是 *Abends*，後者是 *Abende*。

⑨　從 *min uncle* 變為 *my nuncle*。這脫落和黏附的道理也能解釋為什麼人名 Edward 會生出小名 Ned——從 min Ed 變為 my Ned——以及 Oliver、Ann、Ellen 或 Helen 為什麼叫做 Noll、Nan(Nannie、Nancy)、Nell。

⑩　古英語中有些詞首(prefixes)作輕讀，如 a-、ge- 等，後來都消失了。ge-

變弱後，在中古英文中常以 y-或 i-的面貌出現在動詞的過去分詞頭上。

⑪ 比如古英語的/a/後來上升成/o/，於是 OE *lang* 生出 ME *long*，這 long 字至今沒有麻煩。/y/的變化也只是產生了一些有趣的字而已，如標準英語的 busy（＜OE *bysig*）是採了 u 地區的拼法和 i 地區的語音而唸［ˊbɪzɪ:］。喬叟(Chaucer)在《坎特布雷故事集》中寫 bisy。

⑫ 我們採用一般字典所用的簡法來代表複元音。

⑬ 中古英語的長 e 和長 o 各有兩種，嘴唇開閉程度不同。我們把問題簡化了，只講閉式的 ē 和 ō。

⑭ 以希臘文的換寫為例，說到"心理學"等詞的字源，ψυχή 時，Webster、Funk & Wagnalls、Random House 各系列的字典都換寫為 psyché，而 American Heritage 和牛津的 *Dictionary of English Etymology* 卻換寫為 psukhḗ。按 psukhe 是比較語言學上通行的寫法，它的優點是對應準確；但 psyche 是傳統寫法，羅馬時代已開始使用，而且早已變成了拉丁文和英文的一部份。

⑮ 英文也有幾個三文字母，如 TCH(catch)、DGE(judge)、QUE(critique)，但沒有標出單雙文字母以外的音。

⑯ 他講的一個笑話是把 fish 寫成 ghoti。(參考 laugh、women、action 的讀音)。

［附錄二］
詞根與詞幹

孫述宇

一

　　坊間許多教英文的書本，尤其是那些教導學習英文生字以求在托福及其他考試中獲取高分的書籍，都教人如何分析英文字。這些書本差不多都眾口一詞地說，英文字的構成可以這樣分析：

（零至多個）字首＋（一至多個）字根＋（零至多個）字尾

不知道有沒有別的書本並非如此分析；如果有，恐怕也不易為一般人接受。

　　這樣的分析方法，在字首（prefix）和字尾（suffix）方面大致是站得住的。（當然，在 suffix “後綴”之後還有叫做“詞尾”ending 或 termination 的部份，這暫且不論）。但語詞中間的基礎部份不應當是詞根（root），而是詞幹（stem）。若以為這部份是詞根（或字根），而不知其為詞幹，即是不明白根與幹的性質；如此，就不能對語詞結構作妥當的分析。

　　早兩個世紀，受過良好教育的歐洲人一般尚未有詞幹的觀念，他們只說詞根。例如十八世紀在英國政界舉足輕重的徹斯特菲德爵爺（Lord Chesterfield）寫了許多信教導他兒子小菲立，在第十八封信裡他說，若要學習古典語文，應該注意字首與字根，以期事半功倍。他心目中的根是那些基本字；比方他說 *fero* 是其他十六個字的根（“the root of sixteen others”）。他的意思是說，在 *fero* 之前加

- 651 -

上各字首，就會生出 *aufero*、*affero*、*confero*、*defero*、*infero*……等字
——相當於英文字 confer、defer、infer、以及 prefer、refer、transfer
等等。①

這道理大致並沒有錯；他兒子聽了一定得到學習的方便。今天
一般教分析英文字的中文書籍大致亦如此分析，以為語詞除去詞首
詞尾就是詞根了。這樣教，未嘗沒有用處；幾十年來，想必已不知
有多少人以這方法學了許多字。不過，這樣的認識是現代語言學興
起前的認識，它對語詞的分析還不甚到家。

<h1 style="text-align:center">二</h1>

在現代語言學的觀念裡，印歐語言的動詞、名詞和形容詞，其
結構除去前綴（prefix）、後綴（suffix）、詞尾（ending）後，所餘
中間那個收容著基本語意的基礎部份，就是詞幹（stem）。這部份從
前不是稱為根的嗎？現在為什麼學界要改稱之為幹呢？因為學者發
現它內裡還包含著一個更根本的實體，他們把根的名字保留給這實
體。舉個例說，拉丁動詞 "照耀" *lucere*（為了排印方便，本文不使
用辨別元音長短的符號），名詞 "光" *lux*：由於 *lux* 的語音是
/luks/，*lucere* 是 /lukere/，學者判斷兩字所共有的 /luk/（luc）當是
羅馬人心目中具有不甚明確的光亮之意的詞根。這根加上元音 i 就
構成名詞的幹，這幹會衍生 *lux*、*lucem*、*lucis* 等等不同格別的詞形，
而名詞 "光" 的意思也在這時才完全形成；另一方面，這根加上元
音 e 又構成動詞的幹 luce-，這幹配上各種詞尾，就生出不定式
lucere 以及各人稱各時態各語態各情狀的詞形，而動詞 "照耀" 的
意思也至此方才具足。名詞幹 luc(i)和動詞幹 luc(e)上的 i 和 e，叫做
"幹元音"（stem vowel 或 thematic vowel），它們有決定詞形變化
模式的作用，所以語詞會依它們來分類而叫做 "i 類名詞" 或 "e 幹

動詞"等等。幹元音在詞幹與後綴結合時會發生音變；說詞幹時，有時也把幹元音略去不提。

　　詞根是不能再分析的單元。一般說來，詞根比詞幹短小。有少數的詞幹與詞根毫無分別；但在大多數的情形，詞幹總是比詞根長些，因為根的元音可能在幹上伸長，而幹在根的後方多半會有個幹元音，其後還會有顯示語詞性質的後綴。

　　我們且以英文抽象名詞 lucidity 做個例來說明。這個詞末尾的-(i)ty 是個構成抽象名詞的常見後綴，那麼前面的 lucid 是詞根嗎？有些書本說是的。我們若知道 lucid 本身是個形容詞，又存在於動詞 elucidate 與形容詞 pellucid 之內，也就容易以為這是個根了。其實不然。按 lucidity 相等於拉丁文 *luciditas*，它末尾的-tas 是構成抽象名詞的後綴，詞幹是-tat(i)-，可構成各種格別的詞形（tas, tatis, tati, tatem, tate 等）；-tas 之前是形容詞 *lucidus*（即是英文字 lucid 的本源）的詞幹 lucid(i)，這形容詞有個常見的顯示形容詞性質的後綴-ido（也出現在英文字 candid、fervid、rapid、splendid、stupid 所由來的拉丁本字上）；除去這後綴，詞根 luc-就露面了。這個根，是拉丁形容詞 *lucidus*、與上面說到的動詞 *lucere* 和名詞 *lux* 所共有的。

　　倘以為 lucid 就是根了，我們只看得到 lucid、lucidity、pellucid、pellucidity 和 elucidate、elucidation 等字在意義上有共同的來源；但若知道根是 luc-，就更可看見上述這些字與 lucent、translucent、translucency 等字也是同源的。（lucent 是動詞 *lucere* 的現在分詞 *lucens* 所生，*lucens* 的幹是 lucent-。）

　　我們若不憚煩去翻查典籍，還會知道詞根 luc 另有帶後綴-smen 與-stro 等的語形；那麼從拉丁文 *lumen* 以及 *lustrum* 生出的許多英文字，諸如 luminous、illuminate 和 luster、lustrious、illustrous、illustrate 等，我們也明白是與 lucid 等字同源的。

再進一步，知道拉丁根 luc- 的祖先是原始印歐語的詞根 leuk-，我們就更知道從古英語下來的英文字 light 也是個同源詞。（leuk-加上後綴-to，生出古英語的詞 *leoht*。）

三

一些中文書籍把拉丁動詞的幾條詞幹，誤認做幾條詞根。其實一個語詞是不會有多過一條詞根的，因爲詞根就是詞義根本的所在，當動詞的詞形依著人稱和數目以及時態和語態等等而變動時，它的根本意義仍然不會變。偶見的例外是一些叫做"詞形拼合"（suppletion）的情形，如英文動詞 go 採取 *wend* 的過去式 went。②反過來，單一的詞根衍生出許多個語詞，卻是屢見不鮮。

印歐詞根 sta-（"固立不移"之意）是個突出的例子，我們可以拿它來說明一些語詞衍生的問題。英文字產生於這個詞根的，從 stand 和 stud，到 stance 和 constant，到 state 和 statue，到 rest 和 insist，到 constituent 和 prostitution，到 ecstasy 和 system，不知凡幾。

我們且看看這根如何能夠生出這許許多多的字來。拉丁是當今英語字彙的最大來源，在拉丁那邊，sta-首先產生了三個重要的動詞。第一個是加上幹元音 a 而成的自動詞 *stare*，意思是"固立不動"。第二個是以複音的方法（reduplication），在根的前方加上一個音節 si-而構成的 e 幹動詞 *sistere*，它既是表達"站立"的自動詞，又是表達"豎立、放置"的他動詞。第三個是含有"建立、斷定"等意思的他動詞 *statuere*，這詞也許是 *stare* 和 *sistere* 所共有的過去分詞詞幹 stat-構成的，這是拉丁語構造加強（intensive）或重複（iterative 或 frequentative）動詞的方法；但也可能是這共同分詞所生出的名詞"地點" *status* 所構成。這一列三個動詞各自都產生

一大堆英文字。

第一個 *stare*，經過語音變化，成了英文字 stay。*stare* 的現在式詞幹 sta-構成現在分詞 *stans*，它的詞幹是 stant-，中性多數的詞形是 *stantia*，經過音變就生出 *stanza* 和 *stance*。把動詞 *stare* 加上前綴 circum-、con-、in-、或 re-，一批新動詞就生出來了，它們雖然只給了英語一個動詞 rest（來自拉丁 *restare*），但它們的現在分詞卻供應了 circumstance、constance、constant、instance、instant 等字。除了現在式詞幹之外，過去分詞詞幹 stat-也是造詞能手，它在英文字彙中的產品有 status、state、station、stationary、statistic、stature 等等。

第二個 *sistere*，在加上前綴 con-、de-、in-、per-、re-等等之後，形成新的一批動詞 *consistere*、*desistere*……等，這些就是英文動詞 consist、desist、insist……的前身。它們的現在分詞詞幹是 consistent-、insistent-……等，英文的形容詞和抽象名詞 consistent、consistency……就是從這裡來的。所有這些字都直接間接與 "屹立" 或 "建置" 有語意上的關係；值得注意的是，這意思的根本是存在於末尾不顯眼的兩字母 st 之中。

第三個 *statuere*，現在式詞幹是 statu(e)-，過去分詞詞幹是 statut-，那便是英文 statute 和 statutory 的來源。這個動詞同樣能夠與前綴構合而製出新動詞，這時它的根元音 a 變成 i，如 *constituere*、*destituere*、*instituere*……便是。這些新動詞的過去分詞造成的英文字比較多，從它們的詞幹 constitut-、destitut-……生出的英文動詞就是 constitute、institute……；加上後綴-ion，就有抽象名詞 constitution、institution……；再加上形容詞後綴-al（即是拉丁的-alis），就有形容詞 constitutional、institutional……。（institute 和 prostitute 既是動詞，又是名詞③；destitute 則只是個形容詞，不是動詞，儘管英文有個抽象名詞 destitution。） 從這些拉丁動詞

的現在分詞處，英文似乎只得到了 constituent 和 constituency。

　　還有一些帶著詞根 sta- 的英文字是源自拉丁文，但不是直接從上述動詞來的。例如 stable，不論是名詞或形容詞，都來自拉丁──分別源於 *stabulum* 和 *stabilis*。從這形容詞又生出 stability 、establish 等字。

　　英文另有一些 sta- 字是希臘那邊來的，如醫學上的 stasis。還有 static，雖然看似拉丁，但其實與反義詞 dynamic 都是希臘詞，只不過使用了拉丁的拼寫法，以字母 c 代替了 k 而已。ecstasy 也是。

　　此外，從日耳曼語那邊，這個詞根也生出一批英文字。從古英語傳下來的字中，最常見的是動詞 stand，其次是相關的名詞 stead（以及 instead）和 stud。（這裡頭牽涉到根元音的替換。）語源學者說 stow 和 stool 也包含著這個詞根。另外的一批字是 stale、stall、steel、still 等，字義都與 "固立不移" 有關係，學界有人認為它們來自另一詞根 stel-，但也有人認為它們還是 sta- 生出來的。

四

　　上節說過，除非是拼合詞（suppletive），否則一個語詞是不會有多過一條詞根的。但是一個語詞可以有不只一條詞幹。拉丁動詞都有幾條詞幹，它們的現在式詞幹和分詞詞幹都是英語構詞的常用材料，由此而來的英語語詞因此會意義相關而形音卻有出入。

　　在上節的敍述中已可見到這種情形。比方動詞 *stare* 的現在式詞幹是 sta-，現在分詞詞幹是 stant-，過去分詞詞幹是 stat-：現在式詞幹所產生的 stay，在元音之後就沒有什麼輔音；現在分詞所產生的 stance 或 constant，在 a 後都會有輔音 n；過去分詞所產生的 status 或 state，在 a 後都會有 t。

　　拉丁 *manere* 是 "停留、居住" 的意思，過去分詞是 *mansum*。

這動詞加上前綴 re-就產生了英語的 remain；加上 im-、per-等所形成的新動詞，其現在分詞就是英語中 immanent、permanent 等字的來源。由於這些字所採用的是 *manere* 的現在式詞幹 man(e)-，所以它們的字形在 man 之後都沒有別的輔音。但由過去分詞的詞幹 mans-所生的字"居所"mansion，在 man 之後就有 s。

拉丁動詞 *mittere* 的過去分詞是 *missum*。這詞的現在式詞幹加上各種前綴，就生出英文的 admit、commit、emit、intermit、transmit 等字。我們一般有個印象，以為把動詞加上後綴-tion 就可以構成抽象名詞了④；但 admit、commit 等字的抽象名詞並非 admition、commition……，而是 admission、commission……。原因當然是 *mittere* 的過去分詞詞幹是 miss-，上面有 ss 而沒有 t。

有些詞幹的差異更大。如"打碎"的現在不定式是 *frangere*，詞幹是 frang-；過去分詞是 *fractum*，詞幹是 fract-；兩者差別大，有些書本竟以為由這兩個詞幹所生出的英文字——前者是 frangible、fragile、fragment，後者是 fraction、fracture——分屬不同的詞根。這裡頭當然有一些語音變動。fract-除了那具有過去分詞特色的 t 音外，它的 c 與現在式詞幹中的 g 是相當的，兩者同為後顎塞音，只是有聲無聲之別而已。這情形就如"做"字 *agere* 一樣，它的現在式詞幹是 ag(e)- （生出了 agenda、agent 那些字），過去分詞詞幹是 act- （生出了 act、action、actual 那些字）。這樣的拉丁動詞為數頗多，如"觸" *tangere* 和 *frangere* 很相似，它的現在式詞幹 tang-生出英文的 tangent、tangible、contingent 等字，過去分詞詞幹 tact-生出英文的 tact、tactile、contact、intact 等。也許 *frangere* 和 *tangere* 的現在式詞幹中那個多出來的鼻音 n 讓我們疑惑了，但這樣的一個"鼻音中綴"（nasal infix）或鼻音化現象（nasalization）是印歐語言裡很平常的事。英語本身的動詞中，think／thought 和 stand／stood 也有這樣的情形。⑤

英文的 intelligence 和 intellect 是兩個指涉不盡相同而意義相近似的字，它們其實都來自拉丁動詞 *intellegere*，這詞的現在分詞詞幹是 intellegent- 或 intelligent-，過去分詞詞幹是 intellect-。把 *intellegere* 的前綴 intel（即 inter-）去掉，所餘的 *legere* 有閱讀的意思，於是一方面從它的現在式詞幹 leg- 生出 legible、illegible 這些字，另一方面從過去分詞詞幹 lect- 又生出 lectern、lector、lecture 這些字。

五

一詞多幹的問題出在動詞那邊。名詞與形容詞沒有這種問題，它們只有一條詞幹；但它們的詞幹會稍有隱藏而不盡露出。所謂隱而不露，是說在這些語詞的主格（nominative case）上頭我們看不見詞幹的全貌。原因是音變：主格的詞尾（case ending）和詞幹末端的音合併而起變化，有時又有脫落。由於主格的詞形就是字典辭書列出的詞形，也是一般提及這語詞時所舉的詞形，因此我們常會一時看不出或想不起詞幹的真貌。這樣，對語詞衍生的關係就會有誤會或茫然不知。

比方說，有些字典會很簡單地告訴我們說，generic 源於拉丁名詞 *genus*。這是對的。事實上，這兩個字與 gene、genetics、generate、regenerative、general、generous 等字，都有血緣，大家都來自一個有"生長"含義的詞根 gen-。可是，在語音上言之，為什麼 *genus* 這樣的一個拉丁字會生出 generic、general、generate 這樣的字呢？這些字尾巴上的 -ic、-al、-ate 都是常見的後綴，當然各有來歷，可是大家共有的中部音節 -er- 從何得來？為了回答這類很合理的疑問，較完備的字典在說字源時會把詞幹說出。比方在說 generic 時，它們最少也會告訴我們，這詞來自 *genus*，而 *genus* 的詞幹是

gener-；不然的話，就是把 *genus* 和它的衍生格 *generis* 同時列出⑥，讓我們看見詞幹 gener-。

詞幹往往比主格詞形還要長。例如"人"的主格是 *homo*，但詞幹是 homin-，所以會衍生出 hominid、hominoid、hominization 這樣的字。我們看見西洋算命的星座上"女子"是 *virgo*，它的詞幹是 virgin-，所以英語有 virgin 這個字。戲劇是 drama，爲什麼它的形容詞是 dramatic？在後綴-ic 之前的齒音 t 從何而來？原來 *drama* 是個希臘語詞，它的幹是 dramat-。我們若發現從名詞衍生的新語詞，除了前後綴之外尚會比原來名詞多了一兩個語音的話，差不多都可肯定，這些語音是原來名詞的幹上固有的。

爲什麼哲人柏拉圖的形容詞是 Platonic，比 Plato 多了個 n 呢？因爲柏拉圖的名字詞幹末端有這個鼻音。在希臘原文裡，柏拉圖的名字主格已是有鼻音的 *Platon*，斜格也都有這鼻音（*Platonos* 等等）；沒有鼻音的 *Plato* 只是羅馬人的唸法和拉丁文的寫法。英文後來都採取了拉丁方法而稱他爲 Plato。⑦拉丁文愛把詞幹末端的 n 從主格中略去，例如那些-ion 字，它們的拉丁文主格都只到-io 爲止："國家"是 *natio*，"道理"是 *ratio*，"談話"是 *conversatio*，緊隨其後的 n 要在斜格中方才出現。

名詞的主格不但會比詞幹短小，而且會有語音變動。上面已經提到，*homo* 的幹其實是 homin-，*virgo* 的幹是 virgin-。拉丁"名字"是 *nomen*（與古英語的 *nama* 同源），詞幹是 nomin-，所以英語會有 nominate "提名"和 nominal "名義上的"這樣的字；同理，"胃"是 abdomen，但形容詞"胃的"卻是 abdominal。有些字變得更多，如希臘神話中背負大地的巨靈名叫 *Atlas*，詞幹是 Atlant-，大西洋和亞特蘭大等地名都是由此而來的。希臘女人是 *gune*（與英文的 queen 同源），詞幹是 gunaik-，傳統上換寫成拉丁字母 gynaec-，所以婦科是 gyn(a)ecology，女權政治是 gyn(a)ecocracy；男人是

aner，但詞幹是 andr-，所以男性激素是 androgen，而 androgyny 就是植物學上的雌雄同體，以及近年女性主義的非男非女或既男又女的單性。

　　詞幹的存活率比主格高，在後代的語文裡我們常見到詞幹而非主格。譬如拉丁那些以-io 終結的詞，在今天的法、西、英語中都是-ion。拉丁的 "兵士" 是 *miles*，詞幹是 milit-；今天英文字 military、militate 等都顯示這個詞幹，而 *miles* 只見之於男人的名字 Miles。拉丁文裡，山是 *mons*，詞幹是 mont-；死亡是 *mors*，mort-；牛奶是 *lac*，lact-；腳是 *pes*，ped-：在今天的法文裡，這幾個字依序是 *mont*，*mort*，*lait*，*pied*。

註　釋

① 　徹斯特菲德伯爵（Earl of Chesterfield，正名 Philip Stanhope）在文學史上有個惡名，因為文壇祭酒約翰孫（Samuel Johnson）微時曾求助於他，不獲垂青，待編出大字典震動士林時，徹氏為文稱道，約翰孫忿然報之以那封有名的 "我用不著你賞識" 的信。徹氏寫了許多信給他的私生子小菲立，很用心教導他如何獲致成功，教導的特色是重才能重表現而不重道德。（約翰孫看到這些書信出版後，嗤之為教導 "婊子的德性和舞蹈師父的儀態"。）

　　但徹氏是個有本領的人，當政要多年，同時頗有才學。他給兒子的信排滿數百頁現代的書頁，許多是他任國務卿時期公餘之筆，大抵一晚就寫一封，洋洋灑灑，滿紙拉丁詩句似乎都是記誦的。他對語言文字的認識應當很足以代表他的時代。

② 　"是" 字也是拼合的，它的詞形有來自詞根 es-（am、is 以及古時的 *sind*）、詞根 bhu-（be、been）、詞根 wes-（was、were），而 are 更有可能來自另一個根 er-。

　　形容詞的比較級也有拼的情形，例如 good、better、best。這種情形在

- 660 -

拉丁、希臘等古語中更多。

③ 這是因為拉丁文那邊已有由過去分詞詞幹造成的名詞 *institutum*（行為、規矩）和 *prostituta*（妓女）。*prostituta* 是在 *prostituere* 的過去分詞詞幹 prostitut-加上陰性詞尾 a 而成，前綴 pro-是"在前"，*prostituere* 是"置之在前"，*prostituta* 便是"置（身）（門）前的女性"，那當然就不是良家婦女。

destitut-並沒有在英文產生一個通行的動詞。這詞幹在拉丁那邊已產生了一個形容詞，英文把那形容詞承受了。

④ 構成抽象名詞的拉丁後綴原只是-io（詞幹是-ion-），但由於經常出現在過去分詞的詞幹之後，經常都跟隨著 t，羅馬人後來自己也糊塗了，於是有-tio（詞幹是-tion-）這種後綴誕生。

⑤ 拉丁 *frangere* 和英語的 break 同源，都來自原始印歐詞根的 bhreg-，（印歐的 bh 演變成為英語的 b 和拉丁的 f，比如 bher-生出英語的 bear 和拉丁的 *ferre*），但拉丁的 *frangere* 多了個鼻音中綴。另一方面，拉丁 *stare* 與英語 stand 同源，但這回卻是英語的詞有鼻音。

鼻音中綴很容易脫落。*frangere* 中的 n，不僅在過去分詞 *fractum* 中脫落了，在現在式詞幹所生的形容詞 *fragilis*（產生英語的 fragile）中也脫落了。

⑥ 名詞與形容詞的幹在差不多所有的斜格（oblique cases，指主格以外的賓、屬/衍生、予、奪等等格別。有譯為"間接格"，似乎不妥）之中都出現。大抵由於在傳統上衍生格是列在主格之後的第二格，所以文法書和字典都喜歡列出這個格別來顯示詞幹的形狀。有些解說語詞結構的書籍以為衍生格在新詞的形成上特別重要，這可能是一種誤會。衍生格的詞形由詞幹與衍生格尾合成，衍生格尾在新詞的構成上並無作用，要緊的只是詞幹而已。

⑦ 但英國文學之父喬叟既寫 Plato，又寫 Platon。他也把 Cato 依希臘習慣寫成 Caton 和 Catoun。

［附錄三］
英文常用字尾一覽表

一、下列字尾共分名詞、形容詞、動詞、副詞字尾四大類，各類均
　　按字母順序排列。分列於同一條目中的字尾，拼法如有不同，
　　則按使用頻率排列，常用者先列，較少用者列置於後。

二、「字尾」欄右上角標有＊記號者，表示該字尾組成的單字一般
　　較偏難，讀者略微參考即可。

三、「字源」欄中各縮寫字母與其代表語言列出如下，以供參考：

　　OE. = Old English 古英語　　　　　　**L.** = Latin　拉丁語
　　ME. = Middle English　中古英語　　　**F.** = French　法語
　　Gk. = Greek　希臘語

四、「例字」欄中列出例字，盡量以常用重要字彙為主，但有部分
　　較為偏難，乃原字尾偏難所致。

A. 名詞字尾

(1) 表示「人」、「動作者」的名詞字尾

字尾	字源	例　　　　　字	意義用法解說
1. **-ain**	F.	captain 隊長、船長 villain 壞人、惡棍 chaplain 禮拜堂牧師	
2. **-aire**	F.	millionaire 百萬富翁 billionaire 億萬富翁	
3. **-an**	L.	German 德國人	用以表示種族或籍貫

字尾	字源	例　　字	意義用法解說
-ian	L.	barbarian 野蠻人	
-ese	F.	Chinese 中國人	

4. **-ant**	L./F.	applicant 申請人	①也可表示「劑」、「
-ent	L./F.	component 組成要素	器物」等意義
		、成分	②-and, end的形態極少
-and	L./F.	detergent 清潔劑	見，多用於數學名詞
-end	L./F.	multiplicand 被乘數	
		dividend 紅利、被除數	

5. **-ary**	L.	secretary 秘書、書記	
		contemporary 同一時代	
		的人	
		adversary 敵手、對手	

6. **-ate**	L.	advocate 鼓吹者、倡導	
		者	
		candidate 候選人	
		magnate 要人、巨擘、	
		大企業家	

7. **-ee**	F.	employee 雇員	①表示動作的承受者或
		nominee 被提名者	受影響者，與-er反義
		referee 裁判、調解人	②重音絕多在 -ee 上

8. **-eer**	F.	engineer 工程師	①表示「從事…的人」
		pioneer 拓荒者、先鋒	②重音在 -eer 上
		volunteer 志願者	

9. **-er**	ME.	manufacturer 製造人、	也可表示器物
		製造商	
-or	ME.	container 容器、貨櫃	
-ar	ME.	dictator 獨裁者	
-ier	F.	donor 捐贈人	
-eur	F.	burglar 竊盜	
		premier 首相、總理	

字尾	字源	例　　　　字	意義用法解說
		connoisseur 行家、鑑賞家	
10. -ess	F.	actress 女演員 empress 女皇帝 hostess 女主人、女服務員	表示女性
11. -ician	F.	electrician 電氣工、電氣技師 musician 音樂家 physician 內科醫生	①表示「精通之人、能手」的意思 ②多加於以 -ic 或 -y 結尾的名詞上
12. -ist	Gk.	typist 打字員 antagonist 敵手、對手 dogmatist 武斷的人	表示相信某學說的人，或致力於某學科、熟練掌握技術的人
13. -ite	Gk./L.	cosmopolite 四海為家的人 Israelite 以色列人	表示和某團體有關的人
14. -ive	F.	native 土著、本地人 captive 俘虜 fugitive 逃亡者、亡命者	原係形容詞字尾、引申而成名詞字尾
15. -man 　　-sman	OE. OE.	chairman 主席 statesman 政治家 stuntsman 特技表演者	
16. -on	L.	champion 冠軍、鬥士、擁護者 companion 同伴 patron 贊助人、顧客	
17. -ster	ME.	minister 大臣、牧師	

字尾	字源	例　　字	意義用法解說

spinster 老處女、紡織
女工
gangster 強盜集團分子

(2) 表示抽象名詞的字尾

字尾	字源	例　　字	意義用法解說
1. -ace	L.	menace 恐嚇、威脅 grimace 痛苦表情 solace 安慰、慰藉	
2. -ad -ade	Gk. Gk./F.	tetrad 四個(成一組) decade 十年 blockade 封鎖 ambuscade 埋伏 tirade 長篇大論、激 烈演說	①部分與數字有關 ②有時可兼作動詞，如 例字 ambuscade 與 blockade 即是
3. -age	F.	shrinkage 縮小、減少 passage 通過、通道 foliage 樹葉(集合名詞)	表示行爲結果或總稱
4. -al	L.	proposal 提議、求婚 betrayal 背叛 disposal 處理、解決	表示動作或行爲
5. -ance -ancy -ence -ency	L./F. L./F. L./F. L./F.	hindrance 阻礙 forbearance 節制、寬容 constancy 不變、堅貞 resilience 彈性、彈力 tendency 傾向	表示性質或動作
6. -cy	L.	intimacy 親近、交情 advocacy 提倡、鼓吹 bankruptcy 破產	①表示狀態或職務 ②多加於以 -ate 或 -t 結 尾的名詞、動詞、形 容詞上

字尾	字源	例　　　字	意義用法解說
7. **-dom**	OE.	freedom 自由 wisdom 智慧 martyrdom 殉道、殉難	①表示狀態、等級、領土 ②多加於名詞、形容詞上
8. **-hood**	OE.	childhood 幼少、幼年時期 livelihood 生活、生計 likelihood 希望、可能	表示年紀、狀況、親屬關係
9. **-ia**	Gk./L.	mania 瘋狂、狂熱 militia 自衛隊、國民軍 hydrophobia 恐水症	多表示疾病
10. **-ic** 　　**-ics**	Gk. L.	logic 邏輯 magic 魔術、魔力 physics 物理學 aerobatics 特技飛行術	表示學術、技術
11. **-ice** 　　**-ise**	F. F.	avarice 貪婪 caprice 善變、反覆無常 treatise 論述、論文	
12. **-ing**	OE.	ageing 上年紀 clothing 衣服(集合名詞) casing 箱、套、框子	①表示總稱或具體意義 ②多加於名詞、動詞上
13. **-ion**	L.	opinion 意見 diffusion 散佈、蔓延 assertion 主張、斷言 designation 指名、命名	①表示動作及其過程 ②加於動詞之後 ③以 -sion, -tion, -ation 三種形態最爲常見

字尾	字源	例　　　字	意義用法解說
14. **-ism**	Gk.	criticism 批評 exoticism 異國情趣 antagonism 敵對、反對 communism 共產主義	①表示制度、主義、行 　為、狀態 ②加於名詞、形容詞上
15. **-itude**	L.	aptitude 適當性、傾向 rectitude 正直、正確 fortitude 剛毅、不屈 　　　不撓	①表示度量或情況 ②加於形容詞之後
16. **-ity**	L.	brevity 簡短 curiosity 好奇心、稀 　　　奇 elasticity 彈性、伸縮 　　　力	加於形容詞之後，使成 抽象名詞
17. **-ment**	L.	instrument 儀器 fulfillment 實踐、達成 filament 細絲、細線	①表示行為、行為結果 　、工具等 ②加於動詞上
18. **-mony**	L.	harmony 和諧 ceremony 儀式 testimony 證言、宣誓	
19. **-ness**	OE.	friendliness 友善、友 　　　好 abrasiveness 摩擦 adhesiveness 黏性	①表示狀態 ②加於形容詞或分詞上
20. **-o(u)r**	L.	behavio(u)r 行為 ardo(u)r 熱心、熱切 endeavo(u)r 努力、盡力	-or 為美式拼法，-our 為英式拼法
21. **-ry** 　　**-ery**	F. F.	bravery 英勇、美好 treasury 寶藏、國庫	①表示行為、技術、性 　質、總稱、地點等意義

字尾	字源	例　　　　字	意義用法解說
		artistry 藝術才能 machinery 機器(集合 名詞)	②加於名詞、動詞、形 容詞上
22. **-ship**	OE.	relationship 關係 fellowship 交情、共處 workmanship 手藝、技 巧	①表示狀態、性質、職 務、技術等意義 ②加於名詞之後
23. **-th**	OE.	warmth 熱、熱情 breadth 寬、寬度 width 濶、廣博	①表示情況或性質 ②加於動詞、形容詞上
24. **-ty**	L.	cruelty 殘酷 penalty 處罰 bounty 慷慨、賞金	①表示性質或狀態 ②加於形容詞上
25. **-ure**	F.	seizure 捕獲、扣押 disclosure 發覺、暴露 expenditure 開支、經 費	①表示行為及其結果 ②加於動詞或字根上
26. **-y**	L.	modesty 謙遜、樸素 assembly 會議、組合 analogy 類似、相似	①表示狀態 ②加於動詞、名詞、形 容詞之後

(3) 表示「小」的名詞字尾

字尾	字源	例　　　　字	意義用法解說
1. **-cle**	F.	miracle 奇蹟 particle 分子、粒子 speckle 小斑點	表示個體、個別的意義
2. **-cule**	L.	minuscule 小字 molecule 分子 granule 小粒、顆粒	

字尾	字源	例 字	意義用法解說
3. **-el** **-le**	F. ME.	vessel 船隻 model 模型 pebble 小鵝卵石 riddle 謎	
4. **-en** **-in**	OE. OE.	kitten 小貓 maiden 少女 bulletin 公告、告示	
5. **-et** **-ette**	F. F.	cabinet 小櫃子、會 　　議室 banquet 宴會 islet 小島 gazette 公報、報紙	
6. **-ie** **-y**	ME. 	birdie 小鳥 kitty 小貓 pony 小馬	常用於人名的暱稱，如 Sammy, Bobbie, Ronnie 等均是
7. **-kin**	ME.	napkin 餐巾 manikin 侏儒 cannikin 小杯子、小 　　罐子	
8. **-let**	F.	leaflet 小葉子 pamphlet 小冊子 hamlet 小村落	
9. **-ling**	OE.	underling 部下、下屬 seedling 苗、幼木 duckling 小鴨	

⑷ 其他名詞字尾

字尾	字源	例　　　　字	意義用法解說
1. **-ary**	F.	dictionary 字典 vocabulary 字彙、語彙	表示集合體
2. **-ary** **-ory** **-arium** **-orium**	L. L. L. L.	dispensary 施藥所、藥 局 factory 工廠 aquarium 水族館 auditorium 講堂、禮 堂	表示處所
3. **-ful**	OE.	handful 一把、少數 mouthful 一口、少量 armful 一抱、滿懷	①源出 full a.「充滿的」 ②表示「充滿」、「一 　…之量」的意思
4. **-mer***	Gk.	polymer 聚合體 dimer 二量體 plastomer 塑料、塑性 體	表示「部分」的意義
5. **-oid***	Gk.	asteroid 小行星 leatheroid 假皮、人造 皮 paraboloid 拋物線體	①表示「像…似的」或 　「有質量的」 ②加在名詞或動詞之後 ③也可作形容詞字尾
6. **-ology**	Gk.	biology 生物學 zoology 動物學 ecology 生態學	表示學科

B. 形容詞字尾

字尾	字源	例　　　　字	意義用法解說
1. **-able** 　 **-ible**	L. L.	comparable 比得上的 explicable 可解釋的 audible 可聽見的 feasible 可達成的	①表示「能…的」的意思 ②加於絕大多數及物動詞與少數不及物動詞之後
2. **-al**	L.	equal 同等、平等的 partial 部分、偏頗的 confidential 機密的	①表示屬性 ②加於名詞上
3. **-an** 　 **-ian** 　 **-ean**	L. L. L.	republican 共和國的 agrarian 土地、農地的 Parisian 巴黎的 Archemedean 阿基米德的	①表示地名或人名 ②多加於專有名詞上
4. **-ant** 　 **-ent**	L. L.	radiant 發光的 buoyant 有浮力、快活的 diligent 勤勉、用心的 quiescent 靜止、不活動的	①表示性質 ②加於動詞詞幹上 ③與名詞字尾 -ance, 　-ence 同源
5. **-ar**	L.	familiar 熟悉的 spectacular 壯觀的 muscular 肌肉、強壯的	多加於名詞詞幹上
6. **-ary** 　 **-ory**	L. L.	arbitrary 任意、獨斷的 exemplary 模範的 compulsory 強制的 dilatory 慢吞吞、拖延的	表示性質或狀態

字尾	字源	例　　　字	意義用法解說
7. **-ate**	L.	ornate 裝飾、華麗的 sedate 沈著、安靜的 cognate 同族的	表示性質或狀態
8. **-ed**	OE.	aged 年老的 assorted 各式各樣的 sophisticated 複雜、久 　經世故的	加於名詞或動詞之後
9. **-en**	OE.	golden 金製、金色的 earthen 土、土製的 brazen 黃銅製、黃銅 　色的	加於物質名詞上
10. **-ern**	OE.	eastern 東方的 northern 北方的 western 西方的	加於表示方位的名詞上
11. **-fold**	OE.	twofold 雙倍的 threefold 三倍的 manifold 多倍的	①多加於二以上的基數 　詞上，表示倍數 ②也可作副詞字尾
12. **-ful**	OE.	regretful 悔恨、惋惜 　的 fruitful 多產、有利的 bashful 害羞的	①源出 full a.「充滿的」 ②表示「充滿」或「引 　起…的」的意思 ③大多加於名詞或少數 　動詞上
13. **-ic** 　　**-ical**	L. L.	endemic 地方性、固 　有的 epidemic 流行性疾病 　的 economical 節約的 symbolical 象徵性的	①多加於名詞之後 ②轉成副詞時，改爲 　-ically 的形態
14. **-id**	L.	candid 公正、耿直的	表示性質

字尾	字源	例　　　字	意義用法解説
		languid 無力、不景氣的	
		limpid 清澄的	
15. **-ile**	F.	facile 容易、便利的	表示「易於…的」的意思
		hostile 敵視的	
		juvenile 年輕、少年的	
16. **-ine**	F.	divine 神聖、莊嚴的	表示性質
		genuine 眞正的	
		sanguine 血紅色、氣色好的	
17. **-ing**	OE.	pressing 緊迫、切實的	加於動詞上，由現在分詞轉爲形容詞
		agonizing 煩惱、苦悶的	
		unflagging 不衰、不鬆弛的	
18. **-ior**	L.	interior 內部的	原係拉丁文形容詞比較級字尾
		superior 上好、高超的	
		inferior 下等、拙劣的	
19. **-ique**	F.	unique 獨特、唯一的	表示風格
-esque	F.	antique 古代的	
		picturesque 繪畫般、美麗的	
		grotesque 古怪、怪異的	
20. **-ish**	OE.	bitterish 帶點苦味的	表屬性或不強的程度
		selfish 自私的	
		childish 小孩子氣的	
		Polish 波蘭的	
21. **-ite**	Gk./L.	infinite 無限的	
		opposite 反對、相對的	

字尾	字源	例　　　字	意義用法解說
		favorite 中意、珍愛的	
22. -ive 　　-ative	L. L.	massive 巨大、厚重的 diffusive 散佈、普及的 tentative 試驗性、暫時的 deductive 推論、演繹的	①表示關係、傾向、特性 ②多加於動詞或動詞詞幹上
23. -less	OE.	aimless 漫無目的的 groundless 無根據的 odorless 無氣味的	①表示否定 ②加於名詞之後 ③與 -ful 反義
24. -like	ME.	childlike 孩子似、天真的 womanlike 像女人似的 sportsmanlike 有運動家風範的	①表示相似 ②加於名詞之後
25. -ly	ME.	earthly 地球、世俗的 leisurely 從容的 fortnightly 兩星期一次的	①表示「外觀相似的」、「有…性質的」、「反復發生的」 ②加於名詞上
26. -most	ME.	innermost 最內部、深藏的 foremost 最先、第一流的 utmost 最大限度、極端的	表示最高級
27. -oid*	Gk.	asteroid 星狀的 cycloid 圓形的 crystalloid 結晶狀的	①表示相像或質量 ②加於名詞上 ③也可作名詞字尾
28. -ous	L.	advantageous 有益、有利的	①表示「充滿…的」的意思

字尾	字源	例 字	意義用法解說
		circuitous 迂曲的 vigorous 精力充沛的	②多加在名詞上
29. -proof	L.	waterproof 防水的 weatherproof 耐風雨的 foolproof 極簡單、安 全無比的	①表示「防…的」的意 思 ②附在名詞之後
30. -some	OE.	wearisome 使疲倦的 winsome 引人注目、 可愛的 fulsome 過分、令人 生厭的	①表示「像…的」、「 引起…的」的意思 ②加於名詞、動詞、形 容詞上
31. -ward	ME.	backward 向後、落後的 awkward 笨拙的 wayward 任性、無特 定的	①表示方向 ②也可作副詞字尾
32. -y	OE.	foggy 籠罩著霧、朦 朧的 icy 如冰、極冷的 notchy 有凹口的	①大多表示充滿或包含 的意義 ②加在名詞上

C. 動詞字尾

字尾	字源	例 字	意義用法解說
1. -ate -ute	L. L.	accumulate 累積、聚積 alternate 交互、交替 attribute 歸因 persecute 迫害、困擾	與名詞字尾 -ation, -ution 同源
2. -en	OE.	lengthen 加長、延長 worsen 變化、惡化 enlighten 啓發、教化 enliven 使有活力	加於名詞或形容詞上

字尾	字源	例　　　　字	意義用法解說
3. **-er**	OE.	batter 敲打、亂轟 flutter 飄動、飄飛 glitter 閃爍 chatter 喋喋不休	大多表示擬聲或反覆動作
4. **-esce**	L.	acquiesce 默從 evanesce 消散、逐漸 　看不見 convalesce 漸漸康復	大多表示動作開始
5. **-ify** 　**-efy**	L. L.	nullify 使無效、取消 mollify 緩和、撫慰 liquefy 溶解、液化 stupefy 使呆住	多加於名詞或形容詞上
6. **-ish**	F.	cherish 珍愛 diminish 減少、縮小 embellish 裝飾、美化 admonish 告誡	
7. **-ize** 　**-ise** 　**-yze** 　**-yse**	L. L. Gk. Gk.	patronize 贊助、惠顧 summarize 摘要、概述 pulverize 使成碎粉 analyze 分析	①表示「以…方式做」 　、「使成…化」的意思 ②多加在名詞或形容詞上 ③前二種形態，-ize 為 　美式拼法，-ise 為英 　式拼法 ④-yze 和-yse 的形態極 　為少見
8. **-le**	OE.	startle 吃驚、驚嚇 trickle 細流 dwindle 縮小、下跌 dazzle 使眩眼	多表示反覆動作

D. 副詞字尾

字尾	字源	例　　　字	意義用法解說
1. **-fold**	OE.	hundredfold 百倍地 thousandfold 千倍地 manifold 多倍地	①表示倍數 ②加於數詞或個別代詞 　之後 ③也可作形容詞字尾
2. **-ly**	OE.	roughly 約略地 absolutely 絕對、全然 　地 approximately 大約地	多加於形容詞或分詞上
3. **-ward** **-wards**	OE. OE.	southward 向南地 inward 向內地 afterwards 其後	①表示方向 ②加在介詞、名詞、形 　容詞上 ③-ward 的形態也可作 　形容詞字尾
4. **-way** **-ways**	OE. OE.	anyway 橫豎、無論 　如何 sideways 斜地裏 endways 末端朝前、 　筆直地	①表示方向或位置 ②與 -wise 同源
5. **-wise**	OE. OE.	otherwise 不然的話 sidewise 斜地裏 crosswise 交叉、固執地	①表示方向或位置 ②部分可兼作形容詞 ③與 -way, -ways同源

參考書目

1. *The Oxford English Dictionary.* 13 vols. Oxford: Oxford University Press, 1933.
2. *Webster's Third New International Dictionary.* Springfield, Massachusetts: G. & C. Merriam, 1971.
3. *Webster's New World Dictionary.* New York: Warner Books, 1984.
4. Charlton T. Lewis. *An Elementary Latin Dictionary.* Oxford: Oxford University Press, 1891.
5. Karl Feyerabend. *Langenscheidt's Pocket Greek Dictionary.* London: Hodder & Stroughton, 1978.
6. A. H. Irvine. *Thesaurus: A Dictionary of Synonyms and Antonyms.* London: Collins, 1977.
7. Eric Partridge. *Origins: A Short Etymological Dictionary of Modern English.* New York: Greenwich House, 1983.
8. Teresa Ferster Glazier. *The Least You Should Know About Vocabulary Building: Word Roots.* New York: Holt, Rinehart & Winston, 1981.
9. Jean Bouffartigue & Anne-Marie Delrieu. *Trésors des racines latines.* Paris: Belin, 1981.
10. Jean Bouffartigue & Anne-Marie Delrieu. *Trésors des racines grecques.* Paris: Belin, 1981.
11. Donald J. Borror. *Dictionary of Word Roots and Combining Forms.* Palo Alto, California: Mayfield Publishing Co., 1960.

1. 梁實秋主編《最新實用英漢辭典》，台北遠東圖書公司，1972年。
2. 吳金瑞編著《拉丁漢文辭典》，台中光啓出版社，1965年。
3. 吳炳鍾等編修《大陸簡明英漢辭典》，增訂六版，台北大陸書店，1985年。
4. 許章眞編著《托福進階字典》，二冊，台北中西留學書籍出版社，1986年。
5. 李增榮編《英語構詞法例釋》，北平商務印書館，1981年。
6. 橫井忠夫著《英語語源ものしり辭典》，東京大和出版社，1981年。
7. 詹賢鋆著《英語詞素分析──英語單詞簡捷記憶法》，北平商務印書館，1980年。港台版，易名爲《英語詞彙記憶法》，台北書林出版公司，1991年。
8. 許章眞編著《托福字彙研究》，台北書林出版公司，1988年。

本書英文字彙索引

Index

faculty 316
familiar 672
feasible 317, 672
feat 317
feature 317
fellowship 669
ferry 323
fertile 323
fervid 653
filament 668
final 327, 606
finale 327
finance 326, 327
fine 326, 328
finesse 326, 328
finish 326, 328
finished 328
finite 329
flex 331
flexible 331
flexor 330
flexuous 331
fluctuate 334
fluency 334
fluent 335
fluid 335
flume 333
fluminose 333
flutter 677
fluvial 333
fluviology 333
fluviose 333
flux 335
foggy 676
foliage 666
foolproff 676
foot 611, 628
forbearance 666

forbid 132
fore 133
forebear 133
forebode 133
forecast 133
foredoom 133
forefather 134
forefront 134
foregoing 134
foregone 134
foreground 134
foreknow 134
foreman 134
foremost xi, 134, 675
forerunner 135
foresee 135
foreshadow 135
foresight 135
forestall 135
foretell 135
forethought 135
forewarn 135
foreword 135
forfeit 317
forgo 132
forlorn 132
forswear 132
fortify xv, 310
fortitude 668
fortnightly 675
forward 136
found 339
fraction xv, 342, 657
fractional 342
fracture 342, 657
fragile 342, 657
fragment 342, 657
frail 341, 342

frailty 341, 343
frangible 343, 657
freedom 667
freeman 345
friendliness 668
fruitful 673
fugitive 665
fulfillment 668
fulsome 676
fuse xiv, 339
fusion 339
futile 337, 339

G

gangster 666
gazette 670
gender 346
gene 658
genealogy 346
general 344, 346, 658
generate 347, 607, 658
generation 347, 607
generic 344, 347, 658, 659
generous 344, 347, 658
genesis 347
genetics 658
genial 344, 347
genital 348
genitive 607
genius 344, 348
genre 348
genteel 348
gentle 345, 348
gentleman 345
genuflect 330

T

tact 513, 657
tactful 513
tactics 513
tactile 513, 657
tactual 513
tangent 513, 657
tangible 513, 657
tenable 521
tenacious 522
tenacity 522
tenant 522
tend 530
tendency 530, 666
tender 530
tenet 522
tenor 522
tense 530
tensile 530
tension 530
tentative 675
tenure 523
terrify 310
testify 310
testimony 668
tetrad 666
think 658
thought 658
thousandfold 678
threat 545, 547, 617
threaten 547
threefold 420
thrust 547
tirade 666
torch 532, 533
torment 533, 617

torsion 534
tortuous 534
torture 534
torturous 534
trace 535, 541
track 535, 541
tract 535, 536, 541
tractable xv, 541
traction 542
trail 535, 542
train 535, 542
trait 535, 536, 543
transact 235, 249
transcend 234, 235
transcribe 235, 461
transcript 462
transfer 235, 325, 652
transfix 235
transform 235
transfuse 235, 340
transgress 236, 363
transient 236, 354, 356
transit 236, 356
transitory 236, 356
translate 236, 606
transliterate 236
translucency 653
translucent 236, 378, 653
transmit 237, 396, 657
transmute 237
transparent 237
transpire 234, 237
transplant 237
transport 237, 442
transpose 237, 437
transverse 571

traverse 234, 237, 571
travesty 234, 238
treasury 668
treat 543, 617
treatise 535, 543, 667
treaty 535, 543
trek 535, 544
trespass 234, 238
trickle 677
triple 420, 427, 612
triplicate 420, 427
tripod 406
trivia 574, 576
trivial 574, 577
twofold 420, 673
typist 665

U

unanimous 239, 240, 250, 252
underling 670
unequivocal xiii
unexpected xiii
unflagging 674
unicorn 239
unifoliate 239
uniform 240
unify 240, 310
unilingual 239
union 240
unipolar 239
unique 240, 674
unison 240
unit 240
unite 240
unity 240
universal 239, 240,

托福得分六七七・寫書口八談一百字
許章真 說英語論竅門 不是蓋的

▲許章真說，看電視、聽英文歌可以學好英文。
（本報記者 游輝弘攝）

「書林」出版社最近推出「最重要的一百個英文字首字根」，六百多頁，工程頗不小。

書的作者名叫許章真。名字雖陌生，卻也列了個很能打動讀者的資歷：「許章真，截至目前為止世界托福最高分紀錄（六七七分）保持人」。不但任教的補習班拿來當廣告，也開始有電台找他談論「如何學英文」了。

許章真，河南人，今年剛滿卅歲。大學考的是政大西語系，大三降轉到台大外文系，對於「六七七分」成為自己的重要背景資料，多少有些無奈，真說是出版社執著要強調，可是「的確也沒有人考得比這分數高了」。

他先後考過三次托福，四年前當兵時考六六分，後來又考了次六七〇分，最後考到了六七七分。目前他在補習班做按小時計酬的高薪工作，準備存夠學費明年出國讀語言學。剛當完兵時，普林斯頓大學給他最喜歡的獎學金，因為「東亞系」不是他最喜歡的而作罷。

許章真學英文全靠這個月才退休、擔任警察的父親這個興趣與方法得當。方法很奇特，許章真說：「從高二開始，看電視看外國影集時，盡量邊聽邊跟著唸出聲。」

的確是奇特的畫面，看「勇士們」時，許章真也跟著班長、排長發號施令，許章真說：「多虧媽媽和弟弟共看電視時，對我很容忍。」高二、高三下來，他學會會了美國南方腔、英國腔，常用英文跟自己說話，進入政大後，出身嘉義高中的他，贏得全校英語演講比賽冠軍。

大學開始，他買個小收音機，從成天聽美軍電台，熟悉口語英文，經常清晨醒來，發現耳機還插在耳裡，收音機的番言番語未曾停。到現在他只要在家，英語節目一定開著。「聽久了總有幫助的」，許章真覺得英語既是個拼音語言，就該從語音下手去學；而且，學語言必須先學這語言的韻律感。

至於離開學校的人如何進修英文？許章真強調不必拘泥於教學的書，喜歡養魚的就找英文養魚書，喜歡音樂、電腦，就找英文音樂書、電腦書看。滿足了興趣，也增進了英文。

許章真不諱言「好奇」與「崇洋」使他最初對英語產生興趣，隨著年紀漸長，對印度梵文、中國俗文學使也生出興趣，不再崇洋。不論如何，習英語過程使他自信心增強，連年少時的輕微口吃都難他遠去了。

本報記者 黃美惠

許章眞小傳

　　許章眞，祖籍河南伊川，1957 年出生於台灣嘉義，1975 年嘉義高中畢業，考入政大西洋語文系；1977 年轉入台大外文系，1980 年畢業。許君對語言有極濃厚之興趣和造詣，1985 年托福考試得 670 分，並獲美國普林斯敦大學 (Princeton U.) 全額獎學金，因學系不符願望而放棄。1986 年托福測驗成績 677 分爲全世界最高分。先後曾在台北來欣及美加留學英語中心執教四年，主授字彙。著有《托福進階字典》、《托福字彙研究》、《法文字彙結構分析》、《最重要的 100 個英文字首字根》、《托福字彙 600 分》等書。1989 年獲美國賓州大學 (U. of Pennsylvania) 東方語文學系全額獎學金，出國前擬赴澎湖遊覽，1989 年 6 月 27 日在高雄搭飛機失事罹難。

In Memoriam
Chang-chen HSU
August 6, 1957-June 27, 1989

{1}
Hsu Chang-chen, ed. and tr. *Yin-tu hsien-tai hsiao-shuo hsüan [A Selection of Contemporary Indian Fiction]*. Hsin-ch'ao wen-k'u [New Tide Series], 316. Taipei: Chih-wen, 1986. 313 pages.

{2}
_____. *T'o-fu tzu-hui yen-chiu (Mastering TOEFL Vocabulary)*. Taipei: Shu-lin, 1988. viii + 295 pages.

{3}
_____. *Tsui-chung-yao-te i pai ke Ying-wen tzu-shou tzu-ken (100 English Prefixes and Word Roots)*. Taipei: Shu-lin, 1988. xix + 666 pages.

{4}
_____. *Fa-wen tzu-hui chieh-kou fen-hsi -- tzu-shou yü tzu-ken (Les préfixes et les racines de la langue française)*. Taipei: Shu-lin, 1988. xvii + 363 pages.

{5}
_____, comp. and tr. *Hsi-yü yü Fo-chiao wen-shih lun-chi (Collection of Articles on Studies of Central Asia, India, and Buddhism)*. Taipei: The Student Book Company, 1989. vi + 320 pages.

Judging from his phenomenal achievements during the thirty-odd years of his short life, Chang-chen Hsu would undoubtedly have developed into one of the greatest Chinese linguists of all times had he been granted another decade or two to exercise his undisputed brilliance more fully. Celebrated as a virtual folk hero throughout Taiwan for having scored a near perfect 677 on the TOEFL test (apparently the world record) in November, 1987, Hsu was much more than just a master of English test-taking. So multifaceted were his interests and abilities, it is difficult to know how to begin to describe them. Although I hope that someone will one day write Hsu's complete biography, I did not know him personally and, fearing that this might disqualify me from doing justice to this extraordinary young man, do not presume to be adequately equipped to take upon myself this task. My purpose in this brief memorial notice is simply to lament the passing of one of the most enormously gifted graduate students I have ever encountered.

Chang-chen Hsu attended National Chengchi University where he majored in English from September, 1975 to June, 1977. In the fall of 1977, he transferred to National Taiwan University where he continued his study of English and graduated with a B.A. in June, 1980. He was granted a full fellowship from Princeton University but declined it to fulfill his military service obligation and then to continue his unquenchable thirst for language preparation. In June, 1984 he began teaching English at the Y.M.C.A. in Taipei and in August of the same year, he also started working as a TOEFL teacher at the Luxin Language Center. His fame quickly spread as an extremely effective teacher, so that by March, 1985 he had been hired by the Merica English Institute, one of Taiwan's most prestigious foreign language schools, at a salary reportedly equivalent to approximately $6,000 per month (at 1989 values). Other schools and organizations vied for his talents, but the only one with which he maintained a regular relationship was the Buddhist temple at Fo-kuang-shan in Kaohsiung where he instructed the nuns in English. This meant that he was flying from Taipei to Kaohsiung about once a week during the last year of his life. His willingness to teach at a Buddhist temple was not whimsical, however, since by this time he had developed a serious interest in Indian language, philosophy, and literature.

Hsu stayed on longer in Taiwan than many people felt was wise, but he wanted to perfect his language skills before going abroad to receive advanced training. He also had a dream of travelling around the world to record the vanishing tongues of neglected peoples and insisted that he had to save up a huge amount of money to finance these and other researches for the rest of his life after graduate school. By the beginning of 1989, Hsu felt ready to embark on the momentous next phase of his career. He applied to the University of Pennsylvania and was naturally accepted without any hesitation. I secured a full graduate fellowship for him in the Department of Oriental Studies and looked forward with great excitement to having him as a student. A glance at his personal statement will explain why:

> With the advent of Buddhism, Indian civilization exerted a great impact upon a large part of Asia, especially on East and Southeast Asia. Chinese and some other East Asian languages were thus directly and indirectly influenced by ancient Indian languages. It is in the study of these influences that my chief interest lies.
>
> The translations of Buddhist scriptures into the Chinese language beginning in the first century of our era caused the Chinese to take a more self-conscious interest in their own language. The use of Chinese script to render Sanskrit proper names and philosophical terms casts considerable light on the pronunciation of the relevant periods. The sounds given by men of the Han and T'ang dynasties in transliterating Sanskrit words have therefore been treated as data for comparison in the reconstruction of the pronunciation of ancient and medieval Chinese. Scholars like B. Karlgren, H. Maspero, Lo Chang-pei, Li Fang-kuei, E. G. Pulleyblank, etc., have more or less used this approach in their works. However, so far there have only been scanty and unorganized examinations of data in this respect. These data for comparison are furthermore fewer than those afforded by other comparative methods, and their value is further diminished by the fact that we still do not know precisely when a certain transliteration was first used, nor in what dialect. I am interested in looking into this area thoroughly, hoping to produce data leading to a more conclusive result of study.
>
> Another area of interest worthy of extensive survey is the possible syntactical influences that Sanskrit and Prakrit had on Chinese through the translation of Buddhist scriptures. The bulk of extant Chinese Buddhist scriptures translated from ancient Indian languages has scarcely been examined in its syntactic aspect. A thorough study of these materials may help determine the role of this Buddhist literature in the syntactic development of Chinese. For example, it seems that the usage of the preposition *yü* 於 between a transitive verb and an object did not appear in ancient Chinese texts until the third century of our era when translators of Buddhist scriptures like Dharmaraksa (3rd-4th c.) and Kumārajīva (4th-5th c.) started writing such phrases as *hu yü fa-yin* 護 於 法 音 , *chi yü ta-fa-ku* 擊 於 大 法 鼓 , etc. More instances of this nature may be brought forward only after a comprehensive study is completed.
>
> At present, I can read and translate Japanese, French, German and Japanese. I have also been studying Sanskrit and Tibetan for 1-2 years. In addition to these languages, I have taken courses in Latin, Russian and Thai. I wish to continue my study of these and other languages, especially of Sanskrit in which your school has excellent courses to offer.
>
> I am presently taking courses in Chinese and Sino-Tibetan linguistics at National Taiwan University to enrich my background knowledge of the field. On my reading list for early 1989 are also works on syntax, phonetics, phonology and historical linguistics, such as *Introduction to the Theory of Grammar* by Henk van Riemsdijk and Edwin Williams, *Transformational Syntax* by Andrew Radford, *A Course in Phonetics* by Peter Ladefoged, *Generative Phonology* by Sanford A. Schane, *Historical Linguistics* by Theodora Bynon, etc. These works will be able to make up for what lack of formal training one might have in the relevant subjects.
>
> For the past few years I have done quite a bit of research on the cultural and religious transmission between China and India in medieval times. At present I am

writing a series of essays on the Sanskrit education of Chinese monks from the 2nd century to the 11th. A background knowledge in this aspect shall be a great help to the study of the influences of ancient Indian languages on Chinese. I am also planning to translate into Chinese in early 1989 *Gengogaku no tanjō* 言 語 學 の 誕 生 by Kazama Kiyozō 風 間 喜 代 三, and have it published in late 1989. The translation of this Japanese book on historical linguistics shall help me acquire more basic knowledge needed for my study in the future.

Never before had I received an application from a prospective student which demonstrated such breadth of purpose, astuteness concerning critical issues, attention to the need for philological exactitude, and astonishing command of relevant sources and materials. Furthermore, the statement was written in a grammatically correct, succinct, elegant prose that would have been the envy of many native speakers of English. I was absolutely flabbergasted and found it hard to believe that such a person actually existed. Yet there were his GRE scores (480, 780, 600) to corroborate the huge native ability displayed in his statement. Then there were the recommendations from some of Taiwan's most eminent linguists such as Hwang-cherng Gong who casually mentioned that Hsu had consulted him on some Tangut texts he had been looking at and Yü-hung Chang who revealed that Hsu always felt ill-prepared for the tasks which he set himself and that he always competed against himself. It was the overwhelming drive to command all the necessary tools to be an eminent historical linguist and genuine historian of Chinese civilization in the largest sense that seems most to have characterized him, not any desire to intimidate others. Hsu was not a Taiwanese, and yet he learned to speak and understand the Taiwanese language. This is indicative not only of his boundless linguistic ability, but his openness and acceptance of different cultures. Chang-chen Hsu, I salute your gifted, noble soul!

Hsu assumed truly legendary proportions in the eyes of his compatriots. Newspapers wrote articles about him and his picture was posted in bookstores. When I was in Taiwan at the beginning of September, 1989, people were still stunned by his death. Jerome Su, the Managing Director of Bookman Books (Shu-lin) and publisher of several of Hsu's major works, solemnly spoke of Hsu's utter dedication to linguistic scholarship and language pedagogy.

The circumstances of Chang-chen Hsu's death are intensely disturbing. Just before he was set to depart for Philadelphia, Hsu allegedly felt the impulse to do a bit of touring around Taiwan for one last look at his homeland. Apparently, however, when he left Taipei to go to Kaohsiung for a final class at Fo-kuang-shan, he did not tell his friends and relatives that he would make a side excursion to the Pescadores. He must have had deep misgivings about the trip; after changing his airplane ticket **six times** (according to Formosa Airline officials), Hsu reluctantly boarded a Cessna C-440 (flight B-12206) with ten other passengers plus pilot and copilot bound for Wonan. Less than a minute after takeoff at 9:04 a.m. on Tuesday, June 27, 1989, the plane flipped over and fell precipitously out of the sky (having reached a height of only 250 feet), reportedly "for mechanical reasons." It crashed into a new five-story apartment building that was within a thousand meters from the end of the runway. Only one person miraculously walked away from the crash; Chang-chen Hsu and all eleven others on board perished in the flaming wreckage (from *Lien-he Pao / United Daily News* [June 28, 1989], p. 1 and other sources). The news of Hsu's death was broadcast prominently on radio, television, and in the press and an investigation (the results of which are unknown to me) was ordered. The whole episode seems so improbable that it takes on an eerie atmosphere of unreality. And yet I know that Hsu is dead because he is not in my classes and his friends in Taiwan told me that he is no longer among the living.

Every time I look at the pile of books written by Chang-chen Hsu that lies in my office, I am almost moved to tears. Each one of them shows the touch of a master. {1} consists of fifteen carefully chosen stories by Rabindranath Tagore, Rajendra Yadav, Premendra Mitra, R. K. Narayan, and others. They are expertly translated and supplied with excellent, informative notes. At the end of the book is a sensitive afterword which discusses each of the stories and a scholarly appendix on the current Indian linguistic scene. Hsu's ability to capture in these last fifty-some pages of the book the essentials of Indian language, society, and literature is almost breathtaking.

In spite of the nifty English title (more accurately rendered as *Research on TOEFL Vocabulary*) given to it by the publisher, {2} is a meticulous study of the testing procedures and principles employed over a period of several years by the Educational Testing Service. {3} and {4} together amount to a spectacular display of Hsu's seemingly innate sense of linguistic structures. Both are extremely impressive for their accurate bibliographies, precise use of diacriticals, absence of misspellings and other mechanical errors, neat organization, and learned disquisitions. It should be noted that Hsu sought out native speakers (to whom he gives appropriate credit) to vet these and other works of his.

{5} is a virtuoso performance of Hsu's talent for selecting, translating, and copiously annotating the best scholarship in the world on those subjects with which he intended to occupy himself for the next period of his life.

Besides the books sketched above, there was a life of Gandhi, articles in *Chung-wai wen-hsüeh [Literature from China and Abroad]*, *Chung-kuo pien-cheng [China's Border Administration]*, *Shu-mu chi-k'an [Bibliographical Quarterly]*, *Chung-kuo Fo-chiao [Chinese Buddhism]*, and other first-rank journals from Taiwan. It is hard to imagine how Hsu would have had the time to do the research for and write so many fine books and articles within a period of about five years at the same time he was teaching English in several foreign language schools. Hsu's concentration and diligence must have been monumental for him to accomplish so much in such a short time.

Chang-chen Hsu's death is a tragedy of unparalleled dimensions for Chinese linguistics. Because language is so central to civilization and because China's languages are currently in such tremendous flux, Hsu's tragic demise is also a terrible blow to the nation as a whole. More than that, Chang-chen Hsu's premature passing has robbed all humanity of a large-spirited genius and visionary. He would have been able to do so much to heal the wounds between China and the rest of the world simply because he had such a grand capacity to reach out without fear, to seek knowledge with zestful curiosity, and to convey it skillfully to his fellowmen.

My short contact with Chang-chen Hsu has left a deep impression upon me. I am haunted by the flawless, beautiful, gentle, enthusiastic English speaker saying to me over the phone from Taiwan the week before his death, "I am looking forward eagerly to studying with you, Professor Mair." Little did he know that I was equally looking forward to studying with him. When I heard of Hsu's death, I almost collapsed on the spot and even now whenever I think of him I feel painfully bereft.

May China and the world be blessed with other such precious souls, capacious minds, and determined wills to carry on the mission of Chang-chen Hsu! *Requiescat in pace.*

語言叢書

■ 詞典／工具書

書林易解英語詞典 (英-英-漢半雙語詞典)　　　　　　　書林編譯·················550
Bookman English Dictionary for Speakers of Chinese

西文工具書概論 *An Introduction to Reference*　　　　邵獻圖主編·················400
Books in Western Language

兒童英文彩圖辭典 *Children's Picture Dictionary*　　劉勇強編(卡帶 2 捲 300)書 300 台

MLA 論文寫作手冊〈第四版〉　　　　　　　　　　Gibaldi 著，書林編譯········300

例解商用英文表現法　　　　　　　　　　　　　　胡治國編譯···········(精)250

漢英對照成語詞典　　　　　　　　　　　　　　　陳永槙·陳善慈編······(精)350 台
Chinese Idioms & Their English Equivalents

英文姓名寶鑑　　　　　　　　　　　　　　　　　高宣揚·許敦煌編··········100 台

書林簡明語言與修辭學詞典 (英漢對照)　　　　　　黃仲珊·張陵馨編著········300

英語短語動詞用法詞典 *A Dictionary of Phrasal Verbs* 盧思源著·················200 台

英漢漢英新編翻譯手冊　　　　　　　　　　　　　羅斯編·················200 台

英語疑難詞詞典 *Dic. of Problem Words* (英漢對照)　李靜芝譯·················150

多功能實用英文手冊 (英漢對照)　　　　　　　　　楊銘塗著·················300

■ 英語叢書

最新美國口語俚語精選〈修訂版〉　　　　　　　　黃希敏著(卡帶二捲 300)書 150
Modern American Slang & Colloquialisms

最新實用生活美語　　　　　　　　　　　　　　　石素錦編著················
Spoken American English for All Occasions　　　·········(卡帶 3 捲 450)書 350

西洋妙語 1 *Idiom-Magic 1* （英漢對照）　　　　Smithback 著·············120 台

西洋妙語 2 *Idiom-Magic 2* （英漢對照）　　　　Smithback 著·············120 台

西洋妙語 3 *Idiom-Magic 3* （英漢對照）　　　　Smithback 著·············120 台

西洋妙語 4 *Idiom-Magic 4* （英漢對照）　　　　Smithback 著·············120 台

西洋妙語 5 *Idiom-Magic 5* （英漢對照）　　　　Smithback 著·············120 台

英文情書·情詩·情人卡 (英漢對照)　　　　　　屠國元譯·················150
Love Poems for Cards & Letters

英語迷津——相近詞語辨析　　　　　　　　　　　盧思源編著···············250 台

漢英虛詞翻譯手冊　　　　　　　　　　　　　　　黃邦傑編著···············125 台

百行各業英語視窗 (英漢對照)　　　　　　　　　　楊銘塗著·················350
Windows: English for All Occasions

英漢修辭與翻譯　　　　　　　　　　　　　　　　陳定安編著···············200 台

■ 語言學

◎定價如有刊載錯誤或遇有變動時，概以售書時之定價爲準。

國家圖書館出版品預行編目資料

最重要的 100 個英文字首字根=100 English Prefixes
& Word Roots ／許章真編著— —增訂版.
台北市：書林，1997 [民 86]
736 面；21 公分
參考書目：2 面　　含索引
ISBN　957-586-672-X (25K 平裝)
ISBN　957-586-671-1 (32K 平裝)

1. 英國語言－詞彙

805.12　　　　　　　　　　　　85013327

最重要的 100 個英文字首字根〈增訂本〉

編　　　著　許章真(附錄 I, II／孫述宇)
校　　　對　紀榮崧・Andrew Cribb
增　　　訂　孫述宇
出　版　者　書林出版有限公司
　　　　　　100 台北市羅斯福路四段 60 號 3 樓
　　　　　　電　話 02-23684938・23658617 傳真 02-23688929・23636630
台北書林書店　106 台北市新生南路三段 88 號 2 樓之 5　Tel (02) 2365-8617
北區業務部　　100 台北市羅斯福路四段 60 號 3 樓　　　Tel (02) 2368-7226
中區業務部　　403 台中市五權路 2 之 143 號 6 樓　　　Tel (04) 2376-3799
南區業務部　　802 高雄市五福一路 77 號 2 樓之 1　　　Tel (07) 229-0300
發　行　人　蘇正隆
出 版 經 理　蘇恆隆
郵　　　撥　15743873・書林出版有限公司
網　　　址　http://www.bookman.com.tw
經 銷 代 理　紅螞蟻圖書有限公司
　　　　　　台北市內湖區舊宗路二段 121 巷 28 號 4 樓
　　　　　　電話 02-27953656(代表號)　傳真 02-27954100
登　記　證　局版臺業字第一八三一號
出 版 日 期　1988 年 6 月初版，1988 年 10 月增訂，1992 年 9 月增補修訂版
　　　　　　1997 年 1 月增訂版，2011 年 8 月二十刷
定　　　價　400 元
I S B N　957-586-672-X